Alice's Secret

ALSO BY LYNNE FRANCIS
FROM CLIPPER LARGE PRINT

Ella's Journey

Alice's Secret

Lynne Francis

W F HOWES LTD

This large print edition published in 2019 by
W F Howes Ltd
Unit 5, St George's House, Rearsby Business Park,
Gaddesby Lane, Rearsby, Leicester LE7 4YH

1 3 5 7 9 10 8 6 4 2

First published in the United Kingdom in 2018
by HarperCollinsPublishers

A CIP catalogue record for this book is available
from the British Library

ISBN 978 1 52886 349 0

Typeset by Palimpsest Book Production Limited,
Falkirk, Stirlingshire

Printed and bound by
T J International in the UK

MIX
Paper from
responsible sources
FSC
www.fsc.org   FSC® C013056

To my children, for growing up and
giving me the time to write.

PROLOGUE

Summer 1893

Alice felt the hem of her skirt getting wetter and heavier as she brushed through the bracken. This summer had been damp and it had rained hard last night. The fern fronds continued to grow and unfurl across the path, no matter how many of them passed to and from the mill each day. She hated the feel of the sodden wool against her legs. It would bother her all morning until it dried: the smell of the wet cloth, the chafing. She sighed. She'd be working in the weaving shed this morning. It would feel cold at first with the door open, and no easy way to dry off.

Alice clutched her shawl tighter around her shoulders and hooked the basket into the crook of her arm. She lifted it clear of the foliage, which was still heavy with rain. Her work clogs bounced in the bottom of the basket, along with her lantern, and a crust of bread loosely wrapped in rough cloth. Her mother had pressed the bread into Alice's hand with a brusque, 'On your way. You'll not get through the day without it. We'll manage.' Then she'd limped her way painfully to the grate to set the kettle on the hob. Alice's brothers and sisters would have to make do with tea and porridge until tomorrow.

Tomorrow: Alice shuddered. It was the day that they lined up in front of Williams, the overlooker, as he counted the florins, shillings and pennies into their hands. She thought about how Williams used to look meaningfully at her as he dispensed the coins. He'd close her palm around them, letting his fingers linger just that moment too long. She'd been aware of his eyes following her as she moved around the mill or bent to her machine in the weaver's shed. He'd made a point of singling her out for praise for her work, so that the other girls had noticed and teased her, making her anxious. Betty Ackroyd had drawn Alice to one side. 'Alice, you need to watch yourself with Williams,' she'd warned. 'He's got an eye for the young girls here. He don't take no for an answer.'

Despite Betty's warning, Alice had been unperturbed when, as she collected her lantern one evening to start the long journey home, Williams had summonsed her.

'Alice, in here a moment,' he'd said, holding open the door to the office. She'd stepped into the warm glow of the room, startled when the door snapped shut behind her and she found herself pinned against it. She'd tried to shut out what came next – rough bristles against her cheek and neck, panting, heat, hands fumbling at her buttons, tugging at her skirt.

She'd no idea how she had broken free. She dimly remembered Albert coming into the room by the other door – a muffled shout. She remembered fleeing up the path, no time to light her lantern, and having to pick her way home in the dark. She was stumbling, weeping, horrified – frightened of slipping off the path but more fearful of what lay behind.

After that, Williams had started to lie in wait for Alice: pouncing on her in dark storerooms where she'd been sent on pointless errands, trying to corner her on her way home. For weeks, she'd had to submit to his pestering, sickened by his actions, furious with herself. Then she'd found the strength to fight against him, to threaten to report him, to stand up to him. Williams didn't take kindly to having his advances spurned. He made a point of picking on Alice: for faults in her spinning, for talking too loudly, for smiling. She'd shrunk in on herself, making sure that she didn't set a foot wrong, that she left each evening along with Ivy and Betty, parting ways a little further up the path. Williams still found fault. He dropped the coins in her hand on pay day now, glaring at her. He watched her like a hawk, checking to see what time she arrived each morning.

Alice picked up her pace, trying to lift her skirt clear of the bracken. She'd been late twice already this week, her mother too sick to get the children up in the morning. Williams had warned her that one more day's lateness would mean the loss of her job. This morning, she was late again. It was too dangerous to run, the grey stones slippery after the rain, the surface uneven. She'd reached the Druid Stone, only a short distance to go now. She knew every twist and turn of the path, had names for the landmarks along the way. Just the Packhorse Steps to negotiate now. Maybe Williams would be distracted this morning? Maybe she could slip in, unnoticed?

At that moment, her feet flew from beneath her. It was a hard fall. Alice's basket bounced down the steps, her lantern smashed, bread flung into the bracken. The rushing tumble of the river over the falls sounded loudly in her ears. Sharp stones pressed into her cheek; cold, damp moss pillowed her neck. Alice lay still.

PART I

CHAPTER 1

'Oh, my goodness.' Kate, Alys's mother, had stopped, cup halfway to her lips, peering at the screen over the top of her glasses. She'd got a new pair of those ready-readers, Alys noticed. Bright-green frames this time: they worked rather well with her silver hair. Kate said that she kept losing them, so that was why she needed to buy more pairs, but Alys suspected that they were a fashion accessory rather than a necessity. Alys had once picked up a pair belonging to her mother and looked through them. The lenses could just as well have been plain glass for all the difference they seemed to make.

'What's up, Mum?' Alys was only half interested. She was used to her mother's exclamations. Kate had a tendency to be alarmed by the warnings of fraud scams or deadly computer viruses emailed to her by her friends.

'It's your Aunt Moira,' said Kate, glancing up at her youngest daughter over the top of her laptop screen. She paused a moment, arrested – as usual – by Alys's appearance. Wild hair, scraped back into an elastic band, from which crinkly blonde curls escaped at random. Forget-me-not blue cardigan, rather shrunken, buttoned over one of her signature crêpe-de-Chine dresses, orange flowered this time. 1940s vintage, surely. Where *did* she get them from? Kate wondered. And not a scrap of make-up, at a guess. Kate favoured the woven- or knitted-linen look once spring had arrived, in the sort of tasteful shades that also graced her walls. She couldn't understand her daughter's taste and style – or rather, her lack of it. She must have inherited it from her father's side of the family, Kate decided.

'She's had a bad fall. Hurt her hip and shoulder and put her back out. The doctor said she'll need to rest for a couple of weeks at least, but she's got the café to run. Looks as though she might have to close it, just as the holiday season is about to arrive. It's her busiest time – she sounds pretty upset.'

Kate chewed her lip and frowned. She really ought to offer to go up and help her sister out. She mentally ran through her diary for the next few weeks. Since she'd retired, it seemed as though she was busier than ever. Voluntary work at the hospital, her book group and walking group. The garden-committee trip to Sissinghurst, planning and preparations for the village carnival. Kate smiled wryly to herself. When had she become so middle class? 'Must have been when I married David,' she thought, then was dragged back to the present by Alys, saying 'Mum? What should we do?'

'Well, I really should go up and help her,' said Kate, picking up her cup and absently sipping the cooling tea. 'But I've got so much on over the next few weeks. And you know how I feel about Yorkshire . . .' She tailed off, expecting Alys to laugh, but instead her daughter was gazing into space, clearly caught up in her own thoughts.

'I'll go,' she said, unexpectedly.

Kate stared at her. 'But darling, do you have any holiday owing to you? You've only just come back from your trip with Tim? I'm sure Moira would be grateful, but by the sound of it a week, or even two, won't be enough. Although I suppose I could take over after you leave?' Kate mentally prepared herself to go into martyr mode.

'The thing is, Mum—' Alys suddenly looked apprehensive. 'I came here today to tell you something.' She paused. Kate looked at her expectantly, her mind racing ahead. Could Alys and Tim have decided to settle down together at last, start a family? Alys was in her mid-thirties now – she really couldn't afford to leave it much longer. Of course, she'd have to sell that tiny house of hers, lovely garden or not. Heaven knows Tim must earn enough, with that job of his in the city. Maybe Alys was already pregnant? Kate tried to see if there was a bump in evidence, but that shapeless dress made it impossible to tell. She calculated rapidly. It would be an autumn baby, so that would work perfectly. She'd have time to rearrange a few things and she'd still be able to help out at the

Christmas Fair, the carol concert, make the mulled wine and mince pies. The run-up to Christmas was always such a busy time.

'Mum!'

Kate snapped back to attention again. Alys had been talking. 'Mum, did you hear me?'

'Yes, no – sorry, darling. So, where will you and Tim live?'

Alys looked at her blankly. 'Mum, you really *weren't* listening, were you? I told you. I've given up my job. I need a break from Tim, from London. I hadn't planned what I was going to do. A bit of travelling, perhaps. I can delay that, though, and go and help Aunt Moira for a couple of months. I'd be glad to. You know I've always loved it up there. And, of course, I wouldn't expect any payment.'

Alys felt a small burst of excitement at the thought. She'd given up her job as a graphic designer almost on a whim, although the plan had been taking shape in the back of her mind for some time. Days spent staring at a computer screen held no joy for her, and that tricky work issue had finally helped to make her mind up. She'd been putting money aside for a while now, supposedly so she could move from her little house – the closest thing to a cottage that she'd been able to find in London – but really with half a mind to doing something completely different. Travel, voluntary service overseas, who knows? Alys was restless. She knew Kate would say that it was her biological clock ticking and that it was time she settled down and started a family. But she wasn't entirely sure that Tim was the right person for her.

Nice, well-brought-up Tim, with his warehouse flat and a good job in the city that took him abroad a lot. Great salary. Good prospects. She'd purposely set out to look for someone other than the sensitive, creative types that she normally fell for. She'd succeeded. Tim was stable and solvent but he was also boring.

It was Alys's turn to come back to earth with a bump.

'Alys, whatever were you thinking of?' demanded Kate. 'Here we are, with good jobs hard to come by, and you throw yours away! Have you gone mad? I don't know what your father will say!'

Alys allowed herself a wry smile. Her father would be too busy on the golf course or at the Rotary Club meetings to pay much attention to what *she* was up to. As far as he was concerned, his three children were off his hands now they were grown up. He'd step in if he had to, but really, he felt that he'd done his duty by them. Of course, it went without saying that Kate and all of them would be well provided for should anything happen to him.

Alys pushed back her chair and stood up. 'Well, I'd say it's rather good timing myself, considering Aunt Moira's situation. Look, you email her back and say I'll be there by Tuesday. I'll head back to

London, sort out a few things at the house, book my ticket and I'll be on my way.'

And with that, Alys left the kitchen, leaving Kate stunned, staring blankly at her computer screen. The kitchen door opened again. It was Alys, the rucksack that served as her handbag in hand.

'I'll be off, then. There's a train back to London in twenty minutes. If I leave now I'll just make it. Love to Dad. I'll be in touch when I'm in Yorkshire, to let you know how Auntie Moira's doing.' And then Alys was gone.

Kate, still reeling after the swift turn of events, noted that the hem was coming down at the back of Alys's dress. And those army boots looked like they'd not seen any polish in a long, long while.

CHAPTER 2

The interior of King's Cross station seemed to have been rebuilt when Alys arrived there, which was baffling. Surely the last time that she'd been up to Yorkshire it was as reassuringly familiar as it had been for the last twenty or thirty years? She struggled to get her bearings, disconcerted. She queued in WHSmith for a book of stamps, needing to post a letter before she left, only to discover that the new station seemed to lack a postbox. After dragging her suitcase around outside in the pouring rain, in the hope of spotting a familiar red pillar box, Alys gave up, wet through and anxious about time passing.

If she'd been travelling with Tim, of course, he would have been at the station far enough in advance to lunch nearby, having worked out beforehand where to eat. His packing would have been well-practised perfection. He would have had exactly the right amount of clothes, with one set to spare. He wouldn't have had to unzip his case eight times before leaving the house to stuff in more shoes and a hairbrush, then take the shoes out again and put in two jumpers, then take one of the jumpers out and put in a T-shirt instead. Indecision wasn't Tim's thing.

Alys's forward planning had stretched to buying a sandwich in WHSmith along with the stamps, so now she only needed to stand and stare at the departures board along with everyone else. She tried to think back to when she'd last travelled alone. France, Greece, and that ill-fated trip to India – they'd all been with school or college friends. Paris, Venice, Florida – with Tim, or previous boyfriends. Could this really be the first time *ever*?

The train was up on the board, prompting a flurry of activity on the concourse, and a determined rush for the barrier. Alys trekked along the platform to Coach B. It looked as though all the pre-booked seats had been crammed into one carriage, instead of spread out through the train. She settled into her seat with her book, waterproof jacket in the rack above. The letter to Tim was still in her bag so, as soon as she arrived, she'd post it. It stated pretty clearly, she thought, how fondness was not really an option. She was looking for more, or maybe less, than that and so she was going to use this time away to think things through. She allowed herself a small smile, then sighed. It was her way of dodging the issue. In her heart, she knew things were over but she couldn't bring herself to spell it out. She hoped that he'd get the picture, but Tim was used to things going his own way. He'd call, text, email.

Of course, he'd try to change her mind. But she didn't have to reply, did she?

Rain coursed down the window. It was such a long train that her coach was already out in the open, exposed to the elements. Every raindrop reflected the leaden sky. The weather was doing nothing to lighten her mood.

Resolutely, she opened her book. A rare chance to read: something else to be thankful for. This was going to be a journey into a better future, she told herself firmly. No dwelling on past mistakes. It was time to move on.

CHAPTER 3

Alys's book had remained face down on her tray table, spine creased, pages open, for most of the journey. She had read for a while then, once they were clear of London, she'd gazed out of the window, wrapped up in her thoughts, looking back over the past few months, her newly formed resolution already forgotten.

When she was younger, she'd always preferred to do things on the spur of the moment, hated having to plan ahead, have her life mapped out for her. Her friends, and Tim for that matter, liked to sort out their calendars for several weeks ahead. Her friends' lives followed the same routine. Drinks after work on Friday, meet up late on Saturday afternoon for shopping and a gossip about the previous evening, and a discussion about what to wear that evening, probably necessitating the purchase of something new. Recovering from Saturday night on Sunday, maybe the afternoon spent in the pub. Posting up the drunken photos on Facebook to remind themselves that they were having fun. The gym a couple of nights a week to knock themselves into some sort of shape for the holidays, which would be planned months ahead 'so there's something to look forward to'.

Alys's snap decisions – first to leave work and now to go up to Yorkshire – were not as simple as they first appeared, perhaps even to herself. She'd told herself that she was bored in her job, and it was this that was making her feel restless. In addition, though, she had a strange sense of not belonging anywhere anymore.

Late one Sunday afternoon a few weeks previously, as she took the chain off the door to head out to buy some milk, she had realised that the chain had been in place since she went to bed on Friday evening. She'd not left the house, nor spoken to anyone, not even on the phone. Tim was away, and she'd sidestepped texts and emails from friends about meeting up, making vague allusions to visiting family. It was hard for her to acknowledge what lay behind this new tendency to be a hermit. It was true that she'd become increasingly reclusive after her best friend Hannah had gone travelling with Matt, her boyfriend. Their planned six-month trip had already stretched beyond a year. But since Alys had been a teenager, she'd always loved to be out and about, always had a feeling of excitement and anticipation on a Friday evening, wondering what the weekend had in store. Now she couldn't remember when she'd last felt like that, and she was pretty sure that the reason behind the change lay not with her friends, nor with Tim or with her social life, but in a stupid incident at work.

Her company, publishers of a trade magazine, was small and family run: her boss, Charles, was the son of the chairman. He was funny, Alys supposed, if you didn't mind being the butt of suggestive jokes. The general atmosphere in the office was so relaxed that she'd never paid his behaviour much attention, apart from sighing and rolling her eyes along with the other girls at his so-called witty innuendos. She'd met his wife at the Christmas party, and his kids sometimes came into the office during the school holidays. So far, so normal, until she'd noticed that whenever he came to look at work on her screen he started off with one hand on her desk, one hand on her chair, effectively trapping her there. The hand on the chair often strayed to her shoulder. She'd learnt to swivel the chair to reach for something, so that he had to move. She didn't think he suspected that she'd noticed what he was up to.

One evening a couple of months previously, when an urgent deadline meant that they had to work later than usual, he came in with wine, crisps and pizza 'to keep the troops going'. Alys began to feel uneasy as the others finished their work, packed up and started to drift away. She still needed to put the finishing touches to the cover and it looked as though she would be the last to leave. She'd barely sipped her wine, wanting to keep a clear head until everything was signed off, but she noticed that Charles had kept a bottle all to himself and he was well on the way to finishing it.

'I'm done here,' she said at last, shutting down her computer and gathering up her belongings.

'Wait,' he said. 'I just wanted to tell you how pleased I am with how hard you've been working to meet the deadlines. Can I buy you a drink to say thanks?'

'Oh, there's no need, you've already done that,' said Alys, pointing at her wine glass, now half empty.

Charles wasn't going to give up so easily. 'Dinner, then?' he said.

Alys started to put on her coat. 'That's very kind of you, but I really must get going.' She was already heading for the exit but he was there before her, back to the door, arm stretched across the doorway.

'You must have noticed how I feel about you?' He breathed wine fumes into her face.

Alys's heart lurched. 'Well, I—' Was yes, or no, the best answer?

'You *did* know!' he said, triumphant. 'You were just leading me on . . .' Before Alys could protest, he'd pulled her to him and was kissing her hard. Part of her brain was detached, dispassionate, aware of the sour wine on his breath, the prickle of stubble. Alarm bells were ringing in the other half – she needed to make him stop.

She tried to pull away from him, but he was

too strong for her. 'Oh, I've been watching you for so long,' he murmured into her neck. His skin was radiating heat and he was tugging at her buttons, slipping his hand inside the neck of her shirt. Alys felt paralysed. Was this really happening? Could she kick him? Knee him in the groin and make a run for it? Even as she thought these things, images of how the next day would play out were crowding in. Was this going to be the end of her job? The one she took pride in and had worked hard at over the last couple of years, to become part of the close-knit team?

Summoning all her strength she pulled away from him, grabbing his arms and holding them at his sides.

'For God's sake Charles, you're a married man.' It sounded positively Victorian, but it was the best she could come up with. Could she preserve her job by maintaining his dignity?

He just laughed. 'And that's what makes it all the better. No strings attached on either side, eh?'

Alys took a deep breath. There was no way out of this. She was going to have to tell him exactly what she thought of him. At that moment, the door behind him flew open, and a face appeared in the doorway.

Startled, the new arrival said, 'Sorry, sorry. I thought you'd all left. I'll come back. Five minutes?'

Alys seized her chance, pushed past Charles and resisted the urge to hug the cleaner. The poor man looked embarrassed enough already. 'No, it's abso-lutely fine,' she said. 'I was just on my way out.' Then she fled, without looking back.

She ran all the way to the Tube and felt blessed when the train arrived at the platform at the same time as she did. She slept fitfully that night, anxious about the next day, about how Charles might react to her. Would there be a trumped-up dismissal? Or another clumsy attempt at seduction?

Nothing happened. Instead of feeling relieved, Alys found herself jumpy and unable to relax. She wanted to discuss it with him and clear the air, but it was too awkward a topic to broach. How would you start? 'By the way Charles, about last night when you tried it on?' 'How's the wife, Charles? I'd love to catch up for a chat.'

Her inability to take action seemed to have sapped her vitality. Increasingly, she found herself observing, rather than taking part in, social gath-erings. There'd been that after-work drink she'd dragged herself along to, a week or so after the incident, when Laura, one of her workmates had asked her, 'What have you done to upset Charles? I've noticed him picking on you for no reason.' Alys had looked at her in mute astonishment, not sure what to say, indeed, whether it was safe to say anything at all. Laura looked puzzled, then gasped. 'Oh, you weren't treated to one of his late-night working specials, were you? Just ignore it and pretend it never happened. I always say it should be written into the contract. *Clause 2.5. Permission for Mr Rollinson to try it on at least once without employee inflicting grievous injury.'*

Alys was horrified but she tried to give herself a talking-to. Laura had shrugged off Charles's behaviour – why couldn't she? She couldn't get rid of the feeling, though, that Laura should have warned her to be on her guard.

Her feelings started to turn to anger as time passed, but she felt that there was no one she could take her complaint to in a small family firm. It would be her word against that of her boss. Rather than having it out with Charles it felt easier to do nothing. Instead, she brooded on the incident. She no longer looked forward to going into work each day and she was hardly aware of how insular she'd become. She found herself going through the motions of life, following her normal routines, but simply not engaging with them anymore. And soon it became easier to dodge invitations and shut herself away.

The Sunday when Alys, setting out to buy milk, realised that she hadn't left the house or spoken to anyone all weekend, had provided a rare moment of clarity. It had pierced the fug of inertia that had descended upon her. She had decided there and then that the best thing to do was to leave work after all. She was bored in her job, she told herself – blocking out the fact that once upon a time she'd looked forward to each day in the office. She needed a change of scene.

As the plan took shape in her mind, the original reasons were gradually buried, and before long she had convinced herself that boredom and restlessness were her only motivations.

Alys dragged herself out of her reverie, aware that the train had just pulled into a station. She forced herself to focus, looking for the name on the platform. It was Doncaster – they were well on the way. She people-watched from the window as the train waited there for a few minutes. A portly, balding gentleman in a suit drank from his polystyrene coffee cup, gazing intently down the tracks. He turned, and Alys caught a glimpse of an unexpected thin, greying ponytail. As the train pulled out, she saw local buses, the top decks filled with people, heading home after shopping. Who knew where to, or what awaited them there? At the next stop, Wakefield, a man stood in shorts and sunglasses, apparently oblivious to the rain and the fact that all those around him sported coats and umbrellas. Alys was intrigued by these little glimpses into other people's worlds. Who were these people, and what were their lives like? It was a reminder that there *were* other lives apart from her own, equally filled with problems, challenges, achievements, boredom, and happiness.

She changed trains at Leeds, struggling to pull her case out of the rack. She found herself caught up in the confusion of what seemed to be rush hour, even though it was only four o'clock. The train for Northwaite was already standing at the platform, just a couple of carriages this time, heat belting out as though it was a winter's day rather than early April. She took a seat near the door, calculating how many stations there were until her stop. Passengers got on, looked uncertain, asked Alys if they were on the right train. She hadn't a clue, but smiled politely and tried to help.

Once the journey was under way, the elderly man across the aisle tried to draw Alys into conversation. She was guarded in her responses, then felt bad. This was Yorkshire, after all, not London. It was normal here to chat, to be interested in others and what they were up to. This was something she was going to need to embrace: all part of reinventing herself and beginning her new life.

CHAPTER 4

The approach to Bradford held both mosques and mills. It seemed like an odd juxtaposition, the graceful exteriors and gleaming domes of the mosques standing out against the soot-blackened and forbidding Victorian architecture, smoke stacks and minarets paired. No sign of towering office blocks or cranes creating yet more high-rises: this was a landscape new to her. The train rested at the station for longer than usual and, with only a few stops to go now, Alys suddenly felt a flutter of apprehension. *What had she done?*

Rain was still coursing down the train windows when they pulled into Alys's stop. She heaved her suitcase onto the platform. She had received a text from her aunt on the train, saying that she'd send someone to pick her up and that there was no need to get a taxi. Alys headed into the car park and looked around. She hadn't thought to ask for any further details, she'd been so caught up in her thoughts. She'd have to call her aunt and find out who she should be looking for.

She dug into her rucksack, feeling around. She

couldn't locate her phone. 'Damn', Alys cursed under her breath, panic rising in case she'd left it on the train. She rested the rucksack on top of her case and began to dig deeper. It was then that a battered Land Rover, the old, green variety, roared into the car park, and pulled up beside her.

'You must be Alys,' said the driver, leaning across and flinging open the passenger door, without switching off the engine. 'Hop in.'

Alys was rather taken aback. 'How do you know I'm Alys?' she demanded suspiciously. The driver was a man of about her own age, casually dressed in jeans and a jumper, and apparently oblivious to the weather.

He looked her up and down, taking in her rain-soaked hair, the escaped strands which were plastered to her cheeks for once, rather than springing wildly in all directions, the crêpe-de-Chine dress only partially covered by a rather horrid red-and-grey cagoule that had once belonged to her brother, and the army-type boots.

'Your Aunt Moira gave me a pretty accurate description when she asked me to collect you,' he said, with a wide grin.

Alys, feeling her cheeks redden, and trying to hide her embarrassment, attempted to pull her suitcase closer to the Land Rover. There was a grinding noise as one of the wheels caught in the paving stones. She tugged impatiently. The suitcase pulled free of the paving, but left a wheel embedded there and keeled over. Her open rucksack flew off the top of the case and upended itself, scattering her possessions everywhere. Alys watched, horrified, as her phone – clearly not left on the train after all – skidded along the ground and came to a halt perilously close to the grille over a drain.

'Oh crap!' Alys bent down and scrabbled around, trying to gather all her belongings before the rain soaked everything, stuffing them haphazardly back into the rucksack.

'I'm Rob, by the way,' said her driver, who'd now hopped out of the Land Rover, leaving the engine still running, and was trying to help Alys gather her things. She rather wished he wouldn't – the emptying of the rucksack had exposed a muddle of dirty tissues, receipts, scribbled shopping lists, half-full packets of chewing gum and sweets, coins, a pine cone and a less-than-clean comb.

'What about this?' Rob held up a letter, now crumpled and damp, by his fingertips.

'Oh!' Alys almost snatched it from him. 'I meant to post it before I left. Is there a postbox here?'

'Maybe you should let it dry out for a bit first? If it's important.' Rob seemed to have judged from her reaction that it was. 'Here,' he took it back from her and flattened it out on the vehicle's dashboard. 'You can post it up in Northwaite later.'

He turned his attention to her suitcase, heaving it into the back of the Land Rover. 'I see you've come to stay for a bit,' he remarked, looking back at Alys over his shoulder. 'Good job you didn't try to fly up – they'd have charged you excess baggage!'

'It's mainly books,' muttered Alys, on the defensive. It was partly true. Moira had asked for several cookery books for inspiration, and she'd tossed in some travel guides for good measure, so she could start planning for her trip.

'Hope you haven't been waiting long,' added Rob, climbing back into the driver's seat and patting the passenger's seat to encourage Alys to get in. 'The battery was flat, so I had to get a push down the hill and hope for the best. That's why the engine's running, just in case.' And with that he slammed the Land Rover into gear and they were off. The letter to Tim sat on the dashboard, an uncomfortable reminder to Alys of something that she needed to resolve.

She settled herself rather gingerly in her seat, aware that it looked as though it might have held a dog or a muddy jacket until recently. She wrinkled her nose: yes, there was a definite aroma of wet dog. Alys looked away, gazing out of the window. The hill out of the town looked nearly vertical. Rob obviously knew the road well – he drove speedily but carefully. He didn't say another word and Alys began to wonder whether she should try to make conversation. She looked at him surreptitiously out of the corner of her eye, registering wavy brown hair, a checked shirt topped with a ribbed navy sweater (holey at the elbows) and broad hands (none too clean) grasping the steering wheel.

'Um, Rob – is that short for Robert?' she ventured, to break the silence.

'No,' said Rob, shortly.

'Oh.' The silence grew, developing a portentous quality. Alys had the feeling that she had said something wrong.

Finally, Rob sighed, shifted up a gear as the road levelled out, and said, 'Robin'.

'Robin!' Alys tried to stifle a snort of laughter. The name really didn't suit him.

'Ok, I know.' Rob glanced sideways at her. She was relieved to notice the hint of a smile lifting his previously stern expression. 'Blame my mum. When she was expecting me she was stuck at home with bad morning sickness. She fed this robin in the garden every day, apparently. It got so tame that it would fly over to sit on her hand as soon as she stepped outside the back door. She saw it as some sort of good omen, so she promised to name her firstborn after it.'

It was Rob's turn to snort, sardonically.

'Aah, that's a lovely story.' Alys was encouraged by how positively chatty he'd become. 'Well, I don't know who I'm named after. Alice in Wonderland, perhaps?'

'Hmmm, that figures,' said Rob, but before she could ask him what he meant by that, the Land Rover came to a halt and Rob leapt out, leaving the engine still running. He opened her door, and turned to haul her suitcase from the back.

'Don't forget your letter,' he said. 'The postbox is on the main street. Moira will be pleased to see you. That back injury has been making her feel a bit desperate. Can you manage now?' He paused. 'I'll give you a hand with your case onto the path. It's that door along there – the blue one. Don't let Moira lay a hand on this case, mind, or she'll be in hospital.'

Clearly finding this funny, he chuckled to himself, settled back in the driving seat and drove off, leaving Alys to struggle her one-wheeled case along the path that ran between a row of cottages and the church. She had the distinct feeling that she hadn't made a very good impression and she couldn't for the life of her work out why she even cared.

The blue door flew open before Alys reached it, and there was Moira, leaning heavily on a walking frame. Her short wavy hair was threaded with far more grey than when Alys had last seen her, and she looked pale and drawn, but she was beaming from ear to ear.

'I thought I heard Rob's Land Rover,' she said. 'You're here at last. Come in, come in. There's tea, and cake, of course.'

CHAPTER 5

Later that evening, after Moira had shuffled painfully up the stairs to rest in bed, and Alys had made sure that she'd swallowed her painkillers, before arranging her pillows to support her back and ease any pressure on her spine, Alys decided it was time to get her bearings and take a tour of the village before it got dark.

Latching the door behind her, she headed along Church Lane into the cobbled main street. Seen up close, the cobbles came as a shock – she had expected smooth, polished, rounded stones of different hues of brown. She'd seen something like that before, but where? Perhaps in a museum in York, when she was small? The Northwaite cobbles, however, were pretty much uniform in size and looked as though they might have come from a garden centre. Alys wasn't sure that the local tourist authority would appreciate her description, but they'd added nothing to her journey along the road in the Land Rover. She'd be surprised if any of the cars around here still had their suspension intact.

She spotted the postbox: a flat, red panel set

into the grey-stone wall, a tub of bright daffodils beneath it. She hesitated a moment – the letter now looked a bit of a mess. Tim wouldn't be happy. Then she shrugged, and posted it. After all, he'd be even less happy when he'd read it . . .

Turning her gaze to the road ahead, she took in the grey-stone houses fronting the street, hugging it on each side. Window boxes and flower tubs and, in one case, a tiny stone seat, had been squeezed into the available area between the front windows and the pavement, the strong colours of the spring flowers throwing the blackened and weathered stone into sharp contrast. The front doors opened straight into the sitting rooms and, where lights had been turned on inside, Alys could see that the rooms were dominated by huge stone fireplaces that seemed out of place in such small spaces.

Pausing to catch her breath as the road climbed steeply out of the village, she found herself already high up and quite exposed, gazing out at three surrounding and distant hills of a similar height. The road swept off into the distance over one hill, a monument topped a second, moorland the third. Lights were starting to twinkle here and there in the gathering dusk.

Although it was past eight in the evening it was still not quite dark. The light had the strangest quality, tinged with both a grey and a yellow hue. Dark clouds were gathering over to her left and Alys could see a mist sweeping through the valley.

It looked as though rain was heading her way. Her hair, whipped by the wind, was springing free of the elastic band and blowing across her eyes. She shivered, wishing she'd worn something warmer under her cagoule. She remembered Moira's advice before she'd left London. 'Pack some warm clothes. It always feels about ten degrees colder up here.' Perhaps this wasn't the right evening to continue her explorations?

She turned, heading back towards the lights of the village. The last cottage on the high street was more noticeable viewed from this angle. She'd been struck by its ornate stone gatepost and the front door with a carved stone arch above it as she'd headed out of the village. It had seemed unusually grand for a cottage. She now saw that there was a side door, too, with a little niche cut quite high on the wall beside it, similar to the type of thing you might see in a church. This was also decorated with a stone arch, and a pillar candle burned in a glass storm lantern placed in the niche. It was a nice touch, thought Alys, hurrying back towards the haven of Moira's cottage as the first drops of rain began spattering the paving stones. She hoped the flame would survive the coming storm.

CHAPTER 6

The key felt weighty in Alys's pocket, where it sat along with the code for the café alarm on a folded piece of paper that she turned through her fingers as she walked. She felt a mixture of trepidation and excitement: trepidation that she would fumble the alarm code and trigger the alarm, and excitement at getting a proper look at the café for the first time. It lay in the opposite direction to the one she had taken when she had explored yesterday evening. The memory of posting her letter came back to her and she experienced a frisson of worry as she walked. Her letter would be on its way to Tim now. When would the consequences be felt?

At breakfast that morning Moira had said, 'Why don't you take the keys and go and have a look around the café? Then maybe we could think about baking and you could open it on a part-time basis until I'm feeling a bit better, so that my regulars don't think I've abandoned them.'

Then she'd given Alys directions and the instructions for the alarm and so here she was, standing outside the door. The Celestial Cake Café was well placed, on a bend shortly after you came into the village. They must have driven right past it after Rob had collected her from the station the day before, Alys reflected, but she had failed to register it. The café had one large window and a smaller one on either side of the front door, which was set back, providing shelter from the weather. Yesterday's rain had given way to clear skies and a brisk wind that had buffeted her on her walk and Alys appreciated the moment's respite as she prepared to open the door. The door handle, fingerplate and letterbox were made of ornate brass, polished and with a lovely soft sheen that suggested years of use. The exterior paintwork had been freshly done, in a light-sage green to match the door, and 'The Celestial Cake Café' was lettered in a simple black script across the top of the façade. The most striking thing, though, was the pair of white angel's wings that hung in the largest of the two windows. They looked as though they might have been taken from a statue. Alys smiled to herself – she wondered where Moira had got them. They were an original and memorable touch.

She steeled herself to open the door and deal with the alarm but, as Moira had promised, it was perfectly straightforward and, with the beeping of the keypad stilled and the door closed behind her, she could examine the interior at leisure. The whole room was half panelled in duck-egg blue tongue-and-groove, and the upper part of the walls was painted to match. Framed prints of cherubs and line drawings of angels were intermingled with small watercolour sketches that looked as though they might be of the local area: waterfalls, woodland paths and views of greystone cottages. Mismatched wooden chairs painted in a soft palette of colours – blues, greys, greens and stone – had been provided with seat cushions in an Indian paisley fabric that added a bright splash of hot pink, turquoise and orange. There was a window seat under the angel's wings, piled with cushions in the same soft shades as the chair colours, and a wooden serving counter looked as though it had been created from recycled hefty wooden planks, marked here and there with black strips and holes where iron fixings or nails had been removed.

The café interior was L-shaped and the back section held tiny tables and a wood-burning stove. It was now cold but Alys could imagine how the room with its stone-flagged floor would benefit from the heat in the colder months. She peeped out of the narrow window in the sturdy back door to catch a glimpse of a small courtyard, lined with tubs filled with spring bulbs in full flower: scarlet and orange tulips, creamy yellow narcissi and bright-blue grape hyacinths. Scrubbed tables folded against the wall told her that this would be an extra seating space in the warmer months. All in all, Moira had done a wonderful job, Alys thought as she looked around. And the place was spotless, not a crumb or sticky smear to be seen. She tried to imagine what the café must be like when it was busy with the buzz of conversation, the smell of coffee in the air, the serving counter piled high with cakes and biscuits ready for the customers.

One or two people had passed by the café and Alys noticed their curious glances through the window. She decided that it was time to head back to Moira's before it became necessary to turn customers away so, with the alarm reset and the door locked behind her, she turned her steps back up the hill. She felt a surge of impatience. She wished that she was coming straight back, cake tins and boxes already full, ready to open up the café and get to work. As it was, there was much to be done and her head whirled as she mentally listed all the things she would need to ask Moira about. First things first, though. There were cakes to be made.

CHAPTER 7

The larder in her aunt's kitchen was a thing of delight to Alys. A relic of days gone by, its neatly ordered shelves held all manner of ingredients that Moira used for cake making. Apart from paper sacks of flour from a local mill there were eggs supplied by a nearby farm, slabs of chocolate, packs of sugar in shades from purest white through caramel to dark brown, packets of coconut, and oats, and pats of butter wrapped in paper.

Her introduction to this Aladdin's cave of baker's delights had come on her return from the café when Moira, resting on a chair at the kitchen table, had told her to go and open the door in the corner of the kitchen. Half expecting to find a storage cupboard or a hidden staircase, Alys had stood transfixed on the threshold. Within, all was cool, ordered calm. One section was reserved for Moira's own household needs but the rest was given over to baking. Alys didn't need to ask why the butter and eggs were stored there, rather than in the fridge. She knew that it made it much quicker to bring them up to ideal room temperature for cake-making; the larder, which was tiled, was cool in both winter and summer.

Alys could almost feel her fingers twitching as she surveyed the ingredients. She wanted to make a start right there and then, to fill the kitchen with the wonderful aroma of baking. But something told her to proceed with caution. Moira was in pain and although she'd asked for help to run the café, now that Alys was here she could see that her aunt needed help around the house too.

'Let's move you through to the other room,' Alys said, helping Moira up from the hard kitchen chair. 'I'm going to make you a cup of tea, then you can tell me a bit more about the café. And we can make a plan.'

With Moira settled by the wood burner, and tea on the table beside her, Alys sat down on the sofa. 'So, tell me the story of the café. How did you come up with the name? Where did the lovely cushion fabric come from? And the angel's wings?'

Moira eased herself back against the cushions that Alys had stacked behind her, and over the next hour she described how the transformation of the business had come about. She had taken possession of the café a couple of years previously, when the style of the interior had still reflected the previous owner's taste. It had floral wallpaper, rather faded curtains at the windows and the general feel of being stuck in a 1950s time warp.

'I just ripped off the wallpaper and gave it all a lick of paint. The wings came first, though,' Moira said. 'They inspired me to give the café its new identity. I spotted them in an antique shop in Nortonstall shortly after I took over the lease. I just had to have them – they were so unusual. I thought they would be made of wood or plaster and really heavy but they're not. Otherwise, I would have hung them on the wall rather than in the window. Wouldn't like to think of them falling and squashing the customers.' She chuckled, and then winced – her back muscles were very sore. 'I think they must have been carved out of a block of polystyrene and then given a paint job. Maybe they were a prop from a theatre or some-thing?' She paused to sip her tea. 'So, the name of the café came from the wings, really. I liked the way it sounded, too. Alliterative.'

Alys grasped at some half-remembered fact from her schooldays. 'All the C's at the beginning?' she asked. 'Celestial Cake Café?'

Moira nodded. 'Then it was a case of trying to do the place up as cheaply as possible,' she continued. 'The chairs came from a junk shop and I painted them to use up the tester pots I'd bought when I was trying to get the colours right for the walls and the front door.'

'And the cushions?' Alys asked. 'They're such glorious fabrics.'

'Lovely, aren't they?' Moira was smiling. 'I'd had the fabric stashed away for years, wondering what to do with it, and it seemed to work perfectly. Otherwise, I think the place would have looked a bit too tasteful. I wanted it to look smart but also feel relaxed and homely.'

Moira went on to describe how she had built up the business. Apart from the Post Office and a general store, the café was the only other shop in the tiny village. Locals dropped in for bread, for cakes to take home for tea, for a takeaway sandwich as a change from what was to be found in the fridge at home. Wet mornings found them drawn in for coffee and the chance for a chat and a gossip with the other villagers. Her other customers were tourists, who found their way off the beaten track to visit the imposing church with its beautiful stained glass, or hikers striding out on the trails that took them down into the valley and up again, to the open moorland and the Pennine Way.

'I've mainly concentrated on building up the clientele, finding out which cakes people like best,' Moira said, but Alice could tell that despite her modest assertion she was really pleased with what she had achieved. The picture that Moira painted, of a thriving, bustling business with many loyal customers, made Alys all the more determined to have the café open again as soon as possible. Moira was clearly thinking along much the same lines.

'I made a phone call this morning,' she said. 'To Flo, who helps me out when it's busy in the summer. She'd be happy to come in and work alongside you for a while, to show you the ropes, help you with the coffee machine and the cash register until you get the hang of it. And until I feel more able to be there.'

'That sounds great!' Alys was enthusiastic. 'But who's going to look after you? You can't stay here alone all day. You can barely move as yet.'

'It's not quite that bad,' Moira protested. 'I've got a couple of friends in the village who will pop in and help me out – make me some lunch, get me a cup of tea, that sort of thing. And I need to keep moving otherwise I will stiffen up. I can't be just sitting around all day.'

Alys was longing to experience the café routine that Moira had described to her but she insisted on probing further to make sure that her aunt was going to be properly cared for over the coming days. Finally reassured, she got to her feet to prepare some lunch.

'And then,' she announced, 'you're going to have a rest and I'm going to bake.'

Baking had been an important part of Alys's childhood. It wasn't an interest she had inherited from Kate, who had shown only puzzlement when nine-year-old Alys spent her Sunday afternoons turning out fairy cakes and chocolate cake from packet mixes. She'd graduated to homemade scones after a family summer holiday in Devon, where the whole family – apart from Kate – had embraced cream teas with enthusiasm. Kate had got over her worry about the amount of cake that she might be forced to eat, and the number of calories it contained, when she realised that David, along with Alys's older siblings George and Edward, were only too happy to fulfil their duties, and hers too, in that respect. She left her daughter to it, buying whatever ingredients she requested.

By the time Alys was thirteen, she was in demand among friends and family for birthday cakes, millionaire's shortbread, flapjacks, Bakewell tart, and ginger parkin for Bonfire Night. Then, almost overnight, she'd stopped baking. Kate had suspected that it wasn't cool for a Nineties teen-ager to be into baking. The usual teen interests had taken over: music, fashion magazines and flushed and giggly phone conversations achieved by dragging the household phone out into the draughty hallway for some privacy.

However, in her late twenties, Alys had discovered that the ability to bake wasn't a universal skill and her contributions to her friends' Sunday gatherings were always sweet in nature, guaranteeing open-mouthed admiration. So, she hadn't been daunted at the prospect of helping Moira out in the café. In fact, as soon as she had said that she would do it, she had been looking through recipe books and bookmarking her favourite Internet sites, and she was itching to get started. Tim hadn't been a lover of cake or dessert so her baking opportunities had dwindled of late, although her contributions to charity cake bakes at work had always been the first to sell out. Now she couldn't wait to make a start.

Moira had said it would be best to keep things simple at first – maybe two or three cakes and a couple of different types of biscuit. Everything needed to be sold as freshly made as possible and Alys wouldn't have the speed to batch-bake that Moira had developed over the last year or so.

'If only I could stand for any length of time I could be baking while you are at the café,' Moira said, frowning. 'As it is, you'll have to come home and bake once you've closed up the café for the day.'

Alys caught her eyeing her walking frame in a speculative fashion. 'Oh no you don't.' She laughed. 'You'll get better all the sooner if you rest like the doctor said. You don't want to risk a setback. I'll be able to manage, I'm sure.'

'It's the Easter break next weekend.' Moira sighed. 'If the weather's good there'll be plenty of walkers around. It will be a baptism of fire for you, I'm afraid.'

'First things first,' Alys said, determined not to let Moira's worries rattle her. 'I'm going to get baking so that at least there's something to sell. Then I'll get the café open again. It probably won't be operating in quite the way you'd like it, but it will be better than it being closed at such a busy time.'

Moira laughed. 'I consider myself ticked off. You're right. Time to make a start.'

Alys had been planning which cakes and biscuits to make to impress her aunt but on this subject

Moira was firm. 'The regulars have their favourites. They're slow to adapt to change so it will be safest to stick to what they know at first. So, I'm afraid it's biscuits this afternoon – flapjacks and shortbread. Then tomorrow a Victoria sponge, lemon drizzle cake and maybe a coffee-and-walnut loaf. Or something chocolatey?' Moira was suddenly undecided.

Alys's expression must have given her away. 'I know, I know,' Moira said. 'A bit safe and traditional. When I'm up and about properly we can build on these. I can bake them with my eyes closed but I'm really looking forward to trying some new recipes and I'm sure you've got plenty of ideas.'

Ideas were practically bursting out of Alys, but she limited herself to suggesting that brownies were popular with everyone and would fulfil the need for chocolate, and millionaire's shortbread would make more of a treat than plain shortbread and so it was agreed.

CHAPTER 8

Alys answered a knock at the cottage door the next morning to discover Flo standing there, waiting to help Alys carry the cake tins and boxes to the café. A slender lady in her late forties, her brown hair was swept into a casual up-do, Flo looked tanned and healthy, as if she'd just returned from a holiday abroad. As they chatted on their way to the café it became clear to Alys that this was actually a product of being outdoors most days – she learnt that Flo had given up her high-flying job in London ten years ago to live in the country and indulge her passion for riding. Flo made ends meet with a succession of seasonal jobs and, although she wasn't a baker, Moira had said how invaluable she was to the business.

Alys was feeling excited at the prospect of opening up and serving her first customer, but also more than a little nervous. The last time she had worked in a shop was as a schoolgirl, when she hadn't even had to deal with the till, let alone card payments. Moira had sought to reassure her by saying that most people paid by cash which had unnerved her even more – would her change-giving skills be up to it? Luckily, Flo was more than happy to deal with making the hot drinks and managing the till, leaving Alys to serve the customers. Flo also promised to coach Alys in the use of the shiny and impressive coffee machine and talk her through the general routine of the café in their quieter moments.

However, it was as though the villagers had been watching and waiting for signs that the café had reopened. No sooner had Alys checked that the display of cakes and biscuits looked appealing, and turned the sign on the door to read 'Open', than the first customer was across the threshold.

'I was just passing and wanted to come in and see how Moira was doing. Ooh, that Victoria sponge looks delicious. I think I'll just have a little piece. And a pot of tea, please. Now, you must be Moira's niece?'

'Hello Nancy.' Flo swiftly set out a tray with a teapot and cup and saucer for the white-haired lady standing expectantly at the counter. She was so tiny that she could barely be seen over the cake stands. Alys smiled as she selected the largest piece of sponge for Nancy, her first customer of the day.

'Moira's doing well, thank you. And yes, I'm her niece, Alys, and I'll be here at the café for as long as Moira needs me.'

News of Moira's injury and Alys's arrival to help her out had clearly spread like wildfire around the village and the afternoon sped by, with people dropping in to ask about Moira, then staying for cake and to quiz Alys. At five o'clock, Alys turned the sign to read 'Closed'; her face ached from smiling and she didn't think she could bear to repeat why she was there even one more time.

'Now then,' Flo said mischievously. 'Why did you say you were here again?'

Alys burst out laughing. 'Well, I was taking a break from work with the aim of going travelling and so, when Aunt Moira hurt herself, I was delighted to be able to come and help her out. And yes, I love baking'. She smiled wryly at Flo. 'You must be word-perfect, too, by now.'

Alys surveyed what was left of the cakes. 'We've been busy. Thank you so much for your help. I could never have made the teas and coffees, served cake and given everyone my life story at the same time.'

'It went very well,' Flo said. 'It looks as though your cakes are popular. Moira will be jealous.'

'They're all her recipes,' Alys said hastily. 'I just added one or two touches of my own.'

She couldn't help a little glow of satisfaction, though. More than one person had commented on how much they had enjoyed their cake and Alys was particularly pleased to see that all the brownies and millionaire's shortbread had gone. The downside of such a good day was that she needed to go home and bake again, or get up very early in the morning, as Moira had predicted. She'd also learnt a lesson about portion control. She needed to make sure the biscuits were evenly sized and the slices of cake cut with almost mathematical precision: it was clear that her customers were eagle-eyed and they were quick to point out if someone else had a bigger slice. Alys couldn't imagine any squabbles breaking out at the till as everyone had been so warm and friendly today, but it was better to be on the safe side.

After they had cleared up and washed up, Flo helped Alys to carry the cake tins back to her Aunt Moira's then hurried home, promising to be round at eight the next morning to repeat the routine.

'How did it go?' Moira had clearly been waiting anxiously for her return. Alys, who was unused to spending such a length of time on her feet, would have loved to sit down and chat but the thought of more baking to be done, as well as a meal to prepare for them both, made her hesitate.

'We were really busy,' she said. 'Everyone wanted to know how you were, and to pass on their best wishes.'

Moira was impatient to know more. 'Who came in? Which cakes sold best? How did you find it?'

'We've barely anything left,' Alys said, and she couldn't help a big grin spreading across her face. 'So, really, I should set to and get baking. And also make something for us to eat.'

'We've enough food for about a week,' Moira laughed. 'A couple of friends dropped by with a casserole and a pie, so there's no need to worry about tonight's dinner. Have a cup of tea and tell me all about your afternoon.'

Alys could see that Moira wasn't going to be fobbed off so, with the casserole reheating in the oven, she made tea and gave Moira a detailed account of who had been in, who had eaten what and everything that had been said.

'Well done,' Moira said, sitting back in her chair. 'You'll be even busier tomorrow, you know. If you're open in the morning you'll catch the walkers as they go by. I'd better ask Flo if she can sort out some ingredients for sandwiches. And I'm afraid you're right. You'll need to bake as soon as we have eaten.'

That night, Alys fell into bed feeling absolutely exhausted. Three more cakes were waiting to be filled and decorated in the morning, with brownies and millionaire's shortbread divided into portions and cooling on the rack. With flap-jacks still to be made in the morning she fell into a deep sleep, waking in the middle of an anxiety dream about a giant tin of syrup that she was trying to open with an old-fashioned can opener as it didn't appear to have a lid. A sweet buttery aroma was filling her nostrils and down in the kitchen she found Moira propped by the stove, stirring oats into the butter, syrup and sugar mixture that she had already prepared. Alys scolded her but was secretly grateful – there was still a lot to be done before Flo arrived.

Friday was as busy as the previous day but followed a slightly different routine. The early walkers were the first through the door, picking up supplies for their hikes, then locals came in for coffee, with tourists appearing in the afternoon for tea and cake, followed by walkers paying a final visit on their return trip in the late afternoon.

The day had passed in much of a blur for Alys although one worrying fact had stuck in her mind. 'I'll never get the hang of that coffee machine,' she'd complained to Flo as she'd carried a tray of dirty cups and plates through to the tiny kitchen. 'Both my attempts were undrinkable.'

'You will,' Flo soothed. 'We'll have a practise one day when it's a bit quieter. With the Easter holidays here why don't you concentrate on the cake side of things and maybe the teas, and leave the rest to me? You're doing brilliantly. And I can go home and put my feet up – you have to put in all those hours baking at the end of the day.'

Alys would never admit it to anyone, but she hadn't realised just how tiring this was going to be. Baking for friends was one thing. Keeping a café supplied whilst working there as well, was something else altogether. The thought of going home to bake, instead of flopping in front of the TV, was deeply unappealing. But she'd promised Moira that it wouldn't be a problem and, besides, she loved seeing the customers enjoying what she'd made. Plus, Moira had been doing this for ages and she was much older than Alys.

Alys told herself that she would get used to it, and so it proved. After taking the Sunday off her energy levels revived; she found serving in the café less tiring as she became more used to it and she even found time to add a few more cakes to the range, just in time for Easter. By now Alys was getting to know the local customers pretty well, and to understand the walkers a little better. She always smiled to herself as she served them.

'Shall we have this?' They would lust over the lavishly iced coffee-and-walnut loaf, or the Victoria sponge, thickly layered with jam and buttercream. Sanity always prevailed, though, and if they were stopping off before heading out on a hike they bought sandwiches. If they bought something sweet it was 'to top up the energy levels later,' and they settled on sensible flapjacks, millionaire's shortbread or brownies, all folded into brown paper bags and tucked into rucksacks to be enjoyed by the side of a rushing stream, or up on a peaty moorland path. If they were heading home after their walk, they would linger over a pot of tea and a well-earned slice of banana cake or raspberry cheesecake, stretching and easing tired leg muscles as they chatted about their day.

After just over a week, Alys had settled into her new role and anticipated opening up the café each morning with the same sense of enjoyment that she'd once felt about going to her design job. She loved lifting the cakes out of their boxes, positioning them on the special stands on the counter with the biscuits in baskets beside them. The appreciative 'oohs' and 'aahs' of the customers as they walked in and took in the display and the lovely aroma of freshly baked cake never failed to bring a smile to her face. But by the time Moira felt able to come back to work part-time the weekend after Easter, Alys was starting to formulate some more plans.

CHAPTER 9

Although Alys had fallen in love with the café the moment she saw it, once Moira had been back at work for a couple of weeks she plucked up courage to ask her whether she would mind if she made one or two changes of her own. Her inspiration had come on a visit to Nortonstall to collect some baking supplies. To her relief, she'd discovered that she didn't need to take the near-vertical route to the town via the main road. Instead, there was a path that wound its way through the woods, descending level by level on a track that was soft underfoot: here the light filtered green through the trees, and there were glimpses every now and then of the river rushing darkly, and the steep woods rising on the other side of the valley. After the peace and solitude of the path, it was a shock to find herself on the main road, busy with traffic, just outside the town. It was in the window of a Nortonstall charity shop that she'd spotted a lovely vintage cup and saucer, and bought it at once as a present for Moira. Alys could picture it displayed on the grey-painted shelves in the alcove behind the till, beneath the old dark-wood station clock that ticked so peacefully into the room. The cup and saucer had a delicate blue-and-white design of dragonflies, foliage and flowers that looked like orchids. Moira loved it and so did the customers.

So, on her visits to Nortonstall on her rare after-noons off, Alys started to look out for single cups and saucers and mismatched plates. She soon exhausted the stock in the charity shop, but she found a tiny antique shop tucked away up a steep alley off the main street. The doorbell jangled as she absorbed a waft of the smell of old books mixed with the scent of roses, and picked her way through the overflowing shelves, anticipation mounting. After her first visit, when she bore her trophies home, Moira told her that this was the very shop where she had bought the angel's wings. So, the next time that she paid the shop a visit, Alys mentioned this to the owner, and explained why she was on the lookout for vintage china. Before long Claire, the shop's owner, had taken to hunting out suitably lovely bits of china and setting them on one side for Alys. Gradually, vintage milk jugs and sugar bowls had been added to Alys's treasure trove, and she found herself invited for tea with Claire in the tangled garden, draped with wisteria, that swept down from the back of the shop towards the river. Alys took to bringing along a slice or two of cake from the café, ones that she thought Claire might appreciate. She learnt that she could rely on Claire for candid comments on new recipes that she had introduced, appreciative or otherwise. The courgette cake got a thumbs-up for being surprisingly moist, but the beetroot cake had an odd texture and Claire declared a preference for not mixing vegetables with cake too frequently. She would make a pot of Earl Grey and bring out slices of lemon in a dish along with the bone-china plates, cups and saucers that had belonged to her grandmother. They were much-coveted by Alys but she wouldn't dream of mentioning it to Claire. With the sign on the shop turned to 'Closed' they'd sip tea while they soaked up the sun and took in the view down the valley. Alys would try to imagine life back in London, but it was hard. It might as well have been a million miles away, rather than a couple of hundred.

Back in the Northwaite café, the china collection grew until the shelves could hold no more. Moira used the beautiful vintage jugs to decorate the scrubbed tables that the warmer weather had encouraged her to set up in the courtyard. Meadow flowers, such as cow parsley, poppies, cornflowers or whatever happened to be in season, were combined with aquilegia or old-fashioned scented roses from Moira's garden, all spilling over the sides of the jugs in profusion. The villagers exclaimed with delight whenever a new item of china appeared and soon took to bringing in offerings of their own. 'We've had this old thing sitting in the back of the cupboard for years,' they'd say, holding out a beautiful sandwich plate with shaped and gilded edges, decorated with flower borders of yellow-and-white daisies threaded through with forget-me-nots. Or 'This was Mum's Sunday-best cup. She kept it to drink her tea from after church. We know she would have liked you to have it for the café,' as they handed over a bone-china cup and saucer, so delicate you could almost see your fingers through it.

A slice or two of Moira's best chocolate chiffon cake, or a couple of freshly baked scones and tiny pots of homemade jam and clotted cream, neatly parcelled into a brown box, would be waiting when it was time for the donor to leave the café.

Alys persuaded Moira that it was time to release some of the china from the overflowing displays, and use it to serve the customers. At first, Moira was reluctant to make the café reliant on delicate china that had to be washed by hand. But her customers' delighted reactions to the pieces soon persuaded her otherwise and within a day or two her regulars had already earmarked their favourite cups. Matching cups and saucers to the people she was serving soon became a favourite pastime for Alys. Moira still kept a supply of the practical white china on hand though, so that they could offer their customers a choice. She'd realised that the dainty cups with their delicate handles made some of them nervous and clumsy, fearful of breakages.

Alys was disappointed when the café's china

collection had reached capacity and Moira had to beg her to stop buying. 'There'll be no room for our customers at this rate,' she said, laughing. But Alys simply couldn't bear to pass by when she saw a particularly nice piece of vintage china or porcelain for sale and the collection of cups, saucers, plates and bowls continued to grow. Her delight in vintage styling had tapped in to something she hadn't even suspected about herself, and she was hungry for a further challenge. Her disappointment at being urged to stop collecting was relieved a little when, following up on a customer's tip off, she took the train from Nortonstall to Saltaire, and paid a visit to the vintage clothing and fabric stall in Salts Mill. There she snapped up starched white cloths, lovingly preserved and intricately decorated with crocheted panels, lace and embroidery. They were too fine to be laundered for daily use in the café, but Alys had a plan – she was going to offer to supply vintage china and complete table dressings to the weddings for which Moira created towers of cupcakes, or tiered iced sponge cakes, garlanded with sugar-paste roses and iced tendrils and vines. Before long, crates of linen and china were packed and held at the ready in the store room, ready to dress the tables at the many summer weddings for which Moira had already taken orders that year. Alys felt her creative spirit unfurl and spread its wings, rather like the angel's wings that she was hoping to persuade Moira to introduce to the company logo and the cake boxes.

It seemed as though each day her brain was buzzing with a new idea to try out and Moira, now back at work full-time, had to suggest quite forcibly that she should take a day off that didn't involve anything at all to do with the café or with baking, in an effort to get her to switch off and relax. So, as spring turned into summer, Alys went less frequently in search of vintage treasures and began to explore the countryside all around Northwaite, as she had started to do on her very first evening in the village.

CHAPTER 10

'**B**ogbean and myrtle. *Pulmonaria*,' recited Alys to herself as she meandered down the path to the bathing pool. It was her favourite path, the one with the stone she called the fairy slide, where the granite had been worn so smooth by the passage of feet that it was scooped in the centre, with raised sides. It undulated down the hillside, reminding her of the long slide at a theme park somewhere in Cornwall that she'd been to many years before, as a child.

She knew that she was mixing up common and Latin names for plants, but the sound of the words pleased her, making their own kind of rhythm to accompany her as she went along the path. Her aunt had been teaching her, surprised by her lack of knowledge of anything other than the most basic garden flowers. Alys made a point of taking photos of flowers on her phone when she was out and about, then taking them back to Moira so they could check them out against the hand-drawn illustrations in Moira's battered copy of *The Concise British Flora in Colour*.

The pool was in sight below, glinting invitingly

through the trees on this late-spring morning. The water would be freezing, fresh off the moors. She shivered in anticipation. It should be just the right depth at the moment. Any deeper, and she would start imagining moorland monsters lurking down there, their presence protected by the locals who told not a soul about them. Alys smiled to herself. First fairies and now monsters. Her imagination was definitely running away with her. There was something about this area, this valley, though. It felt as though it held so much history, so many secrets.

She shivered again, and shrugged her shoulders in an attempt to break free of the spell it had cast over her. It was a beautiful day, the sort that May offers to seduce you into thinking that summer has truly arrived. The sun was high, the sky all but cloudless and a bright clear blue that stretched upwards into infinity.

Alys crossed the bridge over the stream and stretched out on her back on the grassy bank a little way from the pool. She'd discovered it two or three weeks ago, on one of her walks along the river bank. It was located a little further than she had travelled during her previous explorations, but she soon realised that it could also be reached via the path down the hillside, although this route was less appealing for the journey home when it seemed unaccountably steeper. The pool was a perfect natural formation: a basin formed by rocks, before the water funnelled away and tumbled over stones downstream to Nortonstall, a couple of miles away. The pool always seemed to be calm and still, the water dark and peaceful, and it had suggested itself as the ideal spot for a swim to Alys one day when she realised that the only thing she missed about her trips to the gym back in London was the chance to go swimming. Hauling around sacks of flour, baking, carrying trays of dirty crockery and sweeping the café floor gave her enough of a workout, she reasoned. Swimming would offer some of that nice, gentle relaxation that Moira was recommending.

She gazed up at the sky, watching swifts dart across her vision on high, then swooping low, scooping up insects and shrieking to each other with their high-pitched calls. She was looking forward to the shock of plunging into the pool's icy water, but she wanted to lie there a while first, warming herself in the sun. Bees buzzed busily around the gorse bushes that were scattered around the edge of the grass and on the hillside, which stretched up behind her. Moira had told her about gorse's coconut scent, and she hadn't believed her at first. But now she could smell it quite clearly, wafting over her as she lay there, relaxing into the ground and soaking up wellbeing in every fibre of her body.

CHAPTER 11

As Alys busied herself in the kitchen that evening, chopping onions and garlic, frying, stirring, adding chorizo, tomatoes, Arborio rice and fresh herbs, and absorbing the fragrance filling the room, her mind was drawn back to her afternoon at the bathing pool. It had been an effort to swim in the end, once she'd woken, fuzzy-headed, from her nap in the warm sun. She'd opened her eyes, but couldn't quite take in where she was at first. There was the smell of greenery, of bracken and ferns. Her mouth was dry, and to her horror she realised it was open. She sat up. Had she been snoring? Drooling? Thank goodness there was no one around to see! Her swimming costume felt hot and sticky against her skin, so she unbuttoned her dress and shrugged it off, unlacing her sneakers before she picked her way over the slippery stones at the edge of the pool. Her plain black costume was in striking contrast to her usual attire, chosen because she'd always preferred to be as inconspicuous as possible in the swimming pool at her gym.

Once in the water, she hadn't been able to help

a grin spreading right across her face despite the chill that was starting to numb her whole body. It was a spectacular spot for a swim – about as unlike the gym pool as it was possible to be. She looked up towards the wooded hill on one side of the valley, gorse banks on the other, climbing up to plateaus of fields at the top.

When she turned back, she'd noticed a figure crossing the packhorse bridge. She paid it no attention, imagining whoever it was to be a hiker, making their way over the stream to pick up the Pennine Way. So, she'd been less than pleased when they'd turned off the bridge and headed over towards the pool. With the sun in her eyes, she'd been able to make out little more than the figure of a man, with a dog lead in his hands, but no dog to be seen.

'Hi there,' he said. 'Don't suppose you've seen a dog go past, have you?'

Alys, treading water, felt a little vulnerable. She hoped that whoever it was would move on quickly. She didn't relish getting out of the water in front of him, but she was also feeling distinctly chilly. She shook her head but, before she could respond further, the man went on.

'Oh well, no matter. It won't be the first time she's got home before me.' He paused. 'I've been hearing that you've done wonders for Moira's business. And you seem to be enjoying the country-side. I've noticed you out and about on your walks.'

Alys, still treading water, had manoeuvred herself so that the sun was no longer in her eyes. That, and the turn of the conversation, brought the realisation that the dog walker with the missing dog was Rob. She briefly considered the fact that he'd noticed her out and about. What did that mean, she wondered?

A response was clearly called for. 'D-d-do you ever swim here?' she asked through chattering teeth.

'Are you mad?' Rob laughed. 'Locals don't come in here, except maybe in August, when the water's low enough to paddle. I don't think I've swum here since I was a lad—' he bent to dip a hand in the water and shuddered melodramatically. 'Now I know why!'

Alys laughed, despite herself. 'Call yourself a northerner?' she said. 'I'd have thought you'd be in here every day, breaking the ice in winter to get in.'

'Well, I'll leave you in peace,' said Rob, turning back towards the bridge. 'I'd think about getting out before you catch pneumonia, though.' And with that he was gone, whistling and calling for his dog. Alys had watched him on his way, before turning round and taking a few quick strokes from one side of the pool to the other. Then, floating on her back, she gazed up into the depths of the blue sky. She'd found herself smiling at the turn that the day had taken.

A smile that was echoed now, then quickly erased

as she realised that she'd stopped stirring and was in danger of burning the risotto.

Alys was quiet as she and Moira ate. She poured a glass of red wine for her aunt, but just water for herself.

'Nothing for you this evening?' Moira raised an eyebrow. If her niece was anything to go by, young people had become very abstemious. In her day, you never passed up the opportunity of a glass of wine. Alys had seemed to drink less and less each day since she'd arrived. She was looking better by the day, though, so perhaps there was something to be said for abstinence, Moira thought ruefully. Alys had a light tan, her hair was a little blonder, with threads of red and gold in the mix, and today she positively seemed to glow. She said she'd been for a swim in the bathing pool. Moira couldn't begin to imagine doing such a thing herself. All that water off the Pennines – too bracing by half! Alys was definitely more relaxed in herself, too. No more nervous twisting of rings and bracelets. Although tonight she was a little quiet, a little on edge, perhaps? Moira wondered if something was up – perhaps with that boyfriend back home that Kate had mentioned? Alys herself hadn't mentioned him once in the weeks that she'd been there. But before Moira could think of a way to pose the question without appearing to be nosey, Alys stood up and started to clear the table.

'If you'll be all right, I think I'll just pop out for a bit of a walk. I'll do the washing up when I get back. It's such a lovely evening, but I don't think it's going to last. The forecast said rain for tomorrow. I'd like to make the most of it while I can.'

Alys left via the garden, drinking in the scent of the early roses tumbling on trailing stems along the garden wall. Swifts swooped and called above her, coming closer to the houses as the evening wore on. Jackdaws *chack-chacked* from the church tower. With no clear idea of where she was heading, Alys let herself into the graveyard through the wooden gate and followed the path as it curved around to the back of the church. It was very peaceful, with just the calling of the jackdaws and the occasional *hoo-hooing* of a woodpigeon to disturb the stillness. Some of the older gravestones had fallen, and the words carved on the head-stones around the edges of the graveyard, where it was more exposed to the elements, were illegible.

She settled herself on a seat beneath a yew tree at the heart of the graveyard. Her eye was drawn to a headstone draped in trailing ivy, close to her seat. The setting sun picked out an arched design, carved on top of the stone, which looked strangely familiar. Curious, she got up to take a closer look. The stone was quite weathered, and coin-like shapes of yellow and grey-green lichens spotted its surface. Suckers of ivy had left silvery scars on the stone, an indication that someone had cleared it away in the past. Alys could just make out the name and the date:

1875–1895
Alice Bancroft

Alys felt a chill run through her. She'd died so young! Only twenty years old – fifteen years younger than Alys herself was now. And she had the same first name – well, almost. She shivered. She looked again at the surname – Bancroft – it wasn't familiar to her. But the design on the stone was. She traced it with her finger. Fat seed pods intertwined with trailing tendrils and vines, rather like something that she'd seen on a William Morris print. Surely it was the same as the distinctive carving that she had noticed on the gatepost and around the door of the last house at the top of the village? But why was the stone so intricately carved, and yet there was no message of remembrance? It seemed odd, especially for someone so young. On impulse, she pulled out her phone and took a photo in the fading light, then headed back to the house, resolving to see if she could find out more.

CHAPTER 12

The thought of the gravestone that she had spotted had bothered Alys for a day or so. She examined the photo on her phone, enlarging it as if it might offer up some clues. Was it just that it was always a shock to come across the grave of someone young? That sense of a life lost before it had even been lived?

As the days passed in a blur of early morning baking and serving in the café, followed by the rigorous cleaning demanded by Moira at the end of each day, Alys thought about it less and less.

'It's no good having tables and chairs that stick to you. And crumbs hiding underneath the cushions. It's best to clean up every night, no matter how tired you feel, then you're all set when you come in the next morning,' she'd admonished Alys, who had, at the end of a particularly tiring day, suggested that they could just as easily do all of this in the morning.

It was not until a quiet Thursday, when tourists and locals alike were kept indoors by an afternoon where the rain streamed constantly from a leaden sky, that Alys picked up her phone and flicked idly

69

through her photos in search of blue skies and sunshine.

'Can I look?' Moira peered over her shoulder. Never a fan of the mobile, she was nonetheless captivated by the myriad moments caught by Alys, from the sunny skies snapped from Claire's garden in Nortonstall, to the Pennine crags and wooded valleys around Northwaite.

Alys scrolled through the photos until Moira suddenly called a halt.

'What was that?'

Alys scrolled back. 'Oh, just a gravestone that I spotted in the churchyard here. There was something about it that drew me to it – the carving, I think. I'd seen the same carving somewhere else in the village. And her age. She was so young when she died.'

Moira was quiet for a moment. 'It's odd that you should have fixed on this. She was actually a relative of yours.'

'Of mine?' Alys's eyes widened. 'Here? In Northwaite?'

'Well, yes. The family's originally from round here. You knew that?'

Alys frowned. 'I thought we were from Leeds?'

'We go back a long way around here,' Moira said. 'As far back as I've been able to trace. Your mum and I were brought up in the area as children, until Dad, your granddad, found work in Leeds when we were in our early teens. Our family had lived in Nortonstall until then, but before that our links were all with this village. My grandma Beth lived here in Northwaite, in the very house I live in now. We used to come and visit her from Nortonstall. Her mother, and her grandmother, had both lived here in a house up at the top of the village. My mum said there was some tragedy linked to the family, to do with Beth's mother – your great-great-grandmother. She's the one whose grave you saw. She died so young – I never knew her.'

Alys digested this news. How come she hadn't known that Moira's house was a family one? And that the family had roots in the village? Although that would explain Moira's presence here.

'What did the family do? Were they farmers?' Alys asked.

'No, the women mainly worked at the mill, or were weavers at home before the mills were built. Although one of our relatives, Sarah, was a herbalist – quite well-known locally, by all accounts.'

'What about my great-great-grandma, Alice?' Alys was peering at the photo of the gravestone on her phone again. 'Did she work in the mill?'

Moira hesitated. 'Well, yes,' she said. 'But then she had a baby, Elisabeth, and she didn't carry on after that.' Moira paused. 'I've got a family tree somewhere that I started. Look, let's shut up shop and get off home. It doesn't look as though there's any chance of the rain stopping. I'll dig out that family tree tonight – it might help you to make sense of all those names.'

71

As they set about clearing up, Alys was thoughtful. Moira had mentioned a tragedy, but had seemed rather reticent. What had happened to Alice, and when? Was there a family mystery? She felt a sense of excitement: it all sounded rather intriguing. On top of that, she had now discovered that her roots were in this actual area, something that she had never suspected before. She was looking forward to finding out more.

CHAPTER 13

Alys had been so impatient to see the family tree that when Moira finally placed it in front of her that evening, she felt a stab of disappointment. It had been roughly drawn up on a sheet of paper torn from a foolscap notebook. The names at the bottom of the page, Alys and her siblings George and Edward, and those of Moira and Kate, plus her father David were, of course, all familiar to her, along with Eileen: Kate and Moira's mum. The generations above that included Elisabeth, Eileen's mother, then Alice, Elisabeth's mother, names new to Alys until this afternoon. She skimmed over dates and siblings. Elisabeth had none, but Alice was the eldest of five, born to Sarah and Joe Bancroft. No name was given for the father of Elisabeth, Alys noticed. Beyond that, the piece of paper frustratingly provided no further clues.

'Do you mind if I hang onto this for a bit?' Alys asked as they sat down to eat.

'No, just take care of it. It's the only copy,' said Moira. She was feeling unaccountably tired today and looking forward to an early night. She was thankful yet again for Alys's presence – without her she certainly couldn't have kept the café running. Alys had gone way beyond the call of duty, not only proving herself to be a good baker, but also having a fine eye for how to enhance the business. It wouldn't be long before she would be wanting to be on the move, Moira thought, and she was dreading the day, although she realised that it wasn't fair to try to keep her here. She dragged herself out of her reverie as she became aware that Alys was speaking to her.

'Are you okay?' her niece was asking, concerned. 'You're looking a bit pale, you've barely said a word and you haven't eaten very much.'

'I'm fine,' Moira said, and smiled. 'Just a bit tired this evening. Think I need a long bath and an early night.'

'Well, if you're sure that's all? I hope you're not overdoing it.' Alys rose from the table and started to clear away. She paused, then turned to Moira. 'I'd like to find out more about the history of the area, the mills and such. Get a feel for what it might have been like to live here a hundred or so years ago, now that I've discovered we're all from this area. Have you got any books about it?'

'Local history, do you mean?' Moira settled herself on the sofa. 'No books I'm afraid, but there's a little museum here in the village, and another one over in Nortonstall. There's a lot in both of them about the area. You need to remember that it wouldn't have been like this then.' Moira winced and adjusted the cushions behind her back, which still played up if she had been on her feet all day. 'It would have been an industrial landscape down in the valley, not the beautiful countryside we see now. I expect that the paths that you've been walking are much the same as in the past, though,' she said. 'The workers would have used them to get to the mill from all directions. Lots of children worked there, too. They were employed in the mills because they were small and had nimble fingers. They had to go under the machines to retrieve things, do jobs that adults were too big for. The hours and conditions were awful in the mid-nineteenth century. You should definitely take a look at the museums – you'll learn a lot there. I found it all a bit upsetting, to be honest, but it's worth knowing about, especially while you're here.'

Alys's next half-day off brought more dark clouds and bursts of heavy rain. The thought of exploring the countryside, her normal half-day occupation, didn't appeal. So, she made her way over to Nortonstall and spent a few hours in the museum there. It was housed in an old mill, now mainly given over to workshops and studios, but it gave her an idea of the scale of the place, the forbidding walls and the towering chimney, all set in a cobbled courtyard that must once have rung with the clatter of clogs and the bustle of business. She was sure that the Industrial Revolution must have been on the curriculum at school, but clearly it hadn't stuck in her memory. Now that she was in the landscape that was home to so much of it, her imagination was fired up. She pored over the old black-and-white photos of the area, staring hard at the people captured in them and wondering whether one of them was Alice. She devoured the information about the canals, the weavers' cottages, the different kinds of mill in the area, how Northwaite had declined in importance as Nortonstall had grown, its importance fuelled by the arrival of the railways. She'd found the depiction of a typical working day particularly startling, especially the length of the journey that so many workers in the outlying parts undertook each morning and evening on foot, before they even started their ten-hour day. And once they were at work, they were under constant pressure, bullied by the overlookers to meet deadlines and targets. So that wasn't a new thing, she thought to herself wryly as she lingered over a cup of coffee in the mill café, watching the rain puddling in the courtyard. Life must have been such a struggle in those days. She just hoped that there had been some recompense, something to make life worth living.

PART II

CHAPTER 1

Alice always tried hard to avoid looking at the clock that hung over the door of the tiny schoolroom at the mill. The room had just one small window, high in the wall at one end, opposite the door. It let in a bit of light in the summer, but the room was gloomy in the winter, so the paraffin lamps were always lit. At least it meant that Alice's pupils couldn't gaze idly out of the window. In fact, they were mostly pleased to be there, away from the noise of the mill, the humid heat, the impatient shouts of the overlookers, and the ever-present danger of the machines.

The room had been turned from a storeroom into a classroom when a new law obliged the mill owner, Mr Weatherall, to school the children employed at the mill for half the day. With the village school a long walk from the mill, it made sense to Mr Weatherall to have a schoolroom on site, to make sure that the children were on hand to work all the hours available to them. By the end of the week, the younger ones often fell asleep at their desks, faces cradled on scrawny arms that didn't look strong enough for the work that they had to perform, dazed with fatigue, for hour after hour.

Alice would gladly share small scraps of her lunch with whichever of her pupils looked the frailest and most hollow-eyed that day, even though Alice rarely had enough food for herself. Her income was all they had to support her family. Yet it hadn't always been like this. Alice could remember a time when life wasn't quite such a struggle. A time when her father Joe was around, and Sarah, her mother, had seemed somehow lighter, brighter and more carefree. Alice had an abiding memory from childhood of a gift of a little frog that her father had found by the roadside. Caught unawares, it had been pretending to be a stone, steadfast in its belief that no one could see it, until he had picked it up in his handkerchief and carried it gently home. She hadn't been sure whether to be pleased or alarmed by the gift, reaching out with a hesitant finger to poke the creature, then squealing when it hopped. Sarah came through from the kitchen to see what the fuss was about.

'Take the horrid thing out of here,' she scolded, as Joe tried valiantly to recapture it. 'Whatever were you thinking of, bringing it into the house?'

When Alice's father cornered the frog, he seized it by its hind leg and chased Sarah back into the kitchen, threatening to put it down the back of her dress. Alice squealed again and ran after them.

'Get off with you! What do you think you're playing at?' protested Sarah. Joe held the frog behind his back and leaned in to kiss Sarah. Momentarily distracted, he loosened his grip and away hopped the frog, across the kitchen floor, to take refuge behind the mop.

Alice had few other memories of her father apart from this vivid one. She remembered him as small and wiry, with bright blue eyes in a tanned face. She knew that he had worked away from home a lot, and that there seemed to be hardly any time when Sarah wasn't either pregnant or nursing a small baby. Then, with a family of five to feed, suddenly he wasn't there any more. Alice was so used to her father's absences that it wasn't until the littlest one was starting to walk that she realised that he hadn't been home since she was born. She tried to ask Sarah about it, but her face became shuttered and she turned away. Alice grew up not only unsure whether her father had died or just left them, but with a sense of the impermanence of happiness.

Alice's childhood had been scented by the smell of herbs cooking together in a pot over the fire. From an early age, she'd helped her mother plant and tend coriander, garlic, marigolds, rue, spearmint and tansy in the garden, providing the basic ingredients for the decoctions, pills and potions she prepared so carefully for all those who sought her help. Some of the other herbal ingredients – skullcap, bogbean and bog myrtle

– were better collected from the wild, needing the damp conditions down amongst the woods in the valley, where they thrived in the secret places known to Alice's mother Sarah and the generations before her.

When she was a child, it was normal to Alice that the evenings, whether in the cold depths of winter or the dusky twilight of summer, would bring visitor after visitor to the kitchen door as the workers made their way home from the mill. It was Alice's job when she was small to light the candle that stood in a jar beside the door, to act as a marker for those in search of a remedy for a persistent cough, or for 'spinning jenny sickness', the lung affliction caused by the fine fabric fluff filling the mill air that left them gasping for breath. They came in search of something to ease nervous complaints or for rheumatic joints made painful by long hours held captive at the mercy of the machines.

Sarah patiently spooned potions and creams into the glass jars and pots that her customers brought with them to save a few farthings, offering soothing words to help comfort the distress that was apparent to her on a daily basis. Her skill and sympathy brought visitors to her from beyond the immediate village and she never turned anyone away, day or night. She was driven by something apart from her wish to help others: she had a need to make enough money to be able to keep her family out of the mill where she herself had suffered so much for a time a few years previously. Now the local doctor, made angry by Sarah's success in treating the villagers and therefore taking away what he saw as income rightly belonging to him, had threatened her with investigation by the local magistrate. This uncertainty over her status had driven even loyal customers away, her regular clients now making the trek to Nortonstall for their remedies instead, or trying to trust the local doctor, who favoured mercury and bleeding as cures for most illnesses. Sarah, laid low by illness and exhaustion, was unable to make enough to feed the family. So, it was with a heavy heart that Alice had approached the mill in search of work. An educated pauper, and a girl at that, stood very little chance of any other gainful employment in the immediate area.

On her worst days, when it poured with rain all day and the journey to work left her sodden, mud-spattered and wretched before she even began, Alice would wonder about the living hell that they had all found themselves in, and what the people of these hills and valleys had done to deserve it. On other days, in spring or autumn, when the sun shone and the birds sang as she walked the path to work, life seemed almost tolerable. Hot summer days brought a hell of their own, the temperature inside the weaving shed unbearable, the doors flung open only to allow more sultry heat inside.

Alice knew, however, that she was one of the few

fortunate ones at the mill. Her mother had sent her at a young age to be taught how to read and write by a retired schoolteacher who lived in the village. Elsie Lister had once taught the children of the local landowners at the grammar school. She had seemed an enormous age to the young Alice, but she was probably no more than fifty, worn down by illness, and then by poverty after she became too ill to work. Sarah, Alice's mother, had struck a bargain with Elsie: lessons for Alice in return for herbal remedies, and the deal had stuck over the years it took for Alice to learn the alphabet, perfect her letters, understand punctuation, spelling and all the other things that had enabled her over time to become her mother's scribe and record-keeper. She kept details of Sarah's remedies, transactions and recipes in a hand that matured from a round, childish script to a confident, flowing copperplate. Even when Alice's writing education was complete, she had continued to visit Elsie, reading to her as her eyesight failed, helping with errands and small chores now that she had no other family. She had missed her when she died, for Alice's education had taken her to a place that none of her family could comprehend, and left her isolated there. All she had left to remember Elsie by was a little brooch, an enamelling of a sprig of lavender. Having never seen anything so fine, it had fascinated Alice as a child and Elsie, who must have been aware that the end was close, had gifted it to Alice just before she died. She'd pressed it into her hand, closing Alice's fingers around it, and brushing away her protest.

'What use is it to me, bed-bound all the day and night? Am I supposed to wear it on my nightgown? It needs to be worn – you must take it and be sure to wear it every day, to remind you of what you have learnt and who you are now.'

Alice felt lucky that her period of full-time employment in the mill had been limited and she had been given the chance to teach for part of the day. She loved the time that she spent in the classroom and dreaded having to usher her pupils out, sending them all, herself included, into what she often thought of as the jaws of hell. Alice knew that the mill exploited her. She received very little extra in her pay packet for all her hours of teaching, far less than they would have had to pay a trained teacher to come in from outside. But she so relished the time that she didn't have to spend on the mill floor that she didn't challenge the situation. Which is why she tried hard not to look at the schoolroom clock – not because time was dragging, but because it went by too fast.

CHAPTER 2

Alice suffered mixed emotions when Ramsay, the mill manager, told her that someone had been appointed to teach arithmetic to her pupils. This topic was the least favourite part of her morning and she'd often guiltily allowed reading and writing to expand into the allotted arithmetic hour, simply because she enjoyed teaching these subjects much more. Although she could teach basic sums, she felt unqualified to go much beyond that. She didn't appreciate that her work with Sarah on remedy calculations and costings were as valuable as the hours spent in Elsie's company had been in advancing her reading and writing. But, as Alice realised with a heavy heart, having someone else come in to teach arithmetic would mean that she would have an extra hour or so each day on the mill floor.

For all his brusqueness, Alice had found Ramsay a fair and thoughtful manager, enquiring after her mother's health and occasionally sending a small gift home for her.

'The wife's been jam-making again. Can't abide the stuff mysen. But mebbe the goosegogs will do your ma some good,' he said, thrusting a small pot of delicate-pink gooseberry conserve into Alice's hands as she left for home. Or, 'The hen's been doin' a second shift wi'out us asking it. The wife can't keep up,' handing over half a dozen eggs packed into a straw-filled box with an equal quantity of freshly baked scones on top.

Alice blushed as she stammered her thanks. The gifts were not only kind, but thoughtful. Sarah's illness had left her so low in energy that she could no longer go beyond fulfilling the basic household duties. The fruit and vegetables went unpicked, so the pies, jams and chutneys that had seen the family through previous hard times no longer filled the larder shelves. Alice did her best to fill the gaps when she got home from work, or on her precious day off, taking over all the chores on that day so that Sarah could simply rest. Try as she might, though, she didn't seem to find time to fit in all the extra work. Four-year-old Beattie was too young to help and while Annie and Thomas, who were eight and ten, did what they could, cooking was beyond them. Alice had her sights set on training up her younger sister Ella but, at the age of twelve, she showed no signs of being anything other than the most basic cook or housekeeper. She'd rush through her chores and, before anyone noticed, she'd slipped away through the back door, down the garden path and was off through the back gate, roaming the fields and woods, her thoughts always away somewhere else and no eye on the time at all, except when hunger drove her home, tired and dishevelled at the end of the day. No amount of scolding had any effect. Alice, envying her sister this freedom and having never enjoyed it herself, berated her all the more.

Alice wasn't sure what caused these acts of kindness by old Ramsay and his wife. She tried to hazard a guess at his age – could he be the same age as Sarah? Or older? Maybe they had known each other when they were growing up? She'd mused on it for a while, but there seemed to be no inclination on either side to follow up the gifts. Eventually she'd asked Sarah, half-wondering whether Ramsay was perhaps an old sweetheart of hers. Sarah had laughed, then stopped short, her breath caught.

'No, they're from beyond Nortonstall. I never saw them until a few years back when they came to see me with their daughter. She'd been treated by the doctor out their way, but by the time I saw her there was nothing I could do except give her lobelia syrup and suggest ways they could make her comfortable. Molly was such a pretty girl, but as frail as thistledown by the time she came to me. She'd have been around your age if she'd lived. You'd have transcribed her remedy. Do you not remember?'

Alice didn't, but that was no surprise. She just listed what her mother told her to, and didn't feel as involved with each and every patient as

Sarah did. She remained puzzled, but knew that her mother's care and patience in listening to her patients often gave them as much comfort as the remedy prescribed. The doctors, on the other hand, tended to adopt an overbearing approach to their patients, brooking no argument or questions, and expecting them to do exactly as they said. Sarah's approach was a gentle concern for all issues surrounding the patient's health, with a series of questions designed to probe but not distress, in order to produce a clearer picture of the treatment required. Two patients might seek help for the same complaint, but they rarely left with the same remedy. Sarah's success was the result of seeing beyond the illness to the person and their individual needs, and prescribing accordingly.

CHAPTER 3

Barely a week after Ramsay had told Alice that a new teacher was to be appointed, she found herself being introduced to him.

'This is Richard Weatherall. He'll be teaching arithmetic. You're to show him yon classroom,' and with that Ramsay turned on his heel and was gone, in search of orders to issue on more familiar territory, relating to equipment, cloth orders, and work force.

Alice had expected to find a retired teacher from Nortonstall waiting in the office, happy to have an hour's paid work a day. Instead, the person silhouetted against the window had the bearing of a much younger man. Indeed, as he stepped forward, Alice saw that he wasn't much older than she was. He was slim and pale, with light-brown hair that flopped forward, refusing to hold its shape in the severe style expected of it. His clothes instantly marked him out as a gentleman. Alice's practised eye noted the cut and cloth of his jacket and waistcoat, the fine linen of his shirt. As her eyes travelled the length of him she was surprised to see that his trousers were mud-splattered, his shoes a pair of walking brogues. Richard followed her gaze and laughed.

'Ah, excuse my appearance,' he said lightly. 'I walked Lucy over the moor first thing, then made my way here at once when Father summoned me. There was no time to change, I'm afraid.'

Lucy? Father? Alice was puzzled, and no doubt her face showed it, for Richard smiled and clicked his fingers. Hearing a scrabble and a muffled bark, Alice swung around towards the fireplace where a grey lurcher had been dozing peacefully by the hearth. She bounded up to Richard and butted his leg with her nose until he bent down and fondled her ears. Then she turned her attention to Alice, gazing up at her with beseeching eyes. Alice couldn't help but smile, and stooped to repeat Richard's actions.

'There, best friends already,' said Richard. 'Lucy doesn't take to everyone, you know. It's quite an honour.' He moved on swiftly, seeing Alice blush. 'Do you think it would be all right to bring her into the schoolroom? She goes everywhere with me, you see.'

Alice found her voice at last. 'I'm not sure.' She was doubtful. 'She's rather large. I think some of the smaller ones might be afeared.' As the words came out, Alice wondered at herself for slipping into the local dialect. Was it an instinctive reaction to the 'lord-and-master' situation? She fingered the brooch that pinned her shawl together, a gesture she used to calm herself. Without a doubt,

'Father' must be James Weatherall, the mill owner, and Richard must be his eldest son, recently returned from Cambridge and not proving to be the enthusiastic businessman that his father had hoped for, or so it was rumoured. Rather, he loved to walk the hills, play the piano with his mother and sisters, and write poetry. At least so said Louisa, their neighbour in Northwaite, who was a maid at the big house.

For his part, Richard saw a pale, slim girl with a mass of reddish-brown curls that her work cap failed to contain, dressed in the usual working uniform of the mill girls: a rough long wool skirt and a shirt of a nondescript colour, faded from numerous washes, topped with a knitted shawl pinned tightly at the front. The brooch that held the shawl wasn't the usual cheap and shiny affair, though, but a rather fine enamelled sprig of lavender. Her eyes, first glimpsed when she raised them directly to him whilst fondling Lucy's ears, were the most extraordinary green. Or were they blue? He was fascinated. They seemed to subtly change colour as he looked. Then she blushed again, and he realised that he was staring, as well as babbling some nonsense about the dog.

'I should get back to my class,' said Alice. 'You'd better come and meet them. I set them some reading to get on with.' They would probably have lost interest by now, she reflected, stumbling over difficult words, one or two of them taking the chance for a nap, Charlie Wilmott no doubt teasing

Edith Parker and then sulking when she cut him off with a clever remark that earned her the laughter of her classmates at his expense.

Richard signalled to Lucy to return to her fireside spot, then followed Alice down the narrow corridor, away from the peace of Ramsay's office, past the noisy hubbub of the mill floor, revealed in a flash as a door opened, then hidden again just as quickly as the door snapped shut. Richard suppressed a shudder. The brooding presence of the mill in the valley filled his every day. No matter how far he walked over the moors and through the woods, the chimneys of the valley mills seemed to be always in his sight, even from his bedroom window. Each evening, Father would inform the dinner table of some mill problem or success, of the fluctuating price of cloth, of the need to update the machinery, glancing at Richard to see if he was listening, involved, interested. Richard knew that he was a disappointment. In effect, the mill had paid for his education and was keeping the family in comfort, and his father looked to him to carry on the tradition. But the education that was meant to have prepared him to step into his father's shoes had simply driven him as far as possible in the opposite direction.

'Esther would be far better suited to running the business,' thought Richard ruefully. Trained in the art of home management by her mother, his sister Esther was immensely capable, practical and forward thinking. Richard possessed none of these qualities – his thoughts as he roamed the countryside with Lucy were of a more philosophical nature, and he was far more likely to return home and write poetry than to draw up a plan for the future expansion of the mill. Getting him to teach in the schoolroom was his father's last despairing attempt at getting Richard involved. Mr Weatherall was only too aware that Richard shied away from contact with the workers and locals, nervous of their roughness and down-to-earth demeanour after the rarefied atmosphere of Cambridge. Perhaps meeting the children would help him to understand the mill life a little better?

The chatter from the schoolroom, clearly audible outside, stilled the moment that Alice turned the doorknob. She pushed the door open and stood aside to let Richard enter. Stepping forward, he faced rows of inquisitive faces, feeling his heart sink as he did so. He felt no more connection with the schoolroom than he did with the rest of the mill, but Alice was already introducing him.

'Children, I want you to meet Mr Weatherall. He will be your teacher for arithmetic, starting tomorrow. He will sit with us for the rest of the morning, so he can get to know you a little.' Alice took the teacher's chair from behind the desk and set it at the front of the room, indicating that Richard should sit down. She then stood behind the desk and Richard found himself watching her, rather than the children, as she instructed them on a handwriting exercise, then moved around the room, pointing out lazy loops and sloping verticals, crouching down to a child's level to show how a different way of holding the chalk and the slate would make a difference to the final result. By the end of the hour, Richard had an inkling of the skill involved in teaching a class, and of the love and respect that the children had for Alice. He feared that he would be of very little use in the classroom – he had never taught and had no experience in dealing with children – but his father expected it of him and so it must be.

CHAPTER 4

Alice had been wary of Richard at first, worried that he had been sent by his father to spy on her, to make sure that she was fulfilling her duties in the classroom and teaching the children to a proper standard. She was painfully conscious of her deficiencies when she compared herself to Master Richard, and his fancy education, the likes of which she could barely comprehend. It hadn't taken her long, however, to discover that, fancy education or not, he was totally at sea in the classroom and, it would seem, in life in general.

'Could you help me hand out the slates?' Alice said. Within two days, she had had enough of Richard helplessly watching her, or following her around the schoolroom, hanging on her every word. She no longer worried that he had been sent to report back: rather, she feared *she* was minding *him* until James Weatherall had decided what to do for the best with regard to his future in the mill. Alice's time with the children was limited and precious, and she resented having to waste any of it on Master Richard. She was going to have to come up with a plan.

'Today, Master Richard will work on arithmetic with half the class, while I work on handwriting with the rest of you.'

The children started to mutter their discontent. They wanted nothing to do with either arithmetic or Master Richard.

'Then, halfway through the morning, we will change over,' Alice announced firmly. 'I want you all to listen very carefully to Master Richard. We are very lucky to have him here to help.'

She'd felt shy at first, suggesting that he might devise a lesson, thinking herself presumptuous and hoping he wouldn't take her request amiss. It didn't take her long to discover that he had as little experience of teaching as she had of life at Cambridge. The noise from his group swiftly reached such levels that she had to break off, leaving her group to practise the loops of their 'g's' and 'f's' and intercede before it got too far out of hand.

'I wonder if you might start with something a little more basic?' she suggested, once she realised that Richard had set himself the challenge of explaining long division to his group. Richard looked blank.

'Perhaps if you went back to simple addition or subtraction you could build on that to show how multiplication and division work?'

Richard looked embarrassed and hopeful at the same time. Alice could see he was wondering whether she would step in and take over.

Her cheeks flushed pink, partly at the frankness of his gaze, and partly with annoyance at the difficult position she had been put in. Should she speak to Ramsay? Explain to him that Richard was not well-suited to this role? That he was, in fact, a hindrance to her?

She took a deep breath. 'I think if you tried to make this relevant to their everyday lives it would help.'

Richard still looked uncomprehending so she pressed on. 'I mean, if Charlie earns five shillings a week, and gives his mother three shillings towards the running of the house, and has to pay a shilling in fines and stoppages at the mill' – here all the children laughed, seeing that Alice knew Charlie only too well – 'how much money has he got left? And if he wants to save sixpence, but wants to buy a penn'orth of sweets from Mrs Wrigglesworth's shop' – more laughter – 'how much does he have left then?'

Alice laid the sums out on her slate as she spoke and held it up for the children to see. Richard's confusion seemed to have grown and she felt her impatience rising. With a sharp look, she quelled the giggles and unrest that had broken out in the writing group and thought rapidly.

'We'll change the lesson a bit. I'd like this group' – she indicated the arithmetic group – 'to introduce themselves to Master Richard and tell him about the numbers in their life. So, how old they are, the numbers of brothers and sisters that they have, and the number of people in their family that work in the mill. Then we will put all the numbers together and over the next few weeks we will talk about average numbers, and how to work them out.'

Alice looked at Richard. She hoped he would seize the lifeline she was offering him. At least it would allow him to learn a little about his pupils' lives, and perhaps to see how he could make arithmetic relevant and useful to them.

'And tomorrow, I will ask Mr Ramsay if we can borrow the abacus from his office to help with our sums.' She hoped the novelty would add an extra incentive to get on with things.

As she turned back to her own group, Alice was relieved to see Richard gather his group to him and to hear him start to question them. Even if they got nowhere with the project she'd set them, at least he would start to gain a bit of an insight into their lives.

So how had she moved from irritation to these complicated emotions? When had she stopped feeling annoyed by his uncertainty in the classroom, and started to see it for what it was: shyness and lack of experience? When had she started to respond to his vulnerability, finding herself protecting him from the children? Sharp and canny in spotting weak spots, they soon got over their awe of Master Richard and were quick to tease and fluster him. With no experience of quelling wildness, he was at a loss, until Alice stepped in and exerted discipline. She had no need to raise her voice or threaten – the children instantly understood that she meant what she said. And in any case, they had no desire to displease her.

So why was it that she now approached each day in the schoolroom with a mixture of trepidation and joy, far removed from the calm happiness she had previously felt there? Trepidation that she was somehow stepping out of line in allowing herself to feel on an even footing with Richard? Trepidation that she enjoyed their discussions, conducted in a murmur as the children bent their heads over a work task, or snatched in the brief hiatus at the end of the school morning, once the children had left to devour their lunches and before she and Richard returned to their respective realities?

And joy – joy in discovering that it was possible to talk to Richard without fearing his intent, without him treating her as a possession, something rightfully his to be used and discarded at will. Alice would not let the doubts – troubled thoughts about rightful places and false hopes – rise up and destroy this feeling. She had few enough moments that were hers alone. What harm could it do to keep any doubts to herself and simply enjoy this rare gift – of an educated man treating her like an equal – that had been given to her?

When had he started to lend her books, or suggest a poem that she might enjoy? When did their meetings first stray outside the confines of the working day? When did Richard first talk of a walk he loved to take each Sunday, and when did Alice find herself with time to spare from household duties to surprise him there – careless, as if she had no notion that his path would lead him past where she usually gathered comfrey and woundwort to carry home for Sarah's remedies?

And when had it become apparent that their need to see each other would extend into the dark reaches of the night, into the secret countryside wrapped around the mill, hidden away from family and friends, stepping far outside what either of them knew to be right and proper, so that they might have been the only two people alive?

How had this happened? How had this young man, seemingly so unsuited to the rigours of the mill and to understanding the lives of those who lived there, become so entwined in her life?

Alice pondered the question as she lay in bed, absently turning her locket between her fingers. She hardly felt the weight of it, suspended on its fine gold chain around her neck, and she would have to remember to remove it in the morning when she awoke. For now, she was safe to wear it hidden beneath the high neck of her nightgown. When Richard had given the locket to her, he'd pressed a tiny catch to open it, explaining that it should hold two photos, one of each of them. His photograph, a tiny sepia portrait, still gave her a jolt whenever she looked at it, but she had no picture to put in the locket's empty face, nothing to lock into an embrace with Richard when the two halves were closed together. Alice had never had her photograph taken, and couldn't imagine that she ever would.

PART III

CHAPTER 1

Despite all Alys's research at the museum in Nortonstall, and a follow-up trip to the local museum in Northwaite, she was still no closer to discovering what had happened to cause her great-great-grandmother Alice to die so young. She had only been twenty! Alys could barely remember what her own life had been like when she was that age. She'd have been at college, thinking far too much about enjoying herself and not enough about her degree course. There was no way she would have been fit to bring up a baby. What would her life have been like if she had been born in the 1870s, like Alice, instead of the 1980s?

She was musing on this one evening a couple of days later, after they'd closed up early as more driving rain had emptied the streets of villagers and tourists alike, when she remembered something from her visit to the local museum, something that she had meant to quiz Moira about. 'Wasn't there once a lock-up here in Northwaite? An actual jail?' she asked, as she swept crumbs from under the tables, and straightened the chairs in preparation for the next day.

'Indeed, there was. It's still here, in the basement of Crown Cottage.' Moira laughed at Alys's horrified expression. 'They don't use it any more. Jeff, the builder who lives at the cottage, stores his building materials in there. He's got a few tales to tell about things going bump in the night – ghosts and the like. Especially after he's had a few drinks in The Old Bell.'

Life in the late nineteenth century must have been unimaginably tough, Alys thought, as they locked up the café and prepared to walk home through the deserted, rainy streets. Six-day working weeks and ten-hour days with no welfare state, workers' rights or proper education. Pollution, poverty and, on top of that, prison for poaching a couple of rabbits. She shivered in the pouring rain. No central heating either.

The rain showed no sign of letting up all evening, and darkness fell earlier than usual. Alys listened as the rain lashed against the window. 'I think I'll head for bed now. It's so miserable out there – you'd never think it was June.'

'Chilly too,' said Moira, who had lit the fire earlier and now found herself reluctant to part from it. 'There's an extra blanket or two in the wardrobe if you need them – it definitely feels more like winter than summer.'

Alys woke in near-darkness, heart pounding, feeling under threat. Her head ached and she felt thirsty. At first, she couldn't take in where she was, then gradually the familiar bedroom swam into focus. The gloom was broken by a faint light that was coming through a curtained window, not through the bars of the cell window that she was half-expecting to see. She was in a comfortable bed, not huddled on a hard floor. She tried to reorient herself. She'd had a bad dream, about being imprisoned for something she hadn't done. Alys told herself that her discussion with Moira the previous day about the old lock-up in the village must have permeated her dreams, but her sense of being under threat, of being wrongly accused, wasn't easy to subdue. Uneasy in case she fell straight back into the same dream, she found it hard to return to sleep and when she did, it was fitful, leaving her hollow-eyed at breakfast the next morning.

'Goodness,' said Moira, looking up over the rim of her cup as Alys, yawning, poured herself some tea and settled down to pick at a piece of toast. 'You look tired. Did you have a bad night?'

'I had an odd dream,' said Alys. 'Well, a nightmare, really. Took me a while to get back to sleep. I'll be all right when I've had a shower.' For some reason, she felt unwilling to share any further details of her dream. Somehow, it all still felt too real.

'Sure?' Moira looked doubtful. 'I can manage without you for a bit if you want to catch up on some sleep?'

Alys looked out of the window. The weather had cleared, the sun was shining and it looked set to be a glorious day. She would have dearly loved another hour or so in bed, but she said, 'I'll be fine. Looks like we might be busy today. Give me ten minutes to get ready, then let's bake.'

Alys's assumptions proved correct. The tourists, trapped indoors the previous day by the dire weather, were out in full force. The bell on the café door sounded constantly as customers thronged in, and by the time they shut the doors at the end of the day, the cake stands were bare.

'Every scrap has gone!' Alys was amazed. The day had been so busy that she hadn't had time to think about being tired. Now her legs felt leaden and her eyes gritty and sore.

'An early night for you, I think?' Moira was looking at her with some sympathy. 'We'll have to be up early again to bake in the morning, though. The weather forecast is good until the end of the week.'

Despite her exhaustion, Alys felt a little thrill. The café was doing well and she loved it when there was a constant stream of customers. Plus, she'd got a couple of new recipes that she was looking forward to trying out. The Celestial Cake Café had had a great review in the local press and there'd even been a mention in *The Yorkshire Post*. Alys teased her aunt that they'd be featured on Trip Advisor before long but although Moira smiled, Alys had the feeling that she didn't really know what she was talking about.

The previous night's bad dream felt very much

in the past as she and Moira walked home, the sun still warm on their faces and the air filled with the calls of swifts swooping overhead, delighted by the insect bonanza brought about by the change in the weather. She was still keen to learn more about Alice, and her family history, but this didn't feel like the right moment to broach the subject again, and perhaps Moira wasn't even the right person to ask?

CHAPTER 2

Alys closed the oven door and sighed. The lemon poppy-seed cake had come out of the oven sad. Very sad, in fact: it was decidedly flat and the weight of a brick. She knew it had been a mistake to try out a new recipe she'd found on the Internet – something about it hadn't seemed quite right. No time to start again now, though. She might manage to turn out some flapjacks or coconut cookies instead. They were quick to make, and usually sold well. Alys checked the larder – there were plenty of ingredients here for either recipe. She took butter, sugar, flour, coconut. She'd make the cookies, she decided. Then there'd just be time to check her emails before she set off for the shop.

With the cookies in the oven and the washing-up done, she flipped open the laptop. A succession of pings told her that she had mail – not all of it welcome, she realised as she stared at the screen. There was an email from her mother – without even opening it she felt guilty. She'd contacted her the day after she'd arrived to give her an update on Aunt Moira but now she came to think of it, she hadn't been in touch since. How many weeks had she been here? Her heart sank – her mum was going to be upset with her. She'd send her an email later, she decided, a lengthy one, full of news. She hesitated, fingers poised over the keyboard. Should she open Kate's email or was it going to make her grumpy all day. Reasoning that if she didn't, it would just weigh on her mind anyway, she opened it. *'Hope all is going well,'* it read. *'I know you must be busy but would love to hear your news. How is Moira feeling? Send her my love, Mum xxx'*

Now she felt even worse. The tone was very restrained; really, her mother would have been well within her rights to have a rant. She'd send her some photos along with the email tonight, she decided – she'd take some in the café today. Alys didn't think that her mother would really want to see the photos of flowers and landscapes that had filled her phone since she'd been here. Cakes, the café and Moira it would have to be.

The buzzer on the oven warned her that the cookies were ready. She took them out, inhaling the rich, sweet aroma. They'd need to cool on the baking tray, then on the wire rack, before she could take them to the café. Which meant that she had time to look at the other emails, the ones from Tim.

There were three of them, sent on consecutive days. It dawned on Alys that she hadn't been checking her mail regularly – back in London she would have looked on waking up, at lunchtime and more than once in the evening, not to mention keeping an eye on Facebook and Instagram. She'd gradually stopped doing that while she'd been here, for no reason other than she'd been busy and it hadn't seemed important. And, she realised, she'd barely thought of Tim since she'd posted the letter to him. He'd emailed her pretty swiftly once he'd got the letter, an email in which he had made a lot of sweeping assumptions about what she was thinking, which had only served to annoy her. She'd resisted firing back an answer straight away and had left it a couple of days, then replied with an email focusing on the café and her Aunt Moira and how her help was going to be needed there for a good few weeks. She knew she had rather dodged the issue, and she'd continued to do so, replying to his texts with smiley faces and messages along the lines of '*Must rush – catch up later*', before she'd stopped replying at all. She'd answered a couple more emails, keeping things deliberately light, noncommittal and brief.

So, should she read his latest emails now? And if so, start with the earliest or the latest one? Aware that she had compressed her lips and gritted her teeth, she sighed and opened the last one. Tim had clearly been very wound up by her failure to reply to his previous emails. '*So, I suppose your lack of response is part of your grand plan to have nothing more to do with me? You thought you could just vanish out of my life without giving me a good* reason? I thought better of you Alys. If I sound upset, that's because I am.'

Alys snapped the laptop shut and sat back. Her instant reaction was a feeling of rage, but she fought it down by reasoning that Tim was justifiably annoyed by her failure to respond to his earlier messages. If she replied now, she would have to draft and re-draft before she had crafted a suitable response. Far better to leave it until this evening, she reasoned. And in any case, Moira would be needing her, and the cookies, at the café.

Fifteen minutes later, Alys arrived at the café to find a tractor parked outside and Rob inside at the counter, chatting to Moira.

'There you are,' Moira said. 'Rob has just been asking how you were getting on, and I said you were at home baking.'

Alys opened the cake box and handed it to Moira. 'Here you are. Probably still a bit warm but just in time for the eleven o'clock rush.'

Rob leant over the box and sniffed. 'Mmm – they smell good.'

'Take one,' Moira offered.

'No thanks – I've got my coffee. Better get my tractor off your doorstep,' Rob said with a grin. 'Oh – and next week for the trip?' he asked Moira, who nodded assent as he left.

'What trip?' Alys asked her aunt as she watched Rob swing himself up on to the tractor's seat and set off, his takeaway coffee clutched in one hand.

'Oh, a little surprise,' Moira said. Alys thought she was looking rather pleased with herself. 'I've asked Rob if he'll take you to see something nearby. A sight that's really worth seeing.'

'Not in his tractor?' Alys asked, watching his progress up the village street and admiring the way he deftly skirted his way around the parked cars.

'His tractor?' Moira asked, looking puzzled. 'No, of course not.'

Further enquiry was prevented by the arrival of an influx of customers and Alys immersed herself in arranging the cookies on display and serving coffee, all thoughts of their conversation swept away by a busy day. As they were washing up and tidying at the end of the day, she had a light-bulb moment in relation to the lemon poppy-seed cake recipe and hurried back to Moira's, determined to give it another try that evening. Her emails languished, awaiting responses, completely forgotten.

CHAPTER 3

The surprise trip was to Hobbs Hill, the one place in the area that Alys absolutely must see according to Moira and, as it was best reached by car, her aunt had asked Rob if he could drive her there. Privately, Alys doubted that anything was going to beat the immediate area around Northwaite, but she was happy to have a morning away from the café for a change, especially as the weather was so lovely on the chosen day. As they drove along, sunshine was pouring in through the open window on her side of the Land Rover.

Rob was fiddling with the radio controls. 'Always seem to lose the signal round about here,' he said. Alys was just about to tell him not to bother; that she was happy to experience the full glory of the view in peace, when he picked up a station. Through the static crackle, Alys made out a familiar beat, something that she hadn't heard in a while. She laid her hand over Rob's and he turned to look at her, startled.

'Can we just listen to this for a minute, please?' It was 'Free' by Ultra Naté and she'd loved it when

115

she was at school, dancing around her bedroom to it whenever it came on the radio. Already she could barely keep still in her seat and her fingers were tapping out the rhythm on the door. She was painfully aware that an inane grin was plastered across her face and she fought down the urge to sing along, for Rob's sake, but if she'd been alone she would have been belting it out.

The sentiment felt perfect for the moment. She was free, living her life as she wanted to, doing what she wanted to do. Corny though it was, it felt like a moment of affirmation. Here she was, on the road to Hobbs Hill with stunning views in every direction for miles as the sun burnt off any lingering morning mist. Her spirits soared along with the music, the track finishing just as they pulled into the hill-top parking area. No one else was around yet. Alys flung open the door of the Land Rover and took deep breaths of the air, which was faintly scented with wood smoke that drifted up from the wood burners in cottages far below. As Rob turned off the engine she was initially struck by the silence, until her ear became attuned to faint sounds: a distant tractor ploughing its way through the patchwork of fields down below, a skylark spilling its rapturous song from on high. Rob had already started out up a little grassy bank and Alys followed, feeling the pull in the backs of her calves. Heart pounding and rather more out of breath than she cared to admit, Alys reached the summit. She paused to take in the view, revolving slowly, drinking it in from every direction.

'I never realised it was so beautiful up here. Thank you so much for bringing me!' She turned to Rob and beamed. He looked taken aback and not a little embarrassed, but also pleased and proprietorial.

'We're lucky it's such a glorious day. You really can see for miles. Look.' Rob moved closer to Alys and pointed down into the valley. 'That's Northwaite over there. You can just see the church tower. And there's Nortonstall beyond – it's almost hidden in the bottom of the valley, but you can see where the river runs through it. And see those chimneys along the river?' He pointed out the single brick-built chimneys, in varied states of disrepair, poking up through the trees all the way along the valley. 'Those are all that's left from the days of the cotton mills.'

Alys shivered, whether in response to the realisation of how small she was in such a vast landscape, or simply because her summer dress didn't offer much protection from the brisk breeze on the summit, she wasn't sure. Rob had noticed though.

'You're cold,' he said. 'Sit yourself down here, you'll be out of the wind.' And he steered her to a sunny spot in the lee of the hill. 'Give me a minute. I need to get something from the boot.'

Alys sat in the little grassy dip and hugged her knees to herself for warmth. She'd put on her favourite vintage frock this morning, cornflower blue crêpe-de-Chine, sprigged all over with white daisies, but she wished now that she'd thought to bring the English summer essential – a cardigan.

Rob reappeared with a blanket, a jumper, a flask and a box that looked as though it was from the café. He spread out the rug and offered Alys the jumper. 'Here you go. Found this in the back. Probably smells of sheep but it'll warm you up a bit.' She pulled it on gratefully, feeling warmer in an instant. The wool was a bit scratchy and it did indeed have a smell of the fields but also something else: an indefinable scent that she realised with a start belonged to Rob.

'Thank you.' Alys lay back and stared up into the sky, deepest blue and infinite, with white wisps of cloud scudding across. She searched for the skylark, still pouring out its song from on high, and thought she'd spotted it, a tiny dot hovering, but it was lost again in the blink of an eye. She scanned the sky again for it then raised herself up on her elbows as she caught the scent of coffee.

'This is a treat,' she said, watching as Rob poured coffee from the flask into two takeaway cups, and opened the box.

Rob smiled ruefully. 'You've got Moira to thank for it. She planned ahead, luckily, and gave me this when I picked you up.'

Alys raised her coffee cup and touched it to Rob's. 'To Moira!' she said. 'And what have we here?' She peered into the box. 'Looks like lemon poppy-seed cake!'

Rob looked doubtful. 'Mmm? Cake for breakfast?'

Alys laughed. 'Try it. You'll see. You'll be a convert. It's a recipe I've been trying to perfect for a while and it's already a favourite in the café.'

They sipped their coffee and ate their cake, Alys chasing every last crumb from the box with her forefinger. Warmed by the coffee and the increasing power of the sun, she pushed up the sleeves of the jumper, then eventually pulled it over her head and wrapped it around her neck. Rob rolled up the sleeves of his checked shirt. They sat and gazed at the view in companionable silence, Rob occasionally pointing out one or two more landmarks. Alys had an almost overwhelming urge to lean into him, to rest against his arm and feel the warmth of him against her, to catch his scent. She checked herself just in time, taken aback at the sudden intensity of her feelings and trying to push away uncomfortable thoughts about Tim. At that moment Rob glanced at his watch and sighed.

'I'd like to stay here all day, but I need to drive over Haworth way and check on a delivery that's due. And I promised Moira I'd get you back in time for the late-morning rush.' He turned to look at Alys and, to her surprise, leaned forward and brushed the tip of her nose with his fingers. 'And you're catching the sun. Your freckles are coming out!'

CHAPTER 4

After their trip to Hobbs Hill, Rob had taken to dropping in regularly to the café for a takeaway coffee whenever he passed through the village, continuing to park his tractor outside, to Alys's initial amusement. No one else had batted an eyelid, of course, and soon it was as normal to her as it was to them.

Alys had found herself looking forward to these visits. Although she was busy and exhausted a lot of the time, she missed the company of someone her own age. Most of the customers, local or passing through, were Moira's age or older. The thought of going to a pub on her own, either in Northwaite or Nortonstall, just didn't appeal. So, when Rob suggested another outing, she leapt at the chance. He'd dropped in to pick up a coffee as usual and had turned back just as he was about to leave.

'Don't suppose you fancy a night out in Nortonstall on Saturday?' He'd directed this at Alys, and Moira, overhearing as she was clearing the tables, had suddenly discovered some urgent washing up that needed doing in the tiny kitchen area at the back.

'There's a band on at The Royal. Quite well known, apparently, and trying out some small gigs before they head out on tour. I've not heard of them, but it might make a change?'

He had been quite offhand about it. Alys wasn't sure if he was worried about being turned down publicly, or he was genuinely not bothered whether he, or she, went or not. She'd been in Northwaite nearly two months now, though, and she was ready to try something different.

She looked directly at him, taking in his three-day stubble, hair that looked as though it hadn't seen a comb since he'd got out of bed, and his deep brown eyes. 'This Saturday. Yes, why not? Sounds good.'

Rob looked momentarily startled by her acceptance, then recovered himself. 'I'll pick you up from Moira's. Eight o'clock?'

'See you then,' she said, wondering at their sudden formality.

Rob nodded briefly and left. Alys, watching him go, admired as usual the ease with which he hauled himself up into the tractor cab, then turned to find Moira watching her with a half-smile.

'What?' she demanded, feeling her colour rise.

'Nothing. Nothing at all.' Moira busied herself rearranging cakes on plates and Alys was prevented from interrogating her further by the arrival of a party of walkers, their morning hike over and all of them in urgent need of coffee and cake. It was an hour or so before she had a chance to mull

121

over Rob's suggestion, as she did the washing up, and she was surprised to discover it was quite to her liking. Not just the chance of a night out, but the company involved.

By the time Saturday evening arrived, however, Alys had managed to get herself wound up. What would she wear? Was this an actual date? Was she even in a position to consider dating again? After all, she wasn't sure that Tim had even got the message that she had been trying to convey to him, given that she'd been ignoring his emails. It was more than a bit stressful and not helped by Moira finding it all very amusing.

'For heaven's sake, you're just going to the pub with a friend. You're getting in a state about nothing,' Moira said as Alys, at five minutes to eight, suddenly decided that she needed to change again. Her bed was already piled high with discarded outfits; she had dithered over a dress or jeans, a top and leggings, or something smarter. Did she even *have* anything smarter with her?

'Look, everyone will be either dressed up to the nines or in jeans. Nothing in between. Just go in something you feel comfortable in. And have a nice time!'

The last was said as the doorbell rang and Moira, laughing at the look of panic that swept over Alys's face, propelled her to the door before she could run upstairs for one last makeover.

Rob was wearing a checked shirt and jeans, as

ever. Alys couldn't imagine why she had been getting in such a state. They were travelling in the Land Rover, after all. She felt glad that she'd settled on jeans and a top that she'd actually made herself, from vintage Fifties silk scarves bought at a car boot sale.

'Looking good,' said Rob, and Alys rolled her eyes in embarrassment. She found herself chattering nervously all the way to Nortonstall, and felt a wave of panic again when Rob, as he pushed open the door to the pub, casually mentioned that a few of his friends would be there.

She needn't have worried. Everyone was friendly and open, welcoming Alys into the group as though they already knew her. Once the band had started up, though, they'd had to resort to sign language and Alys was relieved when, as if with one accord, they'd spilled back out into the street and headed over the road to a quieter pub.

'Sorry about that,' Rob said cheerfully. 'I didn't realise they were going to be quite so heavy metal.'

'And loud! I think they thought they were playing at Wembley Arena.' Alys shook her head – her ears were ringing.

With another round bought, she found herself tucked into a window seat, chatting to a couple of girls who had known Rob since school and were now working in Leeds, in marketing and accountancy respectively. They commuted daily and Alys, thinking back to her arrival in Nortonstall by train, thought ruefully that it was quite a different sort of commute to the type she had been used to. Much more scenic, for a start.

Engrossed in conversation about all things cake related, she was startled when Rob tapped her on the shoulder. He waved his phone at her.

'Just had a call. I've got to go.'

She was puzzled. 'A call? Go where?'

'The farm,' said Rob. 'There's a problem with one of the rare breeds. They've called the vet but want me on hand too. Good job I've barely touched this pint. Do you want a lift?'

'Oh.' Alys felt a rush of disappointment. She was enjoying the evening and meeting new people – at the back of her mind she had been looking forward to talking it all over with Rob on the way home.

'Oh, don't go yet,' chorused Rosie and Sian, Alys's new-found friends. 'We'll look after her,' they said to Rob.

Rob looked at her expectantly. 'Sorry, Alys. I need to go *now*. What do you want to do?'

'Stay! Stay!' The girls were laughing and holding her down.

She made a snap decision. 'I'll stay. I can get the last bus or something.'

'Right you are.' Rob was already heading for the door.

'See you next week,' Alys called, but her words were swallowed up in the crowd.

After that, the shine went off the evening. She

enjoyed chatting to Rob's friends, but she was aware of not wanting to miss the last bus back to Northwaite, which went long before the pubs closed. So, at an hour that felt way too sensible, she made her excuses, extracting promises from all of them that they would come and visit the café as soon as they could, and headed for the bus stop. Waiting alongside a family, cheerful after a meal in town, and next to a lovingly entwined teenage couple, she felt suddenly sad. Why was it that the events that were most eagerly anticipated never worked out quite as you hoped?

Rob was cheery the next time he dropped by, which wasn't until mid-week. He seemed to have forgotten all about Saturday night and looked momentarily confused when Alys asked him if his mercy mission had been successful.

'Mercy mission? Oh, the cows. All fine. Pretty much a false alarm,' he'd said. 'Something wrong with the feed, but it's all adjusted now. You can't be too careful with these rare breeds, though.' He paused, as if suddenly remembering something. 'I saw Rosie and Sian. They said how much they'd enjoyed talking to you. Did you have a good time with them after I left?'

Alys felt herself starting to blush as she busied herself taking bags and boxes from the cupboard below the counter to lay out for their takeaway customers. She wondered why he was interested in her opinion of his friends. Did it signify something?

'Why, yes, they were lovely. So welcoming. All your friends seem really nice.' Alys was genuinely enthusiastic. She chided herself for overthinking things. For heaven's sake, whatever was the matter with her? Rob was just being friendly. But was it possible that she was hoping for something a little more than that?

CHAPTER 5

Sun was already pouring through the printed-cotton curtains when Alys awoke. She stretched out in the warmth of the bed and smiled to herself. It was going to be another glorious day. As she started to mentally run through the day ahead, a dawning realisation struck a chill to her heart. She glanced across the room to check that her mind wasn't playing tricks, but there could be no doubt. Her suitcase, lopsided because of its missing wheel, was propped against the wall, waiting to be packed. Alys's time in Northwaite was almost up.

She'd stayed longer than she had originally intended, over three months rather than the two that she had envisaged. Moira had been back on form for a while now and it was time to head back to London and book herself a ticket for the travels that she had only vaguely thought about when she'd packed in her job.

She felt a momentary lifting of her spirits at the thought of blue skies, turquoise sea and white sandy beaches. These images were only too swiftly followed by another featuring a crowded station platform, everyone around her pushing and jostling to board the train, a heavy rucksack making her back run with sweat. She pushed the image away. She'd manage it better this time, not like her trip to India over ten years ago. She was older and wiser, and anyway, the different experiences, the good and the bad, were what made travelling so rewarding. Weren't they?

Alys had a strong suspicion that she might be pursuing the idea of travelling solely because she had mentioned it to so many people – her mother, her aunt, customers in the café – that it would seem odd if she didn't go. It was all very well talking vaguely about her 'travel plans', but she hadn't really got any. It hadn't entered her head once since she'd got to Northwaite, despite lugging several weighty travel guides along for the research that she'd planned to do. If she was honest with herself, she wasn't sure that she wanted to go off on her own on a big adventure. She was very happy here in this little community and, obscurely, she felt a little hurt that, now it was time to go, no one was begging her to stay.

Alys sighed. She glanced around the room, taking in the stripped floorboards, the old pine chest, the faded patchwork quilt on the white wrought-iron bed, which had little hearts fash- ioned into each of its uprights. It was a real wrench. This felt so much like home now, and although she was looking forward to seeing her cats, her garden and her house back in London, she had the strangest sense that everything there was no longer part of her, but belonged to someone else.

Resolutely, she threw back the covers. Today was her last day in the café and she wanted it to be a good one. She'd planned to bake a special cake and hand out slices to the regular customers, as well as make the lemon poppy-seed cake that had quickly become a café favourite. She'd made sure that her aunt had all the recipes for the cakes that she had introduced so there would be no problems with continuity.

'They don't come out as well when I make them,' Moira had complained when they had discussed the recipes.

'That's because you don't make them very often – you usually leave it to me,' Alys teased. 'Come on – you're the master baker here. I bet you'll be making better versions of them by the end of the week.'

Alys had already been embarrassed by the number of customers who had popped in to wish her well. They praised her so often for helping to transform the place that she had blushed and protested, feeling bad for Moira who was busying herself quietly in the background. It was Moira's baking skill that had drawn the customers back since the café had opened, after all. She'd just helped to do a bit of 'window dressing', as she'd been at pains to point out to her aunt. Now she wanted to repay all the compliments with cake, so it was time to shower, dress and head down to the kitchen and bake there for the last time.

More than once over the next couple of hours Alys had had to give herself a stern talking to, to stay focused. Moira had already left for the café, to open up for any early walkers passing through. No sooner had her aunt shut the door behind herself, after a hasty breakfast, than unwelcome thoughts of Tim had popped into Alys's mind. She had messed up so badly in her responses to Tim's efforts to stay in touch that she had found herself promising to meet him for a drink when she was back in London. She wasn't looking forward to it – absence certainly had seemed to make the heart grow fonder in Tim's case but, sadly for him, not in her own.

She wrenched her thoughts back to the task in hand, half fearful that the nature of them might sour her baking. Instead, she started to think about the people she had got to know in the area, in her brief time there, and how friendly and welcoming they had been. Number one, of course, was Moira, who had treated Alys as though she were her best friend and her daughter combined. Then there were the customers in the café, always so chatty and interested in her as well as sharing tales of their own lives, the ups as well as the downs. She was pretty sure that for some of them, the café worked as a much-needed therapy centre. Flo had been such a support from day one in the café, always ready to step in when either she or Moira had needed to take a half-day, and ready to revert to a more full-time role once Alys had left. Then there was Claire, whose shop still drew Alys like a magnet although she had managed to rein in her compulsion to make weekly acquisitions – in any case, Claire had said that she doubted whether there was a single piece of vintage china left anywhere in Yorkshire. She rather thought Alys had bought it all for The Celestial Cake Café.

Last, but not least, there was Rob. She would miss Rob – he was so different from any other men of her acquaintance, past or present, that she didn't know quite what to make of him or, rather, her feelings about him. He was sure of himself without appearing over-confident or overbearing and seemed somehow older than he was, but in a good way. Alys discovered that she had stopped what she was doing and was gazing into the distance with a foolish grin plastered over her face. She shook her head, looked at the kitchen clock, gave a squeak of alarm and redoubled her efforts with the cake mixture.

At ten-thirty, Alys was to be seen hurrying through the village, rather weighed down with bags and cake boxes. She would finish her special cake in the café, she reasoned, as it still needed to cool properly and, in any case, it would have been hard to transport once decorated. She had been determined to incorporate angel's wings into her theme for the cake but she disliked using sugarpaste and lacked the sugarcraft skills to work in pastillage, a sugar-based modelling paste that experts used to make exquisite cake decorations. So, she had settled on something much simpler: a Victoria sponge, sandwiched with jam, cream and local strawberries and dusted on top with icing sugar in the shape of a pair of angel's wings. She had drawn the design herself, basing it on the wings in the café, and cut out a template. Everything she needed was in one of the bags she was carrying and the sponge cakes, which had risen beautifully, were in the boxes. Her mind full of the task ahead of her, she turned on her heels on reaching the café porch and backed through the door to avoid disturbing any of the boxes and packages she was carrying. As she swung around inside the café she was greeted by the sound of clapping, startling in itself, and even more so when combined with the scene that greeted her, so much so that she almost dropped the cake boxes.

Open-mouthed, she stared at the bunch of helium balloons in the shape of aeroplanes that was tied to the counter, the banner strung over the door to the kitchen that read 'Bon Voyage, Alys' but most of all, at the number of people crammed into the café. Moira and Flo, both beaming, were behind the counter and it seemed as though the whole village had popped in to have a final coffee with Alys.

The next hour passed in a blur of kissing of cheeks, answering questions about her plans and saying farewell as customers gradually drifted away to get on with their days. There was another influx at lunchtime, as people dropped in for sandwiches, and even new customers passing through found themselves drawn to enquire what this was all about, before offering Alys their best wishes for her forthcoming adventures.

More than a little overwhelmed, Alys escaped into the kitchen to finally assemble her special cake. Her hands were shaking as she laid the template on top and began to sift the icing sugar that would create the wings. At one point, she had to step back sharply as tears, coursing down her cheeks as she bent over the decoration, threatened to plop onto the sugar and spoil it. She was very touched by all the good wishes showered upon her but once again found herself irrationally upset that everyone seemed happy to wish her on her way, rather than beg her to stay. She knew this was nonsense, that everyone believed that she was doing exactly what she had set out to do from the start. She just wished that she had recognised earlier what was now staring her in the face. She really wasn't ready to leave the café, Moira, Northwaite and all the people she had met there. It was too soon.

CHAPTER 6

Alys was called through from the kitchen to say farewell to Claire, who had dropped in specially to see her.

'I can't stay long,' Claire said, refusing tea but asking for a sandwich to take with her. 'I've shut the shop to take a lunch break but really I ought to get back. Nortonstall is busy today – there are a lot of tourists around. I just wanted to give you this.'

She handed over a package, beautifully wrapped in lilac tissue paper with a pink satin bow. Alys could tell from the slightly awkward shape and the feel of it that it was a piece of china.

'This one's for you, not for the café,' Claire said.

'Oh, it's so beautifully wrapped, I don't want to open it,' Alys exclaimed.

'Open it later,' Claire suggested, then leant across the counter to kiss Alys on the cheek. 'Now, I really must get back but I just wanted to say have a wonderful time. But don't forget your friends – come back and see us as soon as you can.'

Alys felt tears start to her eyes again but to buy herself some time to recover she said, 'Wait, I've got something for you, too.'

She hurried into the kitchen and returned bearing the angel's wings cake, cream and fruit spilling out of the sides where the two sponges were sandwiched together. The template had worked well, Alys thought as she set the cake down on the counter and everyone exclaimed over the design.

'It looks too beautiful to cut into,' Claire protested when Alys insisted that she should take a slice with her.

'Nonsense. It won't keep anyway,' Alys said. 'It's best eaten on the day it's made. But I'll just take a quick picture.'

She did feel very proud of her cake and she remembered that she'd promised to send her mother some more photos. Kate had liked the email that had focused on the café and cakes and Alys realised that she hadn't delivered on her promise to send more along the same lines. Today would be her last chance.

Photo taken, she insisted that Moira cut the cake while she unwrapped Claire's gift. She gasped as she peeled back the layers of tissue. It was a milk jug of the same design as the tea service that had belonged to Claire's grandmother, the one that Alys secretly coveted every time she took tea with Claire.

'It's not—?'

Claire broke in before she finished her sentence. 'No, it's not mine. I'm not that generous, sadly! But I came across this at a house-clearance sale and I've always known how much you loved the design. Nothing else was there I'm afraid, just the jug. But I'll keep my eyes peeled.'

Alys bit her lip. 'It's so lovely. It will always remind me of here, of you, of how lovely everyone has been . . .' She found that she couldn't go on.

'You'll be back, I know you will,' Claire said firmly, taking her sandwich in its bag and balancing her piece of cake in its box on top of it. She turned at the café door and blew Alys a kiss as she left.

By the end of the day, Alys's cheeks were quite pink with emotion and she felt as though she had veered between smiling and tears all day long. At four o'clock, Moira had produced a bottle of prosecco, which she had been hiding at the back of the fridge, and insisted that she, Alys and Flo should share it, sparing a thimbleful here and there for any last-minute regulars who dropped in. Nothing was left of the angel's wings cake apart from a few crumbs; indeed, all the cake stands were bare and only a few pieces of shortbread remained for anyone hoping for a sweet treat at the end of the day.

'We'll clear up,' Moira said to Alys. 'Take your drink out back and just relax for a little while. We're going to eat at the pub tonight so we don't need to rush home and think about making dinner.'

Alys was grateful to have a few minutes to herself, to marshall her thoughts. The courtyard was sheltered and perfect for a day like today, where the sunshine was tempered by a brisk breeze. She sat at a table, shut her eyes and turned her face to the sun. She'd been on her feet since early that morning and she hadn't eaten properly all day, just snatched bites of a sandwich in between talking to customers. Now she could feel her stomach growling and the thought of an early meal at the pub was very appealing. Without bothering to open her eyes she lifted the glass to her lips and took a drink, relishing the fizz of the bubbles and the warming, relaxing feeling as the alcohol took hold. She felt drowsy sitting there, enjoying the sunshine with no sound to disturb her apart from a faint murmur of voices within the café, the buzz of bees visiting the bunches of flowers in jugs on the tables and the calling of swifts as they swooped high above her.

'Alys. Alys, wake up.'

She couldn't work out where she was for a moment, thinking herself in her bed back in Moira's cottage.

'You must have dropped off. Flo's ready to leave. Come and say goodbye.'

Alys blinked and stretched, almost knocking over her glass. It took her a few moments to gather herself, then she stood up and went back into the café. Flo gave her a big hug and Alys made her promise to keep an eye on Moira and to stop her from overdoing things, then she was on her way with a flurry of good wishes for Alys's travels. Alys turned the sign on the door to read 'Closed' and sighed.

'I'm glad that's over. I don't think I can say any more goodbyes.'

Moira, who was busy bringing in the flower jugs from the courtyard, handed Alys her glass. 'Here, finish this. One more goodbye to go, I'm afraid. We're meeting Rob at the pub.'

Alys, gulping down the last of her prosecco, now rather warm, almost choked on the bubbles. 'Rob?' she asked.

'Yes, he couldn't get away from the farm to come in today so he said he'd drop into the pub later to see you.' Moira wiped the counter, scrutinised the room for crumbs and, satisfied, said 'Take one last look around. Then let's go.'

Alys felt quite certain that she didn't want to say goodbye to the café but, to please her aunt, she revolved slowly in the centre of the room, taking in all the features that had so struck her the first time she saw it. The angel's wings hanging in the window, the stone flags, the prints on the wall – and now the shelves of china, washed and ready for a new day ahead.

'Okay, I've got it here,' she tapped the side of her forehead. 'And if all else fails, I've got a lot of it here, too.' She waved her phone at Moira, thinking of all the photos she had taken recently of the café and the cakes.

'Come on then.' Moira propelled her through the door then set the alarm and swiftly locked up. She took Alys's arm. 'I think I need another drink.' And with that, she steered her in the direction of The Old Bell.

CHAPTER 7

Rob had joined them in The Old Bell when Alys and her aunt were halfway through their first drink and discussing whether they should just go ahead and order without him. He'd despatched half of his first pint very swiftly, muttering something about it being a dusty afternoon on the farm, then had gone back to the bar to put in an order for fish and chips all round. Alys was so hungry that she had to stop herself bolting her food when it arrived but she noticed that Moira just toyed with hers and Rob ended up eating most of her chips as well as his own.

'Are you sure you don't want them?' he asked, each time he took a few more on his fork.

'No, honestly, they're yours,' Moira said finally, pushing her plate in his direction. 'I think I ate too much cake earlier.'

Alys was pretty sure that Moira had eaten as little as she had in the café today but she didn't say anything. Instead, she turned to Rob and described the cake that she had made as her farewell to the café.

'Where's my piece, then?' he asked, sitting back

after he'd cleared Moira's chips. He patted his stomach. 'I'm pretty full right now but I'm sure I could squeeze in a tiny piece of cake.'

'Oh!' Alys clapped her hand over her mouth. 'I'm so sorry. I should have saved you a piece. I didn't think.'

Rob raised his eyebrows and sighed heavily. 'I see,' he said meaningfully.

Alys was flustered. Why hadn't she thought to save him some? 'I've got a photo of it,' she said, fishing out her phone and thrusting it under his nose. 'See?'

'Well, that's just made it worse,' Rob said. 'Tempting a man with tales of some special cake that you've made for all your friends, then all you can offer him is a photo of it. A photo, not even the tiniest slice.'

'I could do with another drink,' Moira said. 'Rob, would you mind?' She fished in her wallet and waved a note at him. 'And get one for yourself and Alys while you're there.' She brushed away their protests and stacked the plates as Rob stood up. 'Here, could you take these back too?'

She noticed Alys's quizzical look. 'Sorry, I can't abide plates being left in front of you once you've eaten. They could do with some more help in here.' She looked around. 'And I thought it would give you a break from Rob's teasing.'

But Rob wasn't done. 'It's no good, you know,' he complained once he'd returned with their drinks. He looked at Alys. 'You're about to reduce

140

the number of thirty-somethings in the village by fifty per cent.'

Alys laughed. 'That's a bit of an exaggeration! And if you're including yourself in the total, why, you don't even live in the village anyway.'

'Well, I'm only a few miles away. And anyway, I grew up here, Mum and Dad still live here, so I'm an honorary resident.' He took a sip of his beer. 'So, where do you think you'll head first on your travels?'

'I don't know yet.' Alys was caught off guard. 'I haven't thought that much about it. I'll probably make a spur-of-the-moment decision when I've checked out the flights. Australia, maybe?'

'Australia! So far! I had no idea . . .' Moira looked startled, then collected herself. 'Well, at least you won't have any problems with the language,' she said lamely, grasping for something to say.

'Which part are you thinking of going to?' said Rob, 'I've still got a couple of mates out there from when I was working. I could hook you up with them, so at least you'd have somewhere to stay.' He paused and his expression changed. 'Actually, thinking about it, they might not be quite your cup of tea.'

Alys made a big effort to divert the conversation away from her forthcoming travels or, indeed, anything to do with the café or the village by asking Rob about the farm. He loved to talk about the rare breeds and how passionate he was about preserving them for the future, and her strategy paid off. He was still talking about them as they finished their drinks and he looked at his watch.

'Sorry I can't give you a lift to the station tomorrow, Alys.' Rob got to his feet and prepared to settle his bill at the bar. 'I've got an early start. We're moving the sheep from the high pasture and then I've got to stick around while the bloke comes to service the big combine.'

'No worries, Moira already booked a cab,' said Alys, looking up at him. She felt a terrible pang as she realised that this might be the last time she ever saw Rob.

'Hey, no need to look so sad,' said Rob, bending down to give Alys a hug, just as she rose to her feet, leading to a clumsy embrace that caused a chorus of whoops and catcalls from the regulars at the bar. He dismissed them with an easy shrug, while Alys blushed furiously.

'You'll be back.' Rob's tone was firm. 'You won't be able to stay away. And Moira will be delighted to see you any time, won't you?' He turned to Moira.

'I've already told Alys what a godsend she's been these last few weeks,' said Moira. 'I don't know how I would have managed without her. She didn't just step into my shoes, she did so much more. She brought all the lovely vintage china into the café and as for her cake recipes – well, the place has never been so popular. I hope she knows she's got a home here whenever she wants it?' She turned to Alys with a slightly wobbly smile.

'I can't begin to tell you what a good time I've had.' Alys paused and bit her lip as she thought over the last few weeks and how much seemed to have happened in that time. She thought about trying to summarise all the things that meant so much: the joy the countryside had given her, how much she had loved searching for the vintage china, her delight in trying new recipes for the café, the fun of meeting new people and how welcoming everyone had been. Words failed her so she put an arm around Moira to disguise the fact that she was close to tears herself. 'Come on, time to go,' Alys said, trying to sound brisk and matter-of-fact. 'I've got to finish packing my bag this evening.'

'Ah, your bag. I remember it well.' Rob grimaced. 'Hope you asked the cab company for their strongest driver,' he said, turning to Moira. 'Alys needs a weightlifter to deal with her luggage. She's going to have to master the art of travelling light if she's heading for Australia.' And with a grin and a wave he was out of the door.

Early the following morning, Alys, standing in her room at Moira's and looking out of the window, found herself smiling at the memory of Rob's teasing before she gave herself a little shake. It was time to get on, otherwise the cab would be here and she'd still be in her dressing gown. There was nothing to be done now – the next phase of her life was about to begin.

PART IV

CHAPTER 1

Alice's heart was pounding as she drew closer to her destination. Every beat seemed to shake her chest, her whole frame. It was a cloudy night with no moon to cast its light along the pathway, and the lantern proved a feeble substitute. But Alice was used to being abroad at night. There were heart-stopping moments when her passage would startle a bird from its sleep, sending it blundering from its roost, or cause a nervous deer to break free from the woods and bound along ahead of her, veering from side to side with a flash of its white tail, an instinctive response to the fear of a hunter's gun.

Indeed, poachers were the only people encountered by Alice on her night forays into the woods. They strode past her, caps pulled far down over their eyes in an effort at disguise, rabbits slung from a belt, the gun cocked over a shoulder, where yet more prized specimens hung. Or they would melt away into the woods as Alice approached, blending in with the trees, as unwilling to be seen as Alice was. She was never in any doubt as to their identity, recognising the height, breadth, gait and demeanour of these local men, who were trying to add to their family's larder or to earn themselves a few pence from the local butcher. Alice didn't dwell too long on the rights and wrongs of it. It seemed to her that the valley held an abundance of rabbits and wildfowl, and it puzzled her as to how some landowner could claim ownership of such wild creatures.

For their part, the men grew used to seeing Alice out at night with her lantern and basket, often around the time of the full moon which added extra potency to the herbs gathered then. The poachers gave her little heed as she posed no threat to them. They didn't think to question why a cloudy, moonless night that suited them best for their secret endeavours should also find Alice abroad with her lantern.

Alice had waited until the house was in darkness and all were sound asleep before cautiously rising and slipping out, lantern as yet not lit, shawl wrapped tightly around her, her basket clutched to her. Steady breathing from Sarah's room reassured her that she wouldn't be missed. The moonless night suited her purpose well, although treading the familiar path by lantern light, in haste, was less easy than she expected.

Her pounding heart as she approached her destination was caused by a mixture of exertion, agitation and fear. The deer pool lay far back from the path and was so well hidden that she was convinced that only she, and the deer who drank there, could know about it. It was the perfect spot. She stepped through the almost invisible gap in the trees. It was even darker in here, and she'd extinguished the lantern, keen not to draw attention to her deviation from the path should anyone be watching. Alice stood still for a moment, trying to accustom her eyes to the all-encompassing blanket of darkness. There was just the faintest lifting of the gloom ahead of her, where the absence of trees around the pool allowed some light to penetrate. She took a cautious step or two, breathing deeply whilst trying to remain as quiet as possible.

An awareness of the passage of time increased her anxiety. With her arms stretched out in front of her, she felt her way forwards. Her fingertips brushed the damp ridged softness of leaves, the rasping roughness of bark, felt the electric emptiness of air. Then there was a scent that wasn't damp moss and crushed bracken, but warmer, muskier. Her questing fingertips found a different texture: rough tweed, linen.

She exhaled, releasing some of her pent-up tension.

'Alice', he breathed, reaching out to her through the gloom, drawing her in to him, safe now and all wrapped up in the dark. 'Alice.' Again, breathed into her hair.

CHAPTER 2

As Alice headed down the mill path one late September morning, the sound of someone behind her, slipping every now and then on the loose stones, caused her to look nervously behind and draw back into the bracken, half concealing herself behind a tree, heart beating fast. When she saw Albert, cap pulled firmly over his ears, shoulders hunched into his too-small jacket, and hands jammed into his pockets for warmth, she slipped out from her hiding place directly into his path. He started, having been lost in his thoughts, and then beamed at her.

Alice couldn't remember how long she had known Albert. He'd always been there, finding conkers for her at the edge of Tinker's Wood, in the only spot where the chestnut trees grew; the remnants of the garden of a grand house long gone, perhaps. He'd yelled encouragement when, aged eight, she'd taken on the village boys, becoming Northwaite conker champion for one entire heady autumn. He'd spent hours with her down by the packhorse bridge, racing sticks underneath it in the high, brown waters of a wet spring. Although a couple of years younger than Alice, he'd become bored with the game first, turning his attention to fashioning the stick boats into grand galleons, with twigs for masts and leaves for sails. Once he'd mastered how to keep the boats afloat with their additional load, by dint of judicious carving and whittling, Alice had added precious cargo. Berries became jewels bound for Leeds, the most exotic and far-flung place that either of them could envisage. Petals were bales of fine cloth, while gravel from the bed of the river became gold.

So, spring days turned into summer, and Alice found that household duties kept her at home more and more frequently. Albert stopped loitering by her gate hoping that their idyll could be resumed. Solitary now in his pursuits, he spent his hours perfecting his carving skills with the few tools that he could make or beg, and Alice learnt to look out for offerings left on the gatepost at the end of a long day. A tiny horse, crudely carved from a thin branch of ash. A proper boat, with a hollowed-out hull and a set of twiggy oars. A squat bird, chest daubed red with berry juice, head thrown back and beak wide open in song.

Albert had started work as a millhand as soon as he was old enough, and it was these skills that saved him from the regular drudgery of the life there. His nimble fingers were set to work fixing the machinery that enslaved Alice and the other workers. She was glad for him. He was small for his age and would otherwise have had a dangerous time of it, crawling underneath the working machines to fix broken threads, or collecting the cotton detritus.

When Alice started work at the mill, some of their previous relationship was restored, to Albert's delight. She'd had reason to be thankful, on more than one occasion, that he knew his way around the mill and its people and that he kept an eye out for her. They were always glad to walk down to the mill together in the morning, too. Keeping company on the path made the journey pass quickly and helped Alice keep her mind from its anxious perambulations, the nature of which was causing her to arrive at work each morning besieged by fearful thoughts.

Today, Albert was full of talk about a stone-carving apprenticeship that he harboured dreams of applying for. Alice heard him out, then gently asked, 'But Albert, where will you find the money to bind you to your master? And if you have to travel away from home, to York, to do this, then you must pay your board and lodging too?'

Albert looked crestfallen and walked a few steps in silence, and Alice felt sorry for having spoken so hastily and for having dashed his dreams. 'But perhaps there are foundations you can apply to,' she said. 'Charities that might help fund such an enterprise?'

Albert brightened. 'There must be a way,' he

said. 'I just need to make a plan. Happen I've got a rich uncle hidden away somewhere.'

They both laughed, knowing that the likelihood of Albert making his planned escape was slim. Most of the wages from his employment at the mill went straight to his mother. His father had been left incapacitated after an accident in his job as a drayman, and whatever pay-off they had received in compensation had long since gone. Albert was the main breadwinner and, with no siblings, he was likely to be trapped at home in that role for the foreseeable future.

The roof of the mill below them came into view as the path took its last downward bend. As they got closer, Alice became quiet, her troubled thoughts flooding back. The increasingly autumnal weather had meant that she could use extra layers of clothes to hide the fact that her once-slender figure was now filling out. Soon there would be no disguising her pregnancy, and the knowing looks, the gossip and the shame of it would be more than Alice could bear. But to leave now would mean that her one chance of seeing Richard on a daily basis was taken from her.

CHAPTER 3

Sarah's look spoke volumes of her disappointment, of her despair that Alice was following the path that so many of the village girls before her had trodden.

'Will he marry you?' she asked.

Alice shook her head.

'Cannot or will not?' snapped Sarah, and she seemed almost on the point of striking Alice, who shrank back and shook her head again, mutely.

Her eyes had filled with tears, so she was startled when Sarah reached out and gave her a fierce, rough hug.

'Well, I hope you've known kindness, not cruelty.' Sarah sighed. 'It's a sorry business, but what's done is done and we have to make the best of it. You must leave the mill and, now that I'm feeling better, we'll get by on what my work brings in. Ella is old enough to take your place at the mill, and you must expect to go back when the baby is grown.'

Ella. Alice felt pierced to the heart. She had always held on to a fantasy that none of the rest of the family would have to follow her into the mill, without really thinking about how this might be achieved. Now she had brought down on Ella the very thing that she had so wished to prevent. An unwelcome thought surfaced, and no matter how hard Alice tried to block it out, it persisted. 'Williams,' a voice whispered in her head. 'Williams and Ella.' Ella had only just turned thirteen, so she was eligible for mill work, but the thought of any man taking a predatory interest in her struck a chill to Alice's heart. She reasoned with herself that Ella looked young, and her attitude to life was definitely that of a child. But Alice could even now recognise the hint of a blossoming from girl-hood to womanhood, and it looked as though Ella would be striking in appearance as she grew up. Not beautiful: the Bancroft girls would never be called that, but they had strong features, slender limbs and delicate hands – all the better for mill work, Alice thought in despair. Although it was obvious that Ella and Alice were sisters, their curly, flowing hair marking them out instantly as related, Ella had a dreamy demeanour in contrast to Alice's busy, sharp mind. Her family teased Ella that she must be a woodland sprite who'd adopted their home as hers. When she came back after vanishing for hours on end amongst the woods and fields, she always seemed vague and puzzled as to where she had been and what she'd been doing.

'Ella's away with the fairies again,' was a common refrain in the Bancroft household, but Alice had a very real fear that the mill would crush her restless spirit, and that Williams would prey on her fragility.

'If only I'd thought to teach Ella to read and write, to train her to take over from me as a teacher,' thought Alice, filled with despair. It was too late to remedy this now. Alice had never imagined that she would find herself in such a situation and, although her whole being shrank from accepting it, she resolved to work for as long as she could. In the meantime, perhaps she could think of something that would save Ella from a future in the mill?

CHAPTER 4

The valley view that Richard beheld each day from the window of his bedroom could scarcely have been more beautiful. In the early light of this late-autumn morning, a wisp of mist still hung there, and a dark shadow sliced across the trees on the other side of the valley: blue-green where the sun had yet to strike, a warm golden colour where the sun was already warming the scraps of autumn foliage still clinging to them. The window was slightly ajar, the crisp, clean scent of a fresh morning wafting in. Ordinarily, it would have lifted Richard's heart and raised his spirits, but today he was troubled. He knew that he should leave his desk by the window and go downstairs to join his father for an early breakfast, before heading for the mill. On a normal morning, he would have been in a hurry to do just that, his eagerness to see Alice for a precious hour or two in the schoolroom presenting itself in a boyish enthusiasm that his father mistook to be an eagerness for all things mill-related. As Richard helped himself to breakfast from the covered dishes laid out on the dark-oak sideboard – eggs, cold cuts from the night before, perhaps a slice of pork pie – his father would attempt to engage him in discussions regarding mill business. The cost of transporting their goods by rail from Nortonstall was increasing – did Richard think it would be politic to consider transporting them to a larger town, Manchester, say, in the interest of driving a harder bargain? Would it be worth a trip to Leeds to look at the newest range of looms available, to replace the ones in the western shed that needed to be repaired so frequently?

In the last week, encouraged by what he perceived to be signs that his son might be suitable for grooming to take over the reins of business, his father had started to make bigger plans.

'Time to marry that fiancée of yours,' he said gruffly, never at ease when discussing personal matters. 'You've been betrothed over a year now, so your mother tells me. You can use the top floor here for a time, while we build on the land beyond the stables. I've asked Clarke to come over in the week, to draw up some plans. There's room enough for a house and small garden there – it will be fit for you while there's just the two of you, maybe even three or four. By that time, I'll be ready to retire and this house will be yours.'

Richard had stopped eating, hands resting on his knife and fork at each side of the plate, his breakfast suddenly unappetising.

Caroline. He'd pushed the thought of her from his mind, pleading increasing business duties to excuse the paucity of his letter writing. He had a sudden vision of her, framed against the window in the sitting room of her parents' house in Cambridge, head bent in profile as she read his letter, turning the page back and forth as though she hoped to find some words of intimacy or love secreted somewhere, instead of the stiff prose more in keeping with a business letter. He felt a pang, but nothing more. Not the stabbing, searing, nervous excitement that made him hurry from the house each morning, Lucy at his side sniffing the air for the cocktail of aromas left over from the previous night, while he anxiously anticipated the day's first sighting of Alice. Her pale, often serious face as she talked to the class, the quick smile as she turned towards him, the way her hair curled and sprang free from the clips that were hopelessly inadequate to contain it.

It had seemed no time at all since he'd first seen her, that awkward introduction from Ramsay, yet it was over a year ago now, after he'd reluctantly agreed to do the couple of hours' daily teaching that his father had grimly suggested. By the end of the first month, he'd taken to spending three hours a day in the schoolroom, persuading his father that with the large number of pupils it made sense for him to split the class with Alice, each teaching half, then swapping over. His father, mindful of changes in the law enjoining the need to have children in school, and keen to appear an enlightened employer, was happy to acquiesce.

In any case, now that there were over fifty children in the schoolroom, the task of delivering anything beyond the most basic education lay beyond the skill of Alice alone. She had seemed pleased to have the extra help, and once her initial shyness at the presence of 'gentry' in the room had worn off, she started to treat him as her equal. In fact, it was clear that Richard's expensive and extensive education hadn't equipped him terribly well for the task before him. Alice was the better teacher, with the added advantage of having a rapport with the children. Richard observed her at work, and resolved to learn from her.

He found it hard that she should be forced to take but a short break when her teaching work was done, before she had to take her place on the mill floor. When Richard saw her unfold the cloth from her basket and produce a piece of bread spread with dripping, often the only sustenance she had to see her through the day, he felt deeply ashamed to be heading home to the lunch that awaited him. He dined at a table spread with a white linen cloth, his food was served to him, and washed down with wine in a crystal glass if he so desired. He had quizzed Williams, now the mill manager since Ramsay had retired, as to whether she couldn't take a longer break, since teaching a class full of children was demanding work for a morning.

'Nay, Master Richard,' said Williams. 'It don't do to be soft on her. She's a strong lass, and able.

And now she has thee to help her, why, her work load is even lighter.' Richard didn't like the man's manner, the pleasure it seemed to give him to deny his request. It was clear that the only way he could help was to try to lighten the load; to get there early to help set out what few books there were, plus chalk and slates, and to stay behind to help set the room to rights.

He increasingly found himself thinking of the schoolroom when he wasn't there, at odd hours of the day and night. At first, he laboured under the misapprehension that he had found his true vocation, as a teacher. It wasn't long, however, before he had to acknowledge that the draw was Alice. Her good humour, her gentle chivvying of the tired faces in front of her, her concern for their wellbeing and those of their families, gave him a glimpse into a way of life he had known or cared little about until now. He felt that he was being taught just as much as the children, but on an entirely different set of subjects.

Soon, a meagre three hours a day didn't supply Richard with sufficient oxygen of the type that Alice seemed to provide. Although under no obligation to present himself for work on a Saturday, which was a normal working day for the rest of the mill workforce, Richard found that the weather often meant that his usual lengthy walk with Lucy was out of the question, and he would make better use of his time if he spent it in the classroom. Afternoons, previously spent with his sisters and his mother by the sitting-room fire in genteel pursuits such as reading and writing poetry until the tea tray made its appearance, now found him offering to make himself useful in the mill office, one window of which gave onto the mill floor and allowed him frequent glimpses of Alice, distinguishable from her workmates by her unruly hair that spilled from her cap as she concentrated on the spinning thread.

Despite the punishing pace that the machines forced them to keep up, Richard would frequently catch sight of her, head flung back in laughter at some remark made to, or by, one of her fellow workers. He noticed how their demeanour changed when Williams made one of his regular circuits of the room. Heads were bent demurely, fingers flew twice as fast. Perhaps it was only because Richard was being particularly observant that it seemed to him that Williams lingered as he passed Alice, pausing to address a word or two to her, to which she would respond with that open, fearless look that he, Richard, had come to know so well.

James Weatherall, observing in his turn Richard's developing interest in the goings-on on the mill floor, concluded that the time was right to start drawing him into the plans for expansion, perhaps into a second mill, that he had been brooding upon.

So now the weeks had flown and turned into months, and today Richard was facing a crossroads. It felt as though he had lost Alice from his life forever. She had left the mill and withdrawn up the hill to Northwaite, her kinfolk around her and as cut off from him as if she had moved to London. If he ventured into Northwaite, tongues would wag and, in any case, he had no clue as to which of the cottages was home to Alice. He'd never thought to ask her. His life was mapped out for him: a safe, sensible and desirable marriage to Caroline. He'd met her while he was studying at university and thought she would suit him well, being the daughter of a wealthy Cambridge businessman, who met with his parents' approval. He'd proposed to her before returning home to Yorkshire, without thinking a great deal about it. But what would become of his walks over the moors, the poetry and the music? How would this fit into the life of a mill-owning gentleman? And what of Alice? He was finding it hard to think about her. He skirted the edges of her, only half daring to think of her face, her voice, her hair, her hands, her laugh. How could he go to the mill each day without any of this to sustain him?

He could hear himself duly acquiescing with his father. 'Yes, it would be a good idea to let Clarke draw up the plans.' 'Yes, he must invite Caroline to stay so that more plans could be made, and at her earliest convenience.' 'Yes, he would very much like to see his father's plans for the new mill.' Plans, plans, and yet more plans. All with him at their heart and yet he had no wish to be a part of any of them.

Richard felt as though he was suffocating. He flung the window wide, gasping in breaths of chilly air, trying to still the suddenly panicked beating of his heart. Alice had shown him a way of being different, but it was impossible. Had he the courage to break away? Or was he just caught up in one of those 'interludes' that his Cambridge friends had so often enjoyed?

Richard sighed, closed the window and latched it, then turned to the door. He couldn't stay up here any longer – the day had to be faced. The first working day without Alice at his side. Richard headed down the stairs: breakfast must be endured first. His life was changing and he must decide whether to steer that change, or allow it to overtake him. The day ahead would be long; one of many long days to come, he feared. Days in which he must keep up a pretence. And there was yet another issue to consider – a problem so big he hadn't as yet allowed himself to dwell on it for even a moment.

CHAPTER 5

Elisabeth's birth had coincided with the coldest start to a new year that anyone could remember. Snow had carpeted the ground for weeks, but Alice hardly noticed. Her thoughts and time were taken up with Elisabeth and the strange routine that she brought to Alice's days. Alice had recovered quickly from her confinement, with the help of tonics prepared with great care by Sarah, designed to strengthen her without affecting Elisabeth while she was being nursed. Sarah, though, was troubled that Alice's heart tonic wasn't suitable for a baby, even in the diluted doses that she would have received, and so it had to be withheld. Alice had been taking it for nigh on two years now and Sarah watched her anxiously for evidence of fatigue above and beyond that involved in meeting the demands of a small baby, but the weather and Alice's youth was on her side. Alice was forced to stay at home and rest, and by the time that the snow had eased its grip in early March, she appeared fully recovered.

Life was less easy for Ella, however, who found herself having to negotiate the steep paths, made treacherous and difficult by snow, from the village to the mill. At first, it was the depth of the snow that proved hard to manage, with the journey taking twice as long, and the workers arriving at the mill already exhausted from the effort of the gruelling walk, their clothing dripping wet and their feet frozen. Parties of men were deployed by Mr Weatherall to clear the main paths of the worst of the snow, banking it high on either side in dirty grey mounds, studded with leaves and flecks of soil. Each night, as the temperatures dipped, the paths froze hard where the passage of many feet the night before had turned new snowfall and wet mud to slush. Each morning, the workers were faced with sheets of ice, far too dangerous to traverse even for foolhardy, young mill lads. When they tried to slide down them, they found themselves flung off the path into hard-packed and icy snow, too close for comfort to the encroaching tree trunks, standing black against the white landscape. For the first time in its history, Mr Weatherall had to shut the mill, while he worked out a way for his labourers to get to work that didn't involve them breaking their necks.

Ella was delighted at the news: not only was she spared the arduous journey and the energy-sapping day, but she got to spend precious hours with her new-born niece. Alice and Ella and Elisabeth spent the day snuggled into Sarah's bed, piling on the patchwork quilts from the other children's beds to make as cosy a nest for Elisabeth as possible. Sarah tutted disapprovingly and went about the usual business of the household, stoking fires and preparing food.

'Come and sit with us,' Ella called down the stairs. 'Come and see what baby Elisabeth is doing now.'

'I've no need to see, I can hear her well enough.' Sarah banged pans down, then took up the broom and swept the floor vigorously, scraping chairs against the stone flags while Elisabeth wailed on.

Ella appeared in the doorway, barefoot, hair wild and uncombed, clutching her arms around her chest and shivering dramatically in her long night-gown. 'Come and sit with us, do.'

'And who will get the food ready to feed us on a day like this, with not a vegetable to be had from the garden all week?' Sarah snapped.

Ella came over and stroked her back. 'I'll come and help you in a minute. But first come and see baby Elisabeth.'

Sarah sighed and let herself be led upstairs to the bedroom where the little ones had tucked themselves into the bottom of the bed and were entertaining each other with nonsense stories. Thomas, the eldest of the three, barely had to say more than a few words, or make a face, to set his younger sisters snorting and choking and cover-ing their faces with their fingers. Meanwhile Alice, propped up on pillows, cradled a wailing Elisabeth.

Ella dived back beneath the covers, prompting an even fiercer outbreak of crying.

'Here,' Sarah said, and took Elisabeth from her mother, nestling her into her shoulder and falling into an automatic soothing rocking motion. After a few minutes, as Elisabeth started to settle, Sarah walked up and down, patting her gently on the back.

'Look at you all,' she scolded. 'What if we have visitors? Whatever will they think of us? Still abed at this hour of the day!'

Alice laughed. 'I don't think anyone will be stirring from home today. Look, it's snowing again,' and she gestured at the window. Indeed, it was: thick white flakes were falling hard and fast, swirling against the window as the wind gusted.

Ella patted the bed. 'Elisabeth's asleep. Come and lay her here, and then sit with us.'

Sarah huffed and puffed about floors to be scrubbed and beds to be made, but her token efforts at resistance were overruled and she gave in. The snow did its worst outside, piling thick white drifts high against the walls and the kitchen door. The day never seemed to get beyond the strange half-light of dawn before it plunged back into darkness again, albeit one studded with stars and lit by a frosty moon. Inside, the family were blissfully happy. They built up the fire in the tiny grate, told stories, nursed the baby when she woke, and dozed in the firelight when she slept. Sarah conjured soup from the few wizened vegetables

168

still remaining in the larder and everyone, enchanted by the unusual atmosphere of the day, declared it to be the best soup they'd ever eaten.

As the others dozed around her, Alice smoothed the worn patchwork coverlet, looking at the individual scraps of fabric and remembering. Here was a piece from a dress worn by her mother when Alice herself was small. She had a vivid memory of clinging to Sarah's leg as she stood at the stove, burying her face in the folds of her skirt and staring at the sprigs of cream foliage on the soft blue background. The blue was even more faded now. Sarah had cut the dress down once it became too worn, and turned it into pinafores for the little ones. She'd used the leftover scraps to furnish patches for the quilt.

Alice traced the tiny, perfect stitches with her fingers. Sarah had been quite insistent that Alice should learn to sew beautifully, too. These days Sarah's eyes were too weak and tired to let her create such fine stitching, but Alice was reasonably sure that her standards could match those of her mother. She traced around the hexagonal outline of a few more patches – there was the floral print she herself had worn in a pinafore, handed on to Ella and her younger sisters until it was too worn to be of further use for clothing, but still serviceable enough to create a few of the last patches for the quilt.

Gently, she eased the blanket from around the face of the tightly swaddled Elisabeth. Richard hadn't yet seen his daughter. She had no idea how it would be possible for him to ever see her, or whether he would even want to.

She became aware that Sarah was awake, and watching her. Something in Alice's face made Sarah ask gently, 'What is it?'

Alice turned to her, her eyes huge and dark in the firelight. She'd realised with a sinking feeling of guilt that she'd barely thought of Richard since Elisabeth's birth. 'I was just thinking that Elisabeth might never know her father.'

Sarah smiled wryly. 'No matter. Perhaps it's for the best. She's better off brought up here, with family around her. Times are hard at the moment, with the snow, but the patients will be back. I'll make sure she wants for nothing, and you'll bear that responsibility too.'

Sarah had shown no curiosity as to the identity of Elisabeth's father, and Alice hadn't sought to discuss it with her. She suspected that Ella would have heard gossip from the mill about Williams and herself, and she would have put two and two together, like everyone else. No one would have thought that Alice could have strayed so far beyond her station as to form a liaison with the mill owner's handsome son. Whenever he walked amongst them on the mill floor he generated giggles and blushes amongst the girls. To them, he was a desirable but remote figure, so far removed as to not be worth more than a moment's private fantasy. Yet Williams, who was within their reach, generated no fantasies at all. The girls hushed and bent to their work as he passed, unwilling to catch his eye. There was something unsettling about his demeanour, an air of menace lurking beneath the surface. Unlike the overlookers on the mill floor, Williams never relaxed that stern exterior, never let down his guard to share a joke with the workers under his rule.

Alice thought back to the terror he had aroused in her. It had mysteriously vanished after the fall, when she'd slipped from the packhorse steps and fallen so hard in her rush to work. One of the delivery men, using the old route from the village through habit, had found her by chance. She'd been knocked unconscious, out for quite some time they said. They'd carried her into the mill, without much care as to whether bones had been broken in the fall. It had been Ramsay who had seen to it that she had been placed in the manager's office, setting chairs together to create a makeshift couch, and working quietly at his desk until she roused.

He must have read the fear and confusion on her face as she'd blurted, 'Williams will . . .' somehow convinced in her mind that she was late for work and in trouble. He'd soothed and reassured her, explained how she came to be where she was, and waited until she felt strong enough to stand. Then he'd sent for Albert and instructed him to walk her slowly home and explain to Sarah what had happened. Alice knew she was lucky not to be sent straight to the factory floor, and luckier still when late that night the cramping pains and the bleeding came. Sarah dosed her with a tonic that she'd worked late into the night to create. Both of them knew that they couldn't afford for Alice to miss the wages for another day's work.

Sarah hadn't asked how this had all come about, and for that Alice was grateful. Back at the mill, Alice suspected that Ramsay must have said something to Williams for, to her relief, he left her alone for a while. Ramsay had moved her to work in the schoolroom for half the day, and before very long Richard arrived to join her. Within the month, although Williams was back to his old ways, Alice felt more than able to shrug off his unwanted attention. Even when Ramsay retired, she'd managed to evade Williams successfully. She wasn't sure how she would have coped if things had turned out differently.

Alice, rousing herself from her thoughts, became aware that Sarah was still watching her. She turned to her with a half-smile. 'You're right. It's family that's important.'

CHAPTER 6

As soon as the weather improved, Alice was to be found out and about again. At first, she confined herself to the garden, Elisabeth closely swaddled against the still-cool weather and strapped tightly to her mother. The crisp sunshine lifted Alice's spirits as she busied herself tidying neglected herb beds, the snow having turned the plants to blackened sticks draped in dispiriting flags of grey foliage. As the days passed, she took to venturing further afield, delighted to spot vivid yellow celandines appearing along the grassy banks. Elisabeth's early morning feed, which still took place in darkness, was now conducted to a background of birdsong as the birds staked their territorial claims. Alice preferred to think that they were simply singing to welcome spring.

It was on an unusually mild day that Alice spotted her first primroses at the edge of the woods, where the sunlight warmed the bank for most of the day. She bent to examine the pale lemon-yellow petals set amongst rosettes of crinkled leaves of the freshest green. 'Look, Beth, primroses,' she whispered. 'The first proper sign of spring.' As she straightened up, she became aware of a man's figure between her and the sun. He was in silhouette and at first her heart leapt, thinking it must be Richard. Then, before she even registered his features she noticed his build. Tall and broad, not slender, and dressed in the garb of a working man.

'So,' said Williams. 'This is the bairn half the mill thinks I'm supposed to have given you.' He stepped towards Alice, who immediately stepped back.

'Don't be daft, lass,' said Williams, impatiently. 'You'll at least let me have sight of it?'

Alice hesitated. Elisabeth was tightly bound to her, her face nestled into Alice's breastbone, her body warmed by her mother, their heartbeats echoing each other's. She was content like this and Alice was loath to disturb her. Gently, she turned Elisabeth's head so her face, set beneath Alice's jawline, was towards Williams. He gazed at Elisabeth, then at Alice and abruptly his face, uncharacteristically soft until then, hardened. His brows knitted together into a frown and his jaw set.

'No doubt as to the father, then,' he said. 'Much good it'll do you. You should have used your wits, Alice Bancroft. You could have had yerself a house of your own and a husband with a steady job. Instead, you've got yerself a bastard and another mouth to feed in a house that can barely cope with what it already has. I'll wager your mother's proud of you and your education *now*?'

174

He spat out the last words as he moved away, leaving Alice ashen and shaken. The sun seemed instantly drained of any warmth and his words struck like splinters of ice in Alice's heart. In some ways, he was right. She'd lived the last few weeks in a cocoon of unreality. The landscape that, until a few minutes ago, had looked so lovely, offering the promise of spring, now seemed bleak and threatening. Poverty and hardship, ever at the edges of their lives, seemed to loom closer; Alice's romantic notions about the future, if she'd entertained any, were crushed.

Sarah noticed the change in Alice as soon as she returned home. 'You're as white as a sheet. You shouldn't go walking the paths around and about yet. You're feeding the baby and you need your strength. Sit yourself down and I'll heat some soup.'

Alice shrugged her off impatiently. 'I'm well enough. Don't fuss, it's nothing.' She paused. 'But the primroses are out on the bank near Tinker's Wood. The weather has changed and people will be coming back to see you now that the paths are passable. I can search out plants to gather while I walk with Elisabeth, and we must think about the planting in the herb garden and the vegetable patch.'

Sarah put her hand to Alice's brow. Her cheeks had gone from deathly pale to flushed. 'You've over-tired yourself. Go and lie down for a while. I'll watch Elisabeth. And don't worry. Spring *is* coming, we'll get word out that I'm feeling better now and the patients will return, as they always do. I'll be glad of your help, and Ella will bring in money from the mill. Elisabeth is too small to make a difference to us yet. You're the one keeping her alive, and it's you that must take care of yourself.' And with that Sarah pushed Alice into her room, not unkindly, and closed the door firmly. Alice sank onto her bed, her agitation slowly draining away now that she was back in the safety of her own home. As she drifted into sleep her thoughts turned to Ella. 'I need to make sure she is safe,' she thought. 'I need to talk to Albert, to get him to watch out for her . . .'

CHAPTER 7

Alice stood at the range, stirring the porridge pot and shivering. It was dark, but she had been awake for some time now, disturbed by a fractious Elisabeth, and there seemed little point in trying to get back to sleep with morning so close, and her head full of worries. She turned as Ella stumbled sleepily across the room. From the jug on the side, Ella scooped up a handful of water, collected at the pump the night before, and splashed her face to shock herself into wakefulness to face the day.

'Hurry and get dressed.' Alice stirred the pot vigorously. 'You'll have time to eat some of this to warm yourself before you go. It's still bitter outside.'

Ella yawned and stretched, and went over to baby Beth, now sleeping peacefully in her wooden cradle. She rocked it gently.

'Don't wake her,' Alice warned. 'It's the first bit of peace I've had all night. Now, get on with you.' She gave Ella a little push back towards the stairs.

Ten minutes later she was down again, and Alice

had already set two bowls of porridge to cool at the table. Ella started to spoon hers quickly into her mouth. 'I'll be late,' she mumbled.

'You've got time enough. There's no need to bolt your food like that,' Alice scolded. 'Now listen, I want you to ask Albert to come by one night on the way home. He's not been to see Beth yet, and I want to ask something of him. Will you do that for me?'

Ella was already on her feet, pushing her chair back. 'Of course. We can walk back together. It's nice to have some company when the path is so dark.' She looked out of the window as she pulled on the same rough wool shawl that Alice had also worn for her winter journeys to the mill. 'Dark at night, dark in the morning.' She sighed, picking up the lantern that Alice had already lit for her.

Alice turned Ella towards her, searching her face, troubled by the way the spark seemed to have gone out of her. 'Is all well at the mill?' she asked, trying to keep the anxiety out of her voice.

'Well enough.' Ella turned away to take hold of her lantern and work basket as she unlatched the kitchen door. She paused on the threshold, gazing out into the darkness, then turned and looked back into the kitchen. The fire in the range glowed now, bringing some warmth into the room. All was calm and peaceful, Beth slept soundly, and the younger children weren't awake yet.

'I hate the mill, as you did,' she said. 'But there's nothing to be done.'

Alice caught her arm as she turned to go. 'But there's nothing else? No trouble with anyone at work?'

'Oh, some of the girls are quite snippy.' Ella shrugged. 'But we get along well enough.' And with that she gave Alice a quick hug, then headed off down the path. Opening the gate, she stepped out into the road, blending into a group of other figures, similarly muffled against the cold, as gusty winds blew them along on their journey towards the woods and the mill path.

CHAPTER 8

'You've got a visitor.' Ella came into the kitchen, accompanied by a blast of cold air from outside. She unwound one shawl from around her head and neck, and shook another from her shoulders. Her cheeks were flushed bright red from the bitter wind, and for a moment Alice envied her day away from the confines of the house, even though she knew only too well what it entailed.

Albert loitered shyly in the doorway behind her. 'Come in, come in,' Alice said, tugging Ella further into the room so that Albert could enter. She pushed the door shut and shivered. 'You've brought all the cold in with you.'

She turned to Albert and smiled, genuinely delighted to see him. 'Albert, I've missed our morning walks to the mill. How are you? Come in and warm yourself by the fire – and meet Beth. She's awake – and happy for once.'

Albert hadn't uttered a word. He was overwhelmed at being back in the Bancroft house again and in the presence of Alice, the girl he admired so much. Now she was pulling him into the front room, where Elisabeth was propped up among pillows on the floor near the fire, watched over by Thomas, Annie and Beattie.

'Go along and help your sister in the kitchen,' said Alice, shooing them out. 'Albert has come to be introduced to the baby.' She closed the door firmly behind them.

'Come and sit down.' Alice drew a chair close to the fire as Albert, now quite scarlet with both nervous embarrassment and the sudden heat of the fire, unbuttoned his jacket. He turned his attention to baby Elisabeth, but Alice had other things on her mind. 'Listen,' she said urgently, her voice low. 'I need to ask two favours of you and I don't have much time. Can I ask you to carry this note to Richard Weatherall for me?' And she took a folded piece of paper from her pocket and pressed it into Albert's hand.

'The teacher?' said Albert, puzzled.

'Yes . . . I left some books behind in the schoolroom when I left the mill. I'd like them returned – for Elisabeth when she grows—' It was Alice's turn to blush. She didn't like telling falsehoods to Albert, but wasn't ready to trust him, or anyone, as yet, with the truth. 'He'll probably send you a note back, but I'd like you to give it direct to me, not send it with Ella.' She paused. 'She's a bit of a scatterbrain, as you know, and she might lose it. Will you do that?'

'Yes, of course,' said Albert, only half listening, his eyes sliding towards baby Elisabeth, kicking and gurgling as she watched the flames dance in the fireplace.

'Albert—' Alice laid her hand on his, drawing his attention back to her face at once. Her expression was very serious. 'I need to ask you something else. I'm worried for Ella at the mill. Will you promise you'll keep an eye out for her, as you did for me? With Williams, I mean? I'm frightened he'll try to use Ella to get at me.' Alice hesitated, fighting down terror at the thought. 'I couldn't bear it if she went through what I did.' She sighed, suddenly aware of the enormity of the task.

'Of course I'll watch out for her,' said Albert. 'But Williams shows no sign of being interested in her. In fact, he doesn't seem to have bothered anyone in a while.' Albert mused on this a moment, then turned to Alice, conscious of the trust she had placed in him. 'You're not to worry. I'll keep my eyes open. And Ella does well at the mill. I know she gives the impression of living in a bit of a dream world, but that does her no harm. The others tend to leave her alone and I'm sure she's tougher than she looks.'

Alice felt a wave of relief. This was the first bit of news that she'd been able to get since she'd left the mill, and Ella had been so guarded when she'd quizzed her about her days that Alice had feared the worst. It looked as though mill life, as with the rest of life, rather washed over Ella, who seemed to exist in her own little protective bubble.

The door opened and Sarah and Ella, carrying a tray with glasses and a pitcher, came in followed by a gaggle of young ones.

'What do you think of her, Albert?' demanded Ella. 'Isn't she just lovely?' Albert was confused for a moment: not having had the chance to pay any proper attention to Elisabeth as yet, he thought that she was referring to Alice.

'Why – yes,' he stammered.

Alice laughed and scooped Elisabeth up. 'Here,' she said, thrusting her towards Albert. 'I've kept him talking with news of the mill and we've quite ignored Beth. He's not even held her yet.'

Sarah was busy pouring ale from the pitcher into glasses. 'Our first visitor to see Elisabeth,' she said. 'So we thought it deserved a toast.'

Albert, struggling to balance the baby in the crook of his arm and raise a glass with his free hand, was looking hot and bothered again, but Ella rescued him, and took Beth, who looked as though she was preparing to wail.

'Just look at her perfect little fingers and toes,' she said, waving Beth's podgy hand at Albert. He was grateful to Ella for stepping in. Albert was unused to babies, with no younger brothers and sisters of his own, and felt awkward and clumsy around them. Released from the pressure of hanging onto a wriggling bundle, Albert could relax and enjoy his ale, and observe the room. Alice was revelling in the change from routine that a visitor had brought, especially a visitor as dear as Albert, who was like another brother to her, and Ella was made quite giddy by the general lift in spirits and the delicious warmth that the ale had sent coursing through her. There was such a relaxed atmosphere in the little front room that it was with great reluctance that Albert eventually set down his glass and declared that he must head home. His parents would be wondering at his non-appearance and the lateness of the hour, and his evening meal would be waiting.

'Supper!' Sarah's hand flew to her mouth. She, too, had been caught up in the enjoyment of having company. 'I put a pot to boil on the stove and forgot all about it!' And she leapt to her feet and hurried into the kitchen.

Ella looked up from her fireside seat, Beth on her lap, and waved Beth's hand at Albert as he left. 'I'll see you tomorrow,' she said.

Alice escorted him back to the kitchen door. The front door was reserved for very special company – none of whom had ever shown themselves at the house so far.

Sarah, busily stirring the big pot, looked over her shoulder. 'Come again, Albert. Next time, stay and share our supper.'

Alice opened the door for him and they both drew in their breath as the wind instantly curled around them, wrapping them in a bitter embrace. 'We've not seen the last of winter yet,' Alice said, clutching her shawl around her shoulders and shivering. Then, under her breath so Sarah couldn't hear, 'Remember, watch out for Ella for me. And don't forget my note.'

Albert found himself both nodding and shaking his head as Sarah called, 'Come away inside. You're letting the warmth out and the cold in.' Albert, hearing the door being bolted behind him as he headed off down the path, felt a pang at leaving them all behind. His evening would be a very different affair: his father morose by the feeble fire that he insisted was all they could afford, his mother cowed by a day spent in bitter company. They looked forward to Albert's homecoming to provide relief from the disappointment of their day, and his late return would not be welcomed. A normal evening saw the topic of Albert's day quickly exhausted, to be followed by a silence punctuated only by the ticking of the clock and his father's occasional sighs. Albert was glad that his early starts gave him the excuse to go early to bed, but then he was always troubled with guilt the next morning at not being a better son. The noise and bustle of the mill, although very far from what he wanted to do with his life, allowed him to forget the dreariness of home.

He unlatched the gate, took a deep breath and opened the door, determined to bring some of the jollity of Alice's house into his own. The sight of both parents, grim-faced at the table, plates empty, waiting, did not bode well for a happy evening.

CHAPTER 9

'I'll just take Lucy as far as the mill-top path.' Richard knew he'd sounded plausible. His mother had barely looked up from her seat at the fireside, nor had Caroline or his sister paid him any attention. They were too busy chatting and laughing on the couch, fanning themselves as they teased Mrs Weatherall about her love of a fire in the evening, even when it was well-nigh midsummer. He felt sure that they hadn't sensed the strain in his voice, his desperate need to flee from the suffocating impossibility of this happy family scene. He took deep breaths of the evening air as he stood on the terrace, taking in the sweep of the valley below, the sound of rushing water, the dampness creeping in after the warmth of the day. Lucy whimpered and pawed impatiently at his legs, eager to be away. As he unlatched the gate at the side of the house, Lucy bounded ahead of him onto the track, sniffing the air joyfully. The gathering dusk soothed Richard. There was no one around to see his face, the contortions as he frowned and sighed, pursing his lips as he reconsidered what felt like the indignities of the day. He relived the discussion over the breakfast table, his father full of plans for the new house, his mother trying to interrupt with decisions to be made with regard to the wedding arrangements. Richard's reticence went unnoticed, overshadowed by Caroline's enthusiasm.

Then came the promenade round the garden, Caroline's arm in his as she exclaimed yet again over the view, and the perfect weather. Richard felt sure that he'd made the right responses, gently disengaging himself with expressions of regret about his presence being required at the mill. Caroline had delighted in her day, the chance to have time to get to know his mother and sister properly, his sensitivity in allowing her to do so. Richard should have felt charmed and pleased that all was going so well, that his bride-to-be fitted in so perfectly with his family. Instead, he felt overwhelmed by the effort of keeping up the pretence.

At the mill, Williams had offered congratulations on his forthcoming marriage, having heard that the future Mrs Richard Weatherall was visiting the big house. He'd enquired as to whether 'we might have the pleasure of a visit from your young lady here?' Richard read insolence in the way that he said it, saw arrogance in the raised, enquiring eyebrows, and had to choke back his anger, flushing instead so that Williams laughed as he turned away and headed back to the mill floor.

Richard paused where the path forked and whistled for Lucy. He looked back towards the house – his home – where his family talked, at ease, totally unaware of his turmoil. How could he have imagined that he could make Caroline's visit work? Had he, in fact, imagined anything of the sort? Hadn't he simply refused to think about it, preferred to bury his head in the sand? He'd delayed the visit as long as he could until his mother had reproached him; she'd warned him that if the engagement was allowed to drag on any longer it would cause gossip. Almost two years had passed since he had proposed and he could no longer make the excuse of needing to establish himself in business. Caroline deserved better, he chided himself – he should have broken with her long before this. By sparing himself the embarrassment of calling off the engagement he had made matters so much worse.

Lucy reappeared at his side and Richard turned onto the path that led through the woods high up above the mill. With the trees in full leaf, the gathering gloom made it hard to see and he had to stop to allow his eyes to adjust so that he could press on safely over the uneven surface. His thoughts turned back to the place where they had been all day, throughout the time when he had gone through the motions of appearing to be involved in house decisions, wedding plans, mill matters and dinner table conversation. Alice's face appeared before him, dear enough in itself but doubly so with her daughter – *his* daughter – held up towards him, chubby arms outstretched. Tiny fingers, heart-breaking in their perfection, grasped his, making him feel as though he possessed the hands of a clumsy giant.

How many times had he seen them since Elisabeth had been born? Four? Or was it five? The weather had been against them at first and he'd missed her earliest weeks, unable to find a satisfactory excuse to make his way to Northwaite through the deepest snow that he could remember. Later on, Alice had sought to reassure him, told him that he'd missed little, that Elisabeth had mainly cried and fed, her personality only developing as the weeks passed. Still, he felt cheated, by the passage of time, out of something he would never be able to witness or recreate. Spring had come and all but gone, the days neither long enough nor warm enough for him to catch sight of Alice and Elisabeth together. It was only with the help of Albert acting as their messenger that they'd been able to engineer a meeting one Sunday. Richard had slipped away, after church and lunch, when the family took their customary rest. With Lucy as his pretext, they'd met in a sun-dappled clearing above the bathing pool, well-hidden from the path.

Richard's heart was quite lost at that first meeting. Elisabeth had been calm and cheerful, cooing with delight at the sight of Lucy. Her mother and father found their attention increasingly drawn away from each other, joining instead in adoration of their daughter. As Richard made his way home afterwards he felt bereft, taking no joy in the signs of summer bursting forth all round him. He felt banished, excluded, picturing Elisabeth and Alice heading home to their family, where Elisabeth would be handed around, cuddled and teased. He longed for the next meeting, but his hopes were dashed when the weather turned against them. Subsequent Sundays had brought Richard joy, tinged with sadness each time when he had to leave Alice and Elisabeth, with the knowledge that a whole week must pass before the chance to see them again would arise.

It was amidst the frustration that the waiting caused him that he'd taken it upon himself to make sure Elisabeth's birth was registered, facing down the scolding he received for the tardiness of the notification and for the mother's failure to be present with the baby, which he blamed on illness. He felt a rare moment of pride as he ignored the contempt on the registrar's face. The man clearly didn't believe him but didn't like to challenge him. His own face wasn't well known in Nortonstall, and so he felt confident in describing himself as a schoolmaster to the wretched man, so that he could set about his form-filling duties. It was only as he strode back to the mill from Nortonstall, following the path past the cottages and the school before it turned away into the woods, that he felt a pang, a realisation of how different his life would be if the falsehood he'd just perpetrated were, in fact, the truth. Had he been a schoolmaster he could be living with Alice in a cottage such as the one he had just passed, with his days spent in the schoolroom so close by, Elisabeth playing in the schoolyard, with her brothers and sisters. He'd had no discussion with Alice about the possibility of a future together, nor any real opportunity to do so. Their precious moments together had focused entirely on Elisabeth of late. Alice knew something of Caroline, but they'd spoken little of her while they were both at the mill, and not at all since then. So, it had hit him hard when his hopes of a meeting with Alice and their baby had been dashed last Sunday. Caroline had arrived for her much-heralded visit, and Richard had found himself unable to slip away to see Alice and Elisabeth as arranged. Caroline had said she simply wasn't tired enough to rest, and she would love to walk with him and Lucy in the woods. He'd had to endure her obvious wish that they should spend some private time together, knowing that less than half a mile away Alice and Elisabeth waited for him in vain, and that he was to be denied sight of them for what seemed like an intolerable stretch. He'd managed to slip Albert a brief note for Alice, to explain his absence, but his heart ached with longing and he cursed the situation that he found himself in.

CHAPTER 10

Alice wondered whether she would always remember the moment she found out. Would she always carry that pain with her? Would there be long years of adjusting to it, until it became a tight, hard kernel, buried deep inside, a secret to take with her to the grave?

It was Louisa, their neighbour, who'd told her, pausing as she opened her gate to exclaim over Elisabeth and how she was growing. 'Nearly six months old already! Why, it doesn't seem five minutes since she was born!' Louisa confided that she was dead on her feet. The marriage of Master Richard and that stuck-up Miss Caroline was due to take place on Saturday and it was all bustle and panic at the big house. What with guests from Leeds and Manchester, and the bride's parents coming all the way from Cambridge, there were beds to be made up all over the house and dishes to be prepared for the wedding breakfast. Louisa couldn't see how they would ever get everything done in time, what with Mrs Weatherall changing her mind every five minutes about menus, and who was to have the rooms with the best views.

And had she heard that Mr Weatherall was to give his workers a half-day on the Saturday, so they could come and toast the newly-weds?

Louisa registered the shock on Alice's face. 'I know – it's the talk of the mill. A half-day! That means a whole day and a half at the weekend. And a glass or two of ale thrown in, to boot. Not that *we'll* benefit, mind. It's just another job for us on a day when we'll be rushed off our feet from first light as it is.'

Louisa turned to head up her path when a thought struck her. 'Why don't you come along too? When word spreads around the village, anyone who's able to make it up that path will be there, I'll be bound. Miss Caroline's dress is going to cause a stir. She sent for it to London. I've heard it's one of the new fashions from Paris: all silk and lace.'

Louisa carried on up the path to her front door, bone weary and longing for her bed, with the knowledge of the start of another day but a few hours away. Alice remained rooted to the spot on her own path, Elisabeth clutched to her breast, all thought of what she was supposed to be doing – delivering a remedy to one of Sarah's housebound patients – wiped from her mind. When she'd last seen Richard, in their usual spot above the river, he'd said nothing. Her mind raced. Was it possible that he wasn't planning to go through with it? That he would come and claim her, claim them both, his little family? Even as the thought passed through her mind, she knew the answer, and her mind leapt ahead to what this would mean for them. Her heart felt as if it had been pierced by an arrow, its tip alternately a tongue of flame or a shard of ice. If it hadn't been for the dim awareness of Elisabeth in her arms she would have sunk to her knees. She wasn't sure how long she stood there, motionless, but dusk was falling when suddenly she was aware of Sarah at her side, and of Elisabeth struggling and wailing, pink in the face.

'What ails you? Here, let me take Elisabeth. You'll crush all the breath out of her.' Sarah gently unclenched Alice's hands and released Elisabeth, then put her free arm around Alice and drew her into the house, entreating her to take her arm, to rest her weight on her. Once in the house, she bade the younger ones play with Elisabeth and distract her from her fretfulness, while she cajoled Alice up the stairs and into the bedroom.

'There, there,' she soothed, murmuring into Alice's hair as if she were a small child again, helping her into the bed and under the covers. Alice turned her blank, pale face to the wall. Sarah found her like this when she came up the stairs a little while later, bearing a cup of steaming liquid.

'Drink this. It will help you sleep, help to ease whatever it is that causes you pain.'

In the days that followed, the little house at the end of the village was home to a very subdued family. Sarah yearned to know what ailed Alice, who kept to her bed, quiet and ashen-faced, rousing herself to ask occasionally, 'Has there been word for me?' before sinking back into her reverie when it was clear there was none. Sarah's anxiety over Alice made her short-tempered with the little ones, who crept around and amused themselves as much as possible, glad of the lovely weather that allowed them to be out in the garden, away from the tense atmosphere that pervaded the house.

Elisabeth was probably the most bewildered. She lay beside Alice in the bed, kicking her legs and waving her fists, occasionally turning her head to gaze at her mother. It distressed Sarah to see how quickly Elisabeth picked up on Alice's mood. Getting no response from her mother, she ceased to make eye contact and lay quiet beside her, pupils big in the half-light of the room, already learning what sorrow meant. Sarah had hoped that Elisabeth's presence would rouse Alice but, fearful for the effect on the baby, she started to keep her away, downstairs where the atmosphere was a little more cheerful. Thomas, Annie and Beattie couldn't keep still and quiet for long, and Sarah was relieved to see Elisabeth respond to their high spirits, giggling and beaming smiles at one and all. Sarah hoped it was just over-sensitivity on her part that made her see a reservation, a dark cloud, an anxiousness in Elisabeth's moments of repose, when she would gaze around the room as if looking for something, or someone, lost or missing.

On the third evening, Ella burst in from the mill in her usual fashion, exhausted but delighted to be home. She swept Elisabeth up from the nest of quilts and blankets that Annie and Beattie had created for her and gave her a big kiss, prompting squeals and giggles.

'We're to have a half-day on Saturday,' she announced. 'And we're to go up to the big house to celebrate. Master Richard is getting married and there's to be a party!'

'Can we come? Can we come?' Annie and Beattie clustered around her, tugging at her skirts, trying to catch her hands.

'No, no,' Ella protested, brushing them off as she turned to go up the stairs. 'Mill workers only. At least, I think so,' she added, frowning. 'Maybe the village will be invited too? You'll have to wait and see.'

Sarah stood in the kitchen, listening and wondering. She smoothed her apron and bit her lip, turning automatically to set a pan of water to boil on the range. Could this have anything to do with Alice's grief? She thought for a few moments, then brushed the thought away. From the little that she'd seen of him, Master Richard didn't seem like the sort of man to try to take advantage of the women at the mill. He was nothing like the rough brutes they chose as overlookers. He always looked as though his thoughts were many miles away from the valley, in a much better place.

CHAPTER 11

Ella put her head around the door of Alice's room. 'Are you awake?' She didn't wait for an answer, but pushed the door open further. 'Alice, I have something for you.' There was no movement from the bed. Ella ventured further into the room and sat down. She looked around at the simple furnishings: the bare floorboards with the rag rug beside the bed, the plain jug and washbowl on the stand in the corner, Elisabeth's cot over by the window, a fire burning unseasonally in the grate in an effort to make the room more cheerful. Ella stood up and drew back the curtains. The pale light of a summer's evening illuminated the bed where Alice lay, face still turned to the wall. The covers looked barely disturbed, as if she'd lain there for hours without moving. Ella sat down again and traced over one of the hearts in the wrought-iron bedstead with her finger.

'Alice, I have something for you,' she repeated. She waited, but again there was no response, so she pulled the folded paper from her pocket and gently prised open Alice's clenched fingers.

'Here,' she said, bending and whispering, although she didn't quite know why. 'I think it's important. You should read it.'

When Sarah came up the stairs some time later to see if she could tempt Alice into taking a little soup, she was amazed to find her out of bed, some colour back in her cheeks. She straightened up from the fireplace as Sarah came into the room.

'I'll come down with you,' she said. 'I need to see Elisabeth. I feel like I've been away too long.'

As the day of the wedding drew closer, Alice changed her mind twenty times a day about whether or not to go. The invitation had been extended to the families of mill employees, and it was the talk of the village. In Sarah's house, they could speak of nothing else. Richard's letter – for it was this that Ella had delivered – had lifted Alice's spirits temporarily, but she found herself tossed this way and that on a wave of emotion. One minute she thought she would take Elisabeth and go and see the new bride and groom, standing well away at the back where she couldn't be seen, for to hear second-hand tales of the afternoon would be more than she could bear. The next minute, she was plunged into despair at the thought of what she would witness, and how it would signal the end of all her hopes, frail and insubstantial though they had been. She had memorised every word of Richard's letter before burning it and she went over it in her mind time and again, taking whatever sustenance she could from it.

Sarah's happiness at Alice's apparent recovery was short-lived, and she watched her anxiously, noticing what an effort it was for her to engage in even the simplest tasks. Several times a day she would come across her, lost in thought, staring out of the window or at a wall, her hands arrested in the middle of some semi-automatic task.

Time is a harsh taskmaster. Longed-for events seem to take an age to arrive, then are over in a flash, leaving insubstantial memories in their wake. Dreaded events seem to arrive on wings, then pass with torturous slowness, leaving the smallest details to be relived time and again afterwards.

So it was with Alice. Saturday was upon her before she felt in any way ready for it, and she was still undecided as to what to do.

'Will you come with us this afternoon?' Sarah enquired as she cleared porridge plates from the table.

'I'm not sure,' said Alice, pushing her plate away. She'd eaten barely two spoonfuls, dread and apprehension forming a tight knot in her stomach. 'Perhaps it will rain?' She looked hopefully outside.

'It's a lovely day. The walk and fresh air will do you good,' Sarah said firmly, although privately she wondered whether Alice was strong enough to walk as far as the big house. The mental trials of the last few days had taken their physical toll. She longed to ask Alice what lay behind all this grief and despair, but dare not. Alice seemed too fragile, too close to tears, so she turned her attention instead to Annie and Beattie, who were working themselves into a frenzy of excitement already.

'Can we pick flowers from the garden? For our hair?'

'No, you leave the flowers be. And anyway, any flowers that you pick now will be dead long before you even leave for the party. Now away with you and find something else to do for the morning. I've enough to do here.' Sarah shooed them out of the kitchen, aware that a pile of laundry was waiting to be done once the breakfast dishes were cleared.

Alice stood up slowly from the table. 'I'll find something to keep us all busy. Maybe a walk to look for hedgerow flowers – it won't matter if they spoil.'

'Don't tire yourself, or the little ones. It's going to be a long day for you all,' Sarah fussed, but was glad to see Alice occupied, and just as glad of the chance to get them from under her feet so that she could get her chores out of the way.

CHAPTER 12

T he door finally banged shut, the excited chatter and giggles fading into the distance as the family headed off to walk to the big house. Alice breathed a sigh of relief. When Sarah had asked for the final time, 'You won't come with us?' Alice had shaken her head mutely. Now the house seemed to be listening to the silence, as if in expectation of a sudden return to the normal hustle and bustle, before relaxing into it. Boards creaked and settled. Alice watched a few remaining stragglers hurry past the house, keen not to miss the chance of a drink or two. Occasions for outings and entertainment were few and far between in Northwaite – it was no wonder that the wedding had caused such a stir in the village.

Alice had thought that she would feel better as soon as everyone had gone. She'd looked forward to some time to herself, to peace and a chance to think, other than in the deepest watches of the night, when her thoughts were filled with black despair. The house was always full of people and a whirl of activity, of practical tasks, of chatter. Now, silence crept through all the rooms and filled them up. Suddenly, Alice found it terrifying. She didn't want to be alone with her thoughts. The pain of them was too great, even in the bright light of day. She ran up the stairs – Elisabeth was lying peacefully in her cot, awake from her nap, watching sunlight dance across the ceiling. Alice bent over the cot and Elisabeth turned and smiled at her, reaching out her arms. A few minutes later, mother and baby were hurrying down the garden path, treading in the footsteps of those who had passed not ten minutes before.

The pair hadn't gone very far before Alice caught the sound of a peal of bells, carried softly on the breeze. So, the deed was done. Richard and Caroline were married. She gave a little gasping sob, causing Elisabeth to look up at her, worry again clouding her eyes. Alice hugged her briefly.

'The sun is shining on them,' she said, half to herself. 'Blessing their wedding day. Oh Elisabeth, what's to become of us?'

It was indeed a beautiful day. White clouds scudded across a clear blue sky, and a light breeze blew through the trees. Alice's feet hurried her forwards, past banks of summer flowers, drifts of pink and white. Normally she would have stopped, exclaimed, shown them to Elisabeth. Today, her heart was too heavy. They reminded her that the path from the church would have been strewn with petals of flowers just like these, so that the bride and groom would start out on a happy path. When she was younger, she had waited outside the church, watching happy couples emerge, smelt the perfume of the crushed petals, thought how one day she might be in their place. She knew now that all hope of that was gone.

She heard the chatter of the crowd before she reached the field below the big house. Pausing a moment in the shade of the lane, she looked over the stone wall to take in the scene. The millhands, still in their work clothes, mingled with their families, who were all dressed in their Sunday best, and had walked in from the surrounding villages. The mill girls had plucked flowers from the verges on their walk up from the mill, and used them to dress their hair, or to adorn a buttonhole. The men had made the effort to sluice their faces, hair and hands under the pump before setting off, in an attempt to appear respectable. Children ran about everywhere, threading themselves in and out of the excited knots of people. The chatter was made all the more lively by the ale being dispensed by the jugful. Alice spotted their neighbour Louisa looking flustered, her hair escaping the pins beneath her maid's cap, as she attempted to pour drinks for the mill men, who were bent on teasing her mercilessly. Automatically, Alice looked for Williams amongst them, but she couldn't see him there.

Elisabeth grew restless in her arms and started to struggle, so Alice turned her around to face the crowd. She was instantly captivated by the movement and colour, waving her arms in excitement as a couple of small children chased a yapping dog close to their vantage point.

Holding her firmly around the waist, Alice settled her on top of the low wall, so that Elisabeth's back rested against her. The grey stones, densely covered in thick green moss, made a soft if rather damp cushion. Mother and daughter were partly hidden from view by the branches of the trees that grew all along the lane, shading it from the elements. It was cool here, and calmer. Alice couldn't face going out among the crowd. They would stay here and watch, she decided.

She didn't have long to wait. She noticed that heads were starting to turn towards the house in a ripple effect, and the crowd in the field all hushed as one. Richard and his new bride had stepped out on to the terrace of the big house. Flanked by Richard's parents, they came up to the balustrade and gazed at the crowd below. From this distance, Alice could make out little beyond the fact that Caroline's hair was blonde and all but hidden by her veil, now thrown back to reveal a few ringlets escaping around the edge. Her dress was strange to the eyes of those used to the Northwaite uniform of long skirt, blouse and shawl. White and full-length, it had tight sleeves that puffed out around the shoulders, which had the effect of making her waist look very small. There was a moment's silence, and then someone in the crowd cheered, others clapped and Richard and Caroline smiled, waved and raised their joined hands.

Caroline flung the flowers she was holding to the crowd below, creating an unseemly scramble. Alice could hear the screams of excitement from where she stood. She smiled briefly as the crowd parted and she saw her old friend from the mill, Betty Ackroyd, waving the flowers in triumph above her head.

The next moment, Alice felt as though her legs would buckle beneath her, and she bent forward, sobbing. She clung to Elisabeth, and to the wall, to keep herself grounded. If she hadn't, she felt she would've dissolved into the earth. She focused her gaze on the moss, its vivid green strands arranged in velvety layers on the damp grey stones, and breathed deeply, trying to stop the racking sobs.

'Steady now.' The voice was gruff. 'You'll crush the child. Here—' and Alice felt herself gripped around the waist and lifted upright. She half turned to see who had come to her aid, blinking away the tears that blurred her vision. She started when she recognised Williams, and he saw the change in her face.

'Now, now. Don't be afeared. I was late leaving the mill and had only got this far when I saw you here. You seemed – unwell.' His tone was quite reasonable.

He turned towards Elisabeth. 'She's quite grown since I last saw her.' Alice was briefly reminded of their last meeting, near the primrose bank, and of his words, which had seemed harsh at the time but now seemed so prophetic. Her tears welled again.

'Don't take on so.' Again, gruff kindness. 'How could it ever have been otherwise?' Williams gestured at the field. 'You belong here, with your folk. They belong up there.' They both turned back to gaze at the terrace, where the guests were now being served drinks.

'I must get on,' Williams said. He brandished a rolled sheet of paper. 'The master is expecting the weekly report on production – aye – even on his son's wedding day.' He turned to go, then turned back. 'Will you be all right now? Shall I send someone to fetch your sister?'

Was this concern that Alice read in his eyes?

'I'm well. You must get on.' Alice tried to thank him but the words stuck in her throat. She had a sudden clear memory of Williams at the mill, the struggles, his hot breath on her neck. Clasping Elisabeth, she stepped back, suddenly distrustful.

'I'll be on my way, then.' Williams took a few paces, then turned back towards her again. 'I'll still make an honest woman of you, Alice Bancroft, no matter what has passed before.'

Alice bit her lip and shook her head silently. Was that a threat or a suggestion?

Williams seemed unperturbed. 'Think on it. Times are about to change around here. You might be glad of me afore long,' and with that he turned and walked on.

Alice watched a little while longer from the shady

spot. Shuddering, dry sobs were still racking her body intermittently and she wanted to wait until she felt more composed before returning home. She saw Richard break away from his bride and the guests on the terrace and walk to the balustrade. She could just make out Lucy by his side. He leant over and scanned the crowd, who were now all oblivious to the goings-on at the big house, too involved in their own celebrations to notice him. Was he looking for *her*, she wondered? Was he looking for the little family he'd left behind, *had* to leave behind if his note were true. She liked to think he was, and it saddened her momentarily to think that he wouldn't catch sight of them.

Alice's head ached. The last week had seen all her hopes for the future fade, all her dreams dashed. The little bubble she had been living in had burst. She realised only too well that she now had to find a way to support her family. They couldn't be a burden on Sarah, and on Ella's meagre wages, any longer.

'Come, Elisabeth,' she said, aware of her daughter's fractiousness. She was probably hungry. 'We must go home. We have plans to make.'

Alice took a lingering look out over the field and the big house. Most of those there had formed themselves into tight knots of animated conversation. She couldn't see Sarah, Ella and the little ones, but knew that they would be full of tales of the afternoon when they eventually returned. The group on the terrace of the big house had started to drift inside and Richard was nowhere to be seen, although Caroline was still visible, a bright spot in the afternoon sunshine, surrounded by a little huddle of guests. Alice tried to imagine herself as Richard's bride, standing in Caroline's place on the terrace, wearing her fancy gown. Would she have Elisabeth in her arms? What would she say to Richard's parents, to all their wealthy, distinguished guests? Would she know how to conduct herself, how to charm and flatter and flirt, as no doubt Caroline did?

Alice turned away. Her headache grew worse on the journey home, every step seeming to shake the bones of her skull, to compress them. She'd tried to shut down her fevered imagination but she couldn't stop herself wondering about Richard. Was he distraught too? Was he smiling and accepting everyone's congratulations, all the while wishing himself far away over the moor, Lucy at his side? Or was he squeezing Caroline's hand and thinking what a lucky man he was, looking forward to the secret darkness of their wedding night, to murmured whispers of love, to future happiness, to children, to a rich, contented future?

Alice had thought that seeing Richard and Caroline together might make their marriage easier to accept. That it was better to know, than to imagine. But the reality of them as a couple made the imagining ever more vivid. She longed to be able to shut off her thoughts but by the time she reached home she was sobbing again. It was with a sense of relief that she entered the coolness of the familiar kitchen, drank water, fed Elisabeth and prepared food for the family's return. All the while, her thoughts ran on and on, on a path of their own, a relentless treadmill, a rack on which to stretch and torture herself until she might break.

She was glad when the pale-grey dawn light filtered through the curtains. She had lain awake most of the night, tortured by thoughts of Richard and Caroline on their wedding night. She'd pinched herself, bitten down on her hand, tried silently to distract herself from the mental torment with physical pain. Worried that her tossing and turning would disturb Elisabeth, she'd tried hard to lie as still as possible. She needn't have worried: Elisabeth slept soundly, worn out by the excitement of the evening once the rest of the family had returned from the celebrations, full of tales of who had done, seen or said what. Happily for Alice, few of the tales centred around the bride and groom, instead focusing on gossip to do with the mill or the village. Thomas, Annie and Beattie, over-excited by the novelty of the day, and fuelled by the food that Alice had prepared, ran around like mad things and teased Elisabeth until she was nearly choking from giggling and laughing.

'Enough!' Sarah eventually called a halt. 'Be off with you to your beds. That's more than enough excitement for one day.'

Hands and faces were washed sketchily, and by the time that they had all found their night-clothes, the excited chatter had given way to sleepy mumbling. They fell asleep almost at once, faces still flushed from the excitement of the day.

Now Alice found herself wishing that Elisabeth would wake up, even though she would normally relish any extra minutes of peace that she might get before the day began. She needed something to pull her thoughts away from the terrible repetitive path that they were bound to. She threw back the covers and made her way downstairs, avoiding the creaking floorboards remembered so well from her previous nocturnal journeys. Her trysts with Richard seemed like a very long time ago now. Pausing only to wrap a shawl around her shoulders, she slipped the bolt back and let herself out into the garden. The sun was rising and the scent of damp foliage was carried on the cool air. Alice breathed deeply. Dew covered the grass and she had to stifle a cry as the chill of it struck her bare feet. Lifting the hem of her nightdress clear of the ground, she made her way to the bottom of the garden and leant against the fence, gazing out over the fields and woods.

She picked out familiar landmarks: the church tower, the road climbing away from the village, the gap in the woods where the path dropped down into the mill valley. Down the valley, out of sight, lay the big house. Alice shivered and turned away, looking back towards her own house, still all closed and dark-eyed against the morning. No one stirred, all worn out by the exertions of the previous day. As she was about to start back up the garden, her eye was caught by a movement across the field, along the edge of the wood. A hare, perhaps, taking a leisurely breakfast? She looked again and made out a dog, bounding along beside its master who was striding out in the shadows, his back to Alice as he headed for home. It was Lucy and Richard.

Alice stood and watched them out of sight. Were his thoughts troubled too? Was it thoughts of the little family that he had left behind that had driven him from the marriage bed so early in the morning?

CHAPTER 13

It was less than a week after the wedding, and a miserable wet evening, when Ella came home in a state of some agitation.

'You'd best find some dry clothes,' Sarah observed, taking the sodden shawl from her shoulders and handing her a cloth to dry her dripping hair. Ella wanted to huddle by the range, but Sarah sent her upstairs to change while she lit the fire in the parlour. When the weather changed in these parts, Northwaite, high and exposed on the hill, often bore the brunt of it.

Ella was quiet once she was downstairs again, and Sarah's heart sank. Alice was still very troubled and withdrawn and Sarah didn't think she could cope with more concern and heartache. She wondered how to broach the subject of what was wrong. She didn't have long to wait.

'There are rumours at work,' Ella said abruptly, after sitting in silence for some time.

'What rumours?' Sarah's mind immediately flew to Alice. Had this something to do with her unhappiness?

'That we're to go on short-time,' said Ella.

Sarah was puzzled. 'Are you not busy at the mill?'

'It seems no different to usual. But some say Mr Weatherall isn't getting the price for the cotton that he used to. The bigger mills can undercut him. He doesn't think it's worth running at full production until business picks up again.'

'Is this rumour or fact?' Sarah was already calculating how they would manage if the mill workers were laid off. She could supplement Ella's income with what she earned from her herbalism but, if the local people fell on hard times, then her patients would no longer be able to afford her treatments. Their household income would suffer on two fronts.

Alice came in to the room to find her sister and mother sitting by a cheerful fire, but in less than happy moods.

'Has something happened?'

'No, it's nothing,' replied Sarah, at the same time as Ella said, 'Yes, they're putting us on short-time at the mill.'

'Oh.' Alice, instantly understanding the impact of this, glanced at Sarah. 'When is this to happen?'

'Soon, I think.' Ella looked downcast. 'Some say they have been secretly watching us work and have already picked who will stay, who will go, and who will work part-time.'

'But I thought you said the mill would be on short-time?'

'It will be open as usual, but the workers will be on part-time shifts. Only the overlookers and some others will stay as full-time.'

All three women sat in silence, their thoughts taking them in very different directions. Sarah was wondering about household economies that they might make, mentally reviewing the contents of the larder, thinking about the vegetables they were growing.

Ella was anxiously assessing her conduct at work over the last week or so. They had all been unsettled, made skittish both before and after their half-day wedding holiday. Had she been any better or worse than the others? She hated her job at the mill, but accepted that it was the way things must be. If she lost it, how would they survive?

Alice was rapidly running through possibilities in her mind. She'd thought that returning to the mill would be an option, leaving Elisabeth in Sarah's care when she was a little older, although she worried how Sarah would manage. Now even this possibility was to be closed to her. She had wondered whether they might expand Sarah's herbalism practice, taking small premises in Nortonstall, perhaps. It would have meant a hard walk there and back each day, and problems over what to do with the little ones, but now that didn't seem to be an option, either. Short-time at the mill would mean that the whole area would feel the effect. Money would be in short supply.

The germ of a different idea was growing in her brain, but she fought hard to push it away. Even as she did so, a nagging voice was starting up, telling her that it was the best way to solve all their problems, and to save Ella's job too.

CHAPTER 14

It had been a hot day, even for August, and still the sun seemed in no hurry to descend from the clear blue sky and take to its bed. It was sinking towards the horizon in a blaze of gold that continued to spread warmth right across the countryside around Northwaite. Alice felt sweat trickling between her shoulder blades. Elisabeth was even chubbier now, and walking with her resting on one hip on such a warm evening was proving heavy work. To add to that, Alice felt a sense of nervous apprehension, which was making her heart beat faster. She concentrated hard on the lane, heavily overgrown on each side with the white froth of hedge parsley, threaded through with trailing purple bush vetch. Through habit, she noted a patch of comfrey, pink and purple bells set against large, toothed leaves, a useful supply should their garden crop prove inadequate for Sarah's herbal needs.

The lane, by rights nothing but a track, was little used. Too steep and narrow for a horse and cart to pass, it saw very little footfall, so the vegetation had grown particularly lush and tall. Alice knew all the byways around the area, and who used them and why. They were mainly for getting between the villages, of course, or to work, or for farm workers to reach their fields. This lane was an anomaly, a leftover from times past when it was the only route up to a pair of houses at the top of the track. They had fallen into ruin ten or more years ago, their occupants gone in search of work elsewhere, or passed away, perhaps. It wouldn't be long before the track itself would be absorbed back into the land around it. Alice knew, however, that the passage of one man alone kept it open. A man who chose to live a solitary life in a cottage, once that of a woodcutter, hidden away in the woods bordering the lane. A man who shunned his workmates, but every Saturday, at the end of the working week, found himself drawn to The Old Bell in Northwaite, to sit alone in its darkest corner, nursing his ale and offering a surly nod in exchange for a greeting. Rumours abounded as to the cause of his ill humour. Some folk said that he had been forced to flee from his home in Wales after he'd killed a rival in an argument over a woman. Others said he'd been jilted at the altar and had vowed revenge on all womankind. The only certainty was that no one ever dared to question him and so whatever secret he harboured remained secure.

Alice, pretending to be absorbed in showing Elisabeth the froths of hedge parsley almost overgrowing the track, was aware of this very man coming down the lane towards them. Her heart hammered painfully in her chest, and it required little pretence for her to gasp and jump when he uttered her name: 'Alice!'

She turned to face him, her cheeks flushed by more than the warmth of the evening.

'Ah, you startled me!' She glanced down at Elisabeth who, made uncertain by Alice's reaction, was looking as though she might be about to wail. Her bottom lip trembled.

'Sssh, sssh,' Alice soothed, smiling to reassure her. 'There's no need to be afraid.'

Elisabeth regarded the newcomer gravely, not yet ready to reward him with a smile.

The man's attention, however, was focused on Alice.

'What are you doing here?' It came out in a threatening manner, and he hastened to soften his tone. 'I mean, 'tis rare to find any soul using this track.'

'Oh, you'd be surprised at how often I come here.' Alice hoped the lie couldn't be read in her face. 'There's plants growing here that can't be found anywhere else around.' She saw that Williams, for it was he that she had been waiting for, still looked unconvinced. 'I come here to gather them for remedies. I wanted to check whether the comfrey was still in flower. We've almost exhausted the supply that we grow. And it is – just back there.' Alice waved vaguely back along the track.

Williams's face cleared. He had no reason to suspect her of lying. He nodded his head in an awkward greeting and made as if to move on. Alice thought quickly as to how she might detain him.

'Here, will you hold Elisabeth for a moment? I need to check the bank just here to see if any skullcap is to be found.' And she thrust Elisabeth at a startled Williams.

Taken aback, he was clumsy and awkward, but Elisabeth's attention had been caught by the novelty of a beard, something she had never seen in Sarah's house. She reached out a chubby fist, grabbed hold of it and cooed. Williams, with no experience at all of children, was at a loss as to how to break her grip.

Alice ceased her rummaging in the undergrowth for the non-existent skullcap and straightened up. She laughed, and gently disengaged Elisabeth's hand, but did not immediately move to take her back. Instead she stretched, hands placed in the small of her back.

'She's grown too heavy to carry so far afield,' she remarked. 'I'll have to leave her at home if I'm to come this way again.'

Alice blushed as she spoke, suddenly aware that her remarks were open to interpretation. But Williams didn't seem to have noticed.

'If you've finished your business here, I can help you carry her back?' he suggested, not a little bewitched by the novelty of holding a small, warm, wriggling person in his arms.

And so they made their way down the track, exchanging desultory remarks about the weather and the heat. Alice purposely avoided all mention of the mill or of Richard and the wedding. Williams seemed almost reluctant to hand Elisabeth back once they rejoined the lane, but Alice made an excuse about needing to check one more thing for Sarah before they headed home, and made off across the fields carrying Elisabeth. He stood and watched them go until the sun dipped below the horizon, more than a little bemused by what had just passed, before turning and resuming his journey.

So it was that Alice found occasion to be out and about in other locations where Williams would pass. He had no inkling that his habitual routes had been the object of some attention by Alice. She had reasoned that with Richard now married she was unlikely to be able to find a way of asking him for money to help support his daughter. In any case, such a thing wasn't in her nature. She was proud and determined to manage things for herself. Another option had presented itself to her instead, one which might provide for herself and Elisabeth and keep Ella's job secure. With summer on Alice's side, over the next fortnight Williams came across her in a variety of places around the mill and the village. Making his way back from the packhorse bridge after his weekly check on the water levels upstream, he spied Alice perched on a rock at the water's edge, dangling Elisabeth's feet in the cool water. He paused to watch them from the shade of the path, as Elisabeth squealed and splashed and Alice protested over how wet she was making them both.

He came across her picking wild strawberries along the field path above Tinker's Wood, the path he used to make his way back from the mill long after the others had left it, in no hurry to spend an evening at home with only his own company to enjoy.

He met her as she climbed the steep path out of the valley on the way back from Nortonstall, where he had been on the master's business, and she had been to collect essential supplies for Sarah. They were enjoying such a long spell of fine weather, with unbroken sunshine, fine, high white clouds and warm breezes by day, and clear mild evenings stretching on into the twilight, that it did not seem odd to him that he should see her so frequently, both with and without Elisabeth. The fine weather was a bonus so unexpected that everyone wanted to take advantage of it. The mill workers chafed at being cooped up inside. On their release, they escaped with even more joy than usual, strolling, chattering and laughing as they dawdled their way home, breathing in the scent of the land as it relaxed, as the heat ebbed away but still radiated from the stone walls along their route. More than one romance was born out of these relaxed journeys homeward on such summer evenings. They were a stark contrast to the usual hurried escape, the workers' heads bent and their shoulders hunched as they scurried along, eager for hearth and home. Instead, there was a general lightness in the atmosphere which seemed to affect everyone, and all worries about short-time working were temporarily set aside.

Williams and Alice were very careful around each other. She was uncharacteristically demure, showing only the occasional flash of her old fire, while, for his part, Williams was polite, even deferential. 'A completely different man away from the mill,' Alice reflected, wryly. The tables had been turned. In the mill, Williams was in control, but away from the mill his authority was lost and Alice now had the upper hand. She knew he was confused, recognising that a shift had taken place, but at a loss as to how to account for it. All Williams knew was that as he made his way to and from the mill he was increasingly on the lookout for a slim figure, most usually to be seen walking the paths in a faded blue cotton dress. He liked it better when she was alone. Elisabeth somehow set a barrier between them. But even without Elisabeth there, he found himself frequently tongue-tied, uncharacteristically nervous and somehow wrong-footed. He dreamt of pulling Alice into his arms, of behaving as he had felt it his right to do when she worked at the mill. But faced with Alice in the woods and fields where she was so at home, he found himself unable to lift a finger to even touch her. She was like a nervous deer; one step too close and she would startle back, head tossing, and he would catch a brief glimpse of the fire that he remembered so well.

Williams was a blunt, forthright man, not accustomed to thinking about feelings, his own or anyone else's. In but a fortnight of chance meetings he started to flounder, feeling he was losing his grip on reality. If he'd had more scholarship, or imagination, he might have wondered about enchanted bowers, about whether fairy dust had been sprinkled across his eyes, or a love potion slipped into his ale. Instead, he felt an uncomfortable but not altogether unpleasant quickening of his heartbeat whenever he was away from the mill, a sense of anticipation, an unusual lightness of mood. He started to notice things about his day: the smudgy grey dawn that translated into a golden sunrise day after day as he trod the path to the mill each morning; the sharp stink of a fox that had been casting around outside his door overnight; the cool dampness of the woods; the dew on the grass, sparkling as the drops caught and fragmented the sun's rays. The world smelt fresh, reborn, at that time in the morning, and Williams found himself thinking about Alice. Was she out of bed, tending to Elisabeth, or in the kitchen, splashing her face with water, then opening the back door to gaze out as another glorious day marched in across the horizon? Or was she still sleeping peacefully, cheeks flushed, quilt pulled up beneath her chin, wrapped up in her dreams?

Even so, Williams was taken completely by surprise when Alice said, 'Will you still make an honest woman of me? Would you be prepared to take on Elisabeth as your own? Shall we be wed?'

A fortnight had passed and the weather was on the turn. The villagers had been out collecting brambles from the hedgerows, filling pails and boxes to carry them home to make jams and pies, marvelling at how early they were this year, how the sun's heat had brought them on.

Williams had found Alice blackberrying along the track to his house. Elisabeth was sitting happily in the middle of the track squashing fruit into her mouth with purple-stained fingers, while her mother dropped berries into the white enamel pail borrowed from the scullery and already nearly full to the brim. The blackberrying potential of the track had been forgotten by the village and the profit was all Alice's.

'See how plump these fruits are! How juicy!' Alice held a deep-violet specimen out for Williams to examine. It glistened, picked at the perfect point of ripeness. The warmth of the sun had released its perfume.

'Here.' And before either of them quite knew how it had happened, she'd raised the fruit to his lips, he'd parted them automatically and she popped the berry in. He bit down, releasing a burst of warm, tangy juice, all the time not withdrawing his eyes from Alice's. It was then that she'd asked. Three questions, out of nowhere. And out of nowhere had come his reply. 'Yes, I will. And soon.'

They'd stood back from each other, abashed, neither quite sure of what they'd done, what they'd agreed to. Then Williams reached out and pulled Alice to him. He could feel her trembling, but that sense of urgency from times past, from their days at the mill, suddenly threatened to overwhelm him. He kissed her hard, so hard that her teeth bit against his lip and he tasted blood, its metallic tang mixing with the berry juice. He pulled back, holding her at arm's length, and she gave a sobbing gasp. They were both suddenly aware that Elisabeth, perhaps bored with being abandoned on the path, perhaps sensitive to the charged atmosphere, had begun to cry. Alice broke away to go to her and Williams experienced a surge of irritation. He wanted her back, he wanted her *now*, not to wait until a piece of paper had been signed, an agreement made in that cold, stone church. He made a move towards Alice but she turned to face him, Elisabeth held between them.

'You must go away and think on it,' she said, her face serious. 'It will not be an easy match to make.' And with that she picked up her black-berry pail and made her way up the path, Elisabeth's weight on one hip balanced by the drag of the pail in her other hand.

Williams stood motionless for a time after she had left. He appeared deep in thought, yet he wouldn't have been able to describe a single thing that had passed through his mind. The trees along the side of the track shook in a sudden gust of wind, releasing leaves made yellow and parched by the sun. As they fluttered down around him, Williams looked up at the sky. It was growing darker as the evening drew on, but it wasn't just the night sky that encroached. Storm clouds were brewing, and as Williams turned for home, he felt the first splashes of rain against his face. They hadn't arranged where or when to meet again but, with the shift in the weather, Williams felt the enchantment lift. He smiled grimly. Alice Bancroft would be his, finally.

PART V

CHAPTER 1

Alys had woken early that morning, after a troubled night. Head filled with dreams of the mill, with threads of the other Alice. She'd got up at 2 a.m., in search of a glass of water. Instead of the silence of a Yorkshire darkness, there were loud voices in the gardens at the back, the click and hiss of beer cans being opened, rapid talk. Looking out, she couldn't locate the voices, but her eyes were drawn to the flats across the gardens where a man was framed in the window of a brightly lit room, gazing at a computer screen. Clothes were drying on a washing line strung from window to door. It was an odd glimpse into someone else's world and she pulled away from the window, hoping that she hadn't been seen. She'd forgotten what it was like to live so much on top of everyone, even after such a short time away, and she had struggled to get back to sleep.

She sighed and went down to the kitchen. Her cats, Lottie and Ralph, were very pleased to see her. Lottie was keen to be stroked this morning: behind the ears, under the chin, her fluffy white bib, over and over. Ralph held himself aloof, as usual, but he was back to his old self. Yesterday, they'd both been hesitant, nervous, looking around her to see where the tall, noisy stranger she'd left them with had gone. Seb, the nephew of a friend of Kate's, had been in charge; he was an intern at a newspaper, working for expenses only and sleeping on a friend's floor. He'd been delighted at the offer of a whole house to himself for a few weeks, in return for a bit of cat care. Alys had feared the worst on her return, but he'd left the place clean and reasonably tidy. Better than she would have done at his age, to be fair.

She made tea and toast. There was only some rather elderly white bread in the bread bin. She'd need to do a bit of shopping this morning, stock up again. At least there was jam left in the fridge. Strawberry, but not homemade like she'd become used to at Moira's house.

She took her tea and toast back to bed and settled down, pillows propped, curtains firmly shut. She thought longingly of her casement window back at Moira's, its outside curtain of creeper, the backdrop of trees, hills, weather. If she opened her curtains here, the family across the road would have an unimpeded view of her Saturday morning laziness. She had quite a relaxed relationship with them, although they'd never spoken beyond saying 'hello'. The little kids would wave at her as she watered her window boxes or brought in her shopping. She loved to watch them all out in the street:

the eldest, too-cool-for-school in his designer trainers and compulsory street attire, sent out to watch the others. He'd appeared on crutches for a brief spell, carefully setting them to one side and easing himself onto a kitchen chair outside their front gate, bouncing the youngest, the only girl in the family, on his knee as he supervised her noisy brothers playing football. The little girl greeted her brothers with shrieks and chuckles when they took it in turns to come up and kiss or tease their sister.

Alys guessed that they played in the street because they had no garden. Perhaps the extension, needed to house at least eight people in what would otherwise have been a tiny house, had all but filled it up. Or maybe it was a cultural thing, a way of being sociable in a community, something that a suspicious London seemed largely to have given up on? She herself barely knew the names of anyone in her street apart from her immediate neighbours. Although in the past she had referred to her neighbourhood as her 'London village' she realised now that it could hardly be more different to the friendliness of Northwaite.

At least it was peaceful this morning: no planes on take-off to disturb her. She'd be fine unless the wind changed. Then they'd be back – the smaller ones high and distant, the long-haul flights roaring over and shaking the windows.

Later that morning, Alys stepped out into the back garden, which was lit by a sudden burst of

July sunshine. The bamboo had grown while she'd been away. Great fat shoots pointed at the sky, sprouting antennae as each one started to unfurl. The stems must be at least six or seven metres tall now; they had grown at an alarming rate while she'd been gone. The fig tree had grown a little, too. Trying to unravel the bindweed which clung to it, she managed to snap off one of the figs and felt sad: it had so few. It really ought to be moved to a sunnier spot. Like everything in the garden, it had been planted without a plan; with no thought as to how big it might grow, or how much light it might need.

She found a mysterious replica bird lying on the paving stones. Yellow and purple, with a beady eye and a fat chest, it had a bit of wire instead of feet. Its feathers, such as they were, were tattered and torn. It looked as though it was something that might once have adorned a plant pot. Perhaps it belonged to the fox, a regular visitor by night? It liked odd playthings, and unusual objects had turned up in her garden before: a golf ball, a strange plastic disc, a small doll.

She settled guiltily in the garden with the newspaper, only too well aware that she should really be gardening. The sun had brought others outdoors, keen to make the most of a good day. Alys suddenly felt hemmed in – children were laughing and shrieking in the gardens around her, barbecues were being fired up. She longed for wide-open spaces – how could just a few weeks away have left her feeling like this? 'Time for a walk,' she thought. She'd head down towards the canal. At the end of a day in the office, it had always been balm for her soul. There were plenty of possibilities for getting away from people, and forgetting that you lived in a big city. 'As long as you blot out the noise from the motorway. And the planes,' she thought wryly, newly conscious of the roaring of jet engines as she went in search of her sunglasses.

CHAPTER 2

What did that foliage smell like? Alys struggled to pin it down, closing her eyes to see if it helped bring some images to mind. Pollen, wet dogs perhaps? Down towards the canal it smelt of meadows and summer holidays. Quite different to Yorkshire when she'd left it.

The paths around the canal had changed a lot since Easter. The lacy heads of cow parsley were held aloft on stalks that were taller than she was. And the birdsong was different – no raucous songthrush or persistent chiff-chaff. But there was a bright jay, right by the path, unconcerned. More squawking parakeets than usual. And flocks of noisy black-and-white magpies; a greenfinch, plump and very, very green. A spotted wood-pecker, flying from tree to tree. This year's baby rabbits were already half grown. Now they had plenty of greenery to hide in by the path. She spotted red vetch: single bright flowers on a stem. She slipped a sprig into her pocket. She'd become hooked on identifying the flowers that she saw, but she knew it was wrong to pick specimens in the wild. She should just have taken her usual photo, but she'd left her phone at home.

Alys hadn't passed a soul on the path. It was always quiet – today even more so. The noise as her mobile phone started to ring made her jump. Except, of course, it wasn't *her* mobile – hers was sitting on the table by the sofa. In any case, this one was playing a quite different refrain. But it was clearly a mobile. Alys looked around. It was hard to pinpoint the direction of the sound, but it seemed to be coming from where the tangle of brambles, just bursting into flower by the path, was at its thickest. She crouched down and tried to peer in, but it was too dense. And too thorny to reach in. In any case, the sound had stopped. She guessed the phone hadn't been dropped there by accident. Someone must have been trying to get rid of it.

She pressed on, rounding the corner, the path dropping down towards the canal bridge and the place she thought of as 'her' kingfisher pool. The sight of a heart-stopping flash of turquoise there last September now brought her to this spot every time she walked here, in the hope of a repeat performance. She stopped short. Three or four police officers surrounded a young man, spread-eagled on the ground. More police were walking up the path towards her.

'You'll have to go back the way you came, I'm afraid,' said the tallest and broadest one.

'What happened?' asked Alys, trying to peer around him.

'I'm afraid I can't say.' His tone suggested that further discussion wasn't an option.

Alys wondered whether to tell them about the mobile phone in the brambles, but the Londoner's mantra – 'Don't get involved' – sprang to mind. In any case, she guessed the phone would ring again. They'd probably find it.

Later that day, Alys's neighbour asked her if she'd heard the helicopters circling. 'What with that and the planes, it quite spoilt the lovely afternoon.' She sighed. 'I heard a couple were stabbed a few streets away. Up near the station. One of them's dead, the other critical.' Alys put two and two together and probably made five, but in that instant her mind was made up. London didn't feel like the place she wanted to be any more.

CHAPTER 3

Tim set the glass down in front of Alys. The contents looked suspiciously strongly coloured. Alys favoured crisp, dry whites, pale in colour. This looked too much like a Chardonnay for her liking. She sipped cautiously and tried to disguise a shudder at the unmistakable oily flavour. Cheap, pub Chardonnay. And, as a bonus, he'd bought a large glass.

'Cheers,' said Alys, raising her glass. Guilt over her failure to respond properly to his emails had made her reluctantly agree to meet up with Tim. He'd suggested a drink and so here she was – curious, it's true, to see how she would feel about him after three months apart. He seemed to be having difficulty accepting that, as far as she was concerned, they had split up. He was insistent that the break would have helped their relationship.

Tim got straight to the point.

'So, what's going on?' he demanded. 'You've been away for weeks – months – and I've barely heard a word. Did you lose your phone or something? Although I sent you emails as well that you clearly couldn't be bothered to answer.'

He glared at her. Alys looked at him dispassionately: his lips were narrow, pursed in disapproval; eyes too pale a shade of blue, and rather small, now that she came to think of it. She shook herself: it was unfair of her to be so critical. She was here to give him a second chance, wasn't she?

'I turned my phone off when I got there. It felt like an intrusion, somehow. It was such a wonderful place, steeped in history, cobbled streets and everything. A mobile felt – out of place . . .' she tailed off. Tim was looking at her as though she was mad. She should just have lied and said there was no signal. Truth was, she'd used her phone a lot – well, at least the camera on it. To capture the still, dark woodland, the twisted and exposed tree roots, the waterfalls in every level of spate, the unfamiliar flowers. She'd locked their secrets deep within the phone's digital heart, so whenever she looked at the pictures she had a shock of recognition and it took her right back to the beautiful spots she'd come to cherish so much.

Tim was stony-faced, waiting. Originally attracted to Alys's impulsiveness and scattiness, he was now deeply irritated by it. Why couldn't she be more like him?

Alys stared down at the weathered wood of the table, twiddling the stem of the wineglass with her fingers. When she'd first arrived in Yorkshire, she'd been so caught up in helping Moira, learning about the café and exploring the area, that she'd barely given Tim a second thought. Her London life felt like a distant dream, like something that had once belonged to someone else. She'd actually avoided reading his emails after the first few because she just didn't want to deal with what she might find in them. After all, she'd told him in her letter that she needed a bit of space, some time to think. And in her defence, she had replied at first. Then, becoming annoyed by their increasingly demanding tone, their insistence that Alys was making a mistake and should return, it was true that she'd started to ignore them. It had dawned on her that they were all about Tim; there were no enquiries as to how she was getting on, how Moira's recovery was going, whether she was enjoying working in the café.

Alys pushed back her chair and stood up, her glass of wine barely touched.

'You know, Tim, I came here today prepared to believe that maybe our time apart would have done us both good. I guess I must have changed more than I realised while I've been away. I'm sorry. I don't want things to go back to how they used to be, and I've decided I'm not going travelling either – I'm going back to Yorkshire.'

Until she spoke, Alys had no idea that she had such a plan. The words had just popped out of her mouth. If she was honest with herself, her heart wasn't in finding adventure abroad. She could rent out her London place for twice the rent she'd need to pay there, with a bit left over. But how would she earn a living? Would Moira be prepared to have her back at the café?

It took only a couple of phone calls, an email and an Internet booking, and Alys was back on the train to Yorkshire the next day. Her temporary lodger, Seb, had bucked the interning trend and landed himself a permanent job, along with a salary. So he was keen to move back in and find a friend to help him pay the rent. He was also happy to keep an eye on the cats for the time being, relieving Alys of the guilt she felt about stepping out of their lives once more. Moira, who'd felt bereft when she'd waved Alys off in the taxi to the station only a few days earlier, had laughed and cried down the phone and said that she couldn't be more delighted that Alys wanted to come back to work with her.

'Thank goodness,' she'd said, when she'd recovered herself enough to string a proper sentence together. 'I haven't been able to master the lemon poppy-seed cake recipe at all. The regulars are very put out.'

The spare room was hers for as long as she needed it, Moira added, which would give Alys time to find somewhere to rent now that she was going to be paid a salary.

So far, it had all slotted together incredibly well, and Alys couldn't suppress a smile as she settled back into her seat on the train and contemplated the weeks and months ahead. She could barely acknowledge to herself that, additionally, the thought of something – or should that be someone – was making her return seem even more appealing.

CHAPTER 4

Alys's swift return from London had provoked a lot of good-natured joshing from their regular customers, while Moira was just unreservedly pleased to have her back. After a week of jokes along the lines of how amazing it was that round-the-world trips could be fitted into a weekend these days, Alys was relieved when it all started to die down.

'Don't worry about it,' said Moira, laughing, as Alys tried to remain good-humoured in the face of all the teasing. 'They're as pleased to see you as I am, and they're really chuffed that you've thrown over your exciting travel plans to come back to them.'

Alys raised an eyebrow and was about to respond when the café door opened and Rob appeared. 'Heard you were back,' he said with a grin. 'It's a hard place to leave.'

Alys, who had been expecting another joke at her expense, was rather taken aback. He was right. But how did he know?

'Don't forget – *I* tried to leave once,' Rob went on. 'But the wilds of Australia have got nothing on Yorkshire!' He picked up his takeaway coffee and was heading out of the door when he turned back. 'I did last longer than a weekend, though.' And with a cheery smile, he was gone. They'd had their first encounter, Alys reflected, and she hadn't managed to even utter a word.

Flo had been a source of worry to Alys – after all, she'd agreed to step into Alys's shoes and cover shifts in the café when Alys left. It didn't seem fair to take promised work away from her, but Moira had said rather mysteriously on Alys's return that she had a plan. Moira then began to be away from the café for several hours each day, leaving Flo and Alys to work side by side, and was rather vague about what she was up to. After Alys had fielded a couple of phone calls for her aunt from estate agents and a solicitor she began to have her suspicions but decided to wait until Moira was prepared to share any news.

A month had passed, business at the café had continued to flourish, and Alys felt as though they had worked out a comfortable routine, when Moira said one evening, 'I had an email from Kate. She's going to come and visit for a few days.'

Alys was surprised – it had never occurred to her that her mother would come up north. Although now she came to think about it, she hadn't really told her mother much about the change in her plans. In fact, had she told her *anything*? She thought hard. No, she didn't think that she'd sent her so much as a text in all the time she'd been back.

'Did she say why?' asked Alys.

Moira started to laugh at Alys's reaction. 'To see you, I expect? You're her daughter, remember?'

'But Mum never comes to Yorkshire!' exclaimed Alys.

She'd never understood why Kate seemed to have taken a dislike to her home town, while Moira was still so happy in the area. The reasons weren't at all clear; in fact, Alys wasn't sure that they had ever been spelt out. She was just aware that Kate was decidedly ambivalent about her Yorkshire roots, and it had become a bit of a family joke, without anyone really knowing what lay behind it.

Alys knew better than to ask her mother outright, as she was sure that she'd be fobbed off with some vague wave of the hand and an 'oh, you know, this and that' kind of an answer. Maybe it was time to quiz Moira? They'd taken their evening meal and a couple of glasses of wine into the garden. The day's events at the café had been dissected, the plates cleared and a second glass of wine poured. Moira seemed in no hurry to move indoors.

'I was just wondering—' said Alys, and then paused.

'Yes?' said Moira, waiting and wondering whether she should be alarmed at what might be coming.

'About why Mum seems to dislike this area so much, especially as you seem so happy and settled here.'

'Heavens, I wondered what on earth was on your mind! Well, you know, I haven't really thought about it that much, certainly not recently. That's just the way we are. I suppose Kate, being the eldest, was always pushing boundaries, restless. She didn't like small-town life in Nortonstall and so she was delighted when Dad got a job in Leeds when she was in her teens. She'd never really tried that hard at school and when she had to start a new school in Leeds, she more or less gave up. She was very attractive and she got work very easily. Boutiques were just starting up in those days, in the sixties, and they were looking for girls that looked the part.' Moira paused and took a couple of sips of wine, looking thoughtful.

'I suppose, with Kate gone, my role in the family changed a bit. I went to college for a year, then I took off on an overland trip to India.' Moira laughed. 'Don't look so surprised. It was what lots of students did in those days. Not quite gap-year travel. But then, when Dad died, I was worried about Mum managing by herself, so I came back, went to secretarial college and got a job in Leeds. Then, when Mum died, I used the bit of money I'd inherited to buy this house when it came onto the market. I'd always had my eye on coming back here to Northwaite, but I hadn't really expected this very house, the one that Grandma Beth had lived in, would become my home.'

Moira had revealed a lot about herself in just a few sentences, but there was still a lot that Alys would have liked to ask. She was curious to know more about the India trip, and would have loved to ask Moira why she'd never married, but instead she decided to focus on the one thing that she'd said that she'd found the most surprising.

'Mum was rebellious?' Alys said, aware that she was sounding incredulous.

Moira laughed again. 'Indeed, she was. You'd never know it now, although she's good at getting her own way, of course. I can remember a few terrible rows when she was a teenager, even plates breaking if I remember rightly. I think it was fairly standard teenage stuff: wanting to stay out late, go to see bands in Leeds on a school night, wearing skirts that Dad thought were too short, having unsuitable boyfriends with cars. That sort of thing.'

This was surprising news. Kate had always come down very hard on Alys if she'd shown signs of stepping out of line. You'd have thought that she'd be more lenient, if she'd been rebellious herself, Alys thought. But perhaps it had the opposite effect? Perhaps she remembered what she'd been getting up to at that age and was determined that Alys wouldn't do the same? None of this answered the question of Kate's ambivalence towards her childhood home, though, as Alys pointed out to Moira.

Moira considered. 'I'm not sure if I can put my finger on it. But when Kate met your dad, she was working as an air hostess. She was such a glamorous creature, and I suspect she'd probably invented a whole new history for herself that didn't include living in a small terraced house "up North". So, I guess she wasn't keen on coming back here to show David, and he was so heavily rooted in the South that the question probably never even arose.'

Moira looked with mild amusement at Alys's face. 'Don't look so disappointed. There aren't any skeletons in the cupboard. Just a case of a bit of reinvention, and your mum preferring her new life, I suppose.'

'I was wondering,' said Alys, then paused, unsure of how to phrase her question. 'Was I named after my great-great-grandma Alice? Only, there's a bit of a mystery about her, and I sense that she might have been a bit of a black sheep of the family . . .' she tailed off.

'Oh, but you weren't.' Moira replied. 'It was David's mother's name, too. I think Kate was too terrified to let on that there might be anything in her family background that would make it a less than ideal choice. So, she compromised by settling for a more unusual spelling.'

Moira stopped, seeing Alys's face change. 'Oh, Alys,' she said. 'I've put my foot in it. I didn't mean that to come out as it did. It's a lovely name. And I have a feeling there might be more to the whole family story than meets the eye. My mum always said that her mum, your great-grandma Beth, wouldn't hear a word said against Alice, even though she died when Beth was still a baby. You know, if it's troubling you, why don't you see if you can find out a bit more?'

'You don't have a picture of Alice, by any chance, do you?' asked Alys.

'No, I think only the wealthy sat for their portraits, painted or photographic, in those days,' said Moira. 'I don't suppose a mill worker like Alice would have been likely to have had a photograph of herself. But I do have a box of things passed down the line – don't get too excited,' she warned, as Alys gasped. 'There's not much in there apart from some old book, as far as I remember. I had a quick look at it years ago, then put it in the loft. You can help me get it down tomorrow.'

CHAPTER 5

Could this really hold the clues, maybe even the answers? The box looked insignificant – it was made of cheap plywood, which had split in places – with an ill-fitting lid and an old paper label, mostly worn away. It looked as though it might once have held cotton reels. It spoke of a life spent scrimping and saving, of making do. To Alys, it was as exciting as if it was a treasure chest made of beautifully seasoned wood, and containing the rarest jewels. She hardly dared open it.

Alys sat on the edge of her bed and gazed around. She had always found her room at Moira's calming, peaceful. She would unlatch the door, step in and instantly feel it – like a big sigh leaving her body, her shoulders dropping, relaxing. She'd always assumed the paint colour to be responsible, or put it down to the light in the room, the direction the windows faced.

Perhaps she hadn't fully appreciated the sense of history in this room before? The stripped and polished floorboards and old, pine chest of drawers must have dated back generations, to her great-grandmother Beth's time and even well before that. She'd always assumed that the patchwork quilt on the bed, its faded cotton squares in every shade of blue, must have come from a later era – Moira and Kate's mother's, perhaps? Or perhaps it, too, dated back even earlier? The view out of the window, though – fields stretching out to the distant moorland – must have been the one that Alice saw each day, and Sarah before her, Elisabeth after. The path that Alys took to Nortonstall must have been the one that they had trodden so many times before her, through trees of every season. She felt a sense of anticipation as she turned back to the box. She wasn't sure what she would find in there, only that her instincts told her that it was going to be significant in some way.

Alys expected an aroma of dust and mildew as she lifted the lid away. Instead, the smell of herbs that rose to greet her transported her instantly to sun-drenched meadows. Nestling on a bed of dried foliage that had long ago lost its colour but still held onto a faint scent, was a leather-bound journal, quite obviously handmade. A solid rectangle of brown leather was folded around yellowing pages, which protruded beyond the edges of the cover and were held in place by rough stitches through the journal's spine. A thin leather cord bound around the cover kept it all together.

Lifting the journal from its resting place, she discovered a small, cream fabric bag beneath it, hand-embroidered with a sprig of lavender in greens and purples that had kept their vibrancy over who-knew-how-many years. A dull gleam amongst the papery dried foliage led her to an oval locket, minus its chain and rather battered and misshapen. Front and back were etched with tiny ivy leaves, and a scroll on the front contained the date, 1894, in tiny writing. She tried to open it to see whether it held any photos, to give a clue as to its owner, but the damage it had suffered meant that it remained, frustratingly, clamped shut. Alys was struck by thoughts of who might have placed these items there, before closing the lid and putting the box away for safekeeping. On an impulse, she slipped the locket into her pocket, intending to ask Moira if she knew anything about it, before turning her attention back to the journal. Tugging at the leather cord, she paused to wonder whose hands had tied the loose knot over the years. Sarah? Alice? Elisabeth, perhaps? As the cord fell away and she opened the pages with great care, Alys saw at once the names of herbs, in a neatly drafted ledger of prescriptions, of doses. The names of the patients treated were followed by their ailments: 'Albert Parkin – bronchitis; Florence Broadhurst – rheumatism', along with details of the remedy dispensed, how much they had been charged and whether they had paid. Turning the pages, Alys noticed that some patients had paid their bills in pennies and farthings at different dates, clearly scraping the money together as and when they could. Against the entry for 'Molly Ramsay, daughter of Ivy – lobelia syrup, once daily' there was the sad legend: 'No charge. Beyond help.'

Totally absorbed, Alys went on turning the pages. The herbal described treatment for everything from the mundane: 'John Arkwright – warts upon the hands and nose; bloodroot and tincture of Echinacea' to the more serious 'Margaret Clark – weekly poultice of figwort applied to leg ulcer'.

The centre of the book held a plan of what appeared to be a garden, with herb borders named, and the months for harvest, or perhaps flowering, inked in against each name. A list ran down the side of the page, of place names that Alys recognised from the locality, such as Tinker's Wood. More herbs, ones that weren't named in the garden, were listed here.

Towards the end of the book, Alys found remedies copied out in a careful hand. Some of these pages were clearly much used, being creased and spotted with liquid turned all shades of brown by the passage of time. Amended amounts and faded pencil scribbles were testament to ongoing revisions to the remedies. Two pages were clearly so frequently used that Alys found that she had to peel them apart, terrified of damaging the brittle paper. The remedy on the left-hand page was for a rosemary tonic shampoo, the title of the one on the right read 'Heart tonic' and beneath, in brackets 'Alice's remedy'. Alys started, and nearly dropped the book. She read on through the list of ingredients: skunk cabbage, valerian, hawthorn, pulsatilla, skullcap.

There was a murmur of voices, then footsteps on the wooden stairs. 'Darling, are you up there?' It was her mother's voice.

Alys snapped the book closed, wound the cord loosely around it and pushed it and the embroidered bag back into the box. She put on the makeshift lid, then looked wildly around for a hiding place. Shoving the box underneath the bed, she stood up and prepared to greet Kate, trying not to look as guilty as she felt. Although she had no reason at all to feel that way, it was just that her mother's presence frequently made her feel somehow in the wrong. And today was no exception.

CHAPTER 6

'Alys! Alys, darling.' The door opened and Kate was on the threshold, her loose white-linen trousers combined with a simple knit of a subtle sheen in one of those indeterminate grey-blues that she so loved.

'There you are! Didn't you hear me arrive?'

Alys, engrossed in reading through the herbal remedies, hadn't heard a thing until a few moments ago. She knew that Kate was coming, of course. Moira had told her, or should that be, warned her? Alys feared that her mother would be intent on getting her back to London, and would have a trick or two up her sleeve, no doubt. She'd have to be on her guard. At least Kate was staying at a guest house in Nortonstall and not in Moira's house. With no suitable hotel to be had for miles around, this was the best that Moira had been able to come up with, after Kate had declined the sofa bed, or a swap with Alys that would have given Kate her bedroom and Alys the sofa bed.

'I simply have to have an en-suite, darling,' explained Kate. 'Had one for years now and just can't imagine managing without.'

Alys could visualise Kate's theatrical shudder as she conducted the telephone conversation with Moira. She would have come off the phone saying to David, 'Imagine, she suggested I slept on the sofa bed and shared the bathroom. I might as well take a tent and camp in the woods!' David would have held his counsel, used to Kate's exaggerations. He'd found himself edged out of the en-suite some time ago, forced to trek to the family bathroom when his age-weakened bladder – or perhaps it was the volume of wine that he consumed every night – sent him stumbling to relieve himself in the early hours. He had thought the en-suite would be available to him once a day, but no. 'The floor, David, the floor,' Kate had said briefly. She slept too lightly for secret mutiny to be possible. In fact, Alys guessed that her father had been looking forward to Kate's absence, and would be making full use of the facilities, as well as dropping socks and pants wherever he felt like it, and leaving used plates and dishes stacked in the sink until Kate was due to return, when he would finally get round to stacking the dish-washer. Evenings would, no doubt, be spent stretched full-length on the sofa, wine bottle at his side, cricket on the TV. Unless, of course, it was so long since he'd had the chance to behave like this that he'd forgotten how?

Alys dragged her thoughts back to the present to listen to Kate, who had moved over to the window to gaze out over the fields. 'Moira and I used to share this room when we came to visit Grandma Beth,' she said. 'It's hardly changed at all – and the view certainly hasn't. Nothing but fields for miles around.' It was apparent that she didn't think this was necessarily a good thing.

Alys took a deep breath and decided that she was going to behave beautifully. 'Come on, Mum,' she said. 'Must be time for tea and cake. Moira was baking all morning – I'm pretty sure she made her extra-special layer cake, and there'll be hazelnut brownies too, I expect. We're going to go to the café and have tea there, so you can see the place.' And she linked her arm through her mother's and led her downstairs.

Kate was delighted by the café and exclaimed constantly, and gratifyingly, over the cakes and the china, the wall colour and the wings, the cushions and the courtyard. Moira was quite pink with pleasure and Alys insisted that they sit down together and have tea while she and Flo served the other customers. It wasn't long before a familiar chugging sound in the road outside told her that a tractor was about to pass through – no doubt Rob, who'd already stopped by that morning for his coffee. She looked up, ready to wave if he should glance in but to her surprise he pulled into his usual parking spot outside.

'Well, to what do we owe the honour of this visit?' she asked, as he came in. 'Twice in a day? It must be a record. Coffee?'

She had picked up a takeaway cup and moved

towards the coffee machine when Rob said, 'No, it's cake I'm after, actually.'

'Oh.' Alys was taken aback. Rob didn't appear to have much of a sweet tooth and never bought cakes or biscuits to go with his coffee.

'Yes, there's a birthday over on the farm today. One of the stable lads and no one has done anything about a cake. He looked a bit disappointed so I told the others I'd see if you had anything left as I passed through.'

'That's a lovely idea.' Alys immediately looked for something suitably celebratory among the day's remaining cakes. 'It's been a busy day, I'm afraid. There's not much I can offer you. How about some of Moira's layer cake? She only just brought it in so there's nearly half left. I might have some birthday candles somewhere.'

Alys bent to rummage under the counter and when she raised her head again her mother was standing beside Rob.

'Alys, you must introduce this young man.' She gave Rob a dazzling smile.

Alys took in Rob's puzzled expression and said hastily, 'Rob, meet my mum. Mum, this is Rob.' Kate was looking at her expectantly so she added, 'Rob's a friend of Moira's. He's been kind enough to show me around the area a bit.' She was aware that this sounded a bit lame but Kate clearly had her own agenda that she was intent on pursuing.

'Well, I'm delighted to meet you. Can I repay your kindness to my daughter by asking you to join us for a meal tomorrow evening? I was just discussing with Moira where we might go and it would be lovely if you could come along and make up the numbers.'

Alys could barely hide her astonishment – was this a scheme that Kate had just cooked up or was it something she had talked about with Moira. She glanced back at her aunt who shrugged and gave a wry smile. In the meantime, Kate had extracted a promise that Rob would join them, and had seen him to the door. He was clutching his cake box and rather pink in the face.

'How charming!' Kate exclaimed, watching him leave on his tractor. 'I must say your young man seems very nice. No wonder you were in such a hurry to get back here.'

'He's not my young man, Mum,' Alys protested, but her words fell on deaf ears. Kate had made up her mind that there was something going on and it was going to be hard to dissuade her.

CHAPTER 7

By day two of Kate's stay, Alys's intentions to be on her best behaviour with her mother were being sorely tested. Kate had vetoed a meal at The Old Bell in favour of a restaurant in Nortonstall, and the minute that Alys walked through the door into the hushed atmosphere the following evening, her heart sank. This was clearly the venue for special celebrations, if the scattering of couples, all dressed up and honouring birthdays or anniversaries in more or less unbroken silence, could be said to be celebrating. Kate's party was ushered to a window table – no doubt to make the place look full to any passers-by – presented with leather-bound menus with a flourish, and offered aperitifs. Alys gratefully ordered one, feeling as though she was going to need some extra help to get through the next few hours. They all studied their menus in silence for a while until their drinks arrived and created a diversion. Rob was already looking uncomfortable, tugging at the neck of his shirt as if his tie was choking him. She saw him make a determined effort to be charming as he turned towards Kate.

'So, Mrs Harper, Alys tells me you're originally from this area?'

Alys winced. Not the best start, perhaps, as Kate was notoriously dismissive of her northern roots. But she needn't have worried. Kate had clearly made enquiries from Moira as to Rob's character, and had approved of what she'd heard. Either that, or the few sips of gin and tonic she had taken had gone straight to her head. It seemed she had decided to put a positive spin on what she normally viewed as one of the great handicaps of her life. 'Please, you must call me Kate,' she declared. 'Yes, Moira and I were brought up not far from this very spot,' and she waved her hand vaguely out of the window. 'It was idyllic in many ways,' Kate went on, as Moira's eyebrows shot up. 'But you know what teenagers are like. Can't wait to get away – bright lights, the big city and all that. I headed off to Leeds when I was seventeen, then to London a couple of years after that. I've stayed down south ever since.'

'So, you've not been back until now?' Rob enquired.

'Well, I've visited Moira a couple of times' – Moira's eyebrows rose a fraction more – 'no, let me see, just the once, a few years back. I chose mid-July, banking on good weather, and it poured every day, didn't it?' She turned to Moira, who half smiled. 'I ended up going home early. Not a great one for walking in the rain, you see.' Kate sounded almost apologetic, to Alys's surprise.

She'd always felt herself a duck out of water with her mum, but wondered for the first time whether Kate had, in fact, struggled with her active, outdoorsy family. Her husband was generally to be found out on the golf course, while her kids took to the moors for their Duke of Edinburgh's Award schemes. Kate's idea of a good day out was a successful shopping trip, returning with a car boot loaded with bags from Bluewater or Westfield. Alys suspected that her dad had been drawn to Kate for her style and beauty, but once captured, Alys could see he had become impatient of it and reverted to a life that mostly excluded Kate.

The food arrived with a flourish, tearing Alys away from her thoughts. Her fears about the feel of the place proved justified: the plates were fussily garnished, and although the food was nice enough, it had an old-fashioned feel. Italian, it may have been, but modern Mediterranean cuisine it certainly wasn't. By the time Alys was halfway through her plateful of *Pollo alla parmigiana* she was full up and, moreover, suspected that garlic was oozing from every pore. She tried to avoid catching Rob's eye. She knew she'd have an overwhelming urge to giggle at his expression – he was getting the full focus of Kate on a charm offensive. Alys noted that Moira's plate and her own were half empty; Rob's and Kate's were virtually untouched. Every time Rob lifted his fork to his mouth, Kate interposed a question which he answered politely, and down went his fork again to his plate. Kate's fork, meanwhile, hovered halfway to her lips while she listened intently to his answer, then down it went, untouched, to her plate while she followed up with her next question.

Alys felt action was called for. 'Now, Mum,' she said, 'less of the Spanish Inquisition for Rob. Look at the two of you – your food's getting cold. Moira told me she had some exciting news to share this evening.' She looked at her aunt, who had settled back in her chair, happy to take a back seat, but now visibly pulled herself together. 'Are you ready to tell all?' Alys was impatient to know whether this news had something to do with Moira's absences from the café and the mysterious phone calls she had taken.

'Well, things have been going so well in Northwaite, thanks in no small part to Alys, that I thought the time had come to expand the business,' Moira said. Alys, heart rate suddenly accelerating, noted that Kate looked politely interested, Rob more genuinely so. 'I'm negotiating on some premises just around the corner from here and, if I get them, I'll have the second café in my empire.' She paused. 'And I'm going to ask Alys whether she will run it for me.'

Kate's fork, which had made two or three journeys to her mouth while Moira was speaking, was back down on her plate again. Rob had managed several hearty mouthfuls; now he turned towards Alys and positively beamed.

Kate turned to Alys. 'Well, darling, it looks like you've finally found your niche.'

Alys, startled and not a little overwhelmed by her aunt's trust in her, was too happy to worry whether there was a barbed edge to her words. 'I'm very happy for you. Moira's been telling me what a wonderful help you've been to her and I can see how well you look after your weeks here. The country air obviously suits you. Or perhaps it's something else?' Kate turned towards Rob and smiled, eyebrows raised. Alys blushed furiously, but Rob simply smiled back and said, 'Alys is quite the country girl – she seems really at home here.'

Alys was the centre of attention for a while but she couldn't answer any of Kate and Rob's questions.

'It's a complete surprise to me,' she protested. 'I'll need to talk to Moira about it. But I'm thrilled that you've asked me,' she said, turning to Moira. 'And very excited,' she added, already feeling a thrill as she thought about the challenges that lay ahead. They talked a little more about the premises and how soon Moira might be able to take possession of them then, as the conversation looked set to flag, Alys decided to change the topic before her mother could start quizzing Rob again.

'I found this in the box you gave me,' she said to Moira, fishing the locket out of her pocket and laying it on the table. 'I wondered whether you knew anything about it?'

'Oh, heavens. That's one of the few family heirlooms we have.' Moira looked flustered. 'I thought I'd lost it, and to be honest, I'd forgotten about it.'

'Box?' Kate looked enquiringly from Alys to Moira.

'Just one or two things from the past,' Moira answered hastily. 'An old book. And this. Mum said she never wore it because it was damaged, and it's rose gold, so it was hard to get a chain to match it.'

Alys wasn't sure whether Moira was looking so anxious because of the locket, or because Kate might be angry that she was in possession of a few family things that had once been their mother's.

'Do you know who it might have belonged to?' she asked, hoping her aunt or her mother might be able to shed some light on it.

Kate picked up the locket and turned it through her fingers. 'I remember Mum giving this to you,' she said to Moira. 'I think it must have belonged to our grandma Beth.'

'Would you like it?' Moira turned to Alys. 'It's yours if you would. It seems a shame that it's just been ignored for all these years. It should stay in the family, and be worn.'

'I looked at the date,' Alys said. 'Could it have belonged to Alice?'

Moira, who had relaxed once it was clear that there wasn't going to be a family row over mis-appropriated heirlooms, shifted uncomfortably in her seat. She turned to Kate.

'Alys spotted her great-great-grandma Alice's gravestone in the churchyard. She's curious about her, why she died so young, and about why we moved to Nortonstall from Northwaite. I don't think I've been much help . . .' Moira tailed off.

'Ah, you've discovered our black sheep!' Kate laughed. 'I don't suppose I can be much more help than Moira. I seem to remember Mum saying something about a problem at the mill – a fire – meaning that there were no jobs to be had, and so people left the area. Our Grandma Beth came here to Nortonstall when she was young, with her mum – or wait, was it with her grandma, Sarah? I don't remember. Anyway, Sarah was a herbalist and I think business must have dried up in the village, so she came here. She was quite successful, I think, although the family ended up back in Northwaite again.'

Rob chipped in. 'My great-great-granddad worked at the mill, but when it burnt down he left home and went to train as a stonemason in York. I think a lot of people left – some drifted back later, some didn't.'

Alys, until then focused on her namesake and the fact that both Moira and Kate had neatly side-stepped giving her any more information about her, was distracted by the sudden realisation that other people might have ties to the area as well. 'Wait – so your family have lived around here for years too?' she asked.

'Centuries, more like. We're one of the oldest families in Northwaite. My mum has traced us right back to twelve hundred and something.'

Alys was taken aback. 'Wow, you can actually do that?' Her mind was whirring – she had thought that it was going to be hard to find out more about what had happened just over a century ago, and now that was starting to feel like recent history!

Rob laughed at her reaction. 'You need to talk to my mum. She got the family research bug a while back and now we've got this whole family tree drawn up, framed and hung on the wall at home. She can probably tell you about half the families in the area – we all seem to be related one way or another. You can do a lot of the recent stuff online, but she knows how to dig further back into the past. Have a chat with her if you're interested. She loves telling people all about it.'

'I'd love to,' said Alys, leaning back as her plate was whisked away and replaced by a dessert menu. 'But I don't know where to find her.'

'Oh, you can't miss the house,' said Rob. 'It's the last one as you leave the village on the moor road. The one with a bit of carved stonework over the door.' He paused. 'I usually go over for Sunday lunch. If Moira can spare you from the café one Sunday, why don't you come along?'

Kate cut in, answering on Alys's behalf, 'Why,

266

how kind, I'm sure she'd love to. And I'm sure Moira can manage without her for a few hours.'

Before Alys could speak, Moira had joined in, keen to keep her sister happy. 'No problem. It's a bit quieter now, with fewer walkers when it's hot, plus the school holidays take local people away too. Business picks up again in September. So, pick any Sunday you like. Flo will always be happy to lend a hand, too, if I need her.'

'That's settled, then. I'll talk to Mum and we'll fix a date. Maybe this Sunday?' said Rob who, totally oblivious to Alys's sensation of being rail-roaded by both her mother and her aunt, was busy scanning the dessert menu. He'd had a long and full day on the farm and didn't see any problem in adding pudding to the two courses that he'd already polished off.

Kate, Moira and Alys settled for coffee, Alys resolving to have words with Moira about her colluding with Kate when they got back to the cottage later. But the conversation turned to lighter matters, and by the time they left half an hour later, thankful for the waiting cab, she'd forgotten all about her resolution.

CHAPTER 8

Alys arrived a little early at the gate of Rob's parents' house. She felt a sense of nervous excitement, or was it apprehension? Could it be to do with meeting Rob's parents? Rob clearly saw her as nothing more than a friend, didn't he? So, she didn't need to feel as anxious as she would have felt on meeting a new boyfriend's parents, surely? Whatever it was, she had butterflies in her stomach and wasn't quite sure why.

As Alys raised her hand to lift the door knocker, she took a closer look at the carved stonework arching around the front door. She registered how grand it seemed for a cottage. Garlands of leaves twined around fat seed pods and thistle-like flowers, each detail of the leaf veins and spiky flower heads lovingly carved. Seen in close up, it was even more apparent that the same hand that had carved Alice's gravestone had been at work here.

She lifted the knocker and let it fall, trying to calm her jitters. Rob opened the door with a broad smile, and within moments her nervousness had evaporated, vanquished by the warmth of her welcome. Alys was ushered in, introduced to his mother, relieved of her jacket and box of The Celestial Cake Café macaroons, led into the garden and seated under the shade of a big cream umbrella, with a glass of chilled white wine pressed into her hand. Within moments, she found a dog at her feet, muzzle resting on her shoes and eyes fixed beseechingly on her.

'Just ignore her,' said Rob's mum, who had introduced herself as Julie. She was petite with dark curly hair and had the sort of slim build that made Alys think that she was probably very energetic. A fell-runner, or a regular at the gym, maybe? Alys felt big-boned and clumsy beside her but Julie had welcomed her with such a lovely all-encompassing smile that she felt instantly at ease. 'Derek was supposed to take her for a walk before lunch but he got waylaid by the cricket on TV. She's hoping you're a soft touch.'

'Oh, she's *lovely*.' Alys bent forward to fondle the dog's soft ears, and to chuck her under her chin. 'Maybe Rob and I could take her out after lunch. What's her name?'

'Lola,' said Rob, rolling his eyes. 'Something to do with a song from way back when.'

Lola thumped her tail enthusiastically on the floor.

'I see Lola's found a friend, then.' Derek had come out into the garden, having been dragged away from the cricket by Julie. Alys smiled. He was just an older version of his son: similar jeans and checked shirt, same build, same curly hair but greying a bit around the temples, same brown eyes.

Julie came back out from the kitchen and settled on a chair, glass in hand.

'Right, five minutes while I wait for the vegetables to cook,' she said, glancing at her watch.

'Watch out,' said Rob in a stage whisper to Alys. 'Your turn now for the Spanish Inquisition.'

'Now, now,' scolded Julie. 'Alys must have got used to Yorkshire folk by now. They'll have your life story out of you within ten minutes of knowing you. They're not being nosey, though,' she said, turning to Alys. 'Just friendly.'

'Insatiably curious, more like,' muttered Rob.

His mother shook her head. 'Well, it beats the way they go on down in London. You get on a Tube packed with people and nobody says a word to anyone. If you try to chat to your neighbour, they look at you like you're from another planet.'

Alys laughed. 'I know what you mean.' Although, privately, she felt that maybe city folk had enough interactions to get through in a day without chatting to their fellow passengers – she'd always found the Tube her chance to have some down-time. Time to think, catch up with a book, zone out from the invasion of her personal space by her packed-in fellow commuters.

'So,' Julie said, glancing at her watch again. 'Rob tells me you've been doing a bit of family research while you've been here?'

'Yes,' Alys took a sip of her wine. 'It looks as

though my family go back quite a long way in the area. Well, at least, I've got as far back as my great-great-grandmother. Her name was Alice, too, and she worked at the mill down in the valley.'

'Oh, that'll be Hobbs Mill,' said Derek. 'In those days, just about everyone in the village worked there. Albert, my dad's granddad, was there awhile.'

'I told Alys about all the research you'd done,' said Rob, turning to his mum. 'Maybe there's something in all those papers you have that might help Alys find out some more about her relatives?'

A beeping noise from the kitchen brought Julie to her feet. 'Time for lunch now. But after we've eaten you can make some coffee to go with those wonderful macaroons that Alys brought, and I'll get the boxes down from the spare room. Alys can have a rummage through and see if there's anything there of any use.'

Rob chuckled. 'You've no idea how happy that'll make Mum,' he said, turning to Alys. 'Really, she should have been a historian instead of a school administrator. She's never so happy as when she's going through the Spencer family archives.'

'Get on with you.' Julie rolled her eyes.

'It's true. She even ordered up a map that shows this part of the country well over a hundred years ago. Fascinating, I'm sure.' Rob affected a yawn.

Julie smiled. 'All that research has kept me busy and off your case,' she said. 'But now that it's come to an end, well – better watch out.' And she linked arms with her son as they all drifted through into the kitchen, where a table was set overlooking the garden.

Alys liked the easy way that Rob and his parents related to each other. She felt a pang of envy: it simply wasn't like this in her own family. Kate was permanently over-anxious, David impatient of his wife and overbearing with guests, and Alys would be torn between embarrassment and irritation. Her brothers seemed to just let it wash over them, but she had noticed that they were infrequent visitors, even more so now that they were married. It seemed to her that they used the excuse of their wives' families' commitments increasingly often to avoid Christmas, Easter and birthday gatherings.

The relaxed feeling in the Spencer household persisted throughout lunch. It was a relatively simple meal: roast chicken flavoured with herbs from the garden, new potatoes with garden mint, home-grown vegetables, blackberry crumble. Or rather, bramble crumble, as Rob said she had to call it, now that she was 'up North'. Rob and his father expected a proper Sunday lunch, Julie pointed out, whereas she would have been happy with salad in the summer.

'Salad!' Rob and Derek both looked horrified. 'Nothing there but air!' added Derek.

Julie laughed. It was clearly the response she was expecting. 'Right, time for the archives,' she said. 'Derek, Rob. You're on washing-up and coffee duties.'

272

Alys's offers of help were brushed aside. 'No, guests come here to relax,' said Julie. 'Anyway, it's a family tradition that the men wash up. That's why I've never bothered to get a dishwasher. Got to give them something to do.' And she led Alys along the hallway to the foot of the stairs. 'You can come and help with the boxes, though. More than one, I'm afraid.'

Alys paused at the foot of the stairs, her attention caught by the large, framed family tree that she'd failed to notice as she arrived. 'Oh, Rob told me about this,' she said, peering, fascinated, trying hard to take it all in. Rob, an only child, and his parents were there right at the bottom of a beautifully executed plan, each box filled with italic script detailing the names and dates of birth and death of family members stretching back, as Rob had said, all the way to the thirteenth century. Alys's eyes were drawn to the name she'd heard at lunch.

'Here's Albert,' she said, pointing through the glass. She paused, taking in the dates. 'He died quite young. And he only had one child? That was quite unusual in those days, wasn't it?'

'Yes.' Julie paused, hand on banister, poised to climb the stairs. 'Bit of a tragic story. He died in the First World War. He was in his late thirties, almost too old to enlist, but it seems he insisted on going. There are rumours that he had an unhappy marriage he was trying to escape. He was a great craftsman – a stonemason at York Minster. If he'd lived, I think he might have made a name for himself. He did the beautiful stone carving around the door here.'

Julie headed up the stairs, Alys following. 'We'll just take a couple of the boxes that relate to the time you're looking at,' she said over her shoulder, pushing open the door to the spare room. Alys gasped. One long row of shelves was filled with box files, all neatly labelled in date order.

Julie looked a bit sheepish. 'Rob was right. It did become a bit of an obsession. There's nothing more that I can do really – it's all fully researched. I *so* enjoyed doing it. Maybe I should have been a detective? It's a bit like fitting together the pieces of a jigsaw puzzle. It's so exciting when you find a piece that's been missing.' She looked pensive, then brightened. 'You know, maybe I could help you? I learnt such a lot when I was doing this. And there's so much you can access these days via the Internet.'

Alys felt herself starting to blush. 'That's really kind of you. But I couldn't take up your time. And really, there's only one person I'm interested in. There seems to be a bit of a mystery surrounding her and she died really young, leaving a small baby. I don't know why I'm drawn to finding out more – maybe it's just because we share a name?'

'Oh, now you're making me *very* curious. Don't worry, it's no trouble to give you a few tips to help you get started. Here, give me a hand with the files and we can see if there's anything there.'

By the time Alys and Julie were back downstairs,

the sun had vanished behind dark clouds and the garden was no longer so appealing, so they headed for the sitting room, where coffee was already waiting on a tray with pink, green and lilac macaroons piled on a china plate. Julie caught Alys looking at the cups.

'They're lovely, aren't they?' she said. 'I know what a fan you are of old china. These belonged to my mum and, I suspect, to her mum before her. There's a full set – I think they always kept them for best and hardly ever used them. When Rob told me what you'd done at the café, I decided it was time they came out from the back of the cupboard and saw the light of day on a regular basis.'

Julie and Alys settled themselves on the thick rug that covered the flagstone floor and opened the box files. Derek and Rob took it in turns to peer round the door and offer more coffee or wine but, seeing the two heads bent over a sea of documents, they tactfully withdrew and settled themselves in front of the TV in the other room.

Alys pored over the map that Rob had been so scornful of, marvelling over how little had changed in the village of Northwaite, but struck by how Nortonstall, by no means large today, had expanded since the map had been drawn up.

'It was all because of the mills,' said Julie. 'And the railway. Once that arrived, Nortonstall became a transport hub for cloth from Hobbs Mill, but also for all the mills the length of the valley – about fifteen of them in all. And I suppose these mills needed supplies, and as more workers came to the area, they needed services too, so a whole town grew up.'

Julie flicked through a stack of papers from the box in front of her. There were copies of certificates, of pages of newspapers of the era, lists of businesses and their premises, copies of house deeds and census printouts. 'I got really drawn in,' she said. 'Trying to build a picture of what it must have been like to live here all those years ago.' She paused. 'Actually, in terms of the buildings and countryside, not a lot has changed in Northwaite. Transport, obviously, but the village layout and all the paths to the mill and the next villages are really much as they were well over a century ago. Now, I'm looking for something—' She hunted through a few more documents. 'Ah, here we are.' She extracted a slim book from the pile and handed it to Alys.

'Is it a diary?' Alys asked, fearful of opening it as the cloth binding had split around the spine, exposing the brittle glue and stitching that held the pages together.

'Sort of,' said Julie. 'More a kind of journal, I'd say. It belonged to Albert. We found it in a box of his papers, along with a war medal and some photographs of him in uniform. But I think it dates back further than the war. I had a go at reading it, but I couldn't decipher that much. The ink's faded and his handwriting is hard to read. Maybe you'll have better luck? Since he worked at the mill too, you might find something useful in there?'

Alys turned the pages gingerly, trying hard to quell a growing sense of excitement. 'Don't worry,' said Julie, struggling to her feet and massaging her legs where pins and needles had set in. 'I don't expect you to read it now. You need time and a better light than we have in here.'

With a start, Alys realised it was coming up to half past five. She scrambled to her feet too. 'Oh, I'm so sorry. I've kept you too long!' she exclaimed. 'I had no idea it was so late.'

'You see how addictive it is?' said Julie, and laughed. 'Let's go and see what's happening next door. Odds on, they're both fast asleep.'

Julie knew her family only too well. Both Rob and Derek were, indeed, asleep side by side on the sofa, TV still on. Julie switched it off.

'Good match?' she said loudly. Both men snapped their eyes open, momentarily confused, then obviously wondering whether they could deny having been asleep. Seeing that they'd been rumbled, they yawned and stretched, looking rather sheepish.

'Cup of tea, anyone?' asked Julie, heading for the kitchen. Alys's protestations that she really must be going were overridden and, fortified by tea and the macaroons that had proved to be too much to have after lunch, but now looked rather more inviting, she found herself heading out of the village with Rob, Lola bounding on ahead, delighted that the promised walk had finally materialised.

'How did it go?' asked Rob. 'Find anything useful?'

'You know, I think I just might have done,' said Alys, patting her jacket pocket where Albert's journal was safely lodged. She was looking forward to reading it, planning to hide it away in her bedroom at Moira's and take her time deciphering the fragile pages with their faded script. She savoured the sense of anticipation, but for now the sun had returned and it was a glorious evening. It was the perfect time for a walk, the sky a soft blue, the sun still warm, and the whole of the countryside looking as though it was bathed in a warm glow. Or perhaps that was just a reflection of Alys's mood? She couldn't remember the last time she had felt quite so relaxed and happy. She turned to Rob.

'Race you to Tinker's Wood,' she said, pointing to the band of trees some distance away down the lane. Rob groaned. He hadn't fully recovered from his large lunch and afternoon nap. He would have protested, but he wasn't going to let Alys get the better of him. She was already well on her way, flying down the lane. It wasn't the most elegant of running styles, he noted: her arms were flailing and there seemed to be more upward than forward motion. Her hair was already starting to fly free from the clips that had held it relatively secure all afternoon. He grinned and set off, gathering speed with the incline of the lane. Alys shrieked as she heard his heavy-footed approach. Lola, made giddy by Rob's behaviour, which was quite unlike his normal self, leapt and bounded around the two of them, deliriously happy to be out of the house, the scent of rabbits in the air.

CHAPTER 9

It was several days before Alys found time to settle down and look through Albert's journal. Moira was going out – a very rare occurrence, prompting much teasing about her having a date. She was heading to Nortonstall for an evening of jazz with friends at The Royde Inn.

'I'll get a cab back later,' she said. 'Have a good evening and don't wait up.'

Alys could barely contain herself until Moira was out of the door before heading up the stairs to retrieve Albert's journal from her bookshelf. She had looked at it sitting there every day since bringing it back from Derek and Julie's house. She was half afraid of what she might find within the pages, and half hopeful it would provide some answers to her questions.

With the book clutched close to her chest, she made her way back downstairs and settled into a chair under Moira's reading lamp. Alys had teased Moira about her need for such a strong light when reading, but tonight she was glad to make use of it. The journal's paper had darkened with age, while the ink had faded to a curious brown colour.

The book fell open at the back, where it seemed as though the pages had been pressed firmly open. The date at the top of the page was 5th September, 1914. Alys skimmed over the page, then started again at the top. A chill struck through her as she read. It seemed that Albert was writing a kind of farewell, his own closing chapter. He clearly had no intention of returning from this war that he had signed himself up for. He wrote of how sad he felt *'never to see my boy Walter grow to be a man. Yet if I don't make this effort now, then who knows what the future will hold for him. I can't pretend too much sadness about Violet. I know she will be a good mother to Walter, far better than I have been as a father.'* Here the ink was smudged and Alys struggled to read what came next. There was something indecipherable, then the name 'Alice' which caused her heart to beat painfully in her chest. Had she found a clue already? Could this refer to her great-great grandmother? Or was it a different Alice? She tilted the book this way and that under the light, but the words that came before and after were indistinct. She read to the bottom of the page – there were no further clues but a clear understanding on Albert's part that he would not be returning from what he referred to as his 'last adventure'. There was some reference to making atonement, which was also smudged and perhaps referred to Violet. As far as Alys could make out, rumours of something amiss in his relationship with his wife could well have been true.

She turned back slowly through the pages towards the front of the book. The entries were by no means daily. There was a cluster of them in 1914, in which Albert described his growing conviction that he should enlist in the Yorkshire Regiment, his doubts about his age and fitness, his joy at being accepted, and the plans and preparations he had to make. Alys did a quick calculation – Albert must have been in his mid-to-late thirties. Pretty old to be heading off to war, as Julie had said.

Prior to 1914, there were perhaps two or three entries per year. There was a lengthy description of time spent in York, drawing up plans for restoration work to be carried out at York Minster. In 1905, she found an entry relating to Walter's birth. '*A beautiful boy. We will call him Walter, after Violet's father. Violet is exhausted and must have bed rest for a week. I am not sure how we will afford the care, but at least she is quiet.*' Alys wasn't quite sure what to make of his words. She turned the pages forward again, carefully, but there was no other mention of Violet again, not until the very last entry. It was odd. She turned back again, not quite sure why she was tackling Albert's life in reverse, but unravelling it in this way seemed like the right thing to do.

The early entries were short and matter-of-fact, generally related to business affairs or descriptions of journeys that Albert had undertaken to see potential jobs. A carving for a town-hall door, a fireplace for a wealthy mill owner, restoration work on churches around the county. In 1905 a brief entry read *'Violet and I are to be married tomorrow. I try to rejoice and feel sure it is the right thing. Yet my heart feels as though turned to stone.'*

Alys hoped that Violet had never had cause to pick up this book and read its contents. Surely, she would have been mortified to read these words? As she turned back further through the pages, she stopped, arrested by a sudden thought. Perhaps Violet *had* done just that? Perhaps she had read Albert's journal, hoping for an insight into his mind, and instead found a cold description of his feelings before his wedding night? Perhaps that was why the rest of the book seemed devoid of anything other than the everyday, the mundane, apart from the very last page, where he was clearly making some kind of farewell? And if that were the case, maybe some of his earlier entries would hold better clues to his thoughts and his state of mind?

With renewed purpose, Alys continued to turn back through the book, stopping almost immediately at two pages of drawings. The designs were familiar – garlands of leaves and flowers in a vertical design, close-ups of bursting seed heads, sketches of flower heads from different angles. These were surely sketches for the carved design around Derek and Julie's front door and on Alice's gravestone? Notes on the page appeared to be technical, relating to tools to be used. The design was undated. Alys turned back further, and was halted again, startled by the writing she found. It was sprawling, virtually illegible, looping across the page. She could almost feel the anguish, or perhaps anger, coming off it, before she even read the words.

The entry was a long one, the date 23rd December 1903. Sentences were started, then crossed out, and try as she might, Alys couldn't decipher everything there, but she could read enough to get an inkling of what he was trying to express.

'*So, what has been my great chance in life has also been my undoing. How could I not see that a man such as Williams would never have my best interests at heart? My toil, my tribulations, so far away from home in York, are as naught. Alice is dead and it is all my fault, as surely as if she had died at my hand.*'

Alys stopped, startled, and reread the lines. Whatever could he mean? She pressed on, sure she must be on the verge of a great discovery.

'*In all those months, all those years, I looked forward to coming back, to telling Alice what I had achieved. How I had learnt to write, like her. How I had made something of myself, in the hope that she would be proud of me. Yet all this time she was dead, within three months of my going, from what Ella says. And I the only one who could have saved her.*'

The names 'Alice' and 'Ella' jumped out at Alys. She remembered that Alice had a sister called Ella on the family tree. It *must* be 'her' Alice – surely the coincidence was too great otherwise?

The smudges on the page here convinced Alys that they were tears. Tantalisingly, there were no further clues as to how Albert was involved in Alice's death. Instead, she read in a further entry how he had resolved to do all he could to assist the family and to help Sarah to bring up Beth to whom he was determined to be the best-ever uncle. This was further proof, if she needed it, that he was referring to her ancestors. Sarah was Alice's mother and Beth must be Elisabeth, Alice's daughter. He vowed to raise a stone 'such as no other in the churchyard' on Alice's grave, which he was distressed to see marked only by 'a poor wooden cross', and to bring justice to all who had failed her.

Alys closed the book on her lap, unable to read any more, her head buzzing. What part *had* Albert played in Alice's death? He had clearly once known her well, and he was still welcomed by the family, so they had no suspicion that he was in any way involved in her death. He had created the beautiful gravestone, as well as the door carving, and he seemed determined to help to bring up Beth, who had to be Alys's great-grandmother. Why would he have done this? And who was Williams? Above all, why would Albert believe he was responsible for Alice's death, especially as he had been in York at the time? None of it was making sense.

Alys really wanted to pore over the pages once more in search of further clues. She had a piece of the past in her hands and she really hoped that it might explain whatever mystery there was surrounding her great-great-grandmother and her apparent disgrace. But it was gone eleven o'clock and she needed to be up well before six the next morning to start baking for the day ahead. She needed to save further detective work until she could devote more time to it. Stowing the book back on her shelves, she headed for bed but, despite being tired, she found it hard to settle. When sleep finally came, it was yet again filled with dreams of a darkened cell, shafts of moonlight striking through high bars down onto a stone floor, where a figure lay huddled asleep in a corner. This time, a shadowy figure was trying to get in through the bars, and someone was shrieking.

Alys woke with a start, sweating and with a thudding heart, shrieks echoing in her ears. She listened. All was silent, and the landing light was out. Moira had clearly returned home. Then the eerie cry of an owl from its perch in the church-yard forced a wry smile to her lips. She turned on her side and willed herself back to sleep, aware that her alarm would be waking her again all too soon.

CHAPTER 10

Just over a week later, Alys found herself back at Derek and Julie's front door. She'd managed to spend a couple more evenings poring over Albert's journal but had gleaned little more than she had the first time that she had looked at it. Even so, she was keen to share her discoveries with Julie. She traced the shape of the carving around the door with her finger before she raised the knocker. Albert had carved this, many years before, first drawing out the design in his journal, planning it with the utmost care. But why? For her ancestor, Alice, as some sort of memorial, but then – why here?

Alys was just peering at the detail of a particularly beautiful seed-head when the door was pulled open and Julie caught her in the act. Embarrassed, Alys moved back, blushing, but Julie wasn't at all put out, and stepped over the threshold to join her outside.

'It's beautiful, isn't it?' she said. 'I never fail to look at it when I come home. It's carved with such attention to detail – you can almost feel the love and care that has been poured into it. Anyway, come on in. I've got something to show you.'

Alys had been on the point of telling Julie that this carving seemed significant in Alice's story, but decided that could wait and followed Julie through to the kitchen. A couple of mugs and a plate of biscuits were already set out on the table, along with a pile of documents.

'Tea?' asked Julie. 'Or coffee?' as she flicked the switch of the kettle. 'Or a glass of wine, perhaps?'

'Tea would be great,' said Alys, who secretly longed for the bone-melting relaxation that a glass of wine would bring, but didn't want to make a bad impression. 'No Derek?' she asked, looking around as though she half expected him to pop out from behind the door.

'He's at the pub. He usually meets Rob for a game of darts, or pool, or something. Probably involves staring at some sport. I'm always glad to see him go, and happy to see him back, too! Now, take a seat. I'd have suggested sitting in the garden but it's too chilly this evening. The weather seems to be on the turn already. So, tell me what you've learnt.'

Julie put the mugs on the table and they settled down. Alys explained what she'd found in Albert's journal, the mystery of his belief that he was somehow to blame for her great-great-grandmother's death, and how the stone carving appeared to be some sort of memorial to Alice.

'But what I don't understand is, why *here*?' asked Alys. 'Why *this* house?'

'Well,' said Julie. 'I think I can answer that. After you'd gone the other week I got to thinking about your Alice and wondering if there was anything else in my research that might be useful to you. I looked back through the papers I have that relate to Albert, and this is what I found.' And she pushed the pile of documents over to Alys.

'What are they?' Alys turned them over doubtfully.

'They're the title deeds over the years, telling you who lived in the house. Ignore the ones on top – they relate to the last century – but if you go back a bit, to that one there – that's Albert's.'

Alys turned the top deeds face down and looked at the document that Julie had pointed out. It had a large, red circular stamp across the top, then a great deal of writing in a spidery, flowing script. The heading read: 'Title Deed for Lane End Cottage, Northwaite, dated this day 1 June 1904, being an agreement by Albert Spencer Esq. to purchase said property from Timothy Smallwood Esq. as witnessed by Sutcliffe & Sons Solicitors, Nortonstall.' Alys skimmed over it. Deciphering some of the legal jargon, she managed to work out that Albert had bought the cottage for the sum of 115 pounds.

'That's not all,' said Julie, and she leant over and lifted the deed to show Alys another one, very similar but rather more dog-eared, tucked in further down the pile: 'Being the agreement between Timothy Smallwood and Sarah and Joe

Bancroft for the rental of Lane End Cottage, dated 3 June 1875.'

Alys let out a gasp. 'That's Alice's mother, Sarah.' She looked at the date again. 'She must have moved here before Alice was born. And Joe must be her husband.'

'It turns out Sarah was quite famous in the area,' Julie went on. 'I've found quite a few mentions of her in various documents, local trades-guild journals and the like. She was well known as a herbalist and, by all accounts, she was earning enough at one point to keep the family here after her husband died. She practised from this very cottage, and had a famous herb garden here too.'

'Oh!' exclaimed Alys, sitting back from the table and looking at Julie wide-eyed. 'I've got what might very well be Sarah's herbal back at Moira's. And it's got a plan of her garden in it. It must be this one!' And she gazed out of the kitchen window as if half expecting to see Derek and Julie's garden transform into herb beds before her very eyes.

She looked back at Julie in some excitement. 'I should go and fetch it now so you can see,' she said, and she started to push her chair back.

'No, not now,' protested Julie. 'It sounds fascinating and I'd love to see it another time. But I've got something else to show you.'

She turned back through the documents to the one on top of Albert's deed. It had a very similar format to his, the same large, red circular official stamp, the same flowing script: 'Being the

Agreement between Albert Spencer Esq. and Sarah Bancroft for the rental of Lane End Cottage, dated this day 8 June 1904.'

Alys stared, trying hard to comprehend. 'Wait, so Albert bought the cottage and then—' she paused and flipped back through the papers. 'A few days later he rented it to Sarah?'

'Yes,' said Julie. 'And at a peppercorn rent – look.' By now the documents were spread out across the table and Alys followed Julie's pointing finger to see that the rent that Sarah had paid in 1875 was almost triple the amount she was paying to Albert, over twenty-five years later.

'This ties in with something I discovered.' Alys carefully extracted Albert's journal from her bag. She told Julie what she had been able to learn from Albert's journal, explaining that Albert seemed to feel somehow responsible for Alice's death and showed her the passages in his journal where he vowed to take care of Sarah and her granddaughter Beth. 'And look.' Alys turned the page to show Julie the design for the carving. 'He designed this for Sarah and he carved it over the door here. I guess it was in honour of her profession as a herbalist. Almost like a shop front?'

Julie's cheeks were quite flushed. She loved nothing better than when pieces of research began to slot together and a picture started to emerge. 'Perhaps it wasn't so much in honour of Sarah as in honour of Alice?' she suggested. 'From the sound of it, he couldn't do anything for Alice any more, so he raised a memorial to her in this way, by doing things to help the family.'

A thought struck Alys. 'When Albert bought the house, was Sarah still living there?'

'No, look.' Julie fished out another document. 'Sarah must have left here at the end of 1895. It was rented out to someone else in December 1895 – here's the agreement,' she said, pushing it under Alys's nose.

Alys put her head in her hands. 'Oh, I need to map all this out. I'm getting confused.'

Julie laughed. 'We should draw up a timeline.' She fetched a bit of paper and some coloured pens, and after a bit of intensive plotting it was all making more sense to Alys. 'But what next?' she asked Julie. 'We've built up quite a picture here.'

'There's a key fact missing, though,' Julie pointed out. 'Where did Sarah and her family go between 1895 and 1904? Plus, we don't know what happened with regard to the mill fire. Everyone seems to mention it and the impact it had on the area but it's not clear how it relates to Alice and her family. And we don't know why Albert blamed himself for Alice's death.'

They both sat in silent contemplation of the documents for a few moments, then Julie said, 'There *is* a way of finding out about the fire.'

Alys raised her eyebrows quizzically.

'The local newspaper archive at the library,' Julie went on. 'You can access it all on screen these days. We know what year the fire happened – we can probably pin down the month as well with a bit more research. Then we just need to look at the relevant issue of the paper – the fire's bound to get a mention. I'll explain how to do it, but first I think we need a drink to celebrate. We've uncovered quite a lot this evening!'

Julie poured two glasses of wine from a bottle already open in the fridge. 'Cheers!' she said, raising her glass. 'To Alice.'

'And Albert,' added Alys, savouring the first mouthful of wine and the longed-for feeling of relaxation it brought with it.

CHAPTER 11

Julie had been unable to contain her excitement over the way that Alice's story was starting to take shape, and the role that Albert appeared to have played in it. As her work regularly took her over to Leeds, she'd taken it upon herself to go to the library and locate the newspaper that referred to the mill fire. She'd ordered up a printed copy and given it to Rob to pass on to Alys, without divulging any of the details.

'I think she was a bit embarrassed. Thought she'd overstepped the mark, doing this without asking you,' said Rob as he handed it over.

'That's silly!' protested Alys. 'I'm delighted. I'd never have found time to get over to Leeds myself. Here, why don't we both look through it?'

Absorbed as she was by the newspaper, Alys wasn't aware of the picture they presented to anyone walking into the café. Two heads, one reddish-blonde with wild curls and the other light-brown, separated by barely a hair's breadth as they pored over the pages spread out on the table, searching for the report of the mill fire.

'Hello, Alys.' It took Alys a moment to place what

had once been a familiar voice. She looked up, bemused, then wide-eyed, at Tim, standing silhouetted in the open doorway. He stepped further into the room as Alys started up, narrowly avoiding knocking coffee over the pages, and, for no reason she could comprehend, blushing furiously.

'Tim,' she all but stammered. 'What on earth are you doing here?'

Tim surveyed the scene. 'Well, I thought I'd come up to Yorkshire and see what you found so appealing here. Won't you introduce us?' he asked Alys, looking pointedly at Rob.

'Er, Tim, Rob. Rob, Tim,' said Alys, gesturing awkwardly between them.

'Well, I'd like to say I've heard all about you,' said Tim, taking charge of the situation in the way he always did. 'But I'm afraid that wouldn't be true.'

Rob grinned in a friendly way. 'Can't say Alys has ever mentioned you, either,' he said, turning to Alys and raising an eyebrow.

'Aah, Tim's from London,' said Alys, as if his attire (loafers, chinos, jumper slung around the shoulders of a perfectly pressed shirt) didn't already mark him out as a non-local.

'So, how do you two know each other?' asked Rob, as Tim pulled up a chair and joined them.

Alys blinked rapidly and gazed distractedly around. It was a quiet morning in the café and Moira had seized the opportunity to pop into Nortonstall to stock up on a few things. There were no other customers at present, so Alys couldn't even pretend she had urgent duties to attend to.

She took a deep breath, ignored Rob and addressed herself to Tim. 'How did you find me?' she demanded.

Tim laughed. 'It was hardly a challenge. I just asked your mother.'

Alys groaned inwardly. Had Kate thought it was worth telling Tim where to find Alys, in the hope that he might have one last attempt at persuading her wayward daughter it was time to become a model wife? But really, she'd been through all this with Tim. She glared at him, discouragingly. Why had he even bothered to come?

Rob, receiving no answer to his question, pushed back his chair. 'Looks like you two have some catching up to do. I must be getting on. I promised I'd check up on the sheep over near Barden reservoir.' And without a backward glance, he had gone. Alys felt crushed – he'd offered to take her on a drive later that day, over to the chain of three reservoirs about ten miles away, part of the surrounding area she hadn't yet seen, and she'd been looking forward to it. All of a sudden, the day had taken on quite a different tone.

She noticed a pair of sunglasses on the table. Not Tim's, as they were planted firmly on his head.

'Excuse me a moment,' she said, snatching them up and running outside. Rob had just executed a ponderous three-point turn in the old Land Rover, managing to avoid a sleek, if ostentatious, grey

BMW parked outside. Alys leapt into the road in front of him, brandishing the sunglasses. Reluctantly, Rob wound down his window.

'What's going on, Alys?' he asked. 'I take it Tim's your boyfriend?'

'Yes . . . No! Ex-boyfriend.' Alys screwed her face up into a grimace. She felt a rising sense of panic. She thought she'd made it clear to Tim that it was all over. So, what was he doing here?

'Well, you can't just leave him sitting alone in the café,' Rob pointed out, reasonably. 'You're in charge while Moira is in Nortonstall. Come on Alys, whatever it is I'm sure you can sort it out.'

He put the Land Rover in gear before she had a chance to reply. Alys stepped back, watching him out of sight, then she took a deep breath and went back inside.

'Right,' she said to Tim. 'Now, what's all this about?'

CHAPTER 12

Moira had returned from town to find Alys, looking unusually flustered, trying to deal with a rush of orders from customers on their way to and from walks. Scanning the room for clues to her discomfort, she'd spotted a customer glowering over a cup of coffee and casting furious sideways glances at Alys. He looked rather too well-dressed to be out on a country walk – in fact, he looked as though he would have been much more at home in the Harvey Nicks café in Leeds. Moira guessed that the BMW she'd noticed parked outside belonged to him, and it looked as though he was waiting to talk to Alys. After Alys had managed to serve sandwiches to customers who had ordered cake, coffee to those who had wanted tea, and put the jar of tea bags in the fridge and the milk in the cupboard, Moira decided it was time to act.

She suggested to Alys that she might like to take a walk with her friend, which made Alys feel both relieved and alarmed. After Rob's departure, she'd been resolute in her determination to explain to Tim that, flattered though she was that he had come all this way to visit her, she really had no interest in pursuing their relationship. Events, in the form of a sudden influx of customers, had conspired against her and she'd been forced to break off halfway through her explanations in order to deal with them. Tim, unused to being denied anything, had not taken kindly to being kept waiting.

He was hardly in the best of moods when she had finally escaped from behind the counter. They walked through the village to sit on a bench overlooking the churchyard, the peaceful setting at odds with Alys's feeling of nervous agitation. As she tried to explain her reasons for not wanting to continue their relationship, she nervously twisted her locket between her fingers. She hadn't wanted to damage it by trying to prise it open but she'd found a chain for it in the antique shop in Nortonstall and now she wore it all the time. It hadn't escaped Tim's notice.

'Who gave you that?' He was suspicious. 'Is it new?'

Alys sighed. 'Actually, it's very old. I think it belonged to my great-great grandma, Alice. Moira gave it to me.'

He'd lost interest as soon as he'd worked out that it wasn't the gift of a rival. She suspected it would have been easier for him to accept what she was trying to tell him if someone else had come between them. He seemed to be struggling to understand that her feelings had simply changed.

She began to feel sorry for Tim. He simply couldn't comprehend the fact that she no longer wanted him, nor the life he represented.

'Tim, I'm really sorry if I wasn't clear before. Things have changed. *I've* changed. I love this place . . .' Alys gestured around her, encompassing the distant hills as well as the village. 'And I love what I'm doing here. I see my future here, but I'm sad to say that I don't see you as a part of it any more. I'm really sorry that you had to come all this way to hear me say it.' Alys stood up, feeling a bit shaky and hoping that Tim would accept this without a fuss.

'Has it got anything to do with that bloke I saw you with?' Tim demanded.

'No!' Alys said but, annoyingly, she could feel her colour begin to rise. 'No, Tim. I tried to tell you in the letter I wrote before I even arrived here. And I tried to tell you again in the pub when I was back in London.'

Tim was looking down at his feet and Alys couldn't read his expression.

'Look, it's not you, it's me.' As soon as the words were out of her mouth she realised she was straying into cliché. She needed to be firm and just repeat the message until he understood. 'I'm sorry, Tim. It really is over.' As she said it, she realised with great clarity that for her it had been over a long time ago.

Tim still hadn't looked up. 'I can see I'm wasting my time. Just go away, Alys.'

She felt like stalking off at his words but she knew this meant that Tim was hurting. She just wished that a tiny part of her didn't suspect that he was hurting mainly because he hadn't got his own way. Taking a deep breath, she fought down those feelings, gave his shoulder a brief squeeze, contemplated wishing him the best for his future then thought better of it, and walked slowly back to the café without looking back.

Moira took one look at Alys when she walked in, then took both her hands in hers. 'Look at you,' she said. 'You're shaking like a leaf.' Alys's hands were, indeed, trembling uncontrollably and she felt close to tears.

'Here.' Moira poured Alys a glass of water. 'Now go and sit quietly in the kitchen. I'll tell you when the coast is clear.'

It wasn't long before the BMW could be heard revving up, then it set off down the road over the cobblestones at a pace that was unlikely to do its suspension any favours.

'Right,' Moira said, coming into the kitchen where Alys was washing plates without any apparent sign of knowing what she was doing. 'I think you should take the rest of the day off. Go home and sit in the garden, or go for a walk. The main rush is over here for the day. I can manage by myself.'

CHAPTER 13

So it was that as Tim headed back towards London, Alys found herself sitting in the garden at Moira's cottage, too wound up to know quite what to do with herself. A walk would have dissipated some of her nervous energy but Tim's surprise visit had left her mind in a spin and she couldn't seem to settle to anything. She was sure she'd done the right thing but she didn't like the way it had made her feel.

'If only I'd been clearer with Tim in the first place,' she thought ruefully. She couldn't pass it off, even to herself, as trying to protect Tim's feelings: she knew that she had been guilty of avoidance tactics. She longed to talk things over with her friend Hannah but she was far away in another time zone; even if she managed to get hold of her she couldn't see them being able to have a proper conversation. In desperate need of distraction from her thoughts, she picked up a book and read several pages without taking in a word, then tried a magazine with the same result.

A knock at the door made her start. The thought flashed through her mind that somehow Tim had tracked her down and come back for one final attempt to make her see reason. She opened the door a crack, peering round it cautiously, and was relieved to find that it was Rob on the doorstep, carrying a bottle of wine.

'Moira said I'd find you here. She also said you might need a drink.' Rob brandished the bottle. Alys, thankful of the company, silently blessed Moira's thoughtfulness yet again and threw open the door to let him in.

'How was your trip to the reservoir?' she asked as she took wineglasses from the cupboard, suddenly remembering the path her day was supposed to have followed.

'It was great – the weather was perfect. You could see for miles.' Rob paused, seeing Alys's crestfallen expression. 'Did you manage to get . . . things sorted out?'

Alys made a face. 'I did. Though I'd prefer not to talk about it. I'd rather have had a day out but it's my own fault for not dealing with everything properly before.'

She sighed, led the way out into the garden and poured the wine, passing a glass to Rob before taking a large gulp from her own glass. She sighed again, then settled back into her chair and, for a few minutes, they sat in silence, each immersed in their own thoughts.

'Oh, I nearly forgot.' Rob pulled a newspaper from his backpack. 'You left it behind in the café. I thought it might help to take your mind off things.'

Alys smiled gratefully. It would be good to slip away from the present and distract herself with thoughts of the past. 'Excellent idea,' she said. 'Now, where were we?'

Rob spread out the copy of *The Yorkshire Post* on the garden table. The pages, crammed with dense columns of small type, felt unwieldy in comparison with contemporary newspapers. Rob and Alys worked their way slowly down each column and found what they were searching for on page five, halfway down a long column of text, below a report relating to a meeting at Leeds Town Hall. Rob spotted it first.

'Is this it?' he said, resting his finger on the spot. Alys felt her heart start to race uncomfortably as she bent closer to take a look. Headed 'Mill Tragedy' it read: *A fire at Hobbs Mill in the Lower Royd valley, which started around 8 p.m. on the night of 22 September has claimed the life of Richard Weatherall, aged 25 years, eldest son of James Weatherall of Hobbs Hall, Mill Lane, Northwaite. Mill Manager Owen Williams reported that the fire appeared to have been started deliberately. He, Mr Weatherall and Albert Spencer, the nightwatchman, had fought hard to control the blaze. Mr Richard Weatherall was unfortunately trapped and perished while trying to retrieve vital company papers. Williams commended Albert Spencer for repeatedly entering the burning building in a vain effort to save Mr Weatherall's life. Mr Spencer has been awarded ten guineas for his bravery, which he will use to fund a stonemason's apprenticeship in York with immediate effect. Mr Richard Weatherall's family and his wife Caroline, whom he married just a few weeks previously, are inconsolable. The mill is damaged beyond repair and Mr James Weatherall has expressed his intention to leave the area and start afresh elsewhere.*

A local woman, Alice Bancroft, aged 20 and an ex-employee of the mill, was believed to bear a grudge against her former manager and has been apprehended and held in Northwaite lock-up, awaiting trial for setting fire with intent.'

Alys sat back, took a breath, frowned and looked at Rob. She'd hoped, expected even, something that would set the record straight. But the news was even worse than she could have imagined: Alice had not only destroyed the mill, but someone had been killed.

CHAPTER 14

Alys felt low after Tim's visit, and the news of Alice contained in the newspaper article hadn't helped her mood. She had to fight down an impulse to email Tim to apologise. This was baffling to her: she should have been relieved that she'd found the courage to say what should have been said months ago; instead she felt unsettled and couldn't pinpoint why. Eventually, she confessed her feelings to Moira over breakfast. Moira, not wanting to pry, hadn't asked her anything further about Tim's sudden appearance, and equally sudden departure.

Her aunt stirred her tea slowly, then said, 'Well, I don't know the full story, but perhaps it's just the unfamiliarity of the situation that's unsettling you? You've been so used to having this relationship in the background somewhere, not properly dealt with, that you feel like something is missing? You need to readjust to the situation. Try to give it a few days; I'm sure it will pass.'

It was wise advice. By the time a week had gone by, Alys felt more herself again and had stopped expecting Tim to be standing there every time the café door opened. She had become aware, though, that Rob hadn't dropped by since she had last seen him in Moira's garden.

'What's going on? We've lost our best takeaway-coffee customer,' Moira teased.

'Nothing to do with me,' protested Alys. They were so busy with walkers, even though the school holidays were over, that she didn't have time to dwell too much on Rob's non-appearance. So, when the café door burst open on Saturday afternoon, admitting a giggling crowd of people who greeted her by name, it took her by surprise. It was a moment or two before she recognised Rob's friends, Rosie and Sian, from the night out in the Nortonstall pub, along with several others who'd been there that evening.

'We walked up from Nortonstall. It was so steep!' Sian declared. It was clear from her expression that this wasn't something that she was in the habit of doing. 'Now we're starving!'

Alys was delighted to see them all again and helped them to push several tables together until they had taken up nearly half the space in the tiny café. Then she set about impressing them with a selection of her favourite cakes. Once tea was dispensed, accompanied by exclamations from the girls over the china it was served in, an appreciative silence descended for a short while.

'This is my third cup of tea and my fourth cake,' Rosie groaned, pushing away her plate. 'We'll *have* to walk back now. I can't justify all these calories if we don't!'

'Please, Alys, you *must* bring the café to Nortonstall,' Sian begged. 'I can't manage that hill every time I need some of your wonderful cake.'

'You're in luck,' Alys said, and outlined the plans to open a second premises in Nortonstall. 'There's just one more document to be signed, and then we can make a start.'

By the time the group were all ready to leave – deciding that the bus might be the best option after all as the skies had darkened, threatening rain – Alys had promises of enthusiastic support for the Nortonstall venture.

'Have you seen anything of Rob lately?' Alys asked, as they all gathered their belongings together, hoping her enquiry sounded casual.

'Last I heard, he'd been sent off by his boss to take a look at some cattle down south. Somerset, I think he said. Or was it Devon? Anyway, some more rare breeds to add to the collection over Haworth way. I'm not sure when he said he would be back.'

This came from Chris, whom Alys could remember Rob chatting to at some length that night in Nortonstall.

'Ah, that would explain why he hasn't been in for his daily coffee.' Had her response sounded natural? She hoped so. She waved them off from the café window as they made a noisy last-minute dash for the bus.

She was aware of a feeling of relief: Rob's unexplained disappearance was nothing more than a work trip. Alys decided not to analyse why she was so curious about his whereabouts; in any case, she would soon need to put all her energies into their second café venture. But first, there was just enough time to focus once more on Alice and the mystery of the mill fire. On her next free day, she resolved to take a walk to the site of the ruined mill, in an effort to reconnect with the past, following one of the routes that Alice might have chosen.

There was a definite feeling of summer's farewell as Alys picked her way through the damp, lush fronds of bracken overgrowing the path down through the woods. So few people now passed this way that the path had all but disappeared. In the higher reaches of the wood, spiders' webs were strung from frond to frond, jewelled with moisture droplets that sparkled as they caught the morning sun. Fat-bodied spiders sat proudly dead centre, striped legs delicately hunched, at the ready. Alys let out an involuntary shriek and brushed frantically at herself as she walked into one web, stretched right across the path, sensing it crackle in her hair like an electric charge. Feeling foolish, she looked around in case anyone was watching, then glanced down as a movement caught her eye. It was the spider whose construction she'd ruined, hanging by a thread from a frond. Alys felt guilty – all that work would have to be done once more.

As she pressed on down through the wood, the foliage thinned out and the spider hazard passed. It felt chilly – no late summer sunshine penetrated this far – but dry. Alys breathed deeply, absorbing the scent of the woods: a mixture of earth, moss, bark, leaf. It filled her with a great sense of calm and she imagined it to be like a fragrant guide to the past, holding the history of the trees, the paths and the passage of time, locked within it. She wished she could carry it back with her to Moira's cottage, captured in an old cloudy glass bottle with a ball stopper, held by a rusty metal catch that she could flip back to release the scent whenever she wished.

Alys smiled at her thoughts. The woods always seemed to create these philosophical feelings in her. Her wanderings here over the previous weeks had been accompanied by musings about the craggy cliffs among the trees; mysterious clearings; the raised pool she had found just off the path, but deeply hidden; the hoof prints of deer planted deep in the mud around its dark peaty depths. The silence there had made Alys glance nervously around. She sensed something, the presence of others who had found this place before, who had been here long ago. There was a feeling of anticipation there, as if time was somehow poised, waiting for something to happen. She had no idea what had drawn her from the path in the first place, but she remembered her apprehension as she'd climbed the incline, wondering what she would find on the other side. The deer pool had been a surprise, somehow out of place, yet it must once have had a purpose, now long forgotten.

Today she was intent on exploring the area a little further. She was familiar with the ruined mill: brick towers soaring from the valley floor, sturdy stone bridges, tumbled stone walls. Although she'd come to associate these ruins with Alice, she struggled to place her there when it had been a working mill. She'd seen faded, smudged black-and-white pictures of how the mill had looked in those days: a building several storeys high tucked into this small area of the valley floor; vast theatres of machinery where now there were only trees and ruins, and no sense of the noise, bustle, steam and heat that must have been daily normality six days a week. Now there was just the sound of rushing water, dippers bobbing from rock to rock, the wind whispering and rustling through the trees down the valley.

Alys planned to spend some time just sitting, imagining, absorbing, being there. 'Perhaps we've just lost the power to pick up on the past,' she thought hopefully. 'Maybe it's all still out there, just waiting for us to recognise it, to tap into it.'

The open area where the mill must have once stood had a couple of large flat stones that were perfect for sitting and contemplating. But Alys had a different spot in mind. The main path, such as it was, forked, with one part appearing to lead to a dead end, a crumbling wall. An earlier exploration had shown Alys that in fact the path skirted the wall, and tucked into the lee of it there were tumbled stones and a flat plinth-like rock, perhaps originally a stone door-lintel from the mill. It made a good seat, relatively hidden away, but with an expansive view over the whole mill site. If she had been an artist, it would have made the perfect vantage point to work from, Alys felt sure. Today she hoped it would be her window into Alice's past. More than anything, she wanted to find out what had really happened on that fateful day in 1895. Had Alice really intended to burn down the mill and if so, what could have driven her to do so?

She had come prepared with a rug that she used to cushion her stony seat, a flask of coffee, and biscuits. She settled herself in, poured coffee and sat back, a little shiver of anticipation making her hug her knees into herself. She wondered what anyone would make of her if they stumbled across her, half hidden amongst the bracken and ruined walls.

It was time to absorb her surroundings. She sipped her coffee and looked around. Sunlight was breaking through the trees, there was the sound of running water, and a faint breeze stirred the bracken, still bright green in this sheltered spot. Alys tried to imagine how it must have appeared over a hundred years ago. Right where she was sitting must have been the wall at the boundary of the mill. The huge chimney she had passed was the only remaining complete structure on site – the rest had fallen into ruins and been cleared away, leaving few clues to what might have been. A waterwheel perhaps, sited in that narrow trench? There was the arch of a bridge, now going nowhere. Alys squinted through the trees that had sprung up on site over the years and tried to raise the mill walls in front of her, storey by storey. Somehow, because all the pictures she had seen were black and white, she couldn't make the mill live in present-day colour. It remained trapped in history. She closed her eyes. Could she find her way in via her imagination, through the pictures in her memory?

She relaxed, listening, and gradually the rush of the water transformed into the rhythmic pounding of the spinning machines as the thread wound onto the spools, evenly looping up and down, ready to feed the constant demand in the weaving shed. Small children scurried between the machines, carrying empty bobbins, or cans to collect cotton waste from the nooks and crannies where no adult could safely reach. They looked dirty, hollow-eyed and exhausted, their clothes little better than rags, a strange contrast to the pristine white cotton being spun all around them.

Alys started and opened her eyes – not sure whether she had actually conjured up a vision of the past or whether she was imagining an animated version of something she had seen in one of the museums. The wood felt very still, almost as if a storm was coming, although she could see clear blue sky up around the treetops. Sunlight still glanced down on the water, catching tiny insects performing a late-summer dance in its rays. She closed her eyes again, half reluctant to forsake this for the harshness of the world she had observed, or perhaps imagined, but curious, even so.

PART VI

CHAPTER 1

Alice reached home just as the first fat drops of rain started to fall. Sarah looked up from her seat by the kitchen range, a pile of clothes to be mended, darned and patched at her side.

'I was worried,' she said. 'I heard the wind getting up, and when I went outside the weather had already turned. I hoped you hadn't gone too far afield.'

'Ah, far enough,' said Alice, a little breathless, setting the pail on the scrubbed table and brushing Elisabeth's windswept hair out of her eyes. Sarah looked at her sharply. There was an odd brittleness in Alice's tone, and her colour was high. Her lips looked bruised, but Sarah dismissed the observation as soon as she'd made it, noting how purple Elisabeth's usually rosy lips had become.

'You've let the child gorge on too many berries,' she scolded. 'She'll be crying in the night with belly ache, you mark my words, unless I prepare a draught to settle her stomach.'

Alice was intent on distraction. 'Look,' she said, pointing at the pail. 'See how much fruit I picked. We can make jam tomorrow.'

317

Ella and all the others crowded into the kitchen, exclaiming over the size of the blackberries and helping themselves until Alice protested and slapped their hands away, then covered the pail and put it in the pantry to keep cool until morning. Lightning flashed across the kitchen, followed almost immediately by such a loud clap of thunder that they all cried out, then laughed at each other's alarm. Sarah, observing them quietly from her seat near the range, saw a real flash of fear cross Alice's face.

The others trooped back up the stairs, to continue their dressing-up games before bed, and Alice made to follow with Elisabeth, now scrubbed relatively clean of the purple juice.

'What have you done?' asked Sarah, taking Alice by the arm and turning her so that she faced her.

'You must wait and see. But I hope I have saved us all.' And with that Alice shrugged Sarah off and headed up the stairs. Lightning flashed again, provoking yet more screams and laughter from upstairs, and highlighting her shadow in monstrous form against the staircase wall.

CHAPTER 2

Sarah's hopes that Alice was on the mend, raised by her apparent energy over the last couple of weeks, were dashed the following morning. When Elisabeth's morning murmurings turned into grumbles, then into wails that went unheeded, Sarah rose to find out what was amiss. Alice lay in bed still, cheeks flushed and strands of hair plastered to her face. The tangled bedclothes were evidence of a restless night. When Sarah laid her hand to Alice's brow, it was burning up with fever – as she'd feared.

Sarah scooped Elisabeth from her cot and took her away for the little ones to entertain, then hurriedly prepared yarrow tea for Alice. Ella had already left for the mill, so leaving Thomas in charge of stirring the porridge pot, with strict instructions not to burn either himself or the breakfast, she carried the steaming liquid up the stairs.

'Come now, you must sit up and drink this.' Sarah half lifted, half pulled Alice up until she was propped on her pillows, then sat by her murmuring words of encouragement and stroking her hair back every now and then until every drop had been drunk.

Thomas came up the stairs, Annie and Beattie trooping after him, to declare the porridge eaten and the pot put to soak. Sarah turned to find them jostling for position in the doorway, all wide-eyed and looking anxious.

'It's time to get washed and dressed now,' Sarah said, and shooed them out. She knew that any washing done without the benefit of her first heating the water was likely to be sketchy, but she needed to sit with Alice to make sure that her temperature fell.

Within the hour, Alice's colour had returned to normal and her skin felt cooler and less clammy.

Sarah had reason to be thankful for yarrow's properties in ridding the body of infection. She was still worried as to what ailed Alice, though. The village had been free of contagious illnesses for a long time, and none of the younger children had been sick with any of the usual childhood maladies for some while. Perhaps what Sarah had taken to be a good sign – Alice's energy in going out and about again – had been too much for her and she had simply overdone it?

Sarah stifled a sigh. Her daughter's health was of increasing concern to her. Alice wasn't as robust as you might expect a young woman of her age to be. Sarah had noticed quite early in Alice's childhood that she didn't have the same stamina and energy as other children. She tired quickly, needed more frequent rests, and dark shadows were nearly always smudged below her eyes. Bookish pursuits with old Mrs Lister had suited her well, and Sarah had begun to think that she'd outgrown whatever the problem was. When Alice had started to work full-time at the mill, however, Sarah's hopes had been shown to be premature. She'd returned exhausted each evening, then risen exhausted again to face the new day. It was at this point that Sarah had tried out a heart tonic on her, adjusting the dose and the formula until she found something that seemed to suit her well, and restore some of her equilibrium. Alas, the pregnancy had put an added strain on Alice's body and Sarah had been fearful for her health yet again. The last few months had seen many ups and downs, and as Alice slipped into sleep, still propped on her pillows, Sarah felt an overwhelming sense of sadness. She would fight hard in every way she knew to prevent it, but she had a feeling of foreboding, a fear that Alice's life was not destined to be a long and happy one.

By early afternoon, though, Sarah's fears had dissipated. Alice was up and about, seemingly none the worse for her bad night, all traces of fever gone. She set to work, helping Sarah with the household chores and taking the washing to peg out on the line. The heat of the last couple of weeks had blown away along with the storm and been replaced by a brisk breeze, sunshine and scudding clouds.

'We'll need to keep an eye on it, mind,' Sarah warned. 'It's sunny enough now but it might change at any minute. At least it's a good drying day, while it lasts.'

Alice felt a rising agitation, which she tried to quell by keeping busy. She was aware of Sarah observing her, but her mother didn't say anything, beyond trying to persuade her not to do too much.

'Take it easy, Alice. You've not been well. You don't want the fever to return.' Sarah persuaded her to sit down at the table to help prepare the vegetables for the evening meal.

Alice frowned as she peeled the potatoes, rinsing the residual mud away from the surfaces in a large bowl of water, then setting them aside, now shiny white, to chop. Sarah worked away quietly and watched her, removing the bowl and refilling it with fresh water when she saw that the rinsed potatoes were coming out dirtier than they had gone in. Alice showed no sign of having noticed.

Alice began to chop the potatoes, halving, quartering, then dicing them. Suddenly she flung the knife down and Sarah saw blood smeared over the white cut surfaces of the vegetables, dark-red droplets falling from her fingertips.

'You've cut yourself!' Sarah passed a cloth over to Alice, then went to wring another out in fresh water. She came back to see Alice staring, unseeing, as more drops fell and flowered on the wet surface of the table.

'I'm to be married,' she said abruptly.

Sarah, applying pressure to the cut in an effort to staunch the flow of blood, almost didn't register what she had said.

Alice repeated, 'I'm to be married. To – to Owen Williams.'

Sarah started back and stared disbelievingly at her daughter. Memories of the state that Alice had been in one night on her return from the mill flooded back. Shaken and distraught, she'd appeared on the doorstep, her arms scratched from where she'd struggled home along the path without the aid of a lantern, her face bruised from where she'd blundered into branches, she'd said. Privately, Sarah wondered what else might have caused these injuries. Weeks had followed where Alice hadn't been herself, had been withdrawn, snappy, moody. Then there had been the day when Albert had brought her home from the mill, after the fall, and the terrible night that had followed. The bleeding, the pain, the furious weeping. Sarah knew that Alice believed she'd kept the truth hidden, but Albert had told her everything. She felt a sudden rush of anger, remembering her feelings of helplessness and rage against the person who had done this to her daughter. Against Williams, the man Alice now said she was going to marry.

'*Why*, Alice? Why *him*? When did this happen?'

'It was agreed yesterday.' Alice spoke, looking down at the table, twisting the knife absently between her fingers. Sarah, seeing that the blood still flowed, silently removed the knife and bound Alice's fingers with the wet cloth.

Alice looked up at her. 'It has to be. He wants me. His position is safe at the mill, and it may be that I can get him to make Ella's job safe, too. It's the only way for us all to survive.'

'*No*, Alice.' Sarah felt tears well up. 'No, there *has* to be a better way. We'll manage, we always have. I'll—' She stopped, at a loss as to how to go on.

'You see?' Alice shrugged her shoulders. 'There is no choice. There's nothing else to be done. So many mouths to feed—' She gestured at the doorway. The younger ones had come silently through, leaving their play behind, aware of the change in the tone of the voices in the kitchen.

Alice stood up. 'Come and help me bring in the washing. The rain's on its way.' The children rushed ahead of her into the garden, fighting over who was to carry the wash basket. Sarah turned to look out of the window. Dark clouds had gathered and the first drops of rain struck the windows.

She stopped Alice as she made to follow the children outside. 'He's not Elisabeth's . . .' Sarah stopped, unable to bring herself to continue.

'Father? No!' Alice laughed bitterly, despite herself. 'Maybe it would have been better if he was.' She headed out into the gathering wind. 'It has to be,' she flung back over her shoulder. 'There's no other way.'

CHAPTER 3

Later that week, when Ella arrived home with Albert after the long mill day, Alice was delighted to see him. They found her out in the garden, tying up trailing rose stems blown loose in the recent stormy weather. Autumn's arrival this year had been heralded by days of blustery winds. Ella headed straight into the house, desperate to wash away the dust of the day, but Albert lingered.

'It's lovely to see you,' Alice said. 'You've been quite the stranger.'

Albert looked uncomfortable, staring down at the cap that he was twisting in his hands.

'How are things at the mill? What about your job? Is it safe?' Alice, sensing his unease, hoped that her prattle would relax him, draw him out.

'Is it true?' he blurted out.

'Is what true?' Alice stalled, playing for time, but her heart sank.

'That you're going to marry that – that man. *Williams*.' He all but spat out the name.

Alice flushed. 'Yes, it's true.'

'Ella told me. I couldn't believe it. I know what he did to you. How *could* you, Alice?'

Alice's heart was beating uncomfortably fast. 'I have to, Albert. It's the only way.'

Albert was staring at her. She found it hard to meet his eyes, and when she did, she saw that they were brimming with tears.

'Here, I've got this for you.' He thrust a folded piece of paper into her hand. 'I'll not be acting as a messenger boy for you any more, Alice Bancroft.' And with that he turned on his heel and headed back up the path.

'Albert!' Alice called after him, but he ignored her, shoulders hunched. She feared that he was crying.

She unfolded the note with trembling fingers. It could only be from one person, someone she had never expected to hear from again.

Ella was calling from the house. 'Alice, your food's on the table. Come and eat before it gets cold.'

Slowly Alice refolded the note and slipped it into her apron pocket. It would have to wait, although how she was going to hide the agitation it had caused her from her family, she couldn't begin to imagine. She needn't have worried. Hers wasn't a family to sit in quiet appreciation of their food, but one that talked to, at and over each other. When she entered the kitchen, Sarah already had her hands over her ears.

'Sssh!' She tried in vain to hush them all. 'You

mustn't talk with your mouth full!' She turned to Alice. 'Where's Albert? Will he not stay and eat with us? There's enough to share.'

'He had to go. His parents were expecting him.' The lie tripped off Alice's tongue and Ella gave her a hard look. Alice had a feeling that Albert had confided in Ella on their walk home.

'Did he tell you his news?' Ella said.

'No. He seemed in a bit of a hurry,' Alice said, truthfully.

'He's to be the new nightwatchman at the mill. It means he will have full-time work. He was so worried about how his mother and father would get by if he was put on short-time, and they had to manage on those wages.'

Alice squeezed in between Sarah and Thomas and began to spoon up her stew. But after a few mouthfuls she had to put the spoon down, her stomach churning with anxiety over the contents of the note, its presence like a red-hot ember burning in her pocket. Just as she was wondering whether she could make her excuses and leave the table, Ella leant across and said, 'Oh, Alice, there's some gossip going around the mill that might interest you.'

Alice, apprehensive at what she was about to hear, could only raise her eyebrows and look encouraging. Her mouth was too dry to speak.

'Well, your teacher friend, Master Richard, hasn't been seen around the mill since his wedding. We all thought he and that Miss Caroline had gone off on their honeymoon, but it seems not. Caroline has been up at the big house all this time, moping by all accounts, while Master Richard has been off on his father's business. Although now it seems this mysterious business might not have been at his father's request after all. Louisa overheard Mrs Weatherall having words with old Mr Weatherall about sending their son away straight after his wedding night, and on such a long trip. Mr Weatherall got all indignant and said Richard had volunteered to go, nay, insisted. Said it was vital for the mill that he went to Manchester and Leeds to look at the new machinery that the mills there were using. Now word's all round the mill that' – Ella lowered her voice and mouthed at Sarah and Alice – 'the marriage hasn't been – you know – properly er . . . er . . .' She seemed at a loss for a moment. 'Anyway, so that's why he went away. But he was back in the mill today. He didn't stay for long. He was up in the office and then we all saw him come striding out and he just left, looking very grim. Not like him at all. He's normally very polite to us girls. Now it's got some worrying that the news about the short-time is going to be even worse than we all thought.'

While Sarah's attention was distracted by Ella's tale, Alice had managed to surreptitiously offload most of her stew onto Thomas's plate. He was guaranteed to spoon it up without saying a word, quietly delighted at his luck. Alice was even more conscious of the note in her pocket. Her fingers itched to open it, her agitation rising as she tried to divine its contents by sheer force of will. Then, in an instant, her mood changed. She felt deflated. What possible difference could the note make?

'We've set a date.' She spoke, unheeding, not having been listening to any further conversation.

Ella and Sarah, who had moved on to more mundane matters of village news, both turned to look at her, momentarily uncomprehending.

'The wedding date. It's to be on Saturday afternoon. Just quiet. The church won't have us – because of Elisabeth.' Alice swallowed. 'So he's made other arrangements.'

Sarah looked aghast. 'Saturday! So soon?' She'd hoped for time to persuade Alice not to follow so hasty a course. 'Are you sure? But we must arrange—'

Alice cut in. 'There's nothing to arrange. It will be quiet, like I said. No reason – I mean, need – to celebrate. Just a ceremony.'

'But you must come back here! We can't let it go unmarked! A bride should—'

Alice interrupted Sarah again. 'He doesn't want it. We'll come back to get my things, and Elisabeth's. He's hired help to take them to his place.'

Sarah's thoughts flew to the dark cottage in the woods, glimpsed on her forays to find herbs. She'd always avoided it, not sure if it was the woodland setting, or what she knew of its occupant, that made her fearful. Now she shuddered to think of her daughter, and her precious granddaughter, hidden away behind its shuttered windows.

She started to cry. 'Well, if your mind is made up? You mustn't be a stranger to us here. We want to see you every day. We'll miss you so—' Sarah choked on her sobs and couldn't go on. Ella stared open-mouthed, and all the little ones around the table had fallen silent, unused to seeing Sarah in distress.

Alice threw herself into the business of distracting everyone. She chivvied the children into clearing their plates from the table, persuaded Sarah into the parlour with Ella for company, made her a hot drink with a nip of brandy for medicinal purposes, set Annie to the washing of the dishes, and entrusted the drying to Thomas and Beattie.

Then she shooed them upstairs, to wash hands and faces and get ready for bed. She piled them all into Sarah's bed for a bedtime story, at the end of which Elisabeth was fast asleep, cosy in her nest of children. Alice gently disentangled her and took her to her cot, soothing her brief protests as she felt the chillier air, tucked her in and patted her back to sleep. Alice returned to chase the others into their own beds, blowing out the lamps one by one, and by the time she headed downstairs to join Sarah and Ella, she'd all but forgotten about the note that had seemed so important such a short time ago.

It wasn't until Alice was back in her room,

preparing for bed, that the crackle of the paper in her pocket reminded her. In an instant, her legs felt shaky and she had to sit on the edge of the bed, unfolding the paper with trembling fingers. As she scanned the first few lines, her fingers flew to her mouth to stifle a gasp. She cast her eyes around in desperation. What time was it? She had no way of knowing up in her bedroom. She threw off her apron then, with a quick glance to make sure that Elisabeth slept soundly, she opened the door quietly and crept down the stairs, taking care to avoid making a sound. Pausing only to take a shawl and slip her feet into her boots, quickly lacing them, she unlatched the kitchen door.

It was a clear night, with enough moonlight for Alice to have no need of a lamp. Hastening down the path, she paused at the gate to lift her skirt clear of her boots then ran as fast as she could. Before long, she had to slow down, her breath catching in her chest in sobbing gasps. Pressing her hands into her side, where she could feel a stitch, she forced herself on.

Her mood this time as she approached the deer pool was very different to previous occasions. In her agitation, she paid much less heed to whether or not anyone saw her. Her passage from the main path to the deer pool itself found her stumbling and blundering into brambles, only dimly aware of the scratches to her face and arms.

Alice cast around desperately when she reached

the pool. Was that someone there, half hidden in the shadows against the rocks at the back of the pool?

'Richard?' she called, low and urgent. There was no response, no movement. She sank to her knees on the muddy ground, pressing her hands to her chest to still her pounding heart, and tried to breathe deeply and slowly to calm herself.

She had no idea of the time. In her haste, she'd forgotten to check the clock in the kitchen before she left. Perhaps she was too early and he hadn't got here yet? Perhaps he had been held up at the big house, finding it hard to slip away, waiting for sleep to envelop the house before he could make his escape. In her heart though, she feared he'd been here, waited, and gone. He'd said 'ten o'clock' in his note, but Alice suspected it might well have been that time before she'd read it, perhaps even later. Now it must be nearly eleven. Would he have waited an hour? Or might he still be on his way?

She looked around to see whether he had left any sign that he had been there. But then, why would he? If she didn't come, he would assume that she had nothing to say to him, that his marriage had put paid to their love, that her forth-coming marriage was to put the final seal on the whole hopeless affair. His note had said how desperately he missed Elisabeth, how he missed Alice so much that he had had to take himself far away from his new wife, for fear she would look into his eyes and see what was written in his soul. He'd said how he couldn't bear to think of her married to Williams, of Elisabeth growing up believing him to be her father. But if she was set on that course then he knew he could hardly blame her, although his whole being shrank from the very idea. His note had finished with the line, 'If you do not come, I will not presume to trouble you again but I will carry my love for you with me wherever I go.'

Alice had brought the note with her, and she scanned it over and over again in the dim light, until the words were seared into her brain. She rose from the mud and sought out a more comfortable spot to wait out the night. Surely Richard would come? Surely she hadn't missed her chance of seeing him? For a brief moment, she imagined herself going to the big house, ringing the bell and banging on the door, begging for admittance, making everything come right. She could see it clearly: the forbidding grey-stone wall, the barred gate, the cobbled courtyard leading to the imposing front door. Even if she got that far, stood on the flagged steps and raised her hand to pull the bell cord, waited for the sound to die away inside, for measured footsteps to cross the polished floor, hands to slide the bolt; even then, already placed at a disadvantage because the door stood yet one step higher, she would have to meet the disapproving gaze of the housemaid, falter out her request to see 'Master Richard'.

All nonsense, of course. She could never put herself in such a position. Her rightful place would be down the steps to the side of the building, stone steps worn smooth by the passage of many feet, leading down to the basement kitchen. It was an area that never saw the sun, the air cold whatever the time of year, the grey stones green and slimy with damp. This was not the door at which to enquire for Master Richard either. Alice knew her place.

The first dawn light was breaking through on the horizon when Alice rose stiffly to her feet, hugging her arms about her body, trying to rub some warmth and feeling back into them. She feared Elisabeth would wake before long and she couldn't risk staying a moment longer. Her thoughts during her vigil had taken a desperate turn, and she faced the new day with a very heavy heart. She knew what she must do and it brought her no small amount of fear. Moving slowly at first, until her circulation was working properly again, she left the deer pool and headed for home, her footprints and a discarded, crumpled piece of paper the only sign of her presence.

CHAPTER 4

She'd made it back home before Elisabeth had woken, and had slipped into her own bed, hopeful of an hour or so of sleep before the day began in earnest. Elisabeth had been kind in that respect, but Alice's mind had refused to let her rest. Every time she closed her eyes, images of Williams flashed in front of her: Williams at the mill, his eyes following her wherever she went; Williams's harsh words when she had suggested that her family might provide a wedding breakfast to celebrate their day; Williams taking Elisabeth from her, muttering that she was using her to hide behind; Elisabeth wailing at his rough handling, a brief flash of rage crossing his face before he'd handed her back with bad grace. She tried to push the images away, and relax into much-needed sleep, but it was no good. Were these the thoughts that should be filling the mind of a woman about to be married?

Had some madness overtaken her? What folly was it that had made Williams seem like a saviour? Alice recognised that exhaustion meant that she wasn't thinking straight after her deer-pool vigil, but she began to wonder whether she wasn't, in fact, thinking more sensibly now than she had done for a while. Just because Williams wanted her didn't mean he would be a good husband. True, he had a more secure job than the other mill workers but Alice didn't see him being prepared to share this good fortune with her family. Quite the opposite, in fact. He'd shown worrying signs of intending to keep her from everyone after they were married, making it clear that he expected her to devote herself to the care of the house while he was at work, 'not going gallivanting off to see that mother of yours at the drop of a hat'. He didn't plan to involve her family in any celebration of their wedding, and told her he wanted her out of Sarah's house straight away. The power balance had shifted the minute she'd agreed, nay, proposed to marry him. She could see that now. Even though they were not yet wed, his behaviour towards her had reverted to the way it had been in the mill days. He saw her as his possession. He hadn't tried to force her, mainly because she took pains to keep him at arm's length, but the change in his demeanour was marked.

Somehow, she'd got through the long hours until the mill day was done. Then she'd left Elisabeth with Sarah with the briefest of explanations, although she'd felt sure her face had given far more away than she'd said. It hadn't been difficult to find Williams: she knew his routes and his timings thoroughly by now.

Even through the gathering dusk she'd seen his face lift when he'd seen her. She'd felt a pang then, a worry that she'd misjudged him, but she couldn't let it affect her resolution. She'd told him, as bluntly as when she'd suggested that they should marry. She'd apologised for making a terrible mistake, and told him she was sorry.

He hadn't expected it, but was quick to counter: 'So, you've heard that your Richard is back, have you? Think you can do better than me now? That you can go calling at the big house and take him away from his lovely new wife, do you?'

He took a step forward and Alice backed away, heart beating fast. 'There's nowt there for the likes of you and your bastard. You're lucky I'm even prepared to take her on. There's many a man that wouldn't.'

Alice, stung, could hold her counsel no longer. 'Richard's a better man than you. At least he loves me. And his daughter.' She hesitated, as Williams's brows knitted and his expression became grim. She hadn't intended to say a word about Richard.

'Have it your own way, Alice Bancroft. You'll live to regret it, see if you don't.'

And with that he turned on his heel and headed up the track towards home. The home that would have been his and Alice's and Elisabeth's in a few days' time.

Alice stood and watched him go, then turned slowly homewards herself. He hadn't raged at her, or even struck her, both of which she'd half expected. His threat didn't worry her. The words were those which people flung at each other in anger, to mask hurt pride. In fact, in many respects, she told herself, she'd got off lightly. It was done, and she tried hard to feel relieved.

CHAPTER 5

As Richard let himself out of the side gate, Lucy at his side, he reflected on how different his mood was to that of just a few weeks ago. He'd purposely not asked Caroline to accompany him, ignoring as best he could her hurt look when he said, 'I'll just take Lucy out. I won't be gone long.' Noticing his mother open her mouth to speak, he made a fuss of shooing Lucy from the room, to create a diversion, and slipped through the sitting-room door before anyone had prevailed upon his better nature. He desperately needed some time to himself, to try to work out how to manage the situation. He'd married someone he no longer loved – perhaps never had – to please his family, and in so doing he'd lost not only his one true love, but their daughter too. He'd waited as long as he dared for Alice at the deer pool, but she hadn't come, which meant she wanted nothing more to do with him. She'd be married within the week and there was absolutely nothing he could do about it. He didn't deserve her. He'd been spineless to give in to family and propriety and to marry Caroline. Spineless . . .

Richard realised that he'd spoken aloud; Lucy, by his side, looked up at him, head cocked enquiringly. Richard groaned, and bent to fondle her ears. 'Oh Lucy, what's to be done? How am I to free myself from this situation?' As he straightened up, a glow amongst the trees below caught his eye. Puzzled, he strained to see where it might be coming from. Had someone lit a fire down on the bank of the stream? It seemed unlikely. Poachers were the only ones likely to be out and about of an evening, and they would never risk drawing attention to themselves. Richard's heart lurched as the increasing glow now identified itself as flickering, leaping flames. The light they cast offered the briefest glimpse of a tall chimney, throwing the brickwork into relief. *The fire was at the mill.*

In desperation, Richard cast around for one of the tracks that he knew led downwards off this path; the steep trails that the mill workers used as shortcuts every day. The packhorse steps must be close by – he broke into a run, and at first Lucy bounded along beside him, made joyful by this new game. But she must have begun to sense something was amiss. When he reached the path that he sought and turned sharply to begin a headlong descent, she hesitated, barking a couple of times, torn between keeping him faithful company or turning back. She chose the former, but within the half-hour she was scrabbling back up the path, whimpering, tail and ears down as she headed for home, alone.

PART VII

CHAPTER 1

Alys had been so excited when Hannah's email arrived to say that she and Matt were back from their travels. They were thinking of heading back to Oz to work for a while, but first they were catching up with family and friends. Hannah was travelling up to see her parents in Durham, but she wanted to know if she could come back via Yorkshire and stay with Alys?

She'd arrived at the end of September, looking tanned and fit and full of stories of amazing temples in Thailand and Cambodia, river trips and hangovers in Laos, volunteering at a Vietnamese school, guarding turtle hatchlings in Malaysia. The world had shrunk in Hannah's hands, hundreds of thousands of miles reduced to an admittedly wonderful collection of photographs and clearly fantastic memories. Alys had listened intently, asked questions, determinedly tried to follow the route in her head, although painfully aware that her geographical knowledge was being tested to its limit. At the end of it all, it was clear that Hannah and Matt had had a fabulous time, but it was hard to experience something like that at a distance. The saying 'you had to be there' seemed to apply: it felt no more real to Alys than London currently did.

Maybe it was because she was so busy setting up the new café? Her mind never seemed to be fully engaged with anything else, and she felt very guilty that she could give Hannah so little of her time when she'd been away so long and come especially to visit her.

'Don't worry,' Hannah told her with a laugh. 'I'm going to enjoy exploring the area. You've been pretty bad at keeping in touch since you've been here. I'm keen to see what's kept you so busy.'

Alys and Hannah were camping out in the flat above the new Nortonstall café. It had basic furniture in place, and Moira felt that it would give them more privacy to catch up in a relaxed way than if Hannah had stayed with them in Northwaite. So, while Alys dealt with builders, plumbers and decorators, Hannah took herself off on walks around Nortonstall. Her travels had made her curious and chatty and each day brought her back with tales of where she'd been and who she'd met. Perhaps because these adventures were happening in a landscape that Alys loved and could identify with, she found them far more fascinating than Hannah's more exotic travels. And Hannah had brought an Indian summer with her.

'You must have packed some sunshine in your

rucksack when you left Thailand,' Alys marvelled as day after glorious day unfolded. By the week-end, with the weather still holding good and Flo away on her own holiday, Moira was begging for extra help in the Northwaite café. 'With all this amazing sunshine, I think we're going to be much busier than usual,' she said. 'Is there any chance you could help out?'

Alys had been looking forward to spending a full day with Hannah and had already made plans for what they might do. She tried hard to hide her disappointment. 'I'd be glad to,' she said, 'but I feel bad about Hannah. I've only been able to spend evenings with her so far. I'd planned to do something with her on Saturday before she has to head back to London on Sunday.'

'Leave it with me,' Moira said. 'I'll see if I can sort something out.'

Alys understood her to mean she'd find someone else to help out in the café, and thought no more about it. Until Saturday morning found Rob and the Land Rover waiting outside the Nortonstall café.

'Rob!' Alys was startled to find him there when she came down from the flat to check whether a delivery of tiles had arrived. She hadn't seen him for the best part of a month. And, she realised with a shock, she'd been too busy to notice. With so many things to organise at the new premises, she'd hardly been back to Northwaite for the last few weeks.

'Hello stranger,' Rob said, beaming at her. He looked tanned and fit, Alys noticed. She experienced a sudden rush of feeling. Was it affection? Friendship? Or something a bit more than that?

'I heard how busy you'd been here,' Rob continued. 'It will be nice to have you back in Northwaite again.' He paused, registering Alys's surprise.

'Didn't Moira tell you? She's sent me to collect you. While you help out in the café I'm going to show Hannah the sights of Northwaite – well, a bit further afield, more like. Then we'll all eat together this evening.'

'Oh.' Alys was nonplussed. 'Oh. Okay, hold on, I need to talk to Hannah.'

By the time Alys had climbed the stairs back up to the flat she was feeling decidedly grumpy. It seemed really unfair on Hannah – it was her last full day and they'd planned to spend time catching up, discussing Hannah's plans for the future.

Hannah, however, wasn't at all put out. 'It's great that you're busy and doing so well,' she said. 'And it's really good of Moira to arrange a trip out for me.' She pulled her T-shirt over her head then ran her fingers through her hair as she peered out of the window. 'Ooh, is that my chauffeur, down there by the Land Rover? I think I'm going to enjoy my day!'

Alys, shoving a few things into her rucksack to take to the café, snorted. 'You'll probably get a tour of the best farmland for miles around. But

Rob's done some travelling – spent some time in Oz. You'll have some things in common.'

Hannah registered the tone of Alys's voice and paused as they were about to lock up and head down the stairs. 'All work and no play and all that, Alys,' she said, looking her friend squarely in the eye. 'You're taking life too seriously at the moment. I know you're busy, but you need to organise some time off. It's a shame you can't come along today, too.'

Alys sighed. 'Let me get the café opening out of the way. Things are just a bit too manic at the moment to take a break. Come on, let's get going or else it will be mayhem over in Northwaite.'

Rob gave a start when both girls arrived beside him on the pavement. 'Look at you, you could be sisters,' he said.

Hannah and Alys turned to stare at each other. Alys was pale, any vestige of a tan long since gone due to spending so much time inside, her reddish-blonde hair springing out wildly around her face as usual. Hannah's tan was deep from months of travelling, and her hair, less wild than Alys's but still curly, was dark brown. They both frowned, then burst out laughing. 'It's true, people have said it before but we can never see it,' Alys said. 'Rob, this is Hannah. Hannah – your guide for today – Rob.'

Alys wedged herself into the back of the Land Rover so that Hannah could sit in the front. As she listened to Rob and Hannah chat on the short journey, she reflected that their conversation flowed much more easily than the first time that she'd met Rob. She felt a pang of envy. They were going to have a good day today.

CHAPTER 2

With a sigh of relief, Alys turned the sign on the café door to read 'Closed'. Moira had finished wiping counters and was heading outside to fold up tables and chairs. Late afternoon sunshine still warmed a corner of the courtyard. 'Let's just enjoy the sun for a few minutes before we finish clearing up,' Alys pleaded. 'We've been stuck indoors all day.'

'If I sit down, I'll never get up again.' Moira was poised, cloth in hand, ready to wipe over the outdoor tablecloths. Then she stopped. 'Well, you're right, we need to wait for Rob and Hannah. You make some tea. I'll see what we've got left in the way of cake.'

Half an hour later, when Rob and Hannah made their way through to the courtyard, they found Moira and Alys stretched out in their chairs, eyes closed and heads back against the wall, soaking up the sun's rays in total silence. Empty teacups and plates of crumbs testified to time well spent. 'Sorry we're late,' said Hannah, biting her lip. 'We had such a great day out we lost track of time. It took longer to get back than we thought.'

Moira stretched and yawned, then smiled up at Hannah. 'Where did you go?' she asked.

'Some amazing reservoirs,' said Hannah. 'There were three of them, in a kind of chain along the valley, in the middle of this really unspoilt countryside. We barely saw a soul – it felt like we were the only people left alive on earth! We walked for miles.'

Alys shaded her eyes from the dying rays of the sun. Once again, she experienced a sudden stab of envy. She'd been stuck in a hot café all day, dishing out smiles along with cups of tea and coffee and slices of cake, while Hannah had been out in the fresh air, striding across some of the most glorious countryside around. Which was what her friend had spent most of the past year doing, on her travels. And she was clearly getting on *very* well with Rob. She wondered what Matt would think.

As if reading her mind, Hannah said, 'I took some photos while we were up there and sent them to Matt. To prove you don't have to travel half way around the world to see amazing landscapes.'

Moira stood up and started to fold up the remaining chairs. 'You've been so lucky with the weather, Hannah. It really is spectacular here when the sun shines. It's a real bonus that it's still so lovely this late in the year.'

Alys became aware that Rob's eyes were fixed on her. 'You're very quiet,' he remarked.

Hannah glanced sharply at Alys. 'You're looking

tired. Are you okay?' She turned to Rob, 'I've been telling her she needs a holiday.'

Moira joined in. 'You're right. We're both tired. It's been a busy day today, with this glorious weather. We're not open tomorrow, though. It's the start of our Sunday closing for the autumn – the walkers will have to manage without us for a change. We can both have a rest. And tonight, there's a barbecue at the pub, so we don't have to cook, either!'

Alys tried hard to shake off the return of her grumpy mood. Hannah was her best friend, she hadn't seen her in well over a year and this was their last evening together. She'd no idea where this sudden jealousy had sprung from but it was time she put it back firmly in its box, before it ruined the evening ahead.

'You're right, I do need a break,' she said. She noticed her aunt's worried glance. 'But it's not going to happen for a while – maybe once we've got the new place up and running. Now, tell me more about today.' And she linked arms with Hannah as they all made their way out of the café and up the road to The Old Bell.

It wasn't until much later that evening, as Hannah and Alys headed back to Nortonstall, sleepy in the back of their minicab, that Alys acknowledged to herself that she wasn't just feeling jealous of Hannah because of her travels and lifestyle. It was the evident fascination she had for Rob that she found so galling. During that evening, she'd noticed the ease with which Hannah related to Rob, the way they laughed and joked as if they'd known each other for years. Alys had found herself growing more stiffly formal by the minute, contrasting herself unfavourably with Hannah, so-called sisters or not. The green-eyed monster had climbed back out of his box, but Alys really hoped she'd kept him on a leash so tight that no one there would have suspected. She'd had to move away and chat to another group, huddled under the warm arc of the patio heater as the temperature cooled rapidly under clear late-September skies. At one point, as her eyes strayed back to Rob and Hannah, now convulsed over some shared joke, she'd been aware of a pair of eyes on her, and had turned to catch Moira watching her with a quizzical expression on her face. Embarrassed, she'd felt her face flush and had moved away from the heater, suggesting to Hannah that it was time they made a move.

'You dark horse, you,' Hannah murmured sleepily in the back of the cab. 'No wonder you kept Rob all to yourself. He's gorgeous.'

'What do you mean?' Alys glanced nervously at their cab driver to see if he was listening. Locals loved a bit of juicy gossip.

'Like I said, he's lovely. And obviously smitten with you. He spent most of the time we were out asking me all about you. Lucky that I'm settled with Matt or I might have been rather put out that he wasn't attracted by my overwhelming charm.' She giggled. 'Anyway, fight you for him if anything goes wrong between me and Matt.'

'I don't know what you're talking about.' Alys was very confused. 'I've hardly seen Rob over the past month, since I've been in Nortonstall. And before that, well, he used to come into the café for coffee, and we went out one evening with his friends . . .' She tailed off.

'Well, he's certainly been thinking about you! He said he first knew something was up when he lost his dog and found a water nymph, and then it all crystallised when he discovered the joy of eating cake for breakfast. I've no idea what he was on about.' Hannah chuckled. 'I think he must spend too much time alone in the fields.'

Alys was silent for the rest of the short journey back, but Hannah didn't notice: she'd slipped into a deep sleep and had to be shaken awake when they pulled up outside the door to the flat.

CHAPTER 3

The fire in the open hearth glowed brightly, warming the room while the wind whistled and howled around Moira's cottage. October this year was going out in a stormy blast: the dry leaves swirling around outside sounded like flowing water. The weather forecast had warned of impending snowstorms, the forecaster marvelling over how early snow was blowing in this year. Arctic winds had battered Northwaite all day and Alys was glad to be cosied up in the sitting room, hands cupping a mug of tea. She thought of Moira, who'd braved the elements and taken the evening bus to Nortonstall. She'd been making the trip increasingly often of late – ever since she'd been to that jazz evening back in August. Alys hadn't gone beyond some gentle teasing about what she might be finding so interesting in town these days; she would be only too delighted for her aunt should there be some romance in the air. 'I wish I had a car,' Alys had said. 'I could give you a lift there and back. Save you waiting for buses and paying for cabs.'

'Not to worry,' Moira had replied. 'I've been

thinking about staying over when I go out in Nortonstall and coming back in the morning in time to open up the café.' She blushed when Alys couldn't hide her startled expression and added hastily, 'I mean, when you've properly moved into the flat over the café in Nortonstall. I can stay in the spare room there and catch the first bus back home the next morning.'

Alys hadn't been wholly convinced by this explanation, but didn't enquire further. She started to think about how her own life was unfolding. It felt like a new

Chapter was about to begin. The café in Nortonstall was coming along nicely. Moira had given Alys free rein on the décor, fittings and china. At first, Alys had planned to turn it into a replica of the Northwaite café and had begun to hunt for vintage china so that she could have a stock of it ready and waiting. But before she'd bought more than four or five pieces, she'd had a change of heart. She'd thought about it a while, then plucked up the courage to discuss it with Moira. To her surprise, Moira hadn't been at all put out at the idea of giving the new place a different feel. So, it was now decorated in the Northwaite café's signature shade of grey, but the vintage styling had gone into the heavy-framed mirrors and the ceramic lampshades, which were hung in clusters on wires of varying lengths. Lloyd loom wicker chairs, painted in muted shades of grey, blue and green were dressed with comfy cushions in art-print linens patterned with stylised fruit, flowers and birds. The china was sturdier this time – she'd fallen in love with a hand-thrown range produced by a potter in Nortonstall and had brokered a discount for a range of jugs, plates, mugs and bowls, in return for a credit on the menu and a display of items for sale inside the café. They'd even gone for a different name: 'The Cake Company Café' was emblazoned across the fascia. Without the angel's wings, it had seemed pointless including 'celestial' in the name, and the look of the place was so different that it made perfect sense. One thing that hadn't changed was the range of cakes – Moira and Alys had agreed that the two cafés should offer exactly the same, at least for the present.

So Alys had good reason to feel a sense of satisfaction while she sat by the fire, cocooned from the storm, and contemplated the future. The Nortonstall café had been fitted out in record time, and she was about to concentrate on the flat above, so that she could move in properly and she and Moira could lead their own lives once more. Tonight, though, she was increasingly bothered by her failure to put what Rob used to refer to as her 'Alice mystery' to bed. She was ready to move on to the next stage of her life, but she'd left Alice somehow stranded, exactly where she'd been since the end of August.

Following Julie's advice, she had done another trawl of the newspaper archives and traced one further report relating to the fire. She'd been amazed to see it prefaced with a photograph, the only one that she had ever seen of her great-great-grandmother. Smudged and grainy, it was hard to make very much of it, other than an impression of dark clothing and wavy hair that had pulled free of its confines to frame a pale face seemingly wiped of expression by the camera's flash. Alys had unconsciously twisted her own hair, also springing free from its clips, as she read:

'It has been reported that Alice Bancroft, of Lane End Cottage, Northwaite, has died in the local jail at Northwaite, pending transfer to Leeds Assizes on the charge of setting fire to Hobbs Mill, Northwaite, on the night of 22 September 1895. The fire led to the death of Mr Richard Weatherall, son of mill owner Mr James Weatherall. The death of the accused has been attributed to natural causes: her mother Sarah Bancroft has spoken of a heart condition that had been exacerbated by her recent confinement. The trial will not now take place as all parties concerned consider the matter settled.'

It felt to Alys as though an icy hand had clutched at her heart when she read of Alice's death in prison, in such cruel circumstances. She didn't fully understand the implication of the report, either. Did they mean confinement as in imprisonment, or pregnancy? There was no mention of

357

baby Elisabeth – and if the matter was considered settled, then they clearly saw her as guilty . . .

She couldn't understand why she felt so determined to pursue the matter. Shouldn't she just accept the fact, as the rest of the family seemed to have done over the years, that her great-great-grandmother had been a murderess, and an arsonist to boot, and try to forget about it? She'd tried to reassure herself that it was quite common for families to have skeletons in all sorts of closets that their elderly or long-dead relatives had thought were safely locked away. Yet something within her refused to let it rest. She didn't know why she was so convinced that there was something more to the story, that Alice was innocent and had been harshly judged. She wished that she had the ability to look back into the past and discover the truth. For now, though, it seemed that she had exhausted all the possible avenues to explore.

Alys gazed into the fire, her eyes growing heavy as she relaxed in the warmth. She had the delicious sensation of slipping in and out of sleep, hearing the stormy blasts outside from an ever-increasing distance. The howling of the elements diminished, replaced instead by a melodic humming, with words fading in and out of an unfamiliar and indistinct melody. It was soothing, and Alys was enjoying the sensation.

A part of her knew that she must have fallen asleep, because she was having a dream. A young woman was sitting in a hard, wooden chair by an open fire, stitching and singing to herself as she did so. Her head was bent over her work and Alys could see the gleam of her reddish-brown curls in the firelight. She was absorbed in her sewing, working around the top of a small, plain, cream bag. As Alys watched, the woman stopped stitching and sat back, staring with unseeing eyes into the fire. Alys had the strangest sensation of actually being there, sitting on the other side of the hearth from the woman, so close that she could have reached out to lay a hand on her arm, but she could neither move nor speak. She wanted to turn her head and look around the room, to reassure herself of its familiarity, of her place within it, but she felt paralysed.

The woman shook her head a little, as if to free herself of her reverie, then turned her attention back to her needlework. She turned the work through and Alys saw that, far from being plain, it had a sprig of lavender embroidered on the right side, in tiny stitches of emerald and lilac thread. The woman put her hand in her apron pocket, and at that moment Alys recognised something that her brain had only half acknowledged. The woman's clothing was of a totally different era. She was wearing a long, full skirt of some rough cloth, partly covered by an apron tied around her waist, and a long-sleeved blouse, all in muddy, indeterminate colours. A pair of leather boots peeped from beneath the skirt and when she stood up and moved closer to the fire, Alys could see that they were well worn and patched. The woman stood a moment, hand resting on the mantelpiece, looking at some scraps of paper she had taken from her pocket. She hesitated, made as if to throw them in the fire, then appeared to change her mind. She took up her work, and her seat, again. Alys watched as she folded the scraps of paper, so nearly discarded, into squares.

The scene in front of Alys started to dissolve and fade, and as it did, she discovered she could reach out to the woman, that she had been released from her spell. The woman looked up, as if startled, and a second later Alys realised that she was awake, in her chair by the fire in Moira's sitting room, and alone. The logs still glowed brightly, although there was such a chill in the air it felt as if the room wasn't heated at all.

Alys sat for a minute or two, gathering her senses, trying to work out what was wrong. The room was freezing, despite the fire, and the source of the chill was elsewhere. She stood up, finding her legs unaccountably stiff, and went into the hall. The front door was wide open. Swirls of leaves had blown in on the stone flags and, if she wasn't mistaken, a few flakes of snow were melting there too. Wondering how on earth it could have blown open, Alys hastily closed the door, making sure the latch clicked.

She heard a window banging upstairs, presumably blown ajar by the door-opening gust as it swept through the house. Pausing only to snap on the light, she headed up the stairs. The chill of the upstairs rooms was even more marked. She closed the curtains in her bedroom to block out the rattling of the windows in the gale, then stripped the patchwork quilt from her bed as she turned to leave, welcoming the thought of wrapping herself in it until the sitting room warmed up again. Folding it over her arm, she stroked the folds absently, marvelling at the precise, tiny hand-stitches holding the patches together. A thought struck her. Those neat stitches, that little bag that the woman had been sewing – where had she seen it all before?

Still struggling with the strangeness of the last half-hour, Alys stood and pondered, half expecting to find the woman seated by the fire when she returned downstairs. But now she had remembered where she had seen her handiwork. She retrieved the battered wooden box from under the bed, where she had stowed it away from Kate's all-seeing eyes all those weeks before, and hurried back downstairs, filled with nervous anticipation.

She raised the lid, taking the leather-bound herbal from its resting place, then lifted the draw-string bag, embroidered with a sprig of lavender, from where it lay beneath the ledger. As she did so, she felt something hard inside the bag. She pulled at the string that drew the top together, and upended the bag over her free hand. A brooch tumbled out – an enamelled depiction of a sprig of lavender bound with a cream ribbon. Pretty enough, although the enamel was cracked and crazed with age.

Alys turned the simple piece of jewellery over in her fingers, as if looking for clues. Finding none, she stowed the brooch back in the pouch – and at that moment, her eyes were caught by something that had dropped unnoticed onto her lap from the bag. It was a photograph, tiny and oval, clearly cut down to fit a locket. The portrait was sepia tinted and faded, and showed the sensitive features of a young man with floppy hair, staring, unsmiling, straight at the camera. Alys turned it over, hoping for clues. On the back it had a single initial: 'R'.

'R'? Alys thought rapidly. 'R? Who could it be?'

She was about to return the bag and its contents back to the box, when a sudden thought made her stop. She shook the bag over her hand again. Nothing. She peered inside the narrow opening. Still nothing. Then, handling the fragile fabric very carefully, she turned the bag inside out. Again, there was nothing to be seen: just smooth, cream fabric, so soft it felt like a scrap of silk. Alys looked to see the back of the stitches – somewhere in the back of her mind she held a notion about the needlework skills of the past, about stitches so neat that the front and back would be virtually indistinguishable. But there was nothing to be seen. The bag was lined.

Disappointed and about to give up, she spotted a small opening at the top, where the lining joined the bag. Once, it had been sewn with tiny, almost invisible stitches, but the thread had perished and frayed with time. She teased the stitches further apart, feeling guilty for destroying the workmanship, then managed to push her thumb and forefinger into the gap. She felt the edge of a piece of paper.

Holding her breath, Alys carefully grasped the edge of the paper. Her fingers felt very big and clumsy in such a confined space – she was nervous of tearing the paper as she tugged. It must have been here for some time and she feared it would be brittle and fragile. She thought a moment, then went to the bathroom and retrieved her eyebrow tweezers. Inserting them carefully into the gap, she took a firm grip on the paper and pulled.

The tweezers held several scraps of paper. These were creased where they had been folded, and the handwriting was the same on each one. The words were sparse. 'Sunday 3 p.m.?' appeared on more than one. Just one read 'Deer pool, tonight 10 p.m.' The final one that Alys looked at had a few more words, squeezed onto the scrap in tiny writing. 'Caroline wanted to walk with me. So very sorry. Must talk. R.'

Alys smoothed out the scraps and spread them around her. She frowned. Whatever could they mean? There were six of them in all. Five seemed to be setting up some sort of a meeting, but the scraps held no clue as to day or date, and only one suggested a place. The sixth was the note of contrition, with that initial again, R. And a mention of Caroline. Who was she?

The wind was gusting even more loudly and Alys started to shiver. It was getting late, but her head was full of such jumbled thoughts that there was no prospect of sleep. She got up, put another log on the fire and made herself some tea. Picking up a pen and paper, she settled herself as close to the heat as possible and started to make a list. She needed to spell out what she knew, because currently it was just a tangle of thoughts in her head.

An hour later she had too many questions – and no way that she could see of answering them all. But she had remembered a possible 'R': Richard Weatherall, the son of the mill owner, the man who had died in the fire, the one Alice was accused of killing. If he was the mysterious 'R', the notes seemed to imply that Alice had been seeing him at some point – but hadn't the newspaper report about the fire mentioned that he was married?

With a start, Alys realised that it was 2 a.m. There was no sign of Moira, which was a bit of a worry considering the weather. Fierce gusts of wind were still rattling the windows. 'It's as if someone is trying to get in,' Alys thought uneasily. She needed to get to bed so she could be up in time to bake before opening up the Northwaite café tomorrow, and then to head over to Nortonstall once Moira had reappeared. But she feared it would be a restless night, and not only because of the gale blowing outside.

PART VIII

CHAPTER 1

It was cold. Bitter, damp, bone-chillingly cold. The darkness was unfathomable. They'd given Alice a candle, out of pity, but it was a poor stump of a thing and it had gone out long ago. Alice's cheeks burnt with shame and indignation. She didn't deserve to be here, crouched in the filth in the tiny village lock-up, a rat-infested basement beneath old Smithson's cottage. She tried to drag her thoughts away from the night's events: the horror of the mill on fire, great tongues of flame leaping up into the night sky, the heat driving back everyone who'd rushed to help, labouring to douse the flames with water from the stream. Her throat felt raw from the smoke. She could still smell it in her hair, on her clothes.

Cautiously, she edged her toe forward, probing to locate the basket that lay somewhere on the floor. This was her evidence, her best hope. This was her proof that she'd been doing as she said, gathering herbs for her mother, looking for the skullcap that needed to be picked by moonlight before it was added to the pot, to effect the most potent brew. Her mother would be frantic, wondering where Alice had got to. She'd have seen the glow of the flames lighting up the sky, heard the commotion as people rushed up and down the road, trying to muster help, find buckets or anything that could be used to collect water to quench the fire that was devouring their livelihood. She'd have been soothing Elisabeth, made fretful by Sarah's agitation. The water would have already been on the boil, everything ready for Alice to return with the precious herbs.

Now Sarah would be standing anxiously at the garden gate in the dark, asking anyone who was passing by if they'd seen her daughter, waiting and waiting as the numbers of people returning from the fire became fewer and fewer, until the number dwindled to none. She wouldn't know that Alice, who had been an early arrival on the scene once she'd recognised the fire for what it was, had been pointed out to the local constable by a smoke-blackened figure, wild-eyed and with a cruel twist to his mouth. She wasn't there to see her bewildered daughter seized roughly and thrown into the back of a cart along with her basket. She didn't hear her try to protest, or witness her struggle as her hands were bound roughly with rope and she was pushed into the bottom of the cart with a coarse blanket thrown over her.

'Stay quiet, missie.' The voice had been rough, angry. 'You've caused enough trouble for one night. It's lucky that Williams spotted you before you could scarper.'

CHAPTER 2

Each breath seemed like a cruel one. Each moment of waking, bringing with it the momentary belief that all was normal, a confidence trick. Alice wondered why her heart kept beating, forcing her body to carry on this charade of living.

Richard was dead. Rawson, her jailer, had delivered the news bluntly, unaware of its devastating effect on Alice. He took her silence to be despair over the failure of her murderous plan. Williams lived, rescued from the mill flames by Albert while Richard, who'd been out 'walking his dog,' as Rawson said, had perished.

Alice shut down completely then, all fight gone, huddled into the corner of her cell, refusing all food. She didn't know the manner of Richard's death but, in her imagination, she saw him passing along the route he once would have taken to meet her. She saw his silhouetted figure striding along the moonlit path, Lucy trotting at his side, imagined him stopping, puzzled, as he saw the glow of the fire at the mill down below in the valley. Perhaps at that point it was in its early stages? Just a flicker of flame every now and then, seen and then gone, leaving Richard to wonder whether it was real or imagined. Then he would have realised, and started to run along the path to where it forked down to the mill, skidding on loose stones, Lucy joyful, bounding at his side, enjoying the game, then picking up the scent of smoke on the wind, sensing Richard's agitation, starting to whimper even as she ran. They would have struggled to keep their footing at speed in the dark down the path, Richard's face whipped by low branches he couldn't avoid, having to slow for the steps hewn out of the rocks, ever closer but now seeing the flames leaping higher, roaring as they were fed by the cotton, fanned by the evening breeze. What hope had one man, even two or three, of extinguishing the fire consuming the whole building? Had they even tried – or had they stood there, helpless, watching the catastrophe unfold before them? Had Albert raised the alarm? Had Williams run back and forth from the river with buckets, in a fruitless attempt to throw water over the flames until help arrived from the village? Had Richard tried to get into the office, to retrieve papers – a senseless risk that he thought his father would expect of him? Had Lucy turned tail and fled back up the path alone, arriving back at the big house shaking, traumatised, paws torn, just as word arrived there of the unfolding disaster? Was it at this moment that Alice had paused in her herb collecting and looked up, scenting smoke and seeing a distant glow?

Her head was a fog of grief from which she barely surfaced, day drifting into night and back into day as she trod and re-trod the paths of the life she'd once planned with Richard, her daydreams of a cottage somewhere nearby, children playing in the garden, he a music master, she a herbalist like her mother and grandmother before her, living a poor life but a happy one. Dreams long ago turned to ashes, and leaving what in their place?

Alice could find nothing to lift her from her despair, nothing to bring any glimmer of hope for the future. Sarah begged and begged to be allowed to see her daughter, to bring her some comfort, some news of baby Elisabeth, to bring her a bottle of the heart tonic that she needed to take every day. Rawson was firm, though it grieved him, as he had known Sarah all his life. Mr Weatherall held more than a little sway with the local magistrate, and word had been sent: 'No visitors for Alice Bancroft. No news, nothing from the outside. Solitary confinement until the trial.'

It was perhaps as well that Alice did not know of the growing mutterings against her and her family in the village. With the mill gone, many of the local people found themselves unemployed. The more able-bodied trudged the extra miles to mills further up the valley, in desperate search of a few hours' work here and there. The less able were left with time on their hands, no income, and a growing sense of anger towards Alice, presumed to be the perpetrator of this deed, and the cause of their misfortune. James Weatherall was grief-stricken at the death of his firstborn and, rumour had it – once again carried by Louisa the scullery maid – that he had no plans to rebuild the mill, but would sell the land and leave the area.

Alice seemed unaware of raised voices outside the lock-up, of demands to: 'Let us in. If it's justice you're wanting, we can sort that out. Yon lass must have visited wi' the Devil to do such things.' The lock-up door was sturdy oak, studded and barred, and remained firmly shut in their faces, until the crowd left, muttering, spoiling for trouble. They headed for the inn to further fuel their discontent with ale, wasting what little money they had on the impotent arguments of befuddled brains.

CHAPTER 3

'I hope you have known kindness.' Alice thought back to her mother's words as she huddled in the cold, dank cell. Indeed, she had. She had known cruelty too, but she had mentioned nothing of this to Richard. Nothing of the humiliating tussles that took place when Williams lay in wait for her as she left work, or cornered her in some storeroom, where he had sent her on some pretext or another, right in the middle of the working day.

She had told Richard none of this because she hoped the fact of his existence would help her erase it from her mind. That first night as she had made her way home from the deer pool, part of her in a desperate hurry because she feared that she had lost track of time; and part of her lost, suffused in a glow that both energised her and reduced her to inertia, it was then that she had thought that there might be some happiness to look forward to in her life.

Richard's marriage had almost done for her. She hadn't known it was possible to feel such pain. Such confusion, such abandonment. Amidst this madness, she still didn't know why she had thought it a sensible plan to marry Williams. A belief that he was the one man in the area capable of giving her security for Elisabeth, she supposed. Nothing could be further from the truth. She shuddered. Williams's basic nature was so dark, so damaged, it was hard to see how she could have ever believed he would protect another man's child.

She felt sure that Richard had loved her, and wondered whether, given time, he would have broken the news to Caroline, and to his family, told them of his child and of his wish to be with Alice. God hadn't seen fit to grant him that time, and Alice feared that time had run out for her, too. She closed her eyes, trying to conjure up the faces of those that she loved the best, the faces of Sarah, of Elisabeth, of Richard, of Ella, Thomas, Annie and Beattie, of Albert.

With her last remaining strength, she fought to hold fast to memories of her mother and her daughter and to wish them a future together, a future with as much happiness as her imagination could conjure out of her desperate situation. Her fingers sought the locket, still secure on its chain around her neck. She'd removed Richard's photograph when he married so it was empty now, the case bent and damaged when she had been manhandled into the cart on the night of the fire. But it was Richard's gift to her, the one thing of his she had apart from Elisabeth and she held it tightly, feeling him close as her breath faded and her thoughts pulled her back down the dark avenue of time, to her days in the mill, to the bustle and chatter and the noise of the machines as the thread spooled back and forth across the width of the cloth, the threads pulled taut, warp and weft, ever-growing, ever-changing.

PART IX

CHAPTER 1

The day dawned bright and chilly, the sky a clear, pale blue as if thoroughly washed by the storm of the night before. Alys had been startled when the alarm woke her. She'd actually slept well, far better than she'd expected, despite all the unanswered questions hanging over her when she had gone to bed.

As she headed downstairs, one question was answered, though. Moira hadn't come home. Alys smiled to herself, seeing humour in the reversal of roles between aunt and niece. She'd be able to tease her later in the café. It was a shame that Moira refused to have a mobile, or she could have started the teasing now, by text.

She had further reason to wish Moira had a mobile when, by ten in the morning, she still hadn't shown up at the café, and Alys was eager to get off to Nortonstall. Her new assistants, Dee and Sandy, would have opened up the café when she hadn't appeared, but Alys had appointments booked in to discuss the work to be done to the flat. She fought down a sense of rising irritation – Moira was never unreliable. In fact, now she came to think of it, perhaps she should be worried, simply because this was so out of character?

The door opened and Alys looked up, expecting the first customer of what looked like being a very quiet day.

'Morning,' said Rob cheerfully. 'Just thought I'd let you know in case you hadn't heard? We're marooned here at the moment. The storm brought down trees on both the top and bottom roads. Until they send out cutting equipment from Nortonstall, we can't go out and no one can get in.'

Alys felt a sense of relief. 'At least that explains what's happened to Moira. I'd better give them a ring over at Nortonstall to let them know I'll be even later than I thought.'

'Can't do that either, I'm afraid,' said Rob. 'The landlines are down too – the exchange was flooded. I think you're in for a quiet day. You'll only be seeing walkers for a while yet, and then only from the valley. And from what I hear, with the river in spate after the storm, it's not easy walking either. Well, better get off now – I've got a few trees down to deal with myself.' And with that, he was gone.

Alys felt a mounting sense of frustration, then sighed. There was nothing to be done about it. She called Dee on her mobile to check how things were in Nortonstall, reassured by her new assistant's calm and capable manner. Dee was big, blonde and motherly while Sandy, young enough to be Dee's daughter, was slender and petite with cropped dark hair, huge eyes and a preference for goth-style fashion. They made an odd contrast behind the café counter but the customers loved them. She knew she could trust them to get on with the daily routine so she settled herself at the counter with a cup of coffee, then let her thoughts drift back to the night before. Could she solve the puzzle and unravel the mystery behind Alice's death?

When Julie called in to the café a little later, she found Alys frowning fiercely and gazing at the ceiling while she chewed the end of a pencil.

'Tough crossword?' asked Julie.

'Nothing as simple as that,' said Alys, with some feeling, and she explained the events, and her discovery of the night before, to Julie, and how difficult it was to make any sense of it, with so little to go on.

'Hmmm,' said Julie, once she'd absorbed the information. 'There's an awful lot of speculation going on here. But there's a bit of research you could do that might cast some light on one aspect of it.'

'What's that?' Alys sounded hopeful. 'I haven't been able to think of anything.'

'Elisabeth's birth certificate,' said Julie. 'That should tell you who her father was.'

'Of course!' exclaimed Alys. 'I'm an idiot! Why didn't I think of that? But how do I find it?'

'Easy,' said Julie. 'Like everything these days – you can do it online. I can give you a hand, if you like?'

CHAPTER 2

Nearly a week had passed before Alys found time to meet up again with Julie. Once the road to Nortonstall had been cleared, and Moira had made it back to Northwaite, Alys had been able to head back over to the café, where the demands of the new business and trying to sort out her flat kept her fully occupied. But one evening in the first week of November, she and Julie settled down with a laptop, Alys feeling a mix of apprehension and excitement.

'So, where do we start?' asked Alys.

'Here,' said Julie, typing in an Internet address. 'It's a free site, and quick and easy to do some basic research.' She showed Alys where to type in the information she had – Elisabeth's name and surname, her mother's maiden name and the area where her birth would have been registered.

As Alys pressed 'Find', she could hardly believe how excited she felt. She watched the wheel spin briefly as the search progressed, then the screen changed. Her heart leapt and she scanned the on-screen page. There was an Alice – but not an Elisabeth – Bancroft, born in the West Riding of

Yorkshire. But the date was 1911 and the town was wrong.

'Oh,' Alys exhaled in disappointment. 'It's not her.'

'Don't worry,' said Julie, already busily typing. 'I thought we'd try that site first because it's free. But not all the records have been transcribed and uploaded yet. We'll try another site – there'll be a small charge, but you'll be able to look at other details, censuses and the like.'

Half an hour later, even Julie's optimism had faded and Alys was beginning to wonder whether her ancestors did, in fact, belong in some dream world and not in reality. They hadn't been able to find any evidence of Elisabeth's birth, or of Sarah's family, in the census records of 1891, or of Sarah, Elisabeth and the children in the records of 1901.

Alys frowned. 'There's something odd here. It's almost as though they didn't want to be found.'

'Maybe Alice never got around to registering Elisabeth's birth?' suggested Julie. 'She died when Elisabeth was still very young? And although not wanting to be found wouldn't have been so odd under the circumstances, remember we do have evidence of Sarah on the cottage's title deeds, don't we?'

She saw the disappointment on Alys's face. She'd thought she was about to come one step closer to solving a family mystery but frustratingly it felt as though they had taken a couple of steps back instead.

'Look, I met someone who is an experienced genealogy researcher when I was working on our family tree and she helped me out a few times when I was stuck. She's always very busy but she's also very curious, which is why she's such a great researcher. She loves a challenge, so if we send her as many details as we can, I'm sure she'll have a go at sorting it out. You'll have to be patient, though.'

And so it proved. After a couple of weeks, Julie's friend Tina asked for a few more details, including the names of any men who could possibly be Elisabeth's father, but warned that, in cases where the man didn't want to be named, this section could very easily be left blank on the birth certificate. Alys sent off all the details she had for Richard, which were very few. As an afterthought, she also included Albert. He was an unlikely candidate, but his wish to care for Elisabeth, Sarah and the family kept him in the picture.

CHAPTER 3

November and December had been the busiest months of Alys's life so far. She and Moira had been keen to have The Cake Company Café established by the Christmas period, to take advantage of festive spending by locals and visitors alike. With the Nortonstall café interior fully kitted out, Alys could devote her attention to what turned out to be literally window dressing. She'd called in to see Claire at her antique shop early in November and asked her to keep her eyes open for any vintage Christmas decorations, expecting that at the most she might be able to find the odd bauble or two. At the end of November, just as Alys realised that she would need to start putting up decorations within the week, Claire popped into The Cake Company Café.

'Come over to the shop as soon as you can,' she said, sipping the cappuccino that Alys had made for her. 'I've got something that I think you will be very pleased to see.' Alys could tell by the smile on Claire's lips and the sparkle in her eyes that she had found something that she was excited about, but she refused to be drawn on what it might be and so Alys had to remain patient until mid-afternoon when she managed to slip away from the café with a promise to be back as soon as possible.

A lovely warm glow spilled out from Claire's shop, lighting up the gloomy winter afternoon, and Alys felt a sense of anticipation as she pushed open the door. Claire was talking to a customer on the phone but she smiled at Alys and gestured to her to wait. Drawn as ever to the china section at the back of the shop, Alys picked up a coffee cup and saucer which she guessed belonged to the Art Deco era. The rim featured a geometric pattern of peach and pale-blue bars outlined in gold, with a scattering of gold-and-white blossom below it. It was too small to use in the Northwaite café but Alys was just persuading herself that she could squeeze it in somewhere on the display shelves when Claire appeared at her elbow and made her start so that she almost dropped it.

'Now put that down and come and see what I've found.' Claire was looking very pleased with herself and Alys followed her back through to the counter, where three rather scruffy boxes, their lids loosely secured with fine cotton cord, were set out. The pale, card exteriors offered no clues to their contents, but Alys was intrigued to see straw hanging over the edges of one of the boxes and tissue paper in different colours peeping out of the others. She looked at Claire expectantly.

'Go on – open them up. But be careful, the contents are fragile.'

Alys drew a box towards her and tugged one end of the cord, which fell away, allowing her to lift off the lid. She drew her breath in sharply as she took in what lay inside. The box was divided into twelve compartments by intersecting strips of card. Each compartment contained a nest of crumpled tissue paper and on each one rested a bauble, but baubles unlike anything Alys had ever seen. Some were bright pink or electric blue, shiny and decorated with bold white brushstrokes creating loose approximations of leaves or flowers. Others were pale in colour, mostly silver or gold and moulded or embossed to look like hanging bunches of grapes, cars or animals.

'They're beautiful!' Alys hardly dared to touch them.

'They're made of glass. I think they're mostly 1920s and 1930s, judging by the cars and by the painted designs.' Claire was beaming at Alys's reaction.

'How on earth have they managed to survive so long? And where did you find them?'

'They're from a house clearance. An elderly lady who had lived in the same house all her adult life. They were packed away in the loft. Luckily, after you'd asked me for vintage ornaments, I'd asked around and Reg, a contact of mine in Leeds, phoned me when he came across them.'

Alys was busy opening up the other boxes, finding

two more sets with different designs. One set was painted with rows of horizontal stripes encircling each bauble, the other had a flower or snowflake motif embossed deeply into each ornament.

'It doesn't look as though they've seen the light of day for years,' Alys marvelled.

'Well, I know they'll be going to a good home with you,' Claire said.

'Do you think I'll be able to use them?' Alys was suddenly doubtful. 'I'd hate them to get smashed after they've survived all these years.'

'I thought you could use clear fishing twine to hang them around the top of the window, too high up for anyone to touch.' Claire said. 'You might need to superglue the hangers to the tops of each bauble, though. Those metal loops look like they might be a bit weak.'

They contemplated them for a moment in silence. 'If you don't want them, I won't have a problem selling them,' Claire said, starting to re-pack the boxes.

'No, no, I do!' Alys said hastily. 'I was just getting carried away, imagining putting them up. I think they will look wonderful. Thank you so much for finding them.'

Ten minutes later, Alys was on her way back to the café, the boxes of decorations stowed in a carrier along with the coffee cup and saucer, which she hadn't been able to resist. She had just the spot to display it, in the kitchen of the flat.

The baubles had been hung on the last evening

in November in the Nortonstall café, once Alys had been able to borrow a stepladder tall enough to suit the job. Her assistants Dee and Sandy had volunteered to stay on and help her once the café was closed for the day, and once they had worked out how to hang the first couple, from twine tied onto hooks screwed into the window surround, they'd managed to get a bit of a production line going. Alys had measured and marked the position of the hooks and screwed them in, while Dee and Sandy had glued the bauble tops and then tied twine in differing lengths to each one. They'd teased Alys when she'd been insistent that baubles of the same colour and design shouldn't be hung against each other but they'd all been really pleased at the finished effect. The ornaments revolved a little as they hung, the facets on their surfaces sparkling as they caught the lights in the room.

Once each table had been dressed with a miniature Christmas tree in a pot, topped with a gold gauze bow, and vintage-style card cut-outs of Victorian Santas and ice-skaters had been suspended from the counter and shelves, which were already edged with Christmas lights, Alys pronounced herself satisfied.

'It looks so lovely! Thank you, both of you,' Alys said. 'I just need to make sure Moira doesn't see this before I manage to get round to decorating the Northwaite café.'

Dee and Sandy looked at each other. 'Why don't we do it now?' they asked.

Alys looked doubtful. 'It's getting late. Surely you want to get off home?'

'It's not even eight yet,' Dee said. 'I'll go and get my car while you pack up this stuff ready to go.' She indicated the remainder of the decorations. 'We'll be done by eleven. It will be better to have both places decorated at the same time. It's the first of December tomorrow, after all.'

Alys had been feeling weary but Dee's enthusiasm re-energised her. 'OK. You're right. But I'm going to order in fish and chips and we can eat it before we go.'

That night, at eleven thirty, the three of them stood back and admired their handiwork at The Celestial Cake Café.

'The baubles work really well with the wings,' Dee said. 'And I love these card decorations.' She turned one over in her hands, admiring the printed and gilded decoration. 'These Victorian skater girls are just gorgeous. Where did you get them? I'd like to get some for myself.'

'There's a box left,' Alys said, draining the last mouthful of prosecco that had proved useful in getting them through their final decorating session. 'It's yours – the least I can do for all your help.'

She turned to Sandy. 'And for you . . .' She stopped, at a loss.

'I'll have something from your festive baking course,' Sandy said. 'A cake, mince pies, anything. I won't get round to making my own.'

'The baking course . . .' Alys said. 'The first

one's tomorrow. I nearly forgot. Definitely time for bed.' And they all turned their attention to tidying up.

'Moira is going to be so surprised in the morning,' Alys said. She imagined her aunt's reaction and it helped to lift the fog of weariness as she took one last look around before locking up. By twelve-thirty she had fallen into bed back in Nortonstall, alarm set for six, exhaustion ensuring sleep within minutes.

CHAPTER 4

The baking courses had proved to be a huge success. The Nortonstall café had a large, well-equipped kitchen and Alys had limited the class size to six, to make sure that everyone got their full share of attention. She'd advertised them in the café from mid-November, planning to run just one a week, and they had been slow to fill up at first. But the hanging of the Christmas decorations seemed to spur everyone into thinking about Christmas and by closing time on the first of December, the classes were all full and the length of the waiting list persuaded Alys that she needed to run an additional class each week.

It was too late in the year to make Christmas cakes, but the students learnt how to make mince pies with shortcrust pastry, spiced ginger biscuits and chocolate truffles. The other customers in the café were intrigued by the laughter and the delicious aromas wafting from the kitchen and, encouraged by Dee and Sandy, inevitably ended up peering around the door then popping in to say hello to friends and neighbours who were taking the classes.

'It was like a party in there this morning,' Alys said, flopping into a chair in the café in a quiet moment after the lunchtime rush had died away. 'I couldn't get them to focus at all. It's only mid-December and everyone's over-excited already!'

'We did wonder whether you were passing round the Christmas sherry,' Dee said. 'They sounded like they had the best time, though. And they all looked pretty happy when they came out with their boxes of goodies to take home.'

Alys had wondered whether there were enough hours in the day for her to run the classes as well as bake cakes and biscuits for the café, so she had been delighted when Dee had proved to be a more-than-able baker. With a grown-up family, she had not only accumulated plenty of experience over the years but she had time on her hands and was happy to put in the extra hours over the festive period. She shared the baking with Alys who, once she had sampled Dee's mince pies, also got her to come in to class and run the shortcrust pastry lesson, much to the delight of everyone who knew her.

Moira couldn't have been more pleased with the way that both businesses were going in the run-up to Christmas. 'I can't believe how well you've done,' she said to Alys when she called in to The Cake Company Café after doing some Christmas shopping one afternoon in late December. 'Not just to get the place open in time for Christmas but to turn it into such a popular spot already. All the regulars in Northwaite have been here at least once, you know.'

'It's been lovely to see them,' Alys said. 'And a couple have been on the courses, too.' She sipped her tea and took a forkful of the clementine cake that Moira had brought into the café with her, a new recipe that she was thinking of introducing in the New Year. 'Mmm. This is delicious. It's so nice to taste something fresh and citrusy after all the Christmas flavours.' She lowered her voice for the last few words, wary of her customers overhearing her. They were all still enjoying the cinnamon, nutmeg and spices of the season but Alys's palate was already jaded.

'Well, I'd better be getting back.' Moira gathered up her shopping bags. 'Flo will be wanting to close up and head home. I just wanted to make sure that you are still going to come to Northwaite for Christmas?'

'You bet,' Alys said. 'I can't wait.' Christmas was a beacon of light for her, something to look forward to at the end of the following week. 'Just as long as we don't have to cook anything. And I can put my feet up and do nothing but eat and watch old movies for a couple of days.'

'Tom's going to cook,' Moira said. 'He says we don't need to lift a finger.' Tom, a delightful man of Moira's age, had turned out to be the reason for her increasingly frequent trips to jazz evenings in Nortonstall. Leaving him to do the cooking sounded good to Alys but Moira referred to Tom in such an easy way, a smile playing on her lips as she did so, that it gave Alys a small pang. She was absolutely delighted for them both but suddenly aware of how wrapped up she had been in the business for over three months now. Every day began at six in the morning and finished at around ten in the evening, when she could no longer keep her eyes open. Baking, serving customers and dealing with paperwork seemed to fill all those hours and she couldn't remember the last time that she had had a proper conversation with anyone, or at least one that didn't revolve around cake in some form or another. Even so, she wouldn't have missed a moment. It was the busiest, and most fulfilling, of times.

She waved her aunt off, then got to wondering what on earth she could buy Moira and Tom for Christmas. A couple of nice bottles of wine for Tom, maybe some cook's ingredients, too, and a book for Moira, a nice fat novel perhaps. She should get something for Dee and Sandy, too; a great part of the café's success was due to them, their energy and their rapport with the customers. She put a memo into her phone, knowing that she would never remember otherwise, with so much still to fit in before the holiday arrived. Her mother and father were heading abroad so a card would have to do for them, and she'd long ago given up on buying presents for her brothers. She'd send something to Hannah, of course, but thankfully there was no need to agonise over what to buy for Tim this year.

Her thoughts strayed from Tim to Rob. She'd barely seen him since Hannah's visit in September. She wondered what he was up to and why she hadn't seen him around. She should have asked Moira if he was still buying his coffee in the café every day. At one point, it had seemed as though there might be something between them but now that didn't seem likely. It looked as though neither of them had felt the inclination to get in touch with the other. There hadn't been a moment to reflect on her personal life but, now that she did so, she felt a sense of loss. She was looking forward to Christmas because it would give her the chance to take a break, but would it feel odd, lonely even, she wondered, spending it with a new and happy couple?

Any further thoughts along these lines were suspended by the arrival of the carol singers who, with thirty minutes to spare before their scheduled performance in front of the town's Christmas tree, bundled into the café to buy hot chocolate to warm themselves up.

'It's too cold to stand outside and wait,' one of them explained. 'And the café looked so pretty, all lit up, that we had to come in.'

Alys handed round mince pies and refused to take payment for the hot chocolate, earning her a rousing recital of 'We Wish You a Merry Christmas' before they all headed back out into the street again. Dee, Sandy and Alys took it in turns to wrap up and step outside to listen to a carol or two around the tree. Carols were always uplifting, Alys reflected, and everyone looked so happy standing around the tree and singing. The little children especially looked enchanting, muffled up against the cold and clinging onto a parent's hand as they listened, wide-eyed, entranced by the sparkling lights on the tree. Alys had tears in her eyes but she brushed them away as she came back into the café.

'It's so cold!' she declared. 'Do you think we'll have a white Christmas?'

'No, it's *too* cold!' Sandy and Dee replied at the same time, then burst out laughing.

'I'm going to prepare the kitchen for tomorrow's class if you want to clear up and get away a bit early,' Alys said, surveying the empty café. 'Everyone is listening to the carols, then my guess is, they'll head home.'

'They'll be going to the pub for mulled wine,' Dee said. 'At any rate, that's where I'm going. Sandy? Alys? Do you want to join me?'

Sandy shook her head, saying that she'd promised to babysit for her sister's children and couldn't turn up smelling of alcohol. Alys was tempted and almost agreed, then the thought of the preparation she needed to do before the next day's class stopped her. 'Sorry.' She sighed. 'Not today. But I'll make sure we have a Christmas drink together before the big day arrives.'

CHAPTER 5

On Christmas Eve afternoon, Alys turned the sign on the café door to read 'Closed', picked up her bag and stepped outside to be met by a gust of damp, but not particularly cold, air. It didn't look as though they could expect a white Christmas this year, after all.

The streets were quiet as Alys locked up and headed for the bus stop. It was the end of the afternoon and most people were at home with family and friends, or had gone visiting. She'd sent Dee and Sandy off at midday, promising them that they would have a celebration together in the New Year. The last few days at work had proved too hectic to organise the promised Christmas drink in the end, with customers even dropping in that morning to beg them for a dozen mince pies, gingerbread reindeer and chocolate truffles, to use as last-minute gifts. Alys told herself that a really quiet time was exactly what she had been looking forward to, but now it was almost upon her she had to fight down a sudden wave of loneliness. Christmas was such a family time and, despite the fact that Moira *was* family, they would make rather a small gathering.

The bus drew up at the stop, the driver extra-cheery in his greeting as he was on the last run of the day. As they headed out of town and the bus started the long haul up the hill, it passed houses with curtains left half-open to display trees festooned with Christmas lights, twinkling and winking as rain started to spatter against the bus window. Then all was darkness outside as the bus laboured up the final stretch into Northwaite. Alys jumped off at the first stop, which was closest to The Celestial Cake Café, so she could check whether Moira was still there. But the café was locked up and in darkness. Hunched against the now-driving rain, Alys shouldered her bag and was preparing to head for the cottage when she spotted a note taped to the door.

'In The Old Bell. Join us!' it read.

Alys assumed that this was intended for her, but she wasn't sure she felt like going. She was tired, and had spent all day looking forward to a relaxing evening. A noisy pub wasn't quite what she had in mind. She hesitated, then, reflecting that she'd be at a loose end if Moira wasn't home, and that there would be plenty of time to relax over the next couple of days, she turned her steps up the hill. Within a minute or two, she was pushing open the door of The Old Bell.

A wave of noise and laughter greeted her and she almost turned tail and fled, but Tom, on his way to the bar, spotted her.

'Alys! You made it. You look half-drowned.

Everyone's over in the other bar. Go through and I'll bring you a drink. What'll you have?'

Alys found Moira chatting to some of the regulars from the Northwaite café. It was standing room only, but she managed to stow her bag and coat under a chair and squeeze through the crowd to join them. The glass of wine that Tom brought over helped to soothe some of her tiredness but, after nearly an hour of trying to make conversation over the hubbub, Alys thought about making a break for it. If she said she was leaving, though, Moira and Tom would insist on joining her and she could see that they were really enjoying themselves. So, instead, Alys offered to get the next round and pushed her way through to the bar, standing patiently to wait her turn to be served. She whiled away the time staring at an old photo of the pub on the wall next to the bar. The photo was dated 1895 – she'd never noticed it before. Surely that was the year that Alice had died? There were some indistinct figures in the street, faces pale against dark clothes as they stared at the camera, no doubt a novelty in those times. What if one of them was Alice? She must have walked past the pub many times, although probably without going inside. It wasn't the done thing for women in those days.

'Penny for them.'

Alys jumped. The voice was right in her ear. 'Oh, it's you.'

'Well, that's a nice greeting after all these weeks.'

Rob smiled and Alys felt a sudden rush of complicated emotion. She'd been so tied up with everything involved in getting the new café up and running that she'd barely thought about anything else. Including herself. But Rob was speaking.

'I've been asking Moira about how you were getting on and why we never see you in Northwaite anymore. She said you might be in here this evening.'

It was Alys's turn to be served, finally. As she waited for her drinks she turned to Rob.

'So why haven't you come over to Nortonstall, to the new place? To check out the coffee there?'

Rob laughed. 'I'm not sure they'd be keen to have my tractor on the High Street. Anyway, I've been away myself recently.'

'Away? Anywhere nice?' she asked, trying hard to sound casual.

'London, can you believe.' Rob made a face. 'It was a Rare Breeds Symposium. Why on earth they organised it in London, I'll never know. I don't know how you put up with it down there for so long, Alys. It's so crowded. A bit like being in here tonight!'

They pushed their way back with the drinks and Rob helped her hand them round.

'Rob!' Alys was contrite. 'I didn't get you one! I was so busy memorising the order, I forgot to ask you. Here – I'll go back.'

She turned to go but Rob grasped her arm. 'No need. I've got one. I left it over by the bar. Come with me and we can catch up on each other's news.' He didn't withdraw his grip, instead using it to guide her before him back through the crowd. His drink safely claimed, they wedged themselves into a corner, where the view gave out through the door into the road.

'It's still raining,' Alys remarked. 'I got soaked just walking here from the café.'

'You were pretty drenched the first time I set eyes on you,' Rob said. 'And the second, come to that. The first time it was the rain, the second time because you were swimming.'

The remark hung in the air a moment as they both thought back. Alys felt a response was required, preferably a witty one, but her mind was a blank. She opened her mouth to speak, hoping inspiration would strike, at the same moment as a crowd of new arrivals burst in out of the rain and forced their way into the already crowded space, knocking Alys off-balance and propelling her into Rob.

'Oh!' Alys found herself clutched in a bear hug, which seemed to go on at least a minute longer than it needed to. She wasn't complaining; she was suddenly aware of how long it had been since someone had held her so close. And how nice it felt.

Reluctantly, she disengaged herself. 'Rob, I'm really sorry. My drink's gone all over you.'

His shirt was wet, the checked pattern hiding what was undoubtedly a spreading stain.

'No worries. I'll get you another.' Rob turned for the bar as Moira and Tom appeared.

'Alys, we're going now. It's so busy we can't hear ourselves speak. Do you want to come with us?'

Moira's questioning look moved from Alys to Rob, then back again. Alys was torn. She really wanted to stay and talk to Rob, but the wine she had drunk had started to add to her exhaustion rather than lift it. And the noise level was rising rapidly; they'd be yelling at each other rather than having an intimate chat.

Alys smiled apologetically at Rob. 'I'm really sorry about your shirt.'

He tipped his head and cupped his ear to show he couldn't hear her.

'I must go. I'm really tired,' she yelled. 'And I'm sorry about your shirt.'

He pulled her towards him and spoke into her ear. 'Don't worry. It's crazy in here. I'm meeting Rosie and Sian on New Year's Eve for dinner and a few drinks in Nortonstall. Come along? We'll call by and collect you.'

He made the question sound like a command and Alys, defeated by the noise level, could only nod.

They parted company in a flurry of Christmas wishes, exchanging hugs and kisses. Alys knew she hadn't imagined that, at the last moment, Rob had turned her face towards his and kissed her full on the lips.

She carried the sensation all the way home with

her, quiet as she trudged through the rain, grateful for Tom's presence. It meant that he not only offered to carry her bag, but distracted Moira from asking probing questions. With the longed-for Christmas only a few hours away, she found that she was already looking forward to New Year.

CHAPTER 6

Rosie, Sian and Rob had called for her at the flat in Nortonstall on a bitterly cold New Year's Eve, when a hard frost was already dusting the streets with silver. In buoyant moods, they'd hurried through the streets to the pub, laughing and chatting, their breath hanging in frozen clouds in the air.

The pub had been busy, but nowhere near as crowded as on Christmas Eve in Northwaite. All the tables were booked and food was being served before the main festivities began. It felt like an enchanted place to Alys. A wonderful scent – wood-smoke, perfume, candlewax – filled the dark-painted room, which was lit mainly by candle-light that caught and sparkled in the sequins that most of the women in the room seemed to be wearing. Everyone had dressed up and made an effort: Alys was glad that she'd worn her black-velvet top, the scoop of its neckline edged with sequin-spangled lace. She'd put her hair up and worn her favourite earrings, gold droplets hung with pearls, and Alice's locket.

The four of them joined a large table in the window,

draped with a starched white cloth and set with heavy silver cutlery and what seemed like more glasses than they could possibly need. Alys found herself seated next to Rob, both of them at first a little over-awed by the formal setting. As the waitress poured the champagne and the first sips were taken, the restraint slipped a little and the hum of chatter, mixed with laughter, rose from all the tables.

Alys leant back in her chair and closed her eyes for a moment.

'Are you all right?' She opened her eyes to see Rob watching her with concern.

'Me? I'm really happy. Just taking a moment. This is a lovely place. I've never been here before.'

'It's only been open a few months. It's already got good reviews, though. What with your place and this, Nortonstall's making a mark locally.'

'I always feel so sorry for the people who have to work on Christmas Day and at New Year.' Alys sighed, then brightened. 'But I've got two whole days off. Let's not talk about work. Let's talk about . . .' she paused, considering a topic.

'The future,' said Rob, clinking his glass against hers. 'I have a feeling that this year will turn out to be a good one.'

The rest of the evening had passed in a blur – of banter, chatter and fabulous food and wine. Alys felt as though she was drifting along on a cloud of wellbeing. It was quite definitely the best New Year's Eve she had ever had.

And when she had woken on New Year's Day morning with a pounding head, she hadn't been overly surprised to find someone familiar sleeping in the bed beside her. Someone who groaned as she stirred and turned towards her, wrapping his arms around her.

'Don't get up yet,' Rob said. 'It's too early and my head hurts too much.' He opened one eye. 'Unless you were planning on bringing me coffee and some of that delicious cake. What was it? Lemon poppy-seed cake?'

Alys pulled away, picked up her pillow and threw it at him.

'I'll take that as a no, shall I?' And Rob had drawn her back down into the bed.

It was past midday before Alys surfaced again, protesting as Rob tried to bear-hug her into staying beside him.

'I need water, orange juice, coffee. And food.' Suddenly shy, despite Rob having explored every inch of her body over the previous hour or so, she wrapped herself in her dressing gown and headed for the kitchen to switch on the kettle. The chill of the room struck her and she was just about to alter the thermostat to make the heating come on when movement at the kitchen window caught her eye. Fat, feathery flakes of snow were falling and, judging by the white-ness on the roofs opposite and the pavements down below, it had been snowing hard for the last few hours.

She took orange juice through to Rob, who had fallen asleep again in the few minutes she'd been away. Alys looked at his face on the pillow, turned slightly to the side, his hair tousled and cheeks flushed. She smiled at the sight then, raising her voice, said, 'Hey, sleepyhead! Wake up!'

Rob's eyes shot open and she could see that for a few seconds he didn't know where he was. 'Sorry,' he said. 'I must have dozed off. Mmm. Orange juice. Yes please.' He half sat up, propping himself on one elbow and reached for the glass.

'It's snowing,' Alys said. It was her first experience of snow in the area and she realised that she felt as excited as a child.

'Is it?' Rob said. He looked troubled. 'Has it been snowing long?'

'A few hours I think. Why?'

Rob had gulped his juice, thrown back the covers and was hunting around on the floor for his clothes, scattered the night before.

'I'm going to have to get over to the farm. Check that everything is as it should be. Make sure there's plenty of feed in the barns and the water hasn't frozen over.'

'Oh.' Alys suddenly felt deflated. She'd thought they could have a leisurely breakfast, maybe go out for a snowy walk, then flop in front of the TV or perhaps go to the pub. Although right this minute, having a drink held no appeal whatsoever.

Rob, hopping about on one leg as he tried to get his other leg into his trousers, which was proving difficult as he'd already put his shoes on in his haste, noticed Alys's crestfallen expression.

'I'm sorry, Alys. Snow wasn't in the forecast. It's rather spoilt things – we could have spent the day together.'

Alys surveyed him, dressed in his going-out clothes from the night before. 'You'll freeze if you go out like that,' she commented.

Rob looked down at himself. 'It's OK, I've got my outdoor jacket and boots in the Land Rover. It's parked near Sian's.'

'Why don't I come with you?' Alys went over to her chest of drawers, preparing to pull out a jumper and jeans.

'Oh, I don't know . . .' Rob looked doubtful.

'You don't want me to?' Alys felt awkward. Had she assumed too much?

'It's freezing, we're both hungover and it's pretty boring work.'

Alys felt a sense of relief. She'd wondered whether Rob was embarrassed, maybe didn't want to be seen with her.

'If I give you a hand we'll get it done twice as fast. But before we go, we're going to have coffee. And bacon sandwiches.'

'No time Alys.' Rob was firm. 'I'm worried about the animals. I don't want to leave it another minute.'

'What about a compromise?' Alys thought quickly. 'You go and get the Land Rover, drive past here and I'll run down and join you. It will give me time to get dressed.' And make a flask of coffee, she thought to herself.

'OK.' Rob, already heading for the door, blew her a kiss. Alys grabbed some clothes, flew into the kitchen and quickly made the coffee. Instant will have to do for now, she thought. She would have loved to have a shower but that would have to wait. Food, though, was another matter. She felt light-headed – something was required. As she was standing in the hall, trying to do up her jeans and pull on a sweater at the same time, inspiration struck. She grabbed her coat, keys and phone and was halfway down the stairs before she realised she was in her socks. Cursing, she ran back up to the flat and grabbed her wellies. It was lucky that she kept a pair in Nortonstall as well as Northwaite, she thought, otherwise she couldn't have stepped outside today. Heart hammering, worried that Rob would be waiting impatiently outside or – even worse – would have driven off without her, she stepped outside and gasped as an icy wind blew a flurry of snow into her face. She was in luck – there was no sign of the Land Rover or of any tyre tracks on the road. Fumbling the keys with fingers instantly chilled by the wind she let herself into the café, silenced the alarm and had a quick look to see what the cake tins in the kitchen held. Flapjacks – they would have to do. Syrup and oats: breakfast porridge in a bar, she told herself.

CHAPTER 7

Alys locked up again and stood shivering on the pavement, the flask and bag of flapjacks in hand. Within a minute or two she saw headlights approaching through increasingly blizzard-like conditions as Rob drove the Land Rover along the road at an unusually stately pace.

He leant over and pushed open the door for her. 'In you get,' he said. 'It's as cold inside as out at the moment – I think the heater must have frozen.' He had donned a thick sweater in pale-grey wool flecked with black, its ribbed and zipped collar framing his face.

'Lucky you had a sweater in here,' Alys said.

'It was a Christmas present. Mum would kill me if she knew I was wearing it on the farm.' Rob grinned as he spoke, all the while focusing on the junction ahead of them, braking slowly so that they didn't overshoot it as they came down off the hill. 'Thank goodness the major roads have been gritted,' he commented, as they turned onto the A-road and picked up a bit of speed. There was hardly any traffic around as they left Nortonstall

411

behind and climbed up out of the valley bottom, the sun breaking through as the snow eased. Alys exclaimed at the beauty of the landscape as it was revealed. Snow lay thickly across the moors and sat like white cake frosting along the tops of hedges and the branches of trees. The brilliance of the sun as it reflected back off the sparkling whiteness made Alys's eyes hurt and she longed for a pair of sunglasses. Rob had fished his from the side pocket of the Land Rover and turned to look at her with a smug smile as she groaned, frowned and tried to shield her eyes.

'This isn't helping the hangover,' she complained.

'What have you got in the bag?' Rob glanced down at the paper package on her knee.

'Flapjacks. Do you want one?' Alys held one out to him without waiting for an answer. 'And I've got coffee. Can you drink it while you drive?'

Rob, his mouth already stuffed full of flapjack, could only nod.

Alys carefully poured half a cup into the top of the flask and handed it over. Rob, his eyes firmly on the road, downed it in one and held the cup out for more.

'You're a star,' he said, after he'd eaten a second flapjack and would have drunk all the coffee if Alys hadn't held some back for herself. 'You don't know how much I needed that.'

He was turning off the A-road into a much narrower lane where the snow lay thick and untouched.

'Do you think we'll get through?' Alys asked, suddenly anxious.

'I think so,' Rob said, taking care to stay in the centre, between the high hedges, as he cautiously edged the Land Rover along. 'The entrance to the barns isn't too far along here. We should be okay.'

Alys quickly finished her flapjack, rubbed the crumbs from her mouth and screwed the top back onto the flask. The hedges were too high to afford much of a view, but overhead the sky was now a brilliant blue and, as Rob coaxed the Land Rover along, the warmth of the sun through the windscreen made her wish that she'd taken her coat off earlier in the journey. Rob suddenly stopped the Land Rover, jumped out, went round the back and returned with a spade.

'What's that for?' Alys asked.

'We're here,' said Rob. 'I just need to dig out the gate so I can open it.' With that he vanished through a gap in the hedge ahead. Alys was preparing to climb out and join him when he reappeared, threw the spade in the back, climbed back behind the wheel and edged them through into the barn yard.

Alys had imagined grand, old-fashioned wooden structures and was taken aback at the sight of what appeared to be industrial sheds. 'Are these the barns?' she asked.

Rob noticed her puzzlement and laughed. 'Ah, you imagined Heritage breeds would be kept in tumbledown sheds, looked after by yokels in smocks, didn't you?'

Alys, who had thought that helping him would involve setting to with a pitchfork, tossing hay into cattle stalls, had to confess that she'd expected something like that.

'Come and take a look. It's all state of the art, alarms and everything. These breeds are worth a small fortune so the barns have to be protected, temperature controlled, the lot.'

She followed him across the yard and waited while he punched a code into the door of the biggest barn. 'So, if it's all high tech, why the urgency to get over to see them? I thought they were in barns open to the elements. I'd imagined them all huddled together, shivering in a corner.' They were through the door now and inside the barn, lit by artificial light, where the temperature was a good few degrees warmer than outside.

Rob had the grace to look a bit shame-faced. 'Okay, I'm a bit of a control freak around these cattle.' He gestured at them – the animals had come forward to the front of their pens and set up quite a noise as soon as he and Alys had entered the barn. 'They're my responsibility and I'm always conscious of how valuable they are. They'll have eaten more than usual to keep themselves warm so I need to check whether to replenish the hay before tomorrow. And the water supply comes from outside – it's frozen over before now, so I wanted to double-check everything was okay.'

He was working his way around the cattle, stroking their necks and patting their noses as they jostled each other for his attention. He'd donned a Barbour jacket before leaving the Land Rover and he fished in the pockets frequently, dishing out brown pellets that reminded Alys of the treats she used to give her cats.

'What's in the other barn?' she asked.

'The rare-breed sheep,' Rob said. 'We'll go there next. Why don't you sit over there,' he pointed to a bale of straw. 'And I'll just get this lot seen to.'

Alys did as she was told, watching him work his way around the animals, checking the feed levels and talking to all of them as he went. He was oblivious to her, absorbed in what he was doing, and she enjoyed watching him, sure in everything he did. She hugged her knees to her chest and smiled. She could have stayed like this all day, watching him work, but she also wanted to take him home, join him in the shower and then in her bed. Her face grew hot as she imagined his hands on her body again, his lips on hers. She stood up suddenly and went over to stand close to him, stroking his back. He put his arm around her and pulled her close to his side.

'Getting bored?' he asked.

'No, I'm enjoying watching you,' she replied truthfully. 'But I got to thinking about bacon and eggs. And proper coffee. And . . .' she paused.

'And?' He was smiling as he looked at her and she knew that he knew exactly what she was thinking. He turned her face towards him, kissing her softly then deeply. Lost in the moment, she was vaguely aware of something butting against her arm. Breaking free, she discovered one of the cows busy licking and nibbling at her coat sleeve. Rob laughed and pushed the cow's nose away.

'Let's go – don't want you upsetting the cattle. They're pretty possessive, you know. I'm done here anyway – just need to check the water isn't frozen outside.'

The sheep received a much more cursory visit and within the half-hour Alys and Rob were back in the Land Rover and heading back towards Nortonstall. The changes that snow made to the landscape left Alys feeling disorientated. Landmarks had vanished and instead a vast patchwork of white was spread before her, interspersed with the darker outlines of hedges. Rob knew the route like the back of his hand and their return journey to Nortonstall seemed to take far less time than their outward one. The streets of the town were free of traffic but they'd seen families with sledges heading up towards the hills, well-wrapped against the cold in colourful hats, scarves and jackets.

'What would you like?' Alys asked, as they parked outside the flat. 'Full English? A shower?'

Rob was nodding his head.

'A snowball fight? The pub?'

He shook his head.

'Something else?'

Rob's grin told her all she needed to know.

Back in the flat, both showered and still wrapped in towels and bathrobes, they fell on the very late breakfast that Alys had cooked. Scrambled eggs, bacon, toast, mushrooms, grilled tomatoes and a pot of tea. As Rob pushed his plate away he glanced at the window.

'It's snowing again,' he remarked.

'Oh no.' Alys twisted in her chair to look. 'Does that mean we have to go back to the barns?'

'No,' Rob said, reaching across the table to take her hand and pulling her gently to her feet. 'It means we can spend the rest of the day in bed.'

CHAPTER 8

Alys had been so busy in the run-up to Christmas, and even in the normally quiet January period, that it was only in rare moments that her thoughts had returned to Alice. She'd gone over and over the few scraps of concrete information that she had, trying to tease out anything she might have missed. But closure still eluded her. She was no nearer knowing whether Alice had indeed set the mill on fire and if so, why? Nor who was the father of Alice's baby. She'd found it all so frustrating that it was always much easier to set it aside and bury herself in the demands of the two businesses.

Julie, though, hadn't forgotten, and in mid-February, while Moira took a well-earned holiday and Alys moved back to Northwaite for a couple of weeks to mind The Celestial Cake Café, she dropped in for coffee and to reveal some news.

'Check your email tonight,' she said. 'Tina's sending you something. She wouldn't tell me what it was but she's made an important discovery.' Julie's cheeks were flushed pink either from excitement or from the wind, Alys couldn't be sure.

'She didn't even give you a clue?' Alys immediately wanted to go back to Moira's and retrieve her laptop, but she was working alone in the café that day.

'No, we're just going to have to be patient.' Julie finished her coffee and got up to go. 'Don't forget to let me know, though. Oh, and come for lunch one Sunday with Rob. Derek and I have barely seen him of late.' She raised her eyebrows as she looked at Alys.

Alys blushed to the roots of her hair. She and Rob had spent a lot of time together since New Year and he'd stayed over quite a few times while she'd been in Northwaite. No doubt someone in the village had passed comment to Julie. She'd have to tell him to go and visit his mum – she wouldn't like her to feel neglected.

'I'll take one of those back for Derek,' Julie pointed to an iced gingerbread heart. 'Actually, make that two. I'm not expecting any red roses today – might as well buy my own Valentine's gift.'

Alys felt guilty again, remembering the gift-wrapped box that Rob had given her that morning. She'd lifted the lid to discover a selection of white-chocolate cows, with grey-painted faces and grey markings, as well as pink-and-white daisy chocolates.

'I thought it combined things we both love,' said Rob, looking rather pleased with himself. 'And you'd said how you were sick of the sight of hearts, because of the café.'

'Wherever did you get them?' Alys exclaimed. 'They're wonderful – I've never seen anything like them.' She was already thinking what a good addition they would make to the Nortonstall café, where she was planning to introduce a range of gifts.

'Anything for me?' Rob asked, expectantly.

'Oh!' Alys gasped. Her face was a picture. 'I completely forgot. I was so focused on the cafés . . .' her voice trailed away.

'That you forgot to get anything for me,' Rob helpfully finished off. He shook his head in mock sorrow. 'I won't forget this.'

'Here, have a cow,' Alys thrust the box towards him. 'I'll bring you something back this evening from the café, I promise.'

Rob grinned. 'Don't worry, you can make it up to me another time. But I'm staying over at the farm tonight, remember? Moira's due back.'

'Of course!' Alys struck her forehead. 'How could I have forgotten? There's just too much going on.'

'You work too hard,' Rob said, kissing her on the forehead as he prepared to leave. 'Flo, Dee and Sandy are really good. You can leave them in charge more often than you do.'

Alys smiled ruefully. 'I'm a bit of a control freak, I'm afraid. Ring any bells?'

She pulled herself back to the present as she packed the gingerbread hearts into a box, protecting them with pink tissue before handing them over to Julie. 'There you go. And we'll be there for lunch, this week or, if not, next. I'll let you know.' And she waved Julie goodbye as more customers arrived, intent on getting in out of the winter's chill and finding a seat by the wood burner.

It was nearly 7 p.m. that evening before Alys finally settled at the kitchen table in Moira's cottage and flipped open her laptop. She went straight to her inbox and there it was – tucked in amongst the usual notifications of flight bargains, book deals, and general spam – an email from Tina. She clicked on it, rapidly scanning the text.

Alys sat back, trying to take in the news. Tina had, indeed, solved one of the mysteries. She'd found Elisabeth's birth certificate, dated 1895 as expected. However, she hadn't been registered as Elisabeth *Bancroft*, but as Elisabeth *Weatherall*. So those little scraps of paper, those notes secreted in Alice's embroidered bag, weren't the only tokens she'd had to remind her of a love affair with Richard – she'd had his child. And he'd honoured it, which as Tina pointed out in her email, was unusual, given that not only was he from a very different class to Alice, but he had a fiancée at that point, too. Tina had managed to trace some of the family in the 1911 census, searching by house rather than by family name. She'd found Sarah, plus Annie, Beatrice and Elisabeth all living at Lane End Cottage, under the name 'Bancraft'. It looked as though somewhere along the line the name hadn't been transcribed properly, which explained their failure to find it during their first search. Tina suggested that Sarah had probably taken Elisabeth into the family under the Bancroft family name, presumably to avoid any further trouble after Alice's death. The surname Bancroft had then stuck until she got married.

One of the attachments was a copy of Elisabeth's birth certificate. Alys opened up the document and scanned the neat handwriting. Alice Bancroft was named as Elisabeth's mother, Richard Weatherall, whose occupation was listed as 'teacher', was the father. Also, it was Richard who had registered the birth, which Tina pointed out as worthy of note – he wasn't trying to shirk responsibility. In that era, it was quite usual for the father's name to be left blank, if the parents weren't married.

Alys gazed at the screen for a long time, trying to marshal her thoughts. It was good news, but it also raised other questions. Why would Richard be prepared to acknowledge the baby as his, when he was about to get married to someone else? Had he been going to call off his wedding? How different might all their lives have been if tragedy hadn't struck? If the fire had never happened, if Richard hadn't died, and if Alice hadn't been thrown into prison and perished there. Would they have lived happily ever after? Would Alys herself ever have been born if Elisabeth had been brought up in a different way, in a different place? Alys frowned, and chewed her lip in concentration. But Richard *had* got married, so he must have turned his back on Alice and Elisabeth for some reason?

Alys's reverie was disturbed by the sound of a key turning in the lock. She looked up from the screen, her mind still caught up with the past, finding it an effort to drag herself back into everyday life. Moira was back, struggling to get her suitcase across the threshold. She quickly shut the door behind her against the February chill.

'Look at you – you look great!' Alys exclaimed. Moira's tan was in startling contrast to the pallid winter faces that Alys was used to seeing on a daily basis. She was glowing and relaxed. Shrugging off her coat, she gathered up the bundle of mail that Alys had saved for her and joined her at the table.

'Well, tell all! Was it lovely? Where did you go? What did you do? Shall I make you some tea? I've made cardamom shortbread too, an Indian flavour in honour of your holiday. I'm rather pleased with the way they've turned out. I think I'll start making them for the cafés.'

Moira laughed. 'So many questions! Yes, I'd love tea, and a shortbread. And it's so lovely and cosy in here.' She looked around, feeling the appreciation of returning home after a trip. 'I can't believe how chilly it is outside. Yes, India was wonderful. It's changed so much since I was there last, of course. But we saw so many beautiful things – palaces, forts, temples, sunsets. We crammed so much into the first week, I can't tell you how glad

I was to reach Goa and to be able to just relax by the sea. Such beautiful beaches—' Moira looked wistful. 'It really wasn't long enough.'

'Well, that gives you the perfect excuse to go back again. Did you take lots of photos?'

'Loads! I won't bore you with mine though. Tom's got a good camera – I'll wait and show you the ones he took.'

Alys, curious to know how the relationship had fared on holiday, took this as her cue. She set Moira's tea down in front of her.

'How did it go? Did you two get on all right?'

She was startled to see Moira's tan actually deepen – she was blushing!

'Yes, very well,' she said, then hesitated. 'Actually, Tom asked me to marry him and I said yes!'

Alys was temporarily lost for words, then gathered herself. 'That's such wonderful news! I'm so pleased! When? Where? Have you told anyone else?'

Moira laughed. 'I can't quite believe it myself. It's very *new* news – it only happened yesterday, on our last evening.'

'Oh,' Alys interrupted. 'I can picture it now. A candlelit dinner on the beach under the stars, Tom on his knees in the sand—'

Moira was laughing so much that Alys was worried she might choke. 'I hate to disappoint you, but it was nothing like that. We were stuck at the airport for five hours between flights and it just kind of came up in conversation.'

Alys frowned. 'That's not very romantic.'

'Well, that sums us both up quite well,' said Moira. 'But it *was* Valentine's Day. Does that count as romantic?'

Alys was puzzled. 'You said it was yesterday? How could it have been Valentine's Day?'

'The time difference, remember? I think it was something like 1 a.m. there. Anyway, enough of me – how are things here? How's the business?' Moira gestured at the computer. 'And what are you doing here in front of a screen on Valentine's Day evening?'

'It's all fine here.' Alys ignored the last question, and she proceeded to fill in Moira on how well the businesses had done in the run up to Valentine's Day. 'I have to say, I've had quite enough of heart-shaped cakes and biscuits. Thank goodness for our regulars here in Northwaite. Most of them wanted their tea and cakes as normal: "without any of that romantic nonsense, thank you very much!"'

'Hark at you,' Moira laughed. 'Accusing me of being unromantic when you're just as bad yourself.'

'That's *manufactured* romance,' Alys protested. 'To make a profit. But I suppose I shouldn't complain.'

'Hmmm.' Moira had been leafing through her mail. 'You won't be wanting this, then?' And she held out an envelope to Alys. Quite clearly a card, it had a hand-written address and no stamp. 'Personal delivery, by the look of it.'

It was Alys's turn to blush. Rob must have

slipped the card in among the pile of mail that morning. She ripped open the envelope. To her relief, it wasn't yet another red heart – instead, it featured a cartoon and a rather risqué message that made her snort with laughter as she read it. In time-honoured fashion, there was no signature, just a question mark.

Her relationship with Rob was still very new: she felt protective of it and so before Moira could start to quiz her about how it was going, she turned to the computer screen. 'I've got news too. You know how keen I've been to find out more about Alice and what happened to her? Well, with a bit of help from some friends, I've made a bit of a discovery.' Alys quickly outlined what she knew to Moira.

Moira listened intently, but Alys could see she was struggling a bit.

'Hang on, I didn't know you were doing any of this? And you lost me somewhere, with the bit about some notes in a bag?'

Patiently, Alys started to explain again, but Moira stopped her, yawning. 'It's no good. It must be the jet-lag. My brain's turned to cotton wool. Let's do this tomorrow. I'll probably be wide awake around 4 a.m. if you want to have a go then?'

Alys laughed. 'No thanks! But I need to update Julie, and Rob, too. They've both helped me a lot. Why don't we all get together tomorrow evening, early?'

Moira, suddenly overcome by exhaustion, could

only nod and head for bed. Alys, meanwhile, pottered around a bit longer, her head too full of thoughts to contemplate sleep just yet. Today's revelations had prompted the germ of another idea about Alice and she needed to mull it over. It was close to midnight before she finally headed up the stairs. As she put the card on her chest of drawers, she smiled again at the message. Over the past few months, work had become pretty much all consuming. Maybe it was time to make space for other things in her life now?

CHAPTER 9

There was quite a crowd around the pub table. Alys, Moira, Tom, Julie, Rob – even Rob's father Derek had come along to hear what Alys had to say. They'd spent the last hour hearing about Moira and Tom's holiday, and exclaiming over news of the marriage proposal. If they were secretly thankful that Tom preferred a traditional camera to a digital one, so that his 250-plus holiday photos were still safely on rolls of film waiting to be developed, no one was saying.

During a lull in the conversation, as they gazed into the log fire and contemplated the snow that was starting to settle outside, carried on an icy wind that whistled around the pub, Julie leant forward, unable to contain her impatience.

'Come on then, Alys. What have you – or rather, you and Tina – found out? I'm dying to know.'

Once again, Alys launched into the explanation that she'd tried to give Moira the night before. This time, for Tom's sake, she started at the very beginning, with her discovery in the churchyard of the gravestone that turned out to belong to her great-great-grandmother; how it had made her determined to discover more about her unlucky ancestor; how Julie, Rob and ultimately Tina had helped her to uncover more of the truth and, finally, what she now knew about her great-grandmother Elisabeth's parentage.

Julie could scarcely contain herself until Alys stopped speaking. 'Thank goodness! I'm so pleased you've found a father for Elisabeth.' She paused. 'Although it's a terrible shame that he died so tragically.'

'That's not all, though. I've been doing some thinking about the mill fire.' Alys outlined her deductions. 'The newspaper report on the fire had suggested that Alice had a grudge against Williams, but why? What was her supposed motive for burning down the mill? Albert, who had been there during the fire, blamed himself for Alice's death. He'd referred to Williams in disparaging terms in his journal, and raised a beautiful memorial to Alice. So, it seemed as though whatever Albert knew, he didn't believe Alice to be responsible for the fire and the tragedy. Was Alice just in the wrong place at the wrong time, allowing Williams to frame her for some reason? Or was there something more sinister in all of it?'

Alys's audience looked at her expectantly, waiting for her final revelation.

'I remembered that Albert had said something about holding to account those who had failed Alice. I wondered what he'd meant by it at the time. The name Williams didn't mean anything to me the first time I read his journal, but I went back to it after I read the newspaper report about the mill fire and again last night when I discovered that Richard was Elisabeth's father. Albert was the nightwatchman at the mill, but it wasn't clear to me why Williams would have been there on the night of the fire. I found a reference to Albert paying a visit to Williams after his return to Northwaite, when it seems harsh words were exchanged. Then there was a reference to a newspaper report from 1914 that stated Williams's body had been found in the river in Nortonstall, close to the Packhorse Arms. He'd been drinking heavily and had fallen in. It seemed no one attended the funeral. So, I took a look at the last page of Albert's journal again.'

Alys paused to take a sip of her drink while her audience looked on impatiently.

'Something about Alice had been written there, but I could barely make it out the first time I read it. This time, knowing what I now know, it looked to me as though it said: "With Williams gone, I have avenged Alice and will tell Ella so."'

Alys went on to explain that, with the best will in the world, there was no way now of knowing the complete truth of what had happened. Well over a hundred years had passed and no one was alive who could shed any light on it. The most likely explanation appeared to be that somehow Williams was responsible for Alice being blamed for what happened, while there was a strong possibility that he had started the fire himself. She had learnt enough to be convinced that Alice wasn't an arsonist, or a murderess, and she took some comfort from the fact that Elisabeth appeared to have been loved by both her parents. Although Alice's life had been tragic, Elisabeth had been brought up by the Bancroft family and had thrived. 'If she hadn't,' Alys explained, 'Moira wouldn't be here today, and I wouldn't be either.' She experienced a sense of relief now that she had reached her conclusion. It felt as though she had finally set Alice free.

There was a pause when Alys had finished what she had to say, as everyone digested the story. Rob spoke up first, getting to his feet. 'I propose a toast. To Alys and her detective work – and to her great-great-grandmother Alice, too. They've both been responsible for transforming the area, in quite different ways, and they've made their own mark on history. Without them, our lives would be very different today.' He raised his glass and the rest of the party, smiling and nodding in agreement, echoed his action.

Alys, raising her glass in turn, caught Rob's eye and their gaze locked for a few seconds. It seemed to Alys that her life, already so much more fulfilled since she'd been living here, was about to offer up some very interesting possibilities.

That night, warm and cosy in her bed in Moira's cottage and drifting off to sleep, Alys thought she could hear a melodic humming somewhere in the room. Once again, as her eyes closed, she found herself seated by the fire, a young woman sitting sewing in the chair opposite. Alys struggled to wake herself to speak to her but words wouldn't come. The young woman's attention was caught, though, and she looked directly at her. Alys was convinced she could see her. She smiled calmly at Alys, then looked back down at her work as the humming faded and she was lost to view.

EPILOGUE

The timer beeped and Alys heaved herself out of her chair. She manoeuvred the oven door around her bump. The eye-level oven had not only been a great choice for checking on the progress of the cakes, but it was proving invaluable in the later stages of pregnancy. No bending over and back strain – given that she planned on working until the very last moment, this was a blessing.

She took the lemon poppy-seed cake from the oven and set it down on the work surface. It could cool in its tin for ten minutes or so before she turned it out onto the cooling rack. Alys looked down at the raised golden-brown top, cracked slightly in the centre exposing a sprinkling of dark poppy seeds and releasing a mouth-watering aroma. She was glad she'd found a foolproof recipe. It had become one of the most popular cakes in the Nortonstall café and it was Alys's own personal favourite.

It seemed so long since her first disastrous attempt at baking it, and so much had happened in the meantime. In the last eighteen months alone, her life, which had changed such a great deal since she arrived to help Moira in Northwaite, had simply taken off in a dizzying spiral. Her future was most definitely here, among the very fields, valleys, woods and lanes that had been home to her family, through good times and bad, for so long. The businesses had gone from strength to strength and they had branched out into providing cakes and table settings for weddings, as Alys had planned. Moira and Tom were married now and they'd taken in Lottie and Ralph, her cats from London who'd adapted very happily to country living. Hannah had arrived back in Nortonstall with her boyfriend Matt, declaring that she'd quite fallen in love with the area. They'd bought a house in the countryside near Haworth and proceeded to have a baby. And now Alys's own twins were due at any moment. She could foresee that she and Rob were going to need all the help they could get, but she figured that Julie, Derek, Moira, Tom and now Kate, who had already arrived and was ensconced at Moira's, much to everyone's surprise, would take care of that.

Her scan had shown that she was expecting a boy and a girl, and Alys had already decided on their names: Alice and Albert, who would undoubtedly be Bertie from birth. Rob, who was just generally thrilled with life at the moment, was perfectly happy with her choice but had suggested 'Allie' as a pet name for their daughter. 'Otherwise we'll all get hopelessly confused,' he'd said. Alys could see his point but she hoped that her choice of names would be a fitting tribute to their ancestors. She'd come to feel very close to them, and the bench in the Northwaite graveyard overlooking Alice's gravestone, beautifully carved by Albert, had become her favourite spot to sit and think things through. There was a kind of stillness and peace there. Alys would never have acknowledged this to anyone else, except perhaps to Rob, but she felt so safe there, as though someone was watching over her. In fact, when she was quite sure that no one else was around, she sometimes had conversations with Alice. She didn't expect any response, but she always felt the better for them. Of course, if anyone had spotted her, she knew they'd think she'd gone quite mad.

Alys looked at the kitchen clock. Time to get on – the lemon poppy-seed cake was ready to turn out of its tin, and it was time for the sign on the café door to read 'Open', ready for the start of another day.

RECIPES

Alys's lemon poppy-seed cake

(Serves 12)

Ingredients
50 g poppy seeds
185 ml warm milk
220 g caster sugar
3 eggs, beaten
300 g self-raising flour
200 g unsalted butter, softened
Juice and zest of 1 lemon
100 g icing sugar, sieved

Method
1. Preheat the oven to 180°C/gas mark 4.
2. Lightly grease a small loaf tin.
3. Combine the poppy seeds with the warm milk in a bowl and set aside for 15 minutes.
4. Beat the caster sugar and 185 g of the butter together until light and fluffy. Mix in the eggs. Fold in the flour, alternating with a little of the poppy seed and milk mixture. Stir in the

lemon zest. Beat well, until the mixture is pale and thick.

5. Pour into the loaf tin and bake in the pre-heated oven for 40–50 minutes, or until a skewer inserted into the centre comes out clean. Cool in the tin for 10 minutes, then turn out onto a wire rack.

6. Melt the remaining 15 g butter and add to a bowl along with the icing sugar and around half the lemon juice. Beat until smooth, then drizzle over the cooled cake.

Coconut cookies

(Makes 20)

Ingredients
170 g butter, chopped into small pieces
2 level tbsp golden syrup
110 g desiccated coconut
225 g self-raising flour
85 g caster sugar
Half a level tsp bicarbonate of soda

Method
1. Melt the butter and syrup together in a large pan over a low heat, stirring with a wooden spoon.
2. Remove the pan from the heat, add the coconut and sift the flour and bicarbonate of soda into the mixture. Stir well, add the sugar and stir again.

3. Form the mixture into small balls, using a rounded teaspoon of mixture for each one. Put the balls onto ungreased baking trays, allowing space between them so they can spread.
4. Bake the cookies at 180°C/gas mark 5 for 12–15 minutes. Cool for 10 minutes on the trays then transfer to a wire rack to finish cooling. Store in an airtight tin and eat within three days.

Cardamom shortbread

(Makes 15)

Ingredients
180 g plain flour
125 g butter, softened
55 g caster sugar
6 green cardamoms

Method
1. Cream the softened butter and sugar together until light and fluffy.
2. Remove the seeds from the cardamom pods and crush them into a fine powder using a pestle and mortar.
3. Sieve the flour into the mixing bowl and add the powdered cardamom. Mix well to form a dough.
4. Form the dough into a ball and wrap in cling film. Refrigerate for 15 minutes.

5. Lightly grease two baking trays and preheat the oven to 180°C/gas mark 4. Roll out the dough on a floured surface to 5 mm thick.
6. Cut out using a fluted cutter and place the biscuits on the trays. Bake for 12–15 minutes until pale-golden in colour. Cool on the trays for 10 minutes before transferring to a wire rack to finish cooling. Store in an airtight tin for up to three days.

Chocolate brownies

(Makes 16)

Ingredients
200 g plain chocolate, 70% cocoa solids
110 g unsalted butter, chopped
150 g caster sugar
3 eggs
110 g plain white flour

1. Preheat the oven to 170°C/gas mark 3. Grease and line a 20 cm square cake tin.
2. Break the chocolate into pieces into a heat-proof bowl, add the chopped butter and set over a pan of water, brought to a gentle simmer.
3. Stir gently until the butter and chocolate have melted together, making sure the water doesn't touch the bottom of the bowl. Remove the bowl from the heat and allow to cool for a couple of minutes.

4. Beat the sugar into the chocolate mixture. Add the eggs one at a time, beating well after each addition. Sift in the flour and beat the mixture until smooth.
5. Pour into a tin and bake for 25–30 minutes, until no longer wobbly in the centre. Cool for 10 minutes in the tin then cut into squares and finish cooling on a wire rack.
6. Store in an airtight tin for up to three days.